The Seeds of Aril

R.M. Robinson

firefall™

First Edition: January 2012

Cover Design & Illustration:
Marcia Repaci, North Creek Design

Photography:
NASA; Anja Strømme; WP Armstrong

Editor: Elihu Blotnick

Printed in the USA

isbn: 9780915090228

FIREFALL EDITIONS
Canyon, California 94516-0189

www.firefallmedia.com

Science Fiction by Scientists-tm

The Seeds of Aril
Earth reborn, 20,000 CE,
8,000 light years away.

Iced
Murder at the South Pole,
in light of global warming,

"God help me."

It was a female voice, weak, barely audible above the static. The words were a refrain of resignation and desperation, of infinite sadness and loss.

"Is that all?" Arthur asked Krystal.

"There's more," Krystal answered. "Keep listening."

After several seconds of ghostly crackling, the voice returned. "God," then a pause. "Help me." This time it was a prayer.

"Who is it?" Arthur asked.

Krystal shrugged. "I can't tell. It's coming from a space capsule. It was 5200 light years away at the time the transmission originated. Not one of the Union's. A private vehicle. Very close to Supply Ship 5."

Arthur passed a hand through his graying hair. An inner echo of the weakness and emptiness in the woman's brief plaint moved him to profound sympathy.

"We don't usually get voice transmissions from space capsules," Krystal mused. Her dark eyes were fixed on Arthur. It wasn't the first distress call they'd received from galactic space capsules, but somehow this one seemed to have stirred up long dormant feelings in him.

It was the year 18777. A hundred years had passed since Arthur Mizello and Krystal Charbeau had last visited Supply Ship 6 to conduct routine status checks and review data received in the intervening time. Arthur took care of the warm side of the spacecraft, which held the self-contained biosphere, water production systems, and oxygen storage tanks. Krystal was in charge of the cold storage areas, along with the ship's navigation and communication systems.

Arthur was still tortured by the loss of his wife back in the 22nd century. Though more than 16000 years had past, he had spent much of that time frozen in his capsule's magnetocryogenic chamber. The death of his wife was still fresh in his memory.

Krystal left Earth as one of the thousands of explorers the Union had trained to travel through galactic space, frozen in small vehicles, only unfrozen upon reaching a distant planet to investigate. But Krystal had stopped at Supply Ship 6 along the way and been instantly drawn to Arthur, a serious man with deeply hidden warmth and compassion.

Krystal and Arthur complemented each other. Krystal was darkly clever, constantly conjuring up new ideas and mental games. Technically superior to Arthur and most others she had encountered in her life on Earth, she was supremely confident in herself and her ability to think of novel, often bizarre, solutions to problems. Arthur, on the other hand, was precise and analytical, never venturing to extend his cognitive processes into unknown territory. Whereas Krystal was at ease with all the technology that supported galactic exploration, Arthur was a restless worrier — a fidgety pacer. Even after many millennia he still viewed the entire Union enterprise as a house of cards, apt to fall apart at any moment.

During the times they spent together on the supply ship, they talked about what life had become for them. They had little interaction with other humans. Occasionally, a galactic explorer visited the ship, but those visits were few and far between and lasted only several hours. This would have driven most people crazy, but Arthur and Krystal were not normal humans. Both derived energy from the tantalizing packets of data the ship received sporadically from Earth and nearby galactic space vehicles. They could have spent many weeks poring over the content of those transmissions, but they knew they'd be using valuable oxygen and other life support supplies. Reluctantly, they'd return to their space capsules and launch themselves into orbits shadowing the supply ship, frozen until the next visitor arrived or when it was time again for routine status checks.

This time, Krystal's review of the messages received during the last hundred years had revealed a distress call from an unknown female in a non-Union vehicle. Even with the incredible expanse of time and space that separated them from her, it was difficult to ignore the desperate fight for survival of another human.

"Can you tell the course of her capsule?" Arthur asked.

"According to the data that accompanied the voice transmission, she's moving toward Supply Ship 3."

"That was five thousand years ago. If the vehicle maintained its heading, where would it be now?"

"Pretty close to her destination," Krystal answered.

Arthur estimated the time it would take to transmit a message to the other supply ship. If the woman's vehicle was already close to it, any message they sent would get there long after her expected arrival time.

"Send a message to Supply Ship 3. Find out if she ever showed up there. If she didn't, advise them to search their surveillance data to determine where she might have ended up. If she never made it, advise them to send an emergency message to galactic explorers in the vicinity to search for the vehicle and rescue her if possible."

"Will do," said Krystal. She looked at Arthur with concern. "What bothers me is that we have no information on her or the space vehicle. There shouldn't be lapses in the Union's communication network. When that happens we're all at risk."

She turned back to the console and typed at the keyboard. Her black eyes reflected the faint, pulsating glow of the instrument panel. As she entered commands, new displays appeared on the large monitor. A collection of symbols and numbers scrolled across the screen. The way Krystal worked the computer always amazed Arthur. 22nd century computers featured analog levers and dials, matching in complexity those used in old-fashioned pipe organs. Krystal played the computer as if it was a musical instrument, manipulating the input to produce the broadest range of output. Her deftness made the machine seem an extension of her mind, so contiguous and efficient was the command and control from one to another.

When she finished sending the message to Supply Ship 3, she sat back in her chair and sighed. Arthur took her hand and they

9

strolled together through the silent corridors of the supply ship toward the hermetically-sealed doors of the greenhouse, where a rich assortment of grasses and shrubs gradually replenished the ship's oxygen supply. They examined the plants growing in basins of moist soil on rows of tables. They walked along the interior surface of the rotating cylinder that simulated gravity. To their left was a complex network of pipes, electrical wiring, hoses and valves, intentionally exposed for easy servicing and repair. To their right were the thick crystalline windows that separated them from the empty space outside the supply ship, offering millions of stars in a spectacular view of the sector of the Milky Way galaxy they had occupied for thousands of years.

The star field outside spun in dizzying silence as the cylinder they walked within rotated about the ship's axis. Arthur looked out at a familiar constellation of stars where he knew Supply Ship 3 was located. Somewhere in that direction was a lone female in a diminutive space vehicle, who for some reason had been moved through fear and desperation to pray for help from an ancient god of Earth.

CHAPTER 1

— 2149 —

"Are you as damaged and downtrodden as Earth? Do you feel what the Earth must feel? Are you as flawed and mutilated as our poor planet?" The man standing beneath the blue halogen sign called out in a deep, booming voice, clearly audible above the din of the passing crowds.

"Do you feel lost? Shunned by those around you? Do you have imperfections? Are you ailing, crippled, or handicapped? Has the world passed you by because you are different?"

The sign above the man pronounced, *Captain Warner's New Start for the Disenchanted of Earth*. Captain Warner, in profile, had a hawk-like silhouette accentuated by a close-cropped beard. He wore a blue blazer with a nautical cut and a captain's hat sitting trimly upon his head. Before him on a table hovered a holographic image of a lush tropical garden under a shimmering blue sky with two suns. The Captain gestured endearingly to it as if proudly showing off a newborn infant.

"If you've been cast out, you need a new start — a new start on a new world. Join me and my team on our journey to find a home where there will be no disenfranchised, where everyone will be equal in a world built on mutual compassion and respect."

When Benjamin Mizello happened upon Captain Warner's exhibit, he was searching for perfection, but it was not the tall man that captured his attention. It was a young woman, also approaching the exhibit from the opposite direction. Benjamin's hand instinctively reached for the camera he carried in a bag at his side. She had large fawn-like eyes and there was balance, symmetry and poise in her countenance. The skin of her face was so smooth as to appear artificial, made from wax with the color of moon-glow. Her dark hair framed eyes of deep green, sea water laced with volcanic ash. Captain Warner saw her too and leaned forward planting his fists on the table for support. It was classic predator and prey, and Benjamin fought the impulse to jump between the two, as the woman appeared to be hypnotically drawn to the Captain.

Benjamin had not been looking for perfection in the traditional sense. If so, he would never have found it in Washington DC at the International Galactic Explorers Technology Conference. These annual meetings were organized so that profit-hungry corporations could exchange information, manipulate standards, lobby for industry-favoring legislation, and advertise and market their latest technologies. After long-duration space travel became feasible, a huge industry had developed to support the enterprise, and now the monstrous assembly drew tens of thousands of participants, occupying hotel and exhibit space throughout the U. S. Capitol. The IGET Conferences, with the ultimate goal of providing a means for people to escape Earth and all its problems, featured the kind of contrast, duality, and paradox that defined perfection to Benjamin's artistic eye. The assembly highlighted the cleverest minds and most innovative technology applied to the most desperate and devastating problem Earth had faced — survival of the human race. At the same time, the greed and corruption displayed by the conference attendees were the ideal counterpoints to these lofty endeavors.

Galactic space travel became possible in the latter half of the 21st century when freezing humans safely in suspended animation became routine and safe. Although technology for fast-freezing human tissue had been around for years, damage to the organism during the freezing process could not be avoided. Vital organs froze at different rates and irreversible damage was done before the full frozen state was achieved. Realizing a rapid decrease in temperature simultaneously throughout an organism proved an insurmountable obstacle until the development of magnetocryogenics, the process by which a strong magnetic field instantaneously arrests the motion of molecular material in living tissue.

Instantaneous freezing of organic tissue using strong magnetic fields only solved one part of the problem. Keeping humans in such strong fields for prolonged periods of time was not practical

— on Earth. The temperature in space, however, is nearly absolute zero. A body frozen in space using the instantaneous magnetocryogenic process could remain in such a state virtually forever. This was ideal for the long periods of time required to travel to other planetary systems in the galaxy.

Benjamin paused to let the young woman reach Captain Warner's exhibit first. Seeing that someone had taken his bait, the Captain shifted his attention, speaking directly to her. Only the table separated them now. Benjamin stood to the side for a better view, gauging the light and shadows and the rate of movement, mentally calculating shutter speed and aperture. Was she one of the poor, disadvantaged, weak or sick the Captain was looking for? She certainly did not appear to be. Her clothes were clean, smart, and fashionable, and her hair an exquisite tone of black with purple highlights, evidence of expensive coloring. Always seeking contrast, Benjamin was drawn by the disparity between the naïve, defenseless woman and the Captain's ruthless salesmanship.

"Can I help you, young lady? You look in need, as though life and the world have passed you by. You look…" and here he raised a slender finger aimed somewhere above her head, "…like you want a new start." He paused and, not seeing the desired response, added, "…whether you know it or not."

Benjamin smiled inwardly. The young woman defied the description in every way. Instead of shrinking from the imposing figure, she folded her arms and glared at the Captain. His expression wilted. His predatory aspect was now tempered by a blend of fear and curiosity.

"Can I help you?" he said again, tentatively now, as if he did not want the question answered.

Unconsciously, Benjamin drifted closer to the young woman. She turned and fixed him with a curious stare.

"Excuse me," he stammered. "I was just…" He looked to the Captain, as if seeking help.

The woman stepped back. "Captain Warner, please, tell this young man what you are selling?"

Nervously, the Captain scanned the room. He lifted his hat and wiped a sweating hand through his long gray hair. Sighing, he said, "I am selling...I am selling a new life for those on Earth who haven't had it good here."

Benjamin's eyes focused on the display again, holographic images of lush gardens framed by exotic fruit trees and flowers bursting with color. Frolicking in the garden were men, women, and children, laughing in untroubled bliss. Typical, Benjamin thought, just one of the many groups promising paradise to those disillusioned and defeated by Earth's unrelenting problems. But as Benjamin looked more closely he noticed the figures in the movie were distorted. They limped and staggered. They moved about on shortened or missing limbs. Their arms would not extend. Their heads sagged and rolled.

"Do you have a defect?" the Captain asked.

Benjamin thought for a moment. "We all have defects."

"Let me put it another way," the Captain said. "Have you ever felt left out, alienated, abandoned? Were you an outcast, ridiculed, rejected? Have you lost hope that you'll ever have a normal existence, with a loved one, a family, children?"

Benjamin hesitated. "I guess I don't let my mind work that way. If I did, I'd be depressed, but I try not to evaluate myself by whether I'm accepted by others or not."

Out of the corner of his eye, he saw the young woman staring at him oddly.

"Then you are indeed a fortunate individual," said the Captain.

"Excuse me," the young woman interrupted, her tone changing suddenly. "This new world you're inviting people to join — is it only for the unfortunate?"

"Mostly," the Captain answered slowly.

"So, you're not trying to establish an elite society for a select few with mental or physical superiority. What about beautiful, gifted people, who've never experienced rejection? Would you take them with you?"

The Captain shuffled the brochures on the table before him. "I suppose we'd take anyone who expressed a genuine interest in our colony, but it hasn't happened. Why would it? If you're one of those that succeed at everything they try, who are accepted everywhere, why would you volunteer to spend your life with the mentally and physically challenged?"

The young woman looked puzzled. "Then what about you, Captain? You seem to be a fairly fit person. Are you going to this colony? Will you spend the rest of your life with them?" She gestured toward the images where the scenes of disabled people happily interacting in an alien garden were bizarrely played out.

The Captain responded by working his fingers over a keyboard inlaid into the top of his table. The images changed to show an elderly woman surrounded by handicapped children. "My wife," the Captain said. "She suffered a stroke about fifteen years ago. She has recovered, but is unable to speak. She devotes her life to helping those with physical disabilities. She's the one who came up with the idea of trying to find a new world. I'm going with her. I'm going for her."

The young woman looked deep into the Captain's eyes, searching for something in his face — insincerity, falseness, hypocrisy — but she couldn't find it. In fact, in the few minutes they'd been talking, the Captain had changed from a self-serving carnival pitch-man into an altruistic, sympathetic hero, making a supreme sacrifice for his wife and the neglected souls she cared for.

"I'm sorry," the woman said. "I didn't mean to be cynical and suspicious."

"No problem," answered the Captain. "There are countless reasons to be cynical. Space travel seems to bring out the most desperate people in our society. For thousands of years we've been bound to this planet. Now we have the capability to travel into space in the hope that there is a finite probability, slight as it may be, that a new Earth awaits us out there among the stars."

"May I have a brochure?" Benjamin asked, to break the tension that followed. The Captain handed him one.

Benjamin was reluctant to part from the conversation. He stood awkwardly, wondering what to do or say. Finally the young woman backed away from the table and moved around Benjamin toward the next exhibit. Her shoulder brushed his arm as she passed. Benjamin looked at the Captain, who was watching him with an amused expression. One eyebrow arched up momentarily and Benjamin turned in pursuit of the woman.

When he'd caught up to her, he shouted above the noise of the exhibit hall. "I think I know what you're looking for."

The woman wheeled toward him. He'd dreaded the possibility of seeing annoyance in the dark eyes that turned on him. He wasn't attractive in a way that would give women pause before rejecting him. He was heavy and soft, in a spoiled child kind of way, and his baby face and unkempt hair did little to contradict that image. He hoped his eyes might somehow convey subtle hints of a deeper person within the chubby exterior, but many years of being alone had forced him to accept a harsher reality. He knew that first impressions became fixed in an instant. This striking young woman had now had ample time to size him up. He hoped she'd seen something in him that other women failed to detect.

Stopping him short with her eyes, she replied, "Okay. I'll bite. What am I looking for?"

Benjamin smiled and bowed slightly, "Coffee."

She laughed. "You're right,"

Her smile changed the world.

CHAPTER 2
— 2149 —

Galactic space vehicles with magnetocryogenic chambers began rolling off the assembly line early in the 22nd century. The vehicles were designed with power systems to operate equipment for long periods of time in space. Their navigation systems were capable of working autonomously while space travelers remained in suspended animation. Propulsion systems based on extracting electromagnetic energy from the ambient interstellar medium provided low thrust, which, acting over hundreds of years, were sufficient to gradually accelerate vehicles to a good fraction of the speed of light. Thousands of years of space travel at high speeds offered virtually unlimited opportunities to find and explore other habitable worlds in the galaxy.

While travelers were in space, thermal control was critical. Navigation routes were designed to keep vehicles as far as possible from stars to avoid radiative heating. Still, a small amount of thermal energy from the vehicle's power systems conducted through the surface of the spacecraft might elevate the temperature around the body to unacceptable levels. Thus, travelers were suspended in the middle of cylindrical chambers, held there by thin ceramic rods with soft pads on the ends. After freezing, the chamber was opened to space, and the resulting vacuum insulated the human from potentially lethal warmth conducted through the vehicle's hull.

Galactic space vehicles contained provisions needed by travelers when unfrozen. Food and oxygen were critical. In addition, the capsules carried enough fuel to allow explorers to land on one planet and then return to space again. After each planetary exploration, travelers would have to replenish their supplies at one of seven large supply ships, which carried spare fuel and life-support necessities. Each was cared for by one or two custodians charged with maintaining the vehicle and aiding travelers that happened along.

Galactic space vehicles were also equipped with sensitive radars and laser-based detection systems to anticipate approaching particles that threatened the ship. At the speeds the vehicles traveled, collisions with the tiniest particles could produce catastrophic damage to the craft, its electronics, computer systems, and human occupants. Upon detecting a threat, automated weapons systems built into the ship would fire on the particles to obliterate them prior to impact. At half the speed of light, the detection and neutralization of particles had to be accomplished extremely fast. Multiple weapons were used. A high-energy laser pulse, traveling at nearly the speed of light, was the first line of defense. In case particles survived that, a pulse of high energy plasma was released. Even if particles penetrated that defense, they would be heated by the plasma so that heat-seeking ballistic weapons could be accurately aimed at the target. The system had been successfully demonstrated during test flights within the solar system where the particle population was much higher than the vehicles would encounter in interstellar space.

Outside the exhibit hall it was late spring in Washington, DC, and the air hinted of the warmth and humidity of summer. Benjamin and the woman entered one of the nearby cafes offering outside tables and found one as far from the traffic as possible.

When they were seated, Benjamin said, "I take it you don't approve of space travel."

"Can you blame me?" she answered, nodding toward the convention center. "They're selling dreams to gullible people."

"It may seem like a swindle, but remember not everyone thinks like you."

She looked back at him intently with the same glare she had used on the Captain. Benjamin wondered what he had said wrong. "You presume to know me and how I think," she said.

"It was a guess." He paused to see if the glare would fade. It did. "People who want to go on galactic space voyages are either desperate, delusional, adventurous, or just plane curious."

"And I am none of those?"

Benjamin shook his head slowly, looking at her as if confronted with an object of art, a piece of great beauty and mystery. "No." He paused. "I see you more as an observer — someone who draws knowledge from analyzing human behavior."

She smiled in response and reached across the table with a slender hand. "I'm Ilsa Montgomery."

Benjamin held her hand without shaking it. "I'm Benjamin Mizello, and I'm very happy to be here with you."

They ordered coffee and settled into easy conversation. Ilsa revealed that she was a free-lance writer and an investigative journalist, attending the conference to research the groups organizing space voyages for their members. She was particularly interested in those endeavoring to create new societies with carefully selected and screened members. Some had taken on cult-like qualities and the leaders of one organization were suspected of involvement in a human trafficking ring that enticed women and children from third-world countries, eventually selling them into slavery to wealthy clients.

"And what about you, Benjamin Mizello?" she asked as they started their second cup of coffee. "What brings you to this conference?"

Benjamin smiled and sat back in his chair. "I guess I'm one of the gullible," he answered nodding toward the convention center.

Ilsa smiled back. "I had a feeling."

"I've joined the GSEU, the Galactic Space Explorer's Union. I'm taking the Union's training course in Florida. They sent us up here to the conference to see the technology and get a glimpse of who our fellow travelers in space will be."

"So you're not really one of them," Ilsa said, motioning with her head back toward the exhibit hall.

"Not quite." Benjamin leaned forward again, peering into her eyes. "The Union has only one mission: to explore the galaxy. It has no other goals. No starting new societies, no colonizing distant planets to promote the expansion of humankind. Just exploration."

Ilsa looked puzzled. "What's the point? These voyages take

hundreds or thousands of years. By the time an explorer returns to report any discoveries, the whole world will have changed. If there's anything left of civilization by then, there's no guarantee anyone will care about the Union's mission. You may come back with great news and find no one listening. What's more is that you won't even know anyone when you get back. Do you think you'll just ease into society again thousands of years in the future?"

"No. That's not the point. I will never be able to resume life on Earth when I return. In fact, I may never return. The objective is to send back the information I've gathered in my travels."

"To whom? For what?" Ilsa asked, exasperation in her voice.

"The Union is committed to establishing a permanent repository of all the data we collect. Its vision is that the explorers will transmit data back to Earth at various times so there is a more or less continuous stream of information from all over the galaxy."

Ilsa's eyes narrowed. "So that's it? All this information goes into a permanent repository with no expectation that it'll ever be used by future cultures or inhabitants of Earth? What if they're not ready for it? What if the archive is destroyed in some future war or catastrophe?"

"The archive won't only be on Earth," Benjamin answered. "The primary archive will be here, but back-ups will be kept on the large Union supply ships. The caretakers of those ships are charged with protecting the data indefinitely. They're responsible for ensuring the database stays intact and that new information is added as it comes in. Make sense?"

Ilsa shook her head. "In a way, but I'm still not understanding the rationale for just storing information without knowing that it'll ever be useful."

"It does seem strange. I had the same thought at first, but actually it mimics a well-known process: the genetic code. Every strand of DNA carries genetic information stored for thousands of years. As species evolve, genes retain information about the most primitive life forms from which more complex species evolved. Bits and pieces get added through the millennia. Every strand of

DNA carries all the information coded in an incredibly complex and efficient manner. What the Union is planning is analogous to that process."

Ilsa sat silently, staring back at him, her expression impossible to interpret. "Do you still think it's crazy?" Benjamin asked.

"No. I was just thinking there might be a good article in this."

"Without a doubt," Benjamin said. "I can help you." He paused. "But first you have to help me with my assignment."

"Your assignment?" Ilsa asked. "You mean touring the conference exhibit hall?"

"That's only part of it. The second part of it is for tomorrow, at the Natural History Museum. Will you join me?"

Ilsa was thinking and Benjamin wished with agonizing frustration that he could read her thoughts. "Alright," she said finally. "When are you going?"

"Is 10 AM okay? Meet here for coffee first?"

"Sure," she replied, lifting her coffee cup to toast and seal the deal. Benjamin felt a flutter of excitement. Their eyes locked for a moment.

"So what's with the camera?" Ilsa asked, nodding toward the bag hanging on the back of Benjamin's chair. "Part of the assignment?"

"Not really." Benjamin answered. "That's my day job — when I'm not taking courses to learn how to explore the galaxy."

"You're a photographer?"

"Right." Benjamin said, unable to conceal a hint of pride in his voice.

"What kind of photographer?" Ilsa asked.

"Sort of free-lance, but I'm good enough to make ends meet."

Ilsa sipped her coffee. "If you're doing so well here on Earth in the 22nd century, why throw it all away to explore the galaxy?"

"Can I save the answer until tomorrow? It's a long story and right now we both have to get back to the exhibit hall to finish what we were doing. Now that I know what you're up to, we can help each other."

They returned to the conference center, both still overwhelmed with the scale of the assembly and the level of commotion in the huge hall. As they entered, Benjamin said, "I think I know an exhibit you'll be interested in. I passed it earlier in the day."

"Lead the way," Ilsa said. "I'm lost."

Chapter 3

— 2149 —

The International Galactic Explorers Technology Conference drew many thousands of exhibitors from around the world. Companies touted advanced computers and sophisticated software systems for space vehicles. Some sold the latest lists of potentially habitable planets, gleaned from questionable ground-based observations and dubious scientific analyses. A large part of the exhibit area at the conference was devoted to weaponry needed to protect the space vehicles from collisions with interstellar matter, as well as for defense in the event travelers met with hostile creatures in space.

The exhibit hall was filled with flashing lights, glittering holographic video displays, loud cacophonous music, and the usual collection of humanity's most aggressive, rambunctious, chaotic, and devious people. Animated vending machines rolled through the aisles offering food, drink, and souvenirs, their breast plates alive with scrolling advertisements. Robotic mimes performed life-like impressions of street entertainers, eliciting shrieks from unsuspecting passers by and laughter from the surrounding crowds. Impeccably dressed, beautiful young men and women populated the various booths, enticing guests with glistening smiles and suggestive offers.

Among the many places to eat at the convention, the most popular featured the food to be carried on the galactic space vehicles. Upon being unfrozen after hundreds or thousands of years, galactic explorers could look forward to feasting on vitamin-packed meals stored in special plastic containers that would never deteriorate. So compact were these provisions that the vehicles could carry a full year's worth of life-sustaining food for the galactic traveler. More problematic was water, which had to be replenished during visits to one of the seven Union supply ships.

The Union was the only resemblance of authority in galactic space. A group of wealthy and influential corporate leaders created the GSEU and developed a charter describing the tasks necessary to accomplish the organization's mission. The Union set standards for the design of space vehicles, the way they were manufactured, the types of parts used, and the computer hardware and software that operated them. This was to ensure that travelers encountering each other thousands of light-years from Earth could communicate in a common language, aid each other by sharing parts, and rendezvous at predetermined points in space and time should all other systems fail. The GSEU also constructed and deployed the seven supply ships that were vital sources of food, fuel, and other provisions for space travelers.

A large part of the Union's mission was to train the galactic explorers in the knowledge and skills they would need to survive in space and on the alien planets they would visit. The Union's school in Florida attracted adventurous young men and women, who for widely varying reasons were drawn to the concept of traveling into space with no possibility of returning to friends and family stranded on troubled Earth.

Perhaps the most important part of the Union mission was establishing and maintaining the vast communication system that was to link the space travelers over wide expanses of space and time. To survive for tens of thousands of years, the network had to be extremely robust, with redundant components and multiple pathways linking those components. The primary hubs in space were the seven supply ships, each of which had powerful enough equipment for sending and receiving messages to and from supply ships and galactic space vehicles in their vicinity. Each galactic explorer spacecraft was also a hub in the system, although with less powerful transmitters and less sensitive receivers. Because the occupants of these spacecraft would be frozen most of the time, the vehicles had automated communication systems that operated autonomously and continuously.

Ultimately, information gathered by explorers ended up on Earth via radio links from the five nearest supply ships to the three ground-based radio-telescopes distributed about the globe. The Union also constructed a large radio telescope on the far side of the moon. That location offered an environment free from interference caused by Earth-based radio and TV transmitters. Signals detected by the lunar antenna were carried by optical fibers to the opposite side of the moon where they were relayed to the three radio-telescopes on Earth's surface. All the information received was stored redundantly in computer archives at each of the three ground stations.

Another crucial element of the network was a satellite placed in a stable orbit that would keep it locked at a fixed location between Earth and the Sun. In case world events led to the destruction of all the ground-based data storage facilities, the satellite carried a massive data archive as a back-up. It also had a camera attached to a telescope permanently aimed at Earth. The instrument routinely photographed the planet and transmitted the images to the supply ships. These images constituted another means by which Union explorers in space could monitor the health and well-being of their home planet through the millennia.

In many ways, maintaining the integrity of the ground segment of the communication network was the biggest challenge. The Union realized that communication with the galactic explorer fleet had to be sustained on Earth regardless of the turbulent times the planet might undergo. The ground-based receivers could be destroyed, vandalized, or simply abandoned by future generations of earthlings who were unaware of or had no interest in the Union's mission. Over the passing millennia, the importance those on Earth placed on galactic exploration might wax and wane, but somehow the information the explorers gathered had to be preserved. Also important was ensuring that future generations on Earth understood the official Union language in which all information was recorded. Indeed, knowledge of this elite language would undoubtedly provide Union members on Earth social, political and spiritual power through the ages.

Returning to the exhibit hall, Benjamin and Ilsa strolled through the chaos and confusion of the exhibit space, overwhelmed by the variety of products and services offered. Benjamin took pictures along the way, while Ilsa continuously questioned him about his choice of subjects. He showed little interest in photographing the individual exhibits, many of which were extremely eye-catching and appealing. Benjamin preferred to photograph the faces of people engaged in discussions about the organizations and their visions for new worlds. He tried to capture in visual form the content of the conversation, the intent of the exhibitors, and the mood of the customers. He wanted the pictures to reflect the hardships, the hopes, and the dreams that had brought them to this assembly. Color, contrast, focus, composition, all came instinctively to Benjamin. These were the mechanics of photography. The real challenge was to communicate profound and emotional messages about people and life.

Benjamin stopped in an area near the middle of the massive exhibit hall where large crowds of people jostled for position to observe a large object that sat on a pedestal before them. It was a full-scale model of a galactic space vehicle sliced through the middle to expose a cross section of the craft's interior. The vehicle was conical in shape, with a long cylinder extending horizontally from the narrow end of the cone. This was the space within which the space traveler was frozen, like riding on the point of an arrow shot into space. A manikin had been hung in the center, suspended by almost invisible strands of translucent plastic wire. The cross section revealed the severed ends of massive coils of copper wire that normally wound completely around the cylinder encircling the occupant.

"Those are the coils that create the intense magnetic field applied during the freezing and unfreezing process," Benjamin explained. He pointed to a set of valves at the end of the cylinder. "Those are valves for slowly evacuating the cylinder once the freezing process is complete. After the internal and external pressures have been equalized, a hatch opens exposing the traveler to empty space. The freezing and pressurization process takes about an hour. The batteries powering the magnets have to be completely charged to maintain the field through the entire cycle. Computers within the large conical part of the vehicle control the entire process."

Ilsa walked around to the end of the cylinder where she could get a better view of the interior of the magnetocryogenic chamber. "It looks awfully claustrophobic in there — like one of those old MRI devices."

"It is, but travelers typically don't have to endure it for very long. The procedure is to start the batteries charging up and wait a few minutes for the freezing sequence to start. Then you get inside. You'll be weightless, so you just float through the opening. Once you're in position, the ceramic pins extend to hold you in place. As soon as the freezing starts, you're out cold and feel nothing."

"Are you sure it doesn't hurt?" Ilsa asked.

"Absolutely," Benjamin replied. "I've tried it."

"That just means you don't remember feeling any pain. It may have hurt like hell, but you don't think it did because you don't remember it."

"You might be right, but in that case it doesn't matter if it hurt or not."

Ilsa looked at him strangely. "Of course, it matters if it hurts. Just because you don't remember pain doesn't mean it's not important."

Benjamin held up his hands in surrender. Ilsa peered at the cylinder again. "What's the big red button in there? The eject button? You push it and it shoots you out like a frozen popsicle into space?"

Benjamin laughed. "No. It's just an emergency power down button in case you have to interrupt the freezing sequence for some reason."

"Like if you regain your sanity at the last moment."

Benjamin chuckled again. He admired Ilsa's sense of humor and found himself relaxing in her presence, something he found it difficult to do with most people.

Ilsa moved off, distracted by another exhibit nearby that included a full-scale model of the interior of the space vehicle. Visitors lined up to take turns sitting at the simulated control panel, which was dominated by a large computer screen displaying a spectacular star field. Benjamin saw Ilsa looking at the display and led her over to take a position in the line. Eventually it was their turn and Benjamin motioned for Ilsa to sit at the console. He stood close to her and explained the various controls and gages. He took hold of a joy-stick in the center of the console and manipulated it. The star field on the monitor changed in immediate response. He panned out until the entire galaxy was visible, then pushed a button to produce a three-dimensional grid superposed on the image.

"That's the coordinate system the computer uses to navigate. Enter the location you want on the keyboard and the ship will automatically take you there." Benjamin entered a set of numbers and pushed a button on the console. Ilsa watched the starfield change as if they were traveling through the galaxy, finally stopping near a large orange star. "That's Arcturus," Benjamin said. "It's one of the stars in our immediate neighborhood — easy to see on a warm summer night."

"What if I enter 0,0,0 for coordinates?" Ilsa asked.

"Try it." Benjamin replied. He noticed that a group of other visitors had approached to see what they were doing.

Ilsa entered the numbers and pushed the button. The stars in the display streamed past, slowly at first then more rapidly. The density of stars increased and the luminous streaks on the screen began to merge. "You're flying toward the center of the galaxy," Benjamin explained, now loud enough for others to hear. "The density of stars there is tremendous. The number of stars will grow as we approach the center. I don't know what this simulator will show, but scientists are fairly certain there's a black hole at the center of the galaxy."

The screen became brighter and brighter with the kaleidoscopic stream of multi-colored stars brightening and expanding. Eventually the display became blindingly luminescent and the streamlines coiled into vortices, giving the impression that they were falling into a brilliant whirlpool. The whirlpool tightened and swirled more rapidly and then in one flashing instant went completely black. There was a collective sigh from the crowd followed by an eerie silence as the visitors peered expectantly at the black screen. Then, a moment later the screen reset and they were once again viewing the galaxy as if from a point far away in space. Ilsa rose from the seat smiling. "I guess I crashed it." There were laughs from the crowd as Benjamin took her arm and they strolled away from the exhibit.

Chapter 4

— 2149 —

Given the risks and irreversibility of space travel, galactic voyages were a last resort for humans seeking a better existence. Among those most interested in leaving Earth to find new worlds were religious sects and social groups disillusioned by world events. As the situation on the planet became more desperate, these groups proliferated. Through member donations, many were able to purchase space vehicles and pay for launch costs. These groups sold the hope of finding paradise in a distant part of the universe. The freezing technology made this an easy promise to sell, as the years spent in a frozen state were analogous to death, and the ultimate destination like being born again in heaven. This popular notion brought such groups to the IGET convention. Each set up exhibits promoting the details of their particular brand of paradise awaiting travelers at the end of the ride.

Though many who wished to travel into space were part of large groups, no efforts were made to build craft that carried more than one person at a time. There were several reasons. Smaller craft could accelerate faster, cutting the transit times significantly. Also, in the event of a collision with another space object, the number of casualties would be small. If one vehicle carrying 30 travelers failed along the way, everyone on board would perish. It was more expeditious to travel through space in a tightly knit cluster. This extended buddy-system seemed the best method to ensure the enterprise would not end in catastrophic failure from the demise of a single spacecraft.

In one corner of the exhibit hall, Ilsa and Benjamin came upon an elderly woman sitting at a table with a large computer monitor cycling through a sequence of movies and still pictures. Next to the monitor was a wicker basket filled with medallions similar in size and shape to old-fashioned military dog-tags. The woman deftly braided multi-colored threads of glossy nylon. Ilsa picked up a medallion and ran her fingers across its smooth surface.

"These are rendezvous plans," Benjamin explained. "They store information for travelers who want to meet in space. Mostly they're used by family members to stay in touch with one another. Each tag contains a set of locations at which to meet. Some rendezvous locations are on Earth, others at Union supply ships. The information encoded in these medallions can be downloaded into the computer of any spacecraft and the vehicle will automatically navigate to the arranged meeting point exactly on time."

"I suppose that offers some comfort to travelers," Ilsa mused, "but it seems amazing that people might actually find one another in space after such long times."

"The concept has never been demonstrated," said Benjamin, "but there's no reason it won't work. Sadly, the medallions also function like the military dog-tags of long ago. They carry information to transport a space traveler after death to a designated rendezvous point where family members can perform mourning rituals."

The old woman attached a medallion to the nylon necklace she'd been braiding. Benjamin was struck by the luminescent colors of the necklaces. He extracted a braid from the basket. Each translucent thread showed not only its own color, but the diffused colors from adjacent threads. The overall effect was that each braid shone like an iridescent rainbow. Benjamin could not resist. He picked up another of the shimmering strands and asked, "Are these for sale?"

"They're free if you're a space traveler," the woman answered without looking up. "If not, you can have them for a contribution."

"What am I contributing to?" Benjamin asked, and turned to Ilsa, hoping it hadn't been a stupid question.

"My future purchase of a galactic ship," the woman said.

Benjamin almost chuckled, but something in the woman's tone held him back. Hiding his disbelief, he asked, "You want to go to space?"

She dropped her work on the table, looked up, and gestured

toward the computer, where an image appeared of a small child running through a house.

"Yes — to look for my son. He's in space, and I'm going to find him."

Ilsa broke in at this point, addressing the woman, but looking at Benjamin. "Did he leave a rendezvous plan? Did he tell you where to meet him?"

With a faintly defiant glare, the woman held up a finished necklace with a dangling medallion. "Here is our rendezvous plan."

"Then you'll be able to find him," Ilsa said, "But does your son have a medallion? Does he have the rendezvous plan?"

"No," the woman replied. "That's why I'm giving them out free to space travelers. I'm hoping one of them will meet my son and give him the plan, so…" and here her voice started to break, "…so I can see him again."

"I understand," said Ilsa. "But why doesn't your son have a medallion?"

The computer monitor now showed the child throwing a ball up in the air and catching it. The woman gazed at the image momentarily before answering. "After my husband died, the boy became unmanageable. It was as if he blamed me for the loss of his father. We fought. He was angry. He left. He said he never wanted to see me again."

Ilsa asked, "When did he leave?"

"Eight years ago."

"That's a long time. Do you think it's possible to find him?"

"He'll meet other explorers in space. One of them will give him my rendezvous plan. We will meet somewhere. When I see him again, I will apologize." There were tears now. Her lips quivered. "I have to tell him I love him."

"But the odds," Ilsa said slowly, "the probability of finding your son now in the vastness of space is…"

"I don't care. It's all I have to live for." She raised a bent and arthritic finger. "I want to be frozen in space like him. I want to drift for hundreds or thousands of years. And when I awake, he'll be there. I live for that day."

Benjamin wanted to photograph the old woman, tears streaming down her face, lips attempting to form words that would not come, finger raised crookedly in a futile gesture at the heavens. Instead, he ran his payment card through the scanner on the table and put one of the necklaces on Ilsa and the other on himself.

"We hope you find your son," he said gently. The woman picked up the necklace she had been working on. Her hands were shaking.

Benjamin turned and set off through the exhibit area. Ilsa followed a moment later.

"Another dreamer," she said.

"Or another person with hope."

"What's the difference?" Ilsa asked.

"People with hope have a better chance than dreamers. What are you, Ilsa? A hoper or a dreamer?"

Ilsa was rescued from having to answer by a thunderous boom from overhead. All eyes turned upward to see a plume of steam rising toward the roof of the exhibit hall. Simultaneously, loud electronic music erupted from massive speakers about the hall, the lights dimmed, and multi-colored beams of light coursed through the air illuminating the vaporous cloud. The rays of light moved and flickered at blinding speed, coalescing until a three-dimensional object took shape within the cloud, which now hung just below the ceiling. In the next few moments, onlookers saw the form evolve into a sphere, a planet, looking much like Earth, but noticeably different. As a collective sigh of astonishment emerged from the crowd, the words "New Life" appeared beneath the orb, written in laser-sharp brilliance. Then the music stopped, the dancing beams of light were turned off, and the entire image diffused into nothingness.

Benjamin took Ilsa's hand and they followed the crowd as it collectively moved toward the area in the exhibit hall where the display had originated. Maneuvering through the throngs of people, they finally reached a large exhibit area populated by a half dozen fashionably dressed young men and women, entertaining the crowd with movies and dancing images of a wondrously beautiful planet. At the center of the exhibit, the words "New Life" shone in bright, colorful letters.

"This is just the kind of deception I'm interested in," Ilsa said, raising her voice to be heard among the surrounding din.

Benjamin had been reading the scrolling text beneath one of the holographic displays of the planet they had just seen projected onto the cloud above them. "It says New Life Enterprises has found a new world — just like Earth only unspoiled. They're offering to transport a select group of individuals to this planet to start a colony."

"Are they offering discounted prices? Pay now, enjoy later."

"They claim their scientists have discovered a planet no one else knows about. I really doubt that."

"Like all the rest," Ilsa said, disgustedly. "They're selling dreams. It's that kind of deception I want to expose in my article. I think I'll do more research on New Life to see who's behind it."

"The trouble is that selling false dreams is not against the law," Benjamin remarked, as they moved away from the exhibit.

"Law!" Ilsa exclaimed. "What does the law have to do with this, Benjamin? Don't you understand what's happening? This company is preying upon people who have probably invested all their life savings in the hope that New Life is going to find some idyllic planet in the galaxy where they can live out their fairy tale. Who is going to be around when those people get dumped on some god-forsaken planet with erupting volcanoes and carnivorous reptiles? Or maybe they won't get to any planet. Maybe they'll just die in space after their vehicles fail and they unfreeze in some globular cluster thousands of light years away. What good will the law do them out there? This is not about the law."

Benjamin thought for a moment, intrigued by Ilsa's emotional response. He wondered what in Ilsa's life made her so passionate about injustice, when it was so commonplace in modern society. He stored this thought away and led Ilsa out of the exhibit hall into the bright Washington sunshine.

"It's a great idea to research an article on these businesses. You're right, there's no law in space. Once people leave Earth, nothing protects them but a questionable trust in human character. All that can be done is make sure people who invest in these dreams are aware of the possible consequences."

"Sad, isn't it?" Ilsa said, her eyes following the crowds as they wove through the streets. "How susceptible we all are when a chance is presented to us — an opportunity to live a dream, to get something we've always longed for?"

Benjamin gazed at her, trying to determine if there was a hidden message in her words, but her expression was unreadable. "We either live our lives longing for something better or just accept things the way they are. In either case, we have to be strong and resilient, and ready to deal with whatever happens," he said.

"I hope you keep that in mind when you wake up in your spaceship a thousand light years from Earth and realize you're having second thoughts about exploring the galaxy. How do you deal with that?"

Benjamin smiled, "Turn around and come back to Earth, I suppose. Remember, when you're frozen you have no sensation of the passage of time. One moment I'll be one place, the next moment I'll be somewhere else, and if I choose, I can return to Earth." Ilsa started to protest, but he continued. "I know, I know, it will be thousands of years in the future, but imagine what that will be like. Doesn't that intrigue you? Doesn't it fascinate you? It's like going into a time machine. Snap your fingers and you're there."

"You're there alright," Ilsa said, becoming more agitated. "The trouble with your time machine is there is no way back. You're stuck in the future forever."

"I could say it's better than being stuck in the past," Benjamin replied.

Ilsa dropped her arms to her side and threw her head back in frustration. "Maybe after I write an article on New Life, I'll tackle the GSEU. The Union is no better than these other swindlers. It's selling dreams, and lucky for the Union there are naïve, young adventurers like you ready to sign up."

"I like that," Benjamin replied. "Being called an adventurer. It beats being a photographer."

Ilsa moved closer to Benjamin. She leaned her head and rested it momentarily on his shoulder. "I hear you have to be naked the whole time you're frozen," she said, surprising him.

"Yes," Benjamin stammered. "Completely naked and absolutely alone."

CHAPTER 5

— 2149 —

At the Natural History Museum the next day, Benjamin and Ilsa encountered a very different sampling of humanity. Schools were in session, and most of the midday visitors were boisterous children, disgorged from buses parked in front of the museum. In the corridors Benjamin and Ilsa found themselves dodging excited youngsters enjoying the chaos of the museum and a brief respite from the discipline and order of the classroom.

Walking among the crowds, Benjamin spoke freely about his interest in photography, which he attributed to his parents. His father, Arthur, worked for the U. S. State Department, and his assignments kept the family moving from one location to another. Although trained in diplomacy, Arthur Mizello established a more notable reputation as an interpreter of governments and social structures. His essay series on diverse cultures was uniquely insightful and revealing, drawing parallels and establishing connections between societies that served to unify humanity in remarkable ways. Ilsa was impressed to learn that Arthur Mizello had earned a Pulitzer Prize. She now realized why Benjamin's name had sounded familiar.

An only child, Benjamin had spent much of the day with his mother, while his father performed diplomatic duties. From his mother, Benjamin inherited an instinctive eye for balance, composition, beauty, and esthetics. Forever arranging and rearranging the world around her, she'd been relentless in her pursuit of visual perfection. Whether it was the flowers in the garden, the paintings on the wall, the dishes in the china cabinet, or the fruit in the bowl, she applied the same high standards as well as meticulous attention to detail.

Unfortunately, Arthur's assignments often took them to poverty-stricken places, where nutrition, health, and cleanliness were difficult to maintain. When Benjamin was sixteen, his mother died of a tropical ailment in a remote village lacking medical services. Benjamin was devastated, but his father felt the brunt of the tragedy, blaming himself for his wife's death. After Benjamin entered college, his father was offered and accepted the dubious honor of being the custodian of a GSEU supply ship. He gave all his possessions to Benjamin and spent the next few years in the Union's training course for the dozen people carefully selected to pilot the complex spacecraft supporting galactic exploration. Before his departure from Earth, he and Benjamin spent several days reminiscing about the life they'd shared with Benjamin's mother. Through tears and laughter, they tried to construct a mental barrier to insulate themselves from their shared sadness.

Benjamin understood how empty his father's life had become after his mother died, and he harbored no resentment toward him for leaving. He also understood the impossibility of ever seeing his father again once he left Earth. Benjamin would be dead before Arthur's supply ship had even gotten out of the solar system. Orphaned by disease and the inexplicable attraction of space, Benjamin dedicated his life to photography, having been nurtured on the paradoxical beauty inherent in humanity's struggle to sustain life against impossible odds.

Ilsa found herself drawn to Benjamin's easy-going nature and his willingness to reveal aspects of his private life. He seemed sufficiently comfortable with her and in the course his life had taken, and he hid nothing. This was new to Ilsa, who'd lived long enough to grow wary of the stories people told her. As an investigative journalist, she spent much time extracting information from people trying to suppress or distort the truth. She suspected Benjamin's candor was based on the adolescent notion that other people wouldn't hurt him with the personal information he so freely offered. This was endearing, as it demonstrated an innate confidence and security that Ilsa found rare in someone Benjamin's age.

They walked fairly quickly through the displays of dinosaurs and ancient life forms, of mammals, sea creatures, and insects. When they reached the anthropology exhibits, Benjamin slowed.

Ilsa saw bone fragments from early hominids in glass display cases, dioramas showing how early people may have lived, and colorful timelines painted on the walls indicating when different human species appeared.

"We were told to concentrate on this part of the museum. The Union wanted us to get a feel for the time scales over which we'd be traveling and for the kinds of changes that take place in humans over long periods."

Stopping at one of the timelines, Benjamin pointed out the events identified on the chart. "When you consider the time since the earliest life forms on Earth existed, you have to use a scale of billions of years. When you start talking about human evolution, you have to switch to million-year time scales. But most of those early hominids became extinct. Only one survived to become homo sapiens. That happened in the last 100,000 years."

Ilsa nodded her head with interest. "That's all well and good, but what does it have to do with space travel?"

"The places we're exploring will take thousands or tens of thousands of years to reach. If I decided to come back to Earth, say after 50,000 years, this gives me an idea of the types of changes I might find."

Ilsa moved away from the timeline to one of the dioramas showing a family of primitive people in a cave, huddled around a fire. "These are humans 25,000 years ago," she said. "Big change."

"Not really," replied Benjamin. "They're homo sapiens, just like us. Take them out of their animal skins and dress them in modern clothes and you wouldn't even notice them walking by in the museum. The biggest change in tens of thousands of years has been in human behavior, changes tied to the rise of agriculture, the industrial revolution, and to some extent the environment. Evolution doesn't produce much change in short time scales. It takes millions of years to produce a new species."

"What about races?" Ilsa queried.

"Race differentiation occurs within a species, mostly as a result of environmental factors. If I returned to Earth in 80,000 years, I might very well find a new race of humans living here."

"And there's no way of telling what that future race will be like," Ilsa mused.

"Not unless you can predict the kind of environmental stresses humans might have to adapt to. But, if no dramatic mutation in human DNA occurs as a result of nuclear war perhaps, humans will still be homo sapiens tens of thousands of years from now."

"You're so comfortable talking about unimaginable amounts of time," Ilsa commented. "For those of us who haven't reached the ripe old age of thirty, it's overwhelming."

Benjamin nodded. "There's an analogy that might help. If we have time, I'll take you to the planetarium show at the Air and Space Museum across the mall. Or better yet, come camping with me someplace away from city lights and you can see the night sky. Most of the stars you'll see are within a few hundred light-years of us. The light left those stars in recent history, when humans were fighting World Wars and inventing the computer. But with a really dark sky you can see the Milky Way — light from the myriad of stars that populate our galaxy. That light started on its way tens of thousands of years ago, when homo sapiens was first emerging from Africa and spreading over the globe. If you had a telescope, you could see distant galaxies. That light traversed space while humans were evolving from their pre-hominid ancestors. Light from the more distant galactic clusters, which you can see only with the most powerful telescopes, started on its way when life first appeared on Earth. The parallel between the light we see from objects in space to the time scale of human evolution is completely coincidental, of course, but it puts time and space in perspective. It's like looking down into the Grand Canyon from the rim. The sedimentary layers deeper down in the canyon are from farther back in time."

While Ilsa absorbed this, Benjamin moved to an exhibit showing the earliest examples of written language. "The biggest problem I'd have if I came back in 50,000 years is language. Languages don't last more than 5000 years or so, although a few older dialects may still be used in isolated parts of the world. The Union thought about this too. They've adopted English as their official

40

language, with additional words from other languages when English just didn't work. The official language will be saved in permanent electronic storage; both the written and spoken versions will never disappear. Copies of this electronic "gold standard" will be kept in many places. Hopefully, thousands of years from now people with an interest in speaking to galactic explorers returning to Earth will be able to use the permanent record to bone up on the ancient Union language."

Ilsa was shaking her head. "It's amazing how much thought has been put into space travel. I keep thinking these clever people might use their minds more constructively to solve problems of the here and now."

Benjamin smiled. "No amount of cleverness is going to undo the damage we've done to our planet over thousands of years. Nor can we change the attitude of people whose capacity to live together hasn't improved fast enough to offset the decay of global harmony and cooperation."

They walked toward the museum exit passing a wall filled with photographs. Benjamin had stopped to look at them. Ilsa stood beside him, her shoulder touching his. Arranged on a map of the world showing the location each was taken, the pictures showed men, women, and children, either individually or in groups, with smiling, happy faces. The smiling faces contrasted with the background of the photographs, or often with the physical appearance of the people, which invariably suggested hunger, poverty, and disease. Yet the smiles were genuine, each person looking squarely into the camera and expressing the eerie human ability to laugh even in the face of hopelessness and despair. Interestingly, the pictures seemed to say as much about the photographer as they did about the subjects. The photographer had made no attempt to take the pictures without the subject's knowledge. Instead, there had been a rapport established between the photographer and the subjects, and at some point the picture had been taken, capturing in an instant the person's ability to smile, the photographer's ability to evoke the smile, and the gloominess of the location at which the photo had been taken. The ultimate effect was uplifting, a wall filled with proof that there were connections between people all over the world enabling them to rise above the hardships of life. In small letters near the bottom of the display was written, "Photographs by Benjamin Mizello".

"These are yours?" Ilsa asked Benjamin.

"Yes," he answered, now totally unable to conceal his pride. "The earlier pictures are from the places I lived while growing up. I added more recent images to fill in the blanks. That was harder. I was just a teenager when I began. It was easy to get the subjects to smile then."

"These are wonderful, Benjamin. Thanks for showing them to me." Ilsa stared at the pictures until Benjamin took her arm and led her out the museum exit to the light of the midday sun. They found a bench under a tree in front of the museum and sat watching the children entering and leaving the building.

Ilsa wasn't sure what to say. Many thoughts raced through her mind. Benjamin filled the silence by telling her more about his life. After graduating college, he found there was considerable interest among publishers in the photographs he took in the small towns he'd lived in with his mother and father. Using money his father left him, he traveled the world, creating images depicting the cultural, technological, and biological measures being taken to overcome the growing threat of death and destruction. Life on Earth was on the brink, and Benjamin was on the front lines of humankind's struggle for survival. He was able to show the paradoxical beauty resident in those measures, whether it was urban agricultural high-rises, or the anguish and misery that accompanied the efforts to control birth rates or accelerate death rates, two terms in the same bitter equation. Benjamin's art brought out both the desperation and courage of life pushed to its limits. He unhesitatingly traveled to natural and man-made disaster sites wherever they occurred. After amassing thousands of photographs, Benjamin published a series of books, all with a common theme — that only in hardship and misery can one find the god-like strength and courage that distinguishes humans from all other life forms. Every photograph possessed a stark duality in simultaneously depicting the most beautiful and most ugly in the world, the depressing and uplifting, all at the same time. Indeed, each photograph was life on Earth in miniature, a highly compressed history of civilization from the beginning of time to the present.

Ilsa interrupted Benjamin as he talked about his technique. Shaking her head in frustration, she said, "You have so much talent, Benjamin. Why would you want to travel into space and deprive the world of all you have to offer?"

"I don't take pictures for the world," Benjamin answered. "I do it for myself. I think that's why they're so appealing. I know that sounds selfish, but it's the truth."

"It is selfish," said Ilsa quietly. "So I suppose your decision to travel into space was a selfish one too?"

"Not quite. That relates more to my father." Benjamin stared out across the mall toward the U. S. Capital building, standing out austerely against the blue spring sky. "Before he left we had a long talk about my mother and his feeling of guilt about dragging her and me from one wretched place to another. After she died, he didn't know what to do with his life. He could continue his life's work on Earth, in which case he'd torture himself on a daily basis with memories. Or he could take a desk job in DC and agonize over why he hadn't done that sooner and saved my mother's life. In the end, he took the third option — leave Earth forever."

"That still doesn't explain why you decided to follow in his footsteps."

"Something bothered me about the last conversation I had with my father. Have you ever talked to someone and later worried the other person was trying to tell you something you didn't pick up on — that the other person was skirting a delicate subject hoping you'd guess what it was and coax it out of you? That's what I felt after my father left, and it drove me crazy."

"So you're ending your life on Earth to find your father and ask him what he wanted to tell you?"

"No. I know what he was trying to tell me. He wanted me to join him. I think he hoped I'd express interest in coming with him to explore the galaxy."

"Even if that's true," Ilsa said, "I'm sure your father wouldn't want you to do something so drastic unless you really wanted to."

"I do want to. Not just for him."

Ilsa shook her head again in confusion. "So you still haven't told me why."

"Well, I guess what I'm saying is that what he wanted has become what I want."

"That's not right," said Ilsa quickly.

Benjamin turned toward her. Her eyes were stormy, and he had to look away. "Look," he began, "There were only two people in the world I cared about. One is dead and the other's in space, never to return. I have no family here. We moved around so much when I was growing up that I have no friends either. There's more for me out there, and until now not much to keep me here on Earth."

"Until now?" Ilsa asked.

There was a long pause, after which Benjamin added, "Yes, until I met you."

Ilsa closed her eyes, the lids coming together like the wings of a butterfly. "Benjamin, stop."

Benjamin caught his breath. His mouth closed. "I'm sorry," was all he could think to say.

"That is wrong on so many levels I don't know where to begin."

"I know," Benjamin mumbled.

"No, you don't know, but since we're friends, let me tell you." She looked at him intently. "First of all, I don't believe you made the decision to terminate your life on Earth without considering the possibility of meeting someone who'd make it more important for you to stay on this planet."

"I gave it a lot of thought," Benjamin said, finally finding his voice. "But I never imagined this would happen."

"Benjamin, I've only known you two days, but it's hard to believe you lack imagination."

Benjamin rolled his eyes. "I suppose that's a compliment. Now I'll have to travel into space forever knowing that Ilsa considers me imaginative but dumb."

Ilsa's eyes locked on his and didn't let go. "Benjamin, listen to me. I don't think you should go." She hesitated, still watching him. "I will even go so far as to say I don't want you to leave on your exciting, mind-blowing voyage through the galaxy. Don't go because of your father. And don't not go because of me. Just stop and think what you want to do."

Benjamin stared at the ground as if searching for something written there to help him respond.

"I'm sorry, Benjamin. I shouldn't interfere. I was just trying to make a point — trying to get you to think more carefully."

"I know that. I'm flattered that you're concerned." A cloud had passed over the sun and the sky darkened momentarily. He glanced around. "I hope you know that if the situation were different, I'd very much like to explore a more serious relationship with you."

Now Ilsa looked down and shuffled her feet nervously. "Always the explorer, huh?"

"I think you know what I mean," Benjamin said.

"Yes, I do." She rose, grabbed his hand and walked toward the mall, now filled with mid-afternoon joggers and walkers. Tightening her grip on his hand, she said, "But there's something I haven't told you."

Benjamin didn't answer, but his mood changed visibly. Ilsa turned to face him. He searched her eyes for clues to what she might say.

"Benjamin, I'm married."

Benjamin's head dropped. He mouthed words that didn't emerge. Finally, he said, "You're not wearing a wedding ring."

Ilsa looked at her finger as though confirming the fact. "What's the point? I don't have much of a marriage."

"Why is that? Benjamin asked.

"Because my husband is in a federal prison. He's been there for three years, and will be there for at least another seven."

"Federal Prison?" Benjamin repeated. "For what?"

"My husband committed fraud. He was a hacker. He played

with information in every way one might imagine, even in ways that couldn't be imagined. It took federal prosecutors five years to convict him. The whole time we were together, all he spoke about was how he really didn't do anything wrong, because there were no laws to cover what he did."

"So what does this mean?" Benjamin asked, "It sounds like you never got much from your marriage. Can you get a divorce, or are you just waiting for him to be released?"

She hesitated for a long time, strolling slowly and deliberately, her arm locked in his. "I'm done with him, but he doesn't know it yet. I haven't gotten up the nerve to tell him. In the meantime, I'm concentrating on my writing. I like you Benjamin, but I don't really know how it would work out even if you abandoned your romantic dream of soaring through the galaxy. That's why this discussion is beside the point. You need to be confident that you're making the right decision, whether I stay married or not."

"You're right of course," Benjamin admitted. "But in the past two days we've discussed issues that humanity won't solve in our lifetime. It tires and frustrates me to dissect every major problem and find that ultimately the solution lies with human nature itself. I guess I'm hoping that maybe I'll return to Earth thousands of years in the future and find that humanity, civilization, and society have progressed in tandem, producing a better world than even New Life could ever imagine. I go back and forth on everything else, but I never waiver in my curiosity about whether there's something better, far away in space and time."

Ilsa said nothing. She leaned her head again on Benjamin's shoulder as they walked, both absorbed in their own thoughts, while also wondering what the other was thinking, sharing only the mutual certainty that there'd come a time soon when they'd say good-bye and part forever.

CHAPTER 6
— 2149 —

The Union Supply Ships were marvels of 22nd century engineering and the key to the success of the galactic exploration enterprise. They orbited stars that were sources of energy and power for the craft's life support systems. Supply ships carried self-contained greenhouses within which critical food, water, and oxygen supplies were continuously generated and recycled. The greenhouses were fueled by the stellar light falling on impregnable crystalline windows, which admitted radiant energy to grow a host of life-critical plants. The starlight also illuminated solar panels that generated electricity used to power the ship's systems. Though much larger than the individual galactic vehicles, the supply ships could travel just as fast owing to more powerful engines.

Supply ships were divided into two sections separated by a large heat-insulating gasket. One section contained all the systems requiring warmth and power, such as the greenhouse, computers, and temporary living quarters for custodians and visiting travelers. This section was oriented toward the star about which the ship was orbiting in such a way that the greenhouse remained constantly illuminated by the stellar light. The warm section of the ship was pressurized and maintained at a fairly constant temperature to ensure plants in the greenhouse grew properly. The other section of the supply ship was oriented away from the star. It was unpressurized and open to space. This cold storage area contained all perishable supplies, the cold vacuum of space preventing spoilage and deterioration over thousands of years.

Although primarily deployed for the Union's galactic explorers, other space travelers also made use of supply ships. Thus, the ships were mini-Earths, oases in space where galactic travelers could regenerate and renew rare and precious supplies. Supply ship custodians traveled in their own vehicles. They orbited the same star as the supply ship, but at greater distances to avoid excessive heat build-up in their magnetocryogenic chambers. The lives of supply ship custodians were extremely demanding. They had to visit the supply ship every hundred years for routine maintenance and repairs. They also aided the explorers who arrived to replenish their supplies of food, fuel, and oxygen. Vehicles approaching the ship were detected by the station's surveillance systems, which signaled the custodian of the un-scheduled visit. The technology and computer control had advanced to the point that both the unexpected traveler and the supply ship custodian arrived at the ship almost simultaneously, fully awake and ready for the docking procedure with the station.

For the supply ship custodians then, life was an endless se-quence of freeze-induced oblivion interrupted by occasional arrivals of space travelers or routine visits to check on the supply ship systems. Some custodians also looked forward to the excite-ment of hearing about the exploits of the galactic explorers, either directly or through the continuous stream of data received by the ship's communication system.

Seven supply ships were constructed and launched over a period of about twenty years. The Union deployed the seven ships at locations within the spiral arms of the galaxy where the density of stars is greatest. The supply ships, along with the twelve hundred galactic space vehicles, occupied a volume of space covering about twenty percent of the entire galaxy and including millions of stars.

Advanced computers on the supply ships received and stored data, and clever software routines continuously processed the information, analyzing it and mining it for weak signals, unusual patterns, and unexpected correlations. One of the biggest chal-lenges was to deal with the different times at which the trans-missions originated. Ultimately, computers had to sort the data according to the absolute time it was obtained to construct snapshots of the state of the galaxy through time. Information about the existence of habitable planets was transmitted through the network and presented in such a way that space travelers were not confused by the thousands of years that passed before the message was received. Such old data were not entirely useless because complex mathematical algorithms and sophisticated extrapolations in space and time lent value to it. In the void of space, travelers were otherwise totally information starved. The problem was just an extension of the challenges colonists in the New World faced in communicating with relatives and governments in Europe. One had to take into account all the possible events that might take place during the time required for people, supplies, and messages to travel from one continent to the other.

Supply ships contained the same array of weapons as the individual space capsules, except they were more powerful. For supply ships, the rationale for the weapons was not solely to mitigate against possible collisions with other objects in space. The primary reason was defense against alien attack, as improbable as that event might be. In addition to the standard weapons, the supply ships also carried a dozen nuclear weapons that could be used if all other defenses failed. Because the supply ships carried this nuclear arsenal, being the custodian of a supply ship carried great responsibility. Only the most trusted Union members were given supply ship assignments.

After leaving Ilsa and returning to Florida to resume his training, Benjamin's thoughts turned increasingly inward, dwelling more obsessively on her and less on his future space travels. He continuously reminded himself of his resolve to follow his father into space where together they could engage in the ultimate search for extremes of life in the universe. He resisted the temptation to call Ilsa, as she had made it clear she did not support his commitment to join the Union's mission. She viewed galactic space travel as a form of suicide and refused to invest emotional energy in a relationship that had no future. But Ilsa was the focus of all Benjamin's thoughts as he questioned his own motives. Whenever he played out the life he might lead if he stayed on Earth, Ilsa was the other player on the stage.

Benjamin finally completed his coursework and was ready for the final stage of training, which would take place on the Union's orbiting transfer station and vehicle assembly plant in low Earth orbit. Compared to the instruction he had received for inter-galactic space travel, the Union had poorly prepared him for the flight into orbit. For that, he was dead weight, just another payload to be delivered on thousands of kilograms of rocket fuel. Unlike a payload however, Benjamin suffered through the intense vibrations and G-forces associated with the lift-off and ascent to space. The Union had apparently decided it really didn't matter how much fear and dread the travelers experienced while re-strained helplessly in a tiny metal enclosure attached to enough explosives to vaporize the ship and all of its human occupants.

After the shuttle had docked with the Union station, a green light glowed in Benjamin's module to indicate it was safe to exit. Trembling, he removed the restraining straps and floated toward the exit hatchway. This particular delivery vehicle carried sixteen travelers, four on each of four decks within the cylindrical volume of the launch craft. They took turns propelling themselves into the station where they were guided through a corridor toward the artificial gravity portion of the station. Once they descended the ladder to the perimeter of the rotating cylinder, they signed in and were given instructions on where their quarters were while wait-ing for their galactic voyages to begin. Like the remote outposts on Earth Benjamin had visited, there was a central gathering room where travelers socialized, ate, drank, read, played games, and fought off the inevitable boredom associated with isolation, sensory deprivation, and interminable waiting.

In addition to the explorers, the transfer station was occupied by men and women working in the vehicle assembly plant. They spent their work shifts under weightless conditions in a large bay assembling space vehicles from thousands of parts carefully stored in cabinets lining the interior hull of the station. There were also technicians on route to help construct the Union's large radio telescope on the far side of the moon. It amused Benjamin to find that even here 200 km above the Earth, a well-defined peck-ing order existed, on the bottom of which were the galactic ex-plorers. Others looked with disdain on the young adventurers, destined to be shot into space on impossibly long journeys in unproven vehicles.

Benjamin found a seat at a large table with other explorers and, while eating what might very well be his last meal for thousands of years, listened to the banter of his comrades. The topic was Dr. Andrew Harding, one of the original founders of the Union and perhaps the most knowledgeable and experienced of all its members. After a long successful academic career at MIT, Dr. Harding had resigned and joined a blossoming aerospace company already in the process of developing technology for space travel.

Driven by the fear and desperation of humans suffering the onslaught of unsolvable political, social, environmental, and health problems, Harding's company became increasingly profitable with tremendous worldwide support from wealthy investors. Harding joined with several of these entrepreneurs to spin off the Union because they recognized that long galactic space voyages would be futile without a foundation on Earth. Harding was something of a legend among the explorers. He developed teaching materials and taught classes at the Union academy, but his life took a turn as a result of his wife's much publicized infidelity and a messy divorce. Harding was left owing his estranged wife enormous sums of money, and his daughter, who openly hated her father, used every opportunity to denounce him, to the delight of the paparazzi pursuing her through wild party-filled evenings. Soon after, Harding gave up his teaching responsibilities and announced he would be the custodian of one of the supply ships. Several of the explorers puzzled that Harding had accepted an assignment on the periphery of the Union's galactic network, whereas Arthur Mizello, with far less experience in space technology, had been assigned to the prime location closest to Earth.

A small, dark-haired woman at the table, looking at Benjamin with an amused expression, remarked that she felt better with Arthur Mizello at the central hub of the network. She asserted that Arthur's accomplishments had demonstrated his fundamental humanity, whereas Andrew Harding had only demonstrated his ability to make money and appear frequently in the news.

Some at the table defended Harding and expressed doubt that a diplomat had the right skills to be the custodian of a supply ship, to which the woman smiled and, nodding toward Benjamin, said, "Why don't you ask him. That's his son."

The news was received with considerable scorn by the other explorers at the table and the conversation quickly changed course. Benjamin excused himself and headed for his quarters. The dark-haired woman stopped him. "Sorry to put you on the spot, but I know these guys and I wanted to halt the conversation before it deteriorated further."

Benjamin nodded, but said nothing. The woman took his hand and shook it. "My name is Krystal. I'm a great admirer of your father."

Benjamin mumbled a thank you. They stood awkwardly for a few moments. Up close, Benjamin realized Krystal was older than she looked. Her eyes displayed a wisdom and confidence that belied her youthful appearance. She grabbed Benjamin's shoulder and, holding it firmly as if comforting a child, said, "Stay safe out there, okay?" Benjamin nodded again. The woman turned and walked off.

As he lay in his bunk trying to sleep, Benjamin thought about his father. After the death of his wife, Arthur was susceptible to Union recruitment efforts. The Union felt his knowledge would better prepare space travelers to deal with the strange beings their voyages might lead them to. After teaching for several years, Arthur embraced the opportunity to be a supply ship custodian. Ostensibly drawn by the chance he might apply his skills to intelligent life on other worlds, deep down inside, Arthur also yearned for the loneliness that would validate in some twisted way the suffering he could not overcome after the loss of his wife. Benjamin understood the pressure loneliness could exert on one's psyche and accepted his father's departure with an ease he now found inexplicable. Still, a loose end had to be tied. Benjamin looked forward to seeing his father again and he fell asleep to the faint low-pitched drone of the engines powering the Union transfer station.

Galactic explorers were not told what their first destination would be until just before departure. It was understood they had little recourse once that decision had been made. After Benjamin was introduced to his space vehicle, he sat at the control console and personally tested all the computer functions as he had been trained to do. In testing the software, he learned that his first destination was Supply Ship 2, where he would be directed to a nearby planetary system. This was a typical assignment, as the supply ship custodians had the latest information about nearby stars and planetary systems that might possess life-sustaining atmospheres.

After completing his tests, Benjamin exited the vehicle and made final preparations for his departure. Each traveler was allowed to bring 100 kg of personal belongings. The only limitation was that items had to last for eons in the cold vacuum of space. Some materials would show no particular wear, while others would outgas and slowly lose their chemical integrity. The Union provided travelers with a list of materials most likely to survive. Fortunately for Benjamin, his most prized possessions were the photographs he had taken, all of which were saved in solid-state memory devices weighing very little. Most of his 100 kg was taken up by custom photographic equipment he had collected through the years.

At last the time came for Benjamin to depart. He loaded all his personal effects onto the vehicle, undressed, and stored his official Union jumpsuit in a plastic bag he stowed on the spacecraft. Under weightless conditions, he found it difficult to maneuver his body into the magnetocryogenic chamber that would be his home for the next ten thousand years. Once inside, he initiated the freezing sequence and felt the pressure of the ceramic pins that would hold him in free space at temperatures near absolute zero. His second to the last thought before the intense magnetic field started was of his father. If it had not been for Arthur, Benjamin was sure he would still be on Earth. Ilsa had been right. His last thought before the freezing process began was of her.

CHAPTER 7
— 2150 —

The automatic navigation system and radar-based hazard detection system guided Ilsa's car flawlessly through the desert night, negotiating the curves and obstacles along a road deeply rutted and regularly wiped out by flash floods. She turned down the interior indicator lights to better view the eerie landscape fleetingly illuminated by the car's headlights. Surrounding her was a vast terrain of sand and rock, of earthy luminescent colors in daylight and deathlike darkness at night. The desert unfolding before her was infinite in its scale, interrupted only by unlikely mesas with sheer slopes reaching to unimaginable heights.

She was comfortable with the desert. As a girl, she had often explored many arid regions with her father, a hydrologist who studied ground water and aquifers in the American southwest. Now, the ghostly images gliding past filled her with nostalgic memories of evenings with her father, encompassed by the starkly beautiful desert landscape and crowned by the brilliant stars above.

Her eyes were momentarily distracted by a faint glow from outside, above the quickly retreating shrubs and rock. She opened the window and a stream of warm dry air blew past her. Squinting against the flow, she leaned her head out and looked up to see the black night sky inscribed with an endless sea of powdery light. She pressed a button on the instrument panel and the car glided to a stop, raising a plume of bone-colored sand in the fading glow of the headlamps. The car door rose with a faint hiss and Ilsa climbed out, struck immediately by a strong, steady breeze, warm and dry. She descended the small slope abutting the road and walked among the shrubs until she found a large sandy clearing. Lying face up with hands locked behind her head, she looked at the sky. As her eyes adjusted to the darkness, the familiar constellations appeared and after a while, the Milky Way emerged, a broad band of pallid white across the night sky.

She thought about Benjamin. By now he was on his way, a frozen being drifting through space in a technologically controlled oblivion. What would he find out there at the end of his voyage? What wonders would his travels reveal? What kind of life would he live? She would be long dead by that time. Theoretically, he could spend thousands of years exploring the galaxy. He'd age only during the brief periods he was unfrozen. He would spend several weeks making observations and analyzing data to see if there were any planets capable of sustaining life, or perhaps dock at one of the supply ships and replenish his food, oxygen, and fuel stores. Then he would plot a new course and start again. How supremely lonely a life like that would be. What tragedies, what disenchantment, could drive a soul into a frontier so devoid of life and human spirit? She shuddered to think of it. Would Benjamin tire of it and return to find a futuristic society that would treat him as a freak? Or would he return to find all life on Earth gone, that the planet had become as uninhabitable to humans as was Venus with its poisonous atmosphere, or Mercury with its oppressive heat, or Mars with its immense deserts, now burial grounds for the abundant life that had once flourished there?

Ilsa knew that at some point, if all went according to plan, Benjamin would rendezvous with his father on a distant supply ship. Defying incredible odds, the two would overcome the obstacles of space and time and reunite, creating a glimmer of warmth in the vast coldness of space. It comforted Ilsa to think of it. Perhaps their meeting was only one of many such unions as ubiquitous as the stars themselves. Perhaps the universe was not as cold as the blackness separating the stars made it seem, but rather as deeply warm as the stars themselves. If one could just connect all those specks of love, create a galactic network of compassion and tenderness, the galaxy would be a very different kind of place.

Ilsa glimpsed meteors streaking across the sky. She knew them to be commonplace and terrestrial compared to the luminous stars they strove to mimic. Their transient brilliance mocked life itself, or perhaps humanity, in its feeble attempt to attain majesty for a brief moment. She wondered about life on other planets. Benjamin had explained that most planets capable of sustaining life could be detected fairly easily by the advanced instruments on galactic space vehicles, even if hundreds of light-years away. The real problem with finding such planets was that highly developed life forms probably appear and disappear over tens of thousands of years. The fraction of time during which advanced civilizations existed on a planet was small compared to the age of the universe. This made it unlikely that searchers for life might observe another planet at a similar stage in its biological and technological evolution.

Ilsa was reminded of the fireflies she watched in the trees near her home in Virginia. Each would light up for a second or two and then fade away for a while before lighting again. If each was a civilization that could only observe other populations during the brief time it was lit, then during that moment it might not see any other firefly, even though there were hundreds of them in its vicinity. The lonely firefly would emit its emerald light and fail to illuminate another during that glowing moment. Its light would fade away along with the vanishing hope that other fireflies existed, when the area all about was teeming with thousands of others, all with the same sad notion.

Ilsa gazed at the sky with a new awareness — a recognition that the night sky mixes time and space in such a complex way that no conclusion can be drawn about the existence or non-existence of life forms based on the limited view humans have. Ilsa began to comprehend the incredible attraction Benjamin felt when he decided to embark on his voyage. For him, it was a way to overcome that limitation. Magnetocryogenics allowed explorers to transcend the narrow tunnel that imprisoned them. Ilsa came to understand that galactic space travel was not a form of death, but a new form of life, a life that far exceeded any that Earth-bound creatures could imagine.

Ilsa returned to the car and drove another hour to a small town where she found a reasonable motel to stay in before venturing the remaining forty miles to her destination, the New Life compound. Alone in her gloomy room, Ilsa reflected on the little information she'd found about the organization from public sources. It had been founded by a charismatic young insurance salesman named Charles Stormer. His Eastern European charm and way with words had led to his rapid rise in a powerful insurance conglomerate. He made TV appearances and gained a strong following among people from all over the world. His message was simple. He encouraged his followers to escape the problems of society and the mainstream culture that limited one's horizons. He gained enough supporters to create a new organization, New Life Enterprises, entirely funded by member donations. With those funds, Stormer acquired property in the most remote locations in the country and established self-sufficient societies living in virtually total isolation from the rest of the world. New Life converts had flocked to these places. Though living at one of New Life's compounds was an austere proposition, residents enjoyed peace, quiet, and freedom from news and other impediments to serenity.

Stormer created an executive board for New Life including some of the world's wealthiest and most influential industrialists and politicians. Its power base was so extensive it was able to control communication within the New Life compounds, and residents were restricted to a limited number of radio, TV, and internet options, carefully screened for content by members of the organization's staff.

Eventually however, authorities became suspicious of New Life when complaints surfaced about the organization's heavy-handed recruitment practices. There were reports that recruiters traveled to poverty-stricken parts of the world and coerced desperate individuals, particularly women and young girls, to become members, promising them clean homes and carefree lives. Unfortunately, many of these recruits soon ended up on the streets caught up in drugs and prostitution. New Life denied any responsibility for the fate of these people, but the rate at which the organization was amassing wealth and property was difficult to otherwise explain. Other rumors connected New Life to various paramilitary groups operating in remote areas of the world. These groups were so secretive that no evidence had been produced confirming their existence, much less their association with New Life.

While law enforcement agencies attempted to build a case against Stormer, the organization announced its plans to establish a colony on a distant planet, taking advantage of magnetocryogenic technology. New Life claimed it had discovered a planet capable of sustaining human life, but refused to disclose its location. It began selecting members to travel to this planet and start a new society based on the poorly-defined principles of the organization, which was quickly achieving cult-like status. The mysterious selection process drew from existing members as well as new recruits. Ilsa wanted to learn the criteria used to decide which New Life members were granted the dubious privilege of embarking on the space voyage.

The next morning, she checked out of the motel and after eating breakfast continued her drive. She loved the desert in the morning. The ghostly landscape of the previous evening lay brilliantly exposed before her now, with early morning sun casting dark skeletal shadows around the sparse vegetation. Ilsa marveled that, while the world population grew to staggering numbers, here one still could look for miles in every direction without seeing another person. From this perspective, she could imagine what a space traveler might feel after landing on a planet with no other humans. She wondered what motivated a person to make a life decision that led to such a bleak and hopeless precipice. She shuddered, and thought again about Benjamin.

The car signaled a turn and Ilsa grabbed the steering wheel, guiding the vehicle onto a gravel road that led upward along a gradual slope toward the foot of a low range of mountains. The exposed rock surfaces reflected heat from the strengthening sun. In shadow, nestled at the base of a sheer cliff wall, was a series of low, pale-gray buildings. Ilsa steered the car to avoid the pits and irregularities of the road and before long was confronted by a gate in a long chain link fence that disappeared in both directions. She'd been instructed to phone a number on reaching the entrance, and when she called and announced her name, the gate slid aside. She advanced uphill toward the compound. A half dozen cars were parked in front of the nearest building, along with an unmarked truck, which she supposed was used to bring in supplies.

Ilsa entered through a glass door displaying the New Life logo, the letters NL emerging like sprouts upon a stippled surface. Inside, a woman with graying hair sat at a desk partially hidden behind a computer console. Looking around the obstacle, she smiled and greeted Ilsa pleasantly. "Welcome to New Life, Ms. Montgomery. Mr. Stormer is expecting you. I am his assistant, Ms. Quon. Please follow me."

Ms. Quon led Ilsa down a hallway and stopped at an unmarked door. She knocked gently and opened it, nodding for Ilsa to enter. Ilsa stepped into the room and was immediately taken aback by the large window extending across the far side of Stormer's expansive office, presenting a panoramic view of the desert through which she had just traveled. The various washes and dried river beds stretched out below them, radiating outward from a focus that one could believe was coincident with Stormer's office. He had arranged his desk to face the window, with his back to the door. He introduced himself, shook Ilsa's hand, and invited her to sit on an upholstered chair to one side of the desk.

"Beautiful view, isn't it? In my long career as an insurance salesman, I found it difficult staying at my desk. I had the worst work habits one could imagine. So I designed this place to create a space that would motivate me to stay in my office." He looked at the window and with a sweeping gesture of his hand added, "I think I was successful."

Ilsa smiled, "You certainly were. I'm envious."

She was trying hard to remain objective with Stormer, in spite of all the charges directed against him. He detected her uneasiness and spun his chair away from the window to move closer to her. "But you didn't come here to discuss my view, did you? I was intrigued by our chat on the phone the other day. You're writing an article on New Life. May I ask why?"

Ilsa settled back in her chair. She'd anticipated this question. "I'm not writing an article on New Life. I'm writing about what motivates people to embark on space voyages that might end in disappointment or disaster. I wonder about the circumstances on Earth that push people to an endeavor tantamount to suicide. Because of New Life's public recruitment campaign, I thought I'd focus on its members. I'm also interested in how New Life selects from those wanting to go along."

A wry smile appeared on Stormer's face. Ilsa noticed the intensity in his steady gaze and wondered how old he was. His face looked youthful, except that wrinkles appeared fleetingly as his expression changed. His eyes were hazel, but she supposed could change to a steely gray in the right situation. He had a full head of pewter-colored hair, neatly combed back in a style that was popular in the last century. There was a bird-like energy in the rapidity of his movements, and his hands were constantly busy, arranging items on his desk, twirling a pen, adjusting his clothing.

"Why don't we do this?" Stormer said finally. "Let me give you a tour of our facility. Along the way you will get to meet some of our guests and members of the staff. When the tour is done, we'll discuss your article and agree on the best way to proceed."

Stormer escorted Ilsa into a large courtyard set in the middle of the compound. The buildings were designed to isolate the encompassed area from external view. Only narrow paved pathways separated the structures. The courtyard itself was beautifully landscaped, and Ilsa mused about the quantity of water required to keep the lush vegetation alive. Within the shaded and flowered spaces created by trees and shrubs, Ilsa observed people reading, talking, and strolling in idyllic states of tranquility and detachment. Their clothing was loose-fitting and of light cotton. Her own garments seemed stifling and overly fashionable by comparison. She felt a twinge of envy at the ease with which the New Life residents surrendered to the demands of the desert.

"I know this seems a little monastic," Stormer said. "However, our other outdoor spaces are less soporific. Outside the compound, higher on the slope, is an extensive garden with a variety of crops, totally worked by our guests. And off to the side is a sports area. We've set that apart because our guests can get quite loud during their athletic endeavors, particularly on the soccer field."

Stormer led Ilsa to one of the buildings. Four of its doors opened to the courtyard and a set of windows revealed what appeared to be classrooms within. "We offer a variety of classes for our guests. I can give you a brochure listing the courses."

Ilsa grew impatient. "Mr. Stormer, excuse me, but I have to remind you that I'm here to learn what motivates New Life members to undertake space voyages. I'm not interested in being one of your guests."

Stormer bowed slightly. "I only thought to give you some background into our philosophy and how we treat our members. I was going to explain that we are now offering classes in the knowledge and skills necessary for space travel. We want to be sure our travelers are fully prepared." He indicated a list posted on one of the doors showing the names of those taking a course titled "Preparation for Space Travel."

"Forgive me," said Ilsa, examining the list. "Can you tell me how many of the guests at this compound have been selected for the voyage?"

"About 75 members from this compound have applied, but they may not all end up on the voyage. We are continually training and observing candidates to ensure they are fully committed and…" Stormer hesitated searching for his next word. "…and compatible with other travelers."

"Meaning?" Ilsa asked.

"Our psychologists have emphasized the importance of good chemistry within the group. The fact that all have gotten through our initial screening process is no guarantee they'll get along under the stresses of establishing a new colony."

Ilsa looked to the next building to signal she wanted to move on. "And what happens if they don't get along?" she asked, turning back to Stormer, who followed at a respectful distance.

"We're establishing rules based on the New Life philosophy of harmony and compassion. We don't anticipate serious problems."

"How about enforcement? Will you have a sheriff of the colony, a judge, a mayor?"

Stormer brought his hands together beneath his chin as if in prayer. "Ms. Montgomery, let me ask you a question." He motioned to one of the many benches in the courtyard. "Please sit down. I feel we need to get past the façade and get to the real reason you are here. You must know that we are not the only group preparing to establish a colony in space. Yet for some reason, you are here basing your research on our group. You're asking questions that could be asked of any of the other groups. All will be faced with the same issues and challenges. Why are you only interested in New Life?"

Ilsa squinted under the bright backwash of the buildings on the opposite side of the courtyard. She thought carefully about how best to answer. Finally she said, "I won't pretend not to know about the charges against New Life, Mr. Stormer. Admittedly, the negative attention the organization has received over the past several months intrigues me. I'm a journalist. It benefits me to write about something the public will be interested in. New Life, at least for now, certainly falls into that category."

Stormer sat back and sighed. He seemed fatigued or perhaps disappointed. "Fair enough, Ms. Montgomery. Thank you for being honest. Now I'll be frank with you. New Life has become a bigger organization than even I ever dreamed it would be. As part of that growth, I have had to work with partners all over the world. I will admit to you, and I prefer this remain off the record, that I don't always know what other enterprises my partners are involved in. If I did, and they did not meet my personal standards of integrity, I would sever relationships immediately. Right now, I am too engaged with the space expedition to investigate these charges more thoroughly. I've decided to wait to see what the authorities determine. You have to remember, Ms. Montgomery, that I am one of those embarking on the voyage to the New Life planet. If you are looking for reasons why people choose to leave Earth, I will tell you that I have been motivated by the disappointment of seeing my dream of creating a new society on Earth tarnished by rampant evil forces."

Ilsa observed him closely looking for any signs of dishonesty or deceit, but his demeanor did not change. He appeared to be genuinely disturbed by the accusations against New Life. Not entirely satisfied with his explanation, however, she persisted. "Journeying into space is an expensive endeavor. I can imagine you being tempted by the huge sums of money some partners might bring to the table."

"I suppose that's true. We are all subject to temptation. That is precisely why I am not cutting my ties to contributors based on unproven accusations." Stormer stopped abruptly as if he had just thought of something. "Ms. Montgomery, why are we now talking about the charges against New Life? I thought you were interested in learning about the types of people who want to help colonize a new planet. Are you suggesting there is a link between the two activities?"

The direct question surprised Ilsa. This was, in fact, exactly what she had been after. She became flustered, not knowing what strategy to take now. She tried to conceal the nervousness in her voice. "Maybe it's time for me to meet some of the members selected to travel with you."

"Yes, perhaps it is," Stormer replied thoughtfully. "Very well, Ms. Montgomery." He glanced at his watch. "It's almost time for lunch. We'll eat together in our cafeteria and then continue the tour later. Afterwards, I'll provide you with an office where you can review some materials that might help your research. While you're doing that, I will arrange for interviews with some of our members for tomorrow."

"I hadn't planned on staying overnight."

"Oh, but you should. Even if I was able to arrange interviews for you this afternoon, it would still be too late for you to start your return trip across the desert. We can set you up in one of our guest rooms for the night. You should stay. You'll get a better feel for New Life and its members."

Ilsa was surprised by the offer. "That's extremely hospitable,

Mr. Stormer. I'd love to stay, but I insist on paying. I didn't come here expecting free lodging."

Stormer smiled. "Really, Ms. Montgomery. you don't have to pay. You are my guest. But let us discuss it in the morning. We may both reconsider the arrangement by then."

Ilsa nodded and smiled back. She watched Stormer's fidgety hands as he brushed invisible objects from his clothing. Finally, he rose and offered her his hand. "Ms. Quon can help you if you need to cancel other arrangements you have for this evening."

"No, that won't be necessary."

"A family member or partner you need to call?"

Ilsa smiled, wondering if Stormer's question was an off-handed way of finding out if she were married. "No. No one will miss me," she said, finding herself thinking of Benjamin.

"Very well," said Stormer. "Then please join me for lunch."

To Ilsa's dismay, Stormer drew out the tour. The sun was about to set behind the distant hills before he finally led her to a small office. Several stacks of documents had been arranged on a large desk that filled much of the room. As Stormer left, he promised to return to show her to her room where she could prepare for dinner.

Ilsa scanned through the documents. All dealt with topics of space travel and colonization very generically. There was little specific to New Life. Then she found a blank questionnaire that New Life used in selecting those eligible to join the galactic expedition. With the fading light of day, Ilsa switched on a small desk lamp and began to fill out the questionnaire, trying to imagine there was something on Earth she was trying to escape.

An hour later, Ms. Quon showed up to escort Ilsa to her room. She enjoyed a shower and changed into clothes that had been laid out for her. They were similar to the light linen garments she had seen the other guests wearing.

She was relaxing in a lounge chair when Stormer knocked on her door. He was now wearing a black tee shirt under a light sport coat of pale gray. Again Ilsa found herself amused at the thought that Stormer might be flirting with her. This was unexpected, but Ilsa wasn't uncomfortable with the notion. She wasn't in the least attracted to the tall fidgety man, but the nature of his attention was so subtle, it was difficult to be offended in any way. When Stormer offered his arm to lead her to dinner, she accepted it.

Ilsa was surprised when they did not walk toward the building that housed the cafeteria. Instead, Stormer led her back to his office, which now contained a table set with dinner plates and a small candle. Ilsa was confused and momentarily speechless. Was this part of Stormer's strategy to derail her investigation of New Life? Everything she had planned to say to him seemed inappropriate now, especially when Stormer, standing behind her at the door to the office, switched off the lights. She turned quickly back to him, but could see nothing in the sudden darkness. A moment later, she felt him beside her and he had grabbed her arm firmly. "Don't be afraid," he said huskily. "Please sit down." He guided her into one of the office chairs that had been set before the table. "Look out the window. Let your eyes adjust to the darkness."

Ilsa did as he requested and before long saw an endless sea of stars against the black sky. Soon the faintly glowing band of the Milky Way revealed itself. Seeing it now, while sitting in the air conditioned comfort of Stormer's office, gave it an incongruity that heightened her enjoyment. She noticed off-handedly that music was playing — a soft violin concerto. The combined effect relaxed her and she gave in to the beauty of the moment. She sank back in the chair, knowing very well the vulnerable position she was in. She heard the familiar sound of a wine bottle opening. Moments later Stormer handed her a glass that offered the delicate aroma of a fine red wine.

"I wanted you to experience this," said Stormer softly, as he took the seat next to her. "There is more to research than just reading papers. To understand New Life, you have to understand me and the source of my fascination with the universe. Perhaps by observing the universe as I do night after night, you'll come to appreciate my desire to be more than an observer. Consider the art lover who isn't content just to visit the museum and see great works. Many art lovers, perhaps all lovers, dream of possessing the objects of their passion. This is my passion," and Ilsa could see the silhouette of his arm sweeping across the open window. Stormer tapped his glass against Ilsa's and said, "To passion, in all its many forms."

Ilsa sipped her wine, confused and troubled by the complexity of emotions she was experiencing.

"Let's just drink our wine and savor this moment for a while," Stormer said. "Then Ms. Quon will bring our dinner." Feeling Ilsa's reaction, he added, "Don't worry. Ms. Quon is quite used to my eccentricities. She has worked for me a long time and questions nothing."

Ilsa relaxed and continued drinking her wine in silence, only vaguely aware of Stormer breathing softly next to her. She wondered where his hands were and what they had found in the dark to manipulate. The sky outside had darkened noticeably since she had first entered the room, either because her eyes had become more dark-adapted or because the sun had descended farther below the horizon. The Milky Way became a bright swath of light across the sky, dominating the view in spite of the glistening pinpoints of light from the stars. The high pitched chords of the violins framed the scene before her, enhancing its vividness. Then, almost imperceptibly, she heard, or felt, a low pitched rumble emerge out of the darkness. From the corner of her eye, she saw Stormer lean forward to peer more intently out the window. She followed his gaze and discerned a faint orange glow on the horizon before her. Transfixed by the light, she watched as it strengthened, expanding and becoming a deeper shade of orange. From out of the midst of the red-orange glow, an intense white flame emerged, moving upward, cutting through the diffuse radiance like a bullet. It rose, slowly at first, then gaining speed, like a luminescent finger pointing toward the heavens, leaving crimson chaos in its wake.

Ilsa knew what she was looking at, and found the breath to ask the question, "Is that a rocket launch?"

In the dark, she could only see the silhouette of Stormer's face, faintly cast in red. "Yes." He paused, as if waiting for the answer to cross the gulf between them. "One of ours."

Ilsa looked out again and saw that the white point of light had almost reached the upper limit of the view framed by the window. "Do you mean some are already leaving?"

She heard him continue talking, as if from a distance. "Even though I am considered an old man by most," he was saying, "I feel I have many more years to live. I feel my success should allow me to live my remaining years as I choose, and my choice is to live my life unencumbered by the petty rules of society. I also choose to live my life with people that meet my standards. That is how I decide who is to accompany me on the New Life expedition to space."

As Ilsa listened, Stormer's voice became fainter and fainter and she wondered where he was going that made his voice fade in that way. When she finally realized it was she who was fading, it was too late. The last thing she remembered was a distant feeling of being hungry and annoyance that dinner hadn't been served yet. When she awoke, more than ten thousand years later, she was completely naked, weightlessly suspended in a narrow cylindrical tube, and still hungry.

CHAPTER 8

— 12681 —

Captain Warner and his wife, along with several hundred other travelers, arrived at Supply Ship 5 before beginning their search for habitable planets. The couple, along with two of their companions, docked at the supply ship leaving the rest of the group frozen in their vehicles. The Union had notified the supply ship custodian, Dr. Andrew Harding, of the time of the Captain's arrival. He was already on the ship preparing to meet them.

After emerging from their magnetocryogenic chambers, the four travelers donned one-piece jumpsuits and exited their vehicles. They glided weightlessly into a long hallway leading to the rotating portion of the station that simulated two thirds of Earth's gravitational field. In the comforting clutches of gravity, they embraced one another, marveling that more than ten thousand years had passed and all had survived the voyage not only safely, but with almost no realization that any time had passed. Dr. Harding eyed the travelers warily. These were his first non-Union visitors. The Captain's height and the confident way he moved within his lanky frame surprised Harding. The dark beard and imposing countenance gave him an air of nautical authority. Harding, a short stocky man, who normally exuded strength and determination, was taken aback, unable to intimidate the Captain in any discernible way.

He approached and held out his hand, "You must be the one they call the Captain. Welcome to Supply Ship 5. I'm Dr. Andrew Harding."

"My name is Lance Warner," the Captain said, taking the hand and shaking it vigorously. Harding turned to the others. The Captain stepped quickly between them. With broad sweeping embraces he drew his wife to his right and their two young companions to his left. "Allow me to introduce my wife, Marjorie, and our two friends, Brian and Emily."

Brian, a plump, moon-faced youth, smiled shyly and delicately held out a pudgy hand. Harding responded with a quick hand-shake. He nodded a greeting to Emily, whose hands were twisted into poorly-formed fists tucked under her chin.

Harding turned from the group. "Why don't we go to the galley?" he said. "You must be hungry after your long trip."

Brian laughed loudly, "We ate just before we left. Where's the head?"

Harding frowned and nodded toward a door farther down the corridor. Brian trudged off, and Emily moved closer to the Captain.

"I could use a snack," the Captain said warmly, "and perhaps some rum, which I hope the Union has seen fit to allow."

"As a matter of fact, we have liquor, but our supply is limited."

"I understand," said the Captain. "I will try to control my appetites. As for my wife and my two companions, none of them drink, and I am sure they will allow me their rations."

The Captain's wife nudged him with an elbow, and for the first time Harding realized she was a mute. Her rapid hand movements were obviously strong reproofs aimed at her husband. Harding turned away, but could not suppress a disapproving shake of his head. He considered the madness that must have possessed the Captain to embark on a galactic space voyage accompanied by such needy companions, with hopelessly little chance of colonizing a new planet.

"I assume the others are okay?" Harding asked.

"I checked their status before docking. Of course, I'd like to continue to monitor my people while we're near this star to make sure thermal control is maintained. I assume you can download the data and display it in real time."

"The computer is processing the data now. If anything is out of normal range, we'll be notified. Meantime, I've other activities to tend to. I'll show you the galley and your quarters. At some point, Captain, you and I need to meet in the briefing room. We can check the data on your colonists and discuss your course from here. I also have news from Earth, which of course is over 5000 years old, but it'll give you an idea of what's happened since your departure. It's not particularly uplifting. You might be more interested in reviewing the most recent data we have about nearby planetary systems that look promising."

"Thank you," the Captain replied. "However, I must insist that my wife and our companions also participate in the briefing. I rely on them thoroughly and want to make sure they are kept well informed."

Harding suppressed a scowl and turned away disapprovingly. The Captain continued, "Brian is somewhat of a genius. He has studied all aspects of space travel, stellar evolution, and planetary geology and atmospheres. He's also expert at computers and software engineering. Emily is a biologist, specializing in exobiology and life in extreme environments. When we departed Earth, she was the world's leading expert on observational characteristics used to search for the presence of life on other planets. My wife," and here the Captain paused and pulled the slight woman closer to him, "is my moral and ethical windsock. She is my foundation and provides the base upon which we all stand." The Captain concluded his statement by kissing his wife warmly on the brow. She blushed and feigned to push him away.

Harding perfunctorily showed them the galley and invited them to help themselves, noting that the food and drink were for consumption on the station. Food and supplies needed by the space travelers on their voyage were stored elsewhere in special containers designed to fit into corresponding stowage areas on certified space vehicles.

After fixing tea for herself and Emily, the Captain's wife led the younger woman away while the Captain and Brian sat at the galley table enjoying reconstituted soup and strong coffee. They ate silently, pondering the impossibility of their situation. They were on a spaceship five thousand light-years from Earth, eating food that was ten thousand years old. The human mind was remarkable in its ability to accept the miracles enabled by science and technology. After air travel became routine, people sat comfortably in airplanes without being awed by the thousands of feet of empty space between them and the ground. Elevators ascended and descended through dizzying columns of nothingness with passengers who gave no thought to the trustworthiness of the mechanisms by which physics overcame the limitations of gravity. Communication networks transported voice transmissions and data instantly from one part of the globe to another with few people dwelling on the mysterious nature of the technology. Now, having traveled to a point in space and time so remote from whence they came, the Captain and Brian mulled over what had taken place. No physical or biological laws had been broken. No exotic time warps had been traversed. The speed of light had not been exceeded by their vehicles. It was as if they had died and been reborn at new coordinates in the space-time continuum.

Later, they all assembled in a small briefing room, one wall of which was dominated by a large display monitor. On another wall was a desk and control panel for operating the monitor and accessing the station's computer and memory banks. Brian slid into the seat and confidently entered verbal commands that made the large monitor spring to life. Emily stood behind him, mumbling instructions and reassurances in a language only the two of them could comprehend. Luminous star fields appeared, with some stars marked with vivid blue circles. As Brian zoomed in to view them more closely, each was seen to be surrounded by planetary systems. They peered with curiosity and amazement. One of the barely visible planets in these systems might be the new home they were seeking.

Brian turned to where the Captain and his wife stood shoulder to shoulder with hands linked. "There is evidence of life forms in some of these planetary systems."

"How do you know?" the Captain asked.

"Emily wrote this program. It's an optical search routine that analyzes the light from star systems to determine if they have planets containing organic chemicals. It's amazingly efficient, but it lacks the resolution to determine the specific planet from which the emissions originated."

Harding entered the room and cast a fleeting look of annoyance in Brian's direction. "I see you're familiar with our computer software," he commented.

"Not very difficult," Brian responded without turning around. "Looks like you haven't updated this software in more than ten thousand years."

Harding took a seat at the end of the long table in the middle of the room. "I can give you a quick run-down of the more recent observations later in the briefing. That planetary system you're looking at now is about 200 light-years from here. One of the galactic explorers is on his way there. We should have word back in a few hundred years or so."

"Have you heard anything encouraging from the other explorers?" the Captain asked.

"No, but remember, we're thousands of light-years away from most of the explorer vehicles. It will take some time before we start hearing from them. Also, individual vehicles don't have sufficient power to transmit messages directly to this supply station. For some, the messages have to be transmitted to Earth and relayed to us by more powerful Earth-based transmitters." He paused and watched the quickly changing scenes appearing on the monitor under Brian's fluid control. "Whenever you're ready, we can get started," he added edgily.

Brian and Emily detached themselves from the control console and took seats with the Captain and his wife. Harding leaned forward and planted his elbows on the table. "More than ten thousand years have passed since all of us left Earth. The intermittent nature of transmissions from Earth suggests tumultuous times there. I've used a sequence of images taken from a Union satellite to put together a video. There is far more information available if you're interested. The ship's computers are still processing all the data, but this quick summary will give you an impression of how Earth has changed. The video compresses five thousand years into a fifteen minute clip."

Harding rose and strode to the console where he entered commands and brought the monitor to life again. The initial images showed Earth as they all remembered it, a vividly colored orb marked with familiar land and sea features. Tenuous white clouds extended across the surface like stretched cotton candy. The image jumped and flickered in a way that emphasized the changing features from one frame to the next.

"These images were all taken at the same time of day," Harding commented. "I did that so there is consistency from one frame to the next in terms of light and shadow. Major changes your eyes will naturally lock onto are in the cloud cover, but also watch closely the shifting colors on the land masses. These are indicative of large scale changes in vegetation, most likely in response to climatic variations. If you watch very carefully, there are also variations in the color of the oceans that suggest modifications in the acid or algal content of the seas, again tied to climate variations. As time passes, you'll notice the cloud cover increasing until it eventually blankets the entire globe. This happened about a thousand years after we left Earth. The cloud layer prevents us from seeing the surface, but watch what happens next."

As they all gazed at the flickering image of Earth, the layer of clouds was punctuated by bright flashes of light illuminating large portions of the nebulous mantle from below.

"Lightning?" the Captain asked.

"No," Harding replied grimly. "The extent of the illumination is too great. Those are nuclear explosions. For the first thousand years or so, Union members on Earth sent occasional status reports to the supply ships. We know that during those thousand years there were attempts to launch humans en masse into space. There's a detailed account of those efforts, but none were successful in establishing new colonies on other planets in the solar system. You can read the log if you like. After that, no further attempts were made to escape Earth, as far as we can tell. Space programs were undoubtedly interrupted by cataclysmic wars culminated by the nuclear explosions you just saw. Following this period, there are fifteen hundred years or so where contact with Earth is totally lost. I'll let you watch the remainder of the sequence without comment."

After the flashes of light stopped, the uniform cloud cover over the globe remained unchanged until a thinning appeared near the equatorial regions that allowed a glimpse of the brownish surface below. The thinning deepened and expanded until the surface was exposed in a broad band about the equator. Clouds remained only in narrow wispy strips at higher latitudes. When the last of the clouds disappeared the entire surface of the Earth could be seen. The arrangement of the continents and oceans was familiar enough, but the coloring on the land surfaces was almost uniformly brown. All evidence of vegetation had disappeared. The group watched in reverential silence as seconds went by with no noticeable change in the bleakness of the scene before them.

Eventually, however, an olive-colored patch emerged near the west coast of Africa. This area expanded into a donut-shaped ring that propagated outward. Although the surface within the ring returned to a brownish color in its wake, the ring continued to expand, seeming to jump across the ocean, bringing its transformative green color to the continental United States. As a portion of the ring propagated across South America, a new olive-colored circle emerged in the vicinity of the Peruvian Andes, creating a second ring that expanded into another verdant halo propagating outward. Whenever the ring pattern of the first circle crossed the second circle, a persistent spot, now deep jade in color, appeared at that location. A third ring must have been created on the back side of the Earth because the expanding fronts from that ring appeared. At the spot where any two rings crossed, a permanent green patch appeared, changing gradually from olive to jade and eventually intensifying to an emerald glow. The ring patterns became increasingly more complex to where it was impossible to distinguish individual rings, and the proliferation of emerald-hued spots eventually covered Earth's continents with a lush green carpet. After a while, Earth's surface, save for the oceans, was uniformly wrapped in a fertile blanket that glimmered with the lingering effects of the expanding rings. Still, a steady state had not been reached because the glossy surface began to pulsate as if Earth was being illuminated by a light of periodically modulated intensity. The throbbing continued for a while and then at last clouds began to reappear, coming and going at random locations and times. During the last minute of the imaging sequence, Earth sat in green, blue, and white glory, throbbing gently in a comfortably natural rhythm.

Emily mumbled something that no one understood. Brian translated, nodding in agreement. "Emily says Earth's biosphere exhibited collective behavior."

Harding looked at Brian and Emily curiously. "Meaning?" he asked.

Brian glanced at Emily for guidance and she gave him an approving nod to continue the explanation. "The combined effects of global warming and nuclear war must have produced a profound effect, almost wiping out all visible traces of life. It appears that Earth recovered in such a way as to create a more robust and resilient biosphere. The expanding rings represent the reemergence of vegetation. At first, the emergent growth died out in the wake of the expanding wave fronts, but in some locations the passing of the growth ring launched a resurgence of vegetation. Where the resulting two waves intersected, growth was sufficiently robust to take permanent hold. A positive feedback occurred in which the more persistent regions of vegetation were able to draw more carbon dioxide out of the atmosphere, stabilizing the climate. After a while, probably a couple of hundred years based on the length of time this occurred in the movie, the Earth reached equilibrium."

"Why is that evidence for collective behavior?" asked Harding.

Brian again turned to Emily for encouragement. She nudged him to go on. "It's a global response. It implies transfer of information. If a localized region of Earth experiences a fertile growth spurt, the information about that event gets transferred to adjacent regions."

"That's just spreading of seeds, not transfer of information." Harding said.

"Actually, spreading of seeds is transfer of information," Brian responded. "Seeds are mechanisms by which species reproduce, and critical to that process is the replication of DNA. DNA is the ultimate information transport system. Every strand contains all the data needed to replicate the species. DNA carries the information and seeds carry the DNA. When localized plant growth spreads out over the entire globe, that's collective behavior."

Harding looked skeptical, but grunted in reluctant acknowledgement.

Emily was mumbling again, moving closer to Brian so he could hear her better. "Emily is puzzled though because it appears the sequence of expanding rings started after the clearing of the clouds. The clouds should have disappeared as carbon dioxide was removed from the atmosphere, not before the removal process began. She doesn't understand what cleared Earth of its cloud cover." They looked at Harding, who nodded knowingly.

"We know how that happened from the radio transmissions from Earth that resumed during the recovery stages," he said, glad to be controlling the discourse again. "The missing part of the equation is technology. Global warming and nuclear war did not wipe out civilization. Instead, it went underground for many centuries. That must have been a horrible time for those left on Earth, but fortunately enough knowledge and technology remained. With one major problem to overcome, Earth's population united in its efforts to remove the perpetual cloud cover that hung mercilessly above. Using a combination of mechanical, chemical, and electromagnetic processes, they managed to gradually eliminate the thick layer of water vapor, forcing water to precipitate out, refilling the oceans, lakes, and rivers and kick-starting Earth's hydrologic cycle, so critical to a healthy biosphere."

"What about the pulsing at the end?" the Captain asked.

"It's an eleven-year pulsation, same as the periodicity of the sun. The changes you see are much larger than you would expect from the small variation in solar luminosity through the solar cycle. The messages we've received indicate those on Earth have forced an eleven year cycle in manufacturing and other activities that stress the chemical balance of the atmosphere. They learned that such a rotation allowed time for the balance in Earth's biosphere to be restored before the next industrial growth phase. They tied the timing of the sequence to the solar cycle because there was already a natural rhythm. The Earth is dancing, so to speak, to the rhythm of the Sun, a cosmic pas de deux to retain the natural balance between humanity, the biosphere, and the geosphere. After thousands of years of fighting nature, it appears civilization has finally learned to live in stable partnership with it."

"Amazing," said the Captain softly.

"We can only hope the solution Earth finally devised was a lasting one." Harding manipulated some keys and spoke softly into the microphone at the computer console. The image on the large monitor changed to display a star field. Around one star was a yellow circle. "That's the Sun," said Harding. "Strictly speaking, it's the Sun 5000 years ago. Somewhere near the Sun is that pulsating Earth I just showed you. The messages we're receiving now indicate Earth and the people on it are doing well, but we're looking into the past here. We can only guess the state of Earth now."

They all sat silently for a few moments looking at the insignificant point of light that was at one time their sun. Finally, Harding entered more commands and the image on the monitor disappeared, replaced by a table with several columns of numbers. "Here are some data you will want to study during your time here. It's a list of planets identified as having habitable environments. I've filtered the list to only include those within about 10000 light years of our current position. Select any of the planets in this list and you can access all its data. Brian, I'll leave you and Emily to peruse the list. Call me if you need help."

Brian nodded. "Would it be possible for me to download all the data and information you've received from Earth and take it with me?"

Harding hesitated a moment, then said, "Certainly. There will be an automatic back-up performed in a few hours. I can configure the computer to also back-up to your own storage device."

"Including the Union communications?" Brian asked.

Harding pursed his lips and then sighed. "I'm afraid Union communications are confidential. I cannot allow that."

"Yes, that's what I expected. Why is that?"

Harding shrugged. "We use the Union communication channel

for personal messages among Union members and their families on Earth. By policy, we choose to keep those confidential so as not to inhibit members from communicating information that might be deeply personal."

Brian pretended to understand, but it still puzzled him. Any Earth-bound family members of Union explorers were dead for thousands of years. Why did the Union need to be so protective of those communications?

Harding paused a moment looking at Brian, then rose and left the briefing room. Emily and the Captain's wife came over to stand behind Brian as he returned to his work at the computer. The Captain followed Harding out of the room, saying, "I'm going to get some spirits before Harding changes his mind. You folks figure out where in the universe we're going next."

When the Captain returned, Brian and Emily were still methodically examining the data on each of the planets in Harding's list. "You two should get some sleep. There's no hurry figuring this out. We'll stay here as long as we have to."

Brian and Emily exchanged glances. "If you don't mind, Captain, Emily and I would feel better leaving here as soon as possible. We don't get the feeling Dr. Harding is happy with us on the ship, and that's fine with us because we don't particularly care much for him either."

The Captain stretched and exhaled breath faintly redolent of alcohol. "He's not so bad. He just doesn't know how to deal with people who don't have his intellect."

"A little ironic," commented Brian, "considering he's a Union member whose sworn duty is to explore the galaxy. Did he think all he was going to encounter along the way would be aliens with the mental capacity of Albert Einstein?"

"There's a good chance that's true," said the Captain. "But very soon we'll be many light years away from Dr. Harding and it won't matter one way or another what he thinks. Now I'm going to sleep, and I suggest you two do the same. Remember, being frozen is not the same as sleeping. If you're tired going into the freeze, you'll be just as tired coming out of it, and that may be precisely the time you want all your wits about you."

"Aye, aye, Captain," said Brian lightly.

Later, the four travelers gathered in the kitchen for a quick meal before departure. Brian and Emily had plotted a course that would bring them successively to a series of eight planets, all of which could be explored for habitability. They presented the list to Harding, who wordlessly entered the information into the ship's computer. That data would be transmitted back to Earth, as well as to the two nearest supply ships. The message would be subsequently relayed to other supply ships and galactic explorer vehicles.

Brian looked amazingly well rested as he enjoyed several freeze-dried food packets. The Captain's wife fed Emily, who ate in thoughtful silence. The Captain sipped coffee and stared solemnly at a small monitor displaying the latest transmission from Earth. He thought about going back. The option always lingered in the back of his mind. It was tempting, given the rosy picture that had emerged at the end of the movie. Even if not perfect, wouldn't Earth have far more to offer than any new planet they might find? There was even the possibility that medical science on Earth had advanced to the point where all of his colonists could be cured of whatever disease or genetic disorder had handicapped them. Was he really doing the right thing taking these unfortunate young men and women so far from Earth with potentially catastrophic results? It was a question that haunted him continuously. His only consolation was that all had joined the expedition without coercion and with full knowledge of what the risks might be. He thought of them in their frozen state, drifting obliviously near the station. They'd placed their trust in him to guide them to a new world where they could live a better life with greater promise than the one they'd left.

When the group finished the meal, they climbed the ladder leading to the axis of the supply ship where the weight of gravity disappeared. They propelled themselves carefully back to the docking room to the open ports of their space vehicles. Harding floated into the docking room last. Grasping a safety handle along the hull of the ship, he shook the Captain's hand gently to avoid sending the Captain floating uncontrollably off in a different direction. The official Union handshake was an interlocking of fingers followed by a push-pull motion that would not cause unwanted transverse momentum, but Harding assumed the Captain didn't know the Union's handshake protocol.

"Good luck to you, Captain. I hope you and your friends find what you're looking for out there. Keep in mind that finding a suitable new world will probably be the easiest part of your venture. Overcoming the obstacles of colonization will be a far more difficult and dangerous process."

"I understand, Dr. Harding. Thanks for the advice." With that, the Captain helped guide Brian through the port into his capsule. His wife had already pushed Emily through and then followed her in to help her undress and get situated in her freezing chamber. The Captain waited for his wife to return and then led her into her vehicle to double-check that all the systems in the craft were properly functioning. He tried to find the right words of farewell for a parting that would be for thousands of years, but would only seem like a few minutes. Finally, he exited her vehicle and entered his own with a half-hearted salute to Harding, who remained in the docking station until all four ports had hissed closed.

There was a barely perceptible shudder in the supply ship's hull as the four vehicles detached themselves. Then Harding moved back through the corridor to reenter the gravity-controlled portion of the ship. He would spend the next 24 hours securing supplies, checking the latest data returned from Earth and nearby space vehicles, and transmitting his log entries and other information back to Earth. Then he would enter his own space capsule for freezing until a preset time one hundred years in the future, or upon the arrival of the next visiting traveler or travelers. He knew, however, from transmissions he had already received, it would be the latter that would initiate his next unfreezing sequence. He knew this from confidential Union transmissions, though the person sending them was not a Union member.

CHAPTER 9
— 12699 —

Ilsa awoke in the dark, hearing a faint humming sound and detecting the distinctive odor of ozone. Adding to the eeriness was the total absence of pressure or weight on any part of her body. Panic paralyzed her. She was afraid to move a muscle, fearing no response. After several seconds, her eyes adjusted and small lights and numbers appeared, multicolored and finely etched in the blackness above her. She heard a loud hiss, felt a stream of cold air, and became immersed in blinding luminosity. A pair of hands grabbed her shoulders, pulling her. She was astonished when her body yielded freely without resistance. She floated into a room filled with light. A wave of nausea swept over her. She brought her hands up to cover her mouth, but the rapid motion produced a rotation of her body, suspended in free space. She felt hands again, steadying her, guiding her into a vertical position relative to the room. Before her loomed the smiling face of Charles Stormer.

"My apologies, Ms. Montgomery. I know how disorienting this is to the unprepared, but the sensation will pass. After a while, your balance will get adjusted to the weightlessness and you'll actually find it quite enjoyable."

At the sound of Stormer's voice, Ilsa felt a cold chill. She was completely naked. Instinctively, she brought her arms down to cover her breasts, causing another uncontrolled rotation of her body, which Stormer halted by placing his hand on her bare hips. Seeing her fear and embarrassment, Stormer smiled more broadly. "Come now, Ms. Montgomery, I thought I would get a friendlier greeting from you, given that it has been ten thousand years since we last met."

The breath went out of Ilsa. She felt faint. The disconnected sequence of the last few moments fell into place. Her conversation with Stormer, their dinner together, the scarlet glow of a New Life launch vehicle, and the slightly bitter tang to the wine were as fresh in her mind as if they had just happened. With helpless dismay she took in her surroundings and noted the similarity to the space capsule she had seen at the IGET Conference. Somehow, she was now in one of those capsules, and if she believed Stormer, ten thousand years had passed. Life as she'd known it was gone forever. She might as well be dead. She peered into the sinister eyes of Charles Stormer and saw in them the soul of her murderer. While feeling the need to scream in rage, she grasped the futility of any outburst. Instead, she dropped her arms slowly to her side. Her soul cried out in unfathomable rage, but she assumed an artificial serenity. She stared intently back at Stormer and he turned away.

"Where are my clothes?" she asked coldly.

"They've been safely stowed," Stormer replied. "I'm afraid they're quite out of fashion now. I have a robe for you, but robes don't do well in weightlessness. If you follow me, I'll help you change into something more comfortable." Stormer's eyes scanned Ilsa with little deference to the shame and vulnerability he knew she felt.

He grabbed a series of handles along the bulkhead of the capsule and propelled himself through a hatch leading to a large cylindrical room, narrowing at its far end, where a ladder spun like the hand of a clock.

Ilsa followed, composing her thoughts. Her whole world had fallen apart and receded into oblivion. Her life had no meaning or context now. She contemplated suicide. If she were buried alive, could it be more terrifying? The difference was that here she shared her isolation. Though she despised Stormer more than she believed possible, she knew he wasn't self-destructive. He and his New Life colleagues had enough confidence in the existence of another Earth to undertake this seemingly impossible endeavor. She needed to learn more about their plans.

Stormer negotiated the spinning ladder, disappearing as he descended. Ilsa followed him, intrigued to sense the pull of gravity again as she moved downward. Stepping off, she felt comfortably attached to the floor of a large room, dimly illuminated with white LED lighting. The gravitational field was not as strong as on Earth, and she walked carefully to avoid the momentum of muscles accustomed to greater weight.

Stormer stopped before a wall cabinet at eye-level, opened it and brought out a folded garment. He tossed it to Ilsa, a white linen robe, which she donned quickly, fastening it with metal snaps. The light cloth ended far above her knees, showing a good fraction of her thighs. Stormer watched her intently from across the room. Ilsa glared back defiantly until he turned away, mumbling, "This way, please."

Stormer walked through a doorway to another room with a lounge area, tables and chairs, a galley, and a series of computer desks and large video monitors. A man wearing the same metallic gray jumpsuit as Stormer sat at the table. His face registered overt annoyance and he made no effort to hide the scorn he aimed at Ilsa.

"Ms. Montgomery," Stormer announced, "This is Dr. Andrew Harding. Perhaps you've heard of him. He's not only a business partner in New Life, he's also one of the founders of the Galactic Space Explorers Union."

Stormer waited for a response from Ilsa that did not come. She stood impassively in the doorway. He seemed to be expecting a dramatic outburst from her, but Ilsa refused to be intimidated. She leaned casually against the wall of the cabin with a smile of patient condescension, almost as if bored.

Stormer swept his arm toward the table and said, "Won't you sit down and join us? Now that you can't use anything I tell you to interfere with our mission, I'll be glad to answer questions." He waited, arm extended in a gesture of forced gallantry. Ilsa paused a moment and finally strode to the table, taking the seat across from Harding.

Stormer went to a computer terminal. He spoke commands, producing a radar display on the monitor: concentric circles with radial arms in green sweeping across a background of black. On the display were numerous red dots.

"Each dot represents one of the New Life space vehicles. There are more than 750 of them. The occupants have been frozen since we left Earth. They will be unfrozen when we reach our destination."

"Your flock," Ilsa commented dryly. "Hundreds of innocent people putting their trust in you to find a new planet to inhabit."

"I know what you're thinking, Ms. Montgomery. You think New Life is one of those pathetic groups hoping to establish a Utopian society to live in peace and tranquility. Not true at all. Quite the opposite."

"Why don't you stop playing games, Stormer, and say what you want to say?"

"Very well," he replied. "I'll tell you the plan. Those blissful young people you saw at the compound are not all on our vehicles. Only the women are — about 300 of them. The men were just recruiters. New Life hired them for their appearance and personality. It's amazing really how easily people can be convinced of anything. I'm afraid they'll all be disappointed when they awake to find conditions very different from what they imagined."

Ilsa shook her head incredulously. "Why would you do something so despicable?"

Stormer laughed. "Aside from having 300 beautiful women at our mercy, we do have other plans for the young ladies. You see, the other 450 vehicles contain an army of men trained in survival and paramilitary tactics at another New Life compound. Our hope for a colony on another planet lies with them. They've the strength and skills to overcome incredible obstacles."

Ilsa groaned inwardly. "What kind of colony is that? With all that testosterone, it won't be long before they're killing each other. What about the women? Do they stay home with the laundry while the men are hunting alien wildebeests?"

Stormer grew impatient with Ilsa's sarcasm. "No, Ms. Montgomery. If I may be blunt without disturbing your moral sensitivities, the women will be sexual partners, keeping the men happy and having babies to populate the new colony."

Ilsa's mouth dropped. She was speechless for a moment. "I must be dreaming. This is a nightmare. You intend to start a new world with ruthless mercenaries and kidnapped women." She turned to look at Dr. Harding, who just shrugged. "And what's your role in this astonishingly foolish scheme" she asked.

Harding smiled and for the first time lowered the cup that had been hovering just beneath his lips. He considered the question, "Information control," he answered

"Come again," Ilsa said with a shake of her head.

"Information control is very important in an endeavor like this. My possession of a supply ship means I can provide Mr. Stormer and his fellow travelers the information they need, while keeping others from knowing too much."

"That's ridiculous," Ilsa said. "Your information would be so old no one could act on it."

"Perhaps," said Harding, "but the first part of my role is more important. If for some reason Stormer's efforts to start a colony fail, his group will return to this supply ship and I'll direct them to another promising destination — maybe one already settled."

Ilsa glanced back and forth between Harding and Stormer, her exasperation uncontrollable. "So it's not enough for you to deceive young women and force them to serve you and your frozen hooligans. You might actually hijack the successful efforts of other colonists. That's the plan?" She spat the words out.

Harding just shrugged.

"So what's in it for you?" Ilsa asked him, her journalistic instincts returning.

Harding leaned back in his chair. "Let's just say Mr. Stormer helped me a long time ago and I'm repaying him."

Ilsa looked at Stormer, who was smiling smugly. "I hope you understand now, Ms. Montgomery. What a wonderful exposé you could've written ten thousand years ago. Pulitzer Prize material. Now the information is useless to you."

"Then why entertain me with your arrogant rambles? You could've killed me and left me in the desert."

Stormer sighed. "What fun would that be? I like you, Ms. Montgomery. You and I will make a great couple, side by side starting a new world together. Perhaps our children…"

Ilsa rose from her seat, spilling the table, amazed at how easy it was in the reduced gravity of the ship. She lunged at Stormer, surprising him with the fury of her attack. He fell backward in his chair. Ilsa was thrilled to see the fear on his face. She had him by the throat, not really applying pressure, but enjoying the panic in his eyes. Then she felt Harding's arms around her waist, pulling her up in a move more sexual than combative. He held her against his body as she struggled to get away, then finally threw her to the floor. She slid across the slick metallic surface and crashed head first into the wall. A stinging pain went through her lower lip and she tasted blood. She lay there face down and motionless, sobbing uncontrollably. An enormous fatigue overcame her. She wished she could sleep. Her body went limp.

"Are you sure you want to deal with her?" Harding asked Stormer. "She can be easily disposed of."

Stormer composed himself. "She'll be worth the trouble," he said. "I'm sure of it."

"Let's carry her to her quarters." Harding said.

Ilsa remained limp as the two men dragged her across the floor like a corpse in a body bag. A hatchway hissed open and she was thrown through the opening. Another hiss followed and the room was dark and silent. A faint iridescent glow emanated from LED lights embedded in the ceiling. Occupying the small room was a cot with pillow and blankets. Ilsa crawled over and lifted herself onto the cot with just enough strength and will to position the pillow beneath her head and carelessly cover herself with the blanket. Her knees drawn upward, she wept silently. She could not bring herself to do anything but lament her fate. She hoped sleep would offer relief from her tormented thoughts, but that did not happen. Instead, her panic made her more alert and agitated. She recalled the sensation upon waking in the space capsule, of having been buried alive in a tomb of infinite dimensions. The indicator lights in the confinement cylinder had glowed with a life of their own, tiny souls hovering in the blackness of space. Her life now had no more meaning than those dim pinpoints of light, helplessly bound to sources of power beyond their control.

Ilsa finally drifted off to sleep, hypnotized by the steadfast glimmer of those luminous specks.

She was awoken by the sound of the door opening. Light entered the room from the corridor. Stormer appeared, holding an object in his hand that she first took to be a flashlight. "It's time to get up, Ms. Montgomery. You might want to have something to eat. You won't eat again for five thousand years."

Ilsa blinked at him, not moving. "In case you're wondering," he said, "this is an electromagnetic pulse weapon. Your violence earlier makes it impossible for me to trust you. Please, get up and follow my instructions."

Ilsa recalled her outburst and regretted it. The extra care Stormer was taking now would make it even more difficult to escape. She rose from the cot and followed him into the galley where she ate perfunctorily, ignoring Stormer sitting across from her. She mused bitterly about the capacity of living organisms to execute the routine activities necessary to sustain life, even when external conditions made those functions completely meaningless. People often spoke of the spirit living after the physical being has perished, but few spoke about how physical needs persist long after one's spirit has been destroyed.

Harding entered and filled a cup with coffee from a machine built into the wall of the galley. He leaned back on the counter and addressed Stormer. "I've given you all the information you need to proceed to your next destination. It's been uploaded to your computer. All the other vehicles have been programmed to follow yours. There's no reason for you to remain here and use up valuable oxygen supplies on my ship."

"Very well," said Stormer. "We'll be off. As soon as I'm certain about the success, or lack of success, of our mission, I'll send you a message."

With that, he rose from his chair and, still holding the weapon, motioned for Ilsa to follow him. She trembled uncontrollably. Somehow she had thought she'd have more time before being frozen again. Unsteadily, she stood and took one final glance around the room, looking for some diversion or excuse to buy her extra time, but the room was totally void of any source of comfort or chance of escape.

They proceeded to the ladder, Ilsa walking steps ahead of Stormer. He stopped her before she started up. "You might want to take off your robe now." She turned and gave him a hard stare. "Very well. Suit yourself," he said with a sardonic smile.

She ascended the rungs, feeling dizzy and disoriented, as if she were falling backward. Stormer climbed up and held her in place with one hand against her lower back. She hurried upward, desperate to escape his touch. Nearing the top, she became lighter and launched herself upward with a gentle pull on the handrail. She bumped her head against the wall of the cylindrical corridor that led back to the docked vehicles. Stormer gave her a shove and she found herself floating freely toward the docking room. To her dismay, the robe she was wearing seemed to have a life of its own. The cloth floated up entangling her arms. The lower half of her body was uncovered and in full view of Stormer. She extracted her arms from the garment and flung it back toward him, but he easily batted it away. She drifted the remaining distance to the docking area. Stormer pressed a switch and a hatchway opened, revealing the interior of the space vehicle. She maneuvered into it, trying not to scrape against the metallic edges of the hatch. She found herself in the capsule's control room. At its far end was the hatchway of the confinement chamber she'd occupied for the last ten thousand years.

"Put your arms straight down at your sides and make your body rigid," Stormer commanded.

In a dream-like trance, Ilsa did as she was told. Stormer hooked his feet in a pair of handles on the wall. With his legs locked, he reached over and grabbed Ilsa's waist, lifted her, and steered her feet first into the cylindrical opening of the chamber. Her body tensed. He squeezed harder and in a moment she was through the narrow opening, stopping only when her heels bumped against the far wall of the cylinder.

"Hold still," Stormer said. "I'm activating the ceramic pins."

Ilsa heard a faint whirring sound as multiple blunt protrusions pressed into her head, torso, legs and arms.

"Now relax," Stormer commanded. "We will meet again, Ms. Montgomery, in a seemingly short time."

Ilsa heard a loud hum and a red LED display in front of her said, "CHARGING." A moment later, the hatch at the end of the magnetocryogenic chamber above her head closed and darkness enveloped her. She could see nothing except the multi-colored indicator lights embedded in the walls.

Panic overcame her. She'd never felt so helpless. She wanted to scream out in agony. Directly in front of her, a series of digits counted down by seconds. If this was the time until the batteries were fully charged and the freezing sequence commenced, she had less than twenty minutes.

Ilsa struggled to turn about in the chamber, but the pins restricted her. Under her right hand she felt a mushroom shaped protrusion about the size of her fist. She remembered the large red button she had asked Benjamin about at the IGET Conference. She'd joked that it was the ejection button, but he'd told her it was a switch to interrupt the freezing process in an emergency. Stormer had either forgotten about it, or wasn't worried Ilsa would activate it. If she pressed it, would alarms go off? Where was Stormer? With the end of the cylinder closed, she could hear nothing from the other part of the space capsule. Would he wait until the freezing process was completed before returning to his own vehicle? Or would he board his capsule and launch both simultaneously, even before Ilsa had been completely frozen? In any case, she had to take a chance. She could wait till the last possible minute and then hit the power off switch. If she kept from being frozen, she'd have more time. She waited, watching the countdown clock.

With ten minutes still remaining, she felt the vehicle vibrate, sensed a slight acceleration, and realized her capsule was detached from the supply ship and moving rapidly away. This was encouraging. Stormer was less likely to notice when she aborted the charging sequence. She placed her closed fist over the mushroom-shaped button and prepared to depress it at the last possible moment. Now only sixty seconds remained. She wondered how far her vehicle had moved away from the supply ship. She could sense the accelerating speed transmitted through the craft's hull.

With one second to go, she slammed her fist down. Instantly the LED display changed from "CHARGING" to "STANDBY". The ceramic pins withdrew. She could move more easily again. Reaching above her she felt about the circular hatch at the end of the cylinder and found another button. When she pressed it, the hatch opened. She kicked her feet against the cylinder to propel herself out of the chamber.

Once in the larger part of the capsule, she sighed, relieved, and composed herself. There was no way of telling whether Stormer or Harding knew she had aborted the freezing process.

Ilsa floated to a bank of stowage compartments built into the hull of the vehicle. The compartments were filled with food and survival gear. In one, she found a plastic pouch with the clothes she'd been wearing when she visited the New Life compound. She tore open the package. The garments floated weightlessly about her in ridiculous shapes. She saw the necklace Benjamin had given her at the IGET Conference. Ilsa caught hold of the medallion and ran her fingers along its smooth surface, comforted by its flawless solidity. The necklace had attracted Benjamin's artistic eye then, but it had lost its brilliance here in the dim light of the capsule. Ilsa pulled the strand over her head and positioned the medallion to lie against her chest, but without gravity the object hovered several inches away from her skin.

In the next compartment, Ilsa found a microfiber jumpsuit similar to the one Stormer had been wearing. With considerable effort, she maneuvered and twisted herself into the suit and zipped it up. She felt comforted by the texture of the cloth against her flesh. Though not cold inside the capsule, the exposure of her skin to the air as she moved about chilled her. She pushed herself gently toward the capsule's control console and pulled herself into the seat, buckling herself in with the safety harness. She sat for several moments gazing at the monitor, displaying row upon row of meaningless numbers. She knew her capsule was part of

Stormer's fleet, pre-programmed to follow the course he had selected. She needed a way to detach her vehicle from the others, even though by doing so she'd be alone and hopelessly lost in space.

Some of the numbers on the monitor were understandable. Next to the word "OXYGEN" were the digits "14423". The number decreased by one every few minutes. The rate of decrease was reassuring. Ilsa estimated there were about 70 hours of oxygen left in the vehicle. She needed to conserve her supply, not knowing how much she'd need later. At some point, she'd have to return to the cylinder and start the freezing process again to be able to survive until her next destination was reached, wherever that happened to be — unless she just gave up and let the oxygen run out, releasing her from a more uncertain, more terrifying fate. It was only a fleeting thought however, not because of any misguided sense of optimism, but more because the complex array of electronics in front of her seemed to offer infinite possibilities and a finite amount of hope.

The medallion, which had been floating just below eye level, drifted into view. She wondered how its information allowed one space traveler to meet another at a prearranged location and time. Benjamin had lectured her about DNA and how it was nothing more than a complex mode of communicating information about an organism from one generation to another. She understood that the information was coded in chemical bonds within the molecular structure of DNA. The information in the medallion must be similarly coded into the lattice of its metallic structure. How would her son have extracted the information?

She unhooked the harness and floated nearer to the console. Running her hands gently over the displays and switches she found a narrow slot whose length matched the shorter dimension of the medallion. She removed the necklace and inserted the rectangle into the slot. It was a perfect fit. She heard a faint click. She tugged slightly on the medallion, but a mechanism in the console had locked it in place.

The display on the computer monitor changed. It showed a

series of rows now. At the beginning of each were the letters "SS" followed by a single digit. The remainder of the row contained four numbers. Ilsa guessed that "SS" stood for "Supply Ship" and the single digit denoted different ships at which the old lady hoped to meet up with her son. Three of the four numbers must be the ship coordinates, like those Benjamin had used in the simulator at the conference. The fourth number might be the time of the rendezvous. If so, then all Ilsa had to do was determine how to reprogram her vehicle to navigate to one of those destinations.

At the left end of each row was an icon resembling a control button. Realizing the screen was touch-sensitive, Ilsa placed a trembling finger on the button next to "SS6". A message appeared: "Invalid Location. Destination can not be reached at the time specified." She pressed a button next to the message that read "CANCEL" and selected the next location: "SS1". Again, the "Invalid Location" message came up. Her heart sinking, she pressed the button next to "SS3". To her surprise and relief, the message now read, "Calculating...".

Moments later, it read, "SS3, ETA 21326.37648. PROGRAM?" Next to it was a button saying simply "OK". She stared at the screen for several seconds. She wasn't sure how to interpret the number, but if the five digits to the left of the decimal represented years, then the ETA for her arrival at SS3 was dishearteningly more than 8000 years away. She let out a deep breath and pressed the "OK" button. She had to believe the freezing process would make the time lapse imperceptible. A message appeared immediately: "Initiating". On the control console, lights changed from green to red, and the numerical display altered itself rapidly. She felt a mild vibration transmitted from the body of the capsule, followed by a change in the vehicle's acceleration. The capsule was altering its course.

She watched the numbers on the display until the maneuver was completed and the red lights turned back to green. She heard a click and reached over and pulled the medallion from its slot with no resistance. She held the smooth metal to her lips and kissed it lightly, her eyes closed in silent thanks. Now it was time to return to the cylinder and reinitiate the freezing process.

She removed the jumpsuit, stowed it back in its pouch, and reluctantly released the medallion into the same compartment. She floated to the freezing cylinder. With tremendous force of will, she projected her body feet first into the claustrophobic opening. After trying several switches with no discernible results, she found a button which read in faint blue light, "POWER". On pressing it, she heard a hum. The display that read "STANDBY" in green changed to "CHARGING" in red. The countdown clock now said 30 minutes. When it reached 20, a red light appeared and the countdown stopped. With a start, she remembered the ceramic pins were still retracted. There was probably an interlock that halted the charging process until the traveler was fully in place with the ceramic pins extended. She tried several switches embedded in the chamber wall, but with no success. Finally, she found a button where she should have suspected it would be: at her left hand diametrically opposite the emergency power off button, similar in shape but smaller. Before pressing it, she puzzled at a message in green that had been activated when she was trying different switches. It read simply, "TRANSMIT." Ignoring it she pressed the button at her left hand and the ceramic pins extended, pressing into her skin. The countdown clock started again. She remained still, heart pounding.

"God help me," she said to the emptiness around her. A moment later she closed her eyes and sighed weakly. "God," and after a pause added, "Help me." Minutes later, she heard a loud, ear-shattering bang and the last thought she had was that Benjamin had been wrong. It hurt like hell when the magnets turned on, magnetic shock being little different from electrical shock. Ilsa lost consciousness. A short time later the external hatch of the cylinder opened. Surrounded by cold empty space, her body tissue froze from the outside in, the magnetic field remaining on until the process was complete.

She was suspended by the cylinder's ceramic pins, her body at nearly absolute zero now, accelerating rapidly toward a dubious rendezvous in space.

Andrew Harding was nearly ready to board his vehicle to depart Supply Station 5 for another hundred years. He stopped at the computer console to check the status indicators. The message light was on. With a voice command, he played the message. "God help me," a female voice said. Several seconds later, the message repeated. "God, help me."

Perplexed, Harding gave added commands to the computer. A radar display appeared showing the location of Stormer's fleet of vehicles. One vehicle was separated from the others, highlighted by a red blinking circle. Harding spoke a command to the computer and a list of numbers appeared on the screen next to the object.

"Damn," Harding whispered under his breath. The vehicle was on a course to Supply Ship 3. He wondered how the destination had changed. Speaking another command into the computer, a new stream of data appeared on the screen. Embedded in the text was the name of the passenger of the vehicle: Ilsa Montgomery.

"Damn," Harding repeated. "Damned, fool," he added thinking about Stormer's misguided attempt to kidnap the woman and bring her along on the expedition. To unfreeze her just to gloat about what he had done and terrorize her with threats and innuendos was risky and unnecessary. The woman was obviously more resourceful than Stormer realized. Harding's first thought was to wake Stormer and have him intercept the woman and put her back on course. Ms. Montgomery had heard enough of their plans to make trouble for them. Though Harding had many followers in the Union, he knew the custodians of Supply Ship 3 would not take well to what Stormer had done.

Harding resolved that the safest course of action was to destroy Ms. Montgomery's vehicle. She was still within reach of the supply ship's directed energy weapon, which could fire an electromagnetic pulse strong enough to neutralize the capsule's power systems. Though it would do little structural damage, without power the ship would be unable to navigate and defenseless against incoming particles. Ms. Montgomery, if she survived the EMP blast, would drift through space, frozen forever, until the vehicle collided with something or was captured by the gravitational pull of a star and fell into its vaporizing heat.

Harding spoke new commands and a set of red cross-hairs appeared on the screen. With the joystick he positioned them over his target. Then he said in a firm voice, "Charge EMP."

There was a whirring sound from the ship. After thirty seconds a message appeared in large green letters, "EMP WEAPON ARMED."

"Fire EMP," Harding commanded.

There was no sound and no vibration as an invisible burst of concentrated radiation emanated from the supply ship at nearly the speed of light. In seconds the pulse reached Ilsa's vehicle. As it passed through the spacecraft, it created current surges that burned the electrical components and reduced the circuit boards to cold, useless masses of metal and silicon. Ilsa remained frozen in the confinement cylinder, but the vehicle was powerless to either guide or protect her.

Harding commanded his computer to display the status of the vehicle, still appearing weakly in the radar scan. The words appeared: "NO DATA". Harding exhaled loudly. Methodically he went through the remaining checks. Finished, he sent a message to Stormer explaining that he'd been forced to terminate Ms. Montgomery because she'd somehow managed to reprogram her vehicle. He concluded, "Her death is on your hands," knowing Stormer would see the message when he was unfrozen at his destination.

"Damned fool," Harding said to himself again, and then continued his preparations for departure from the supply ship.

CHAPTER 10

— 18215 —

During his stop at Supply Ship 2, Benjamin was directed to a planet 2000 light-years away. Observations made by custodians of the supply ship showed the planet possessed a rich oxygen atmosphere sufficient for life. Even so, Benjamin followed Union procedures and made more extensive observations upon arrival before venturing to land on its surface.

It had a large moon with a high reflectivity. The light from that imposing object would dominate the night sky. Like Earth, the planet sported an intrinsic magnetic field, which focused energetic particles from the planet's sun, producing rings of auroral luminosity persistently suspended over the north and south poles. The numerous crater-like features on the planet's surface indicated it was young with abundant volcanic activity. The biggest obstacle for Benjamin though was the planet's high surface temperature, well over 100 degrees Fahrenheit. Only at the high latitudes was the temperature tolerable for humans.

Benjamin considered the risks of landing. The computer programs on the vehicle were optimized to search for level landing sites near the equator. Measurements of the high latitude regions were less reliable because of the oblique viewing angle. Given the dangers, he could easily justify aborting the mission. However, the observations intrigued him, and he couldn't afford to wait until enough data were acquired to confirm the safety of the landing site.

He strapped himself in the console chair and reclined it. The entire landing sequence was under computer control. Never one to enjoy thrill rides, Benjamin tensed every muscle in his body and clenched his eyes tightly shut. The kinetic sensations were so intense he could do nothing else. Only when he felt the sudden deceleration caused by the deployment of the parachute did he open his eyes. He activated the external video camera as the vehicle descended. The planet's bizarre landscape appeared on the video monitor, filling him with awe. Vast fields of black lava extended to distant volcanic peaks set against an azure sky. The rockets blasted intense streams of superheated air downward, battling the relentless pull of gravity and slowing the capsule's fall. His video image was obliterated by a great plume of black ash rising from the planet's surface. The abrupt cessation of the roaring engines and the gentle thump of the vehicle on the ground told Benjamin he'd landed safely. He sat still for a while, listening carefully. All he heard was residual hissing from the rocket engines and a crackling sound as the capsule's metallic hull came to thermal equilibrium with the planet's atmosphere.

Rising from his seat, Benjamin savored the sense of control gravity brought to his equilibrium. He moved unsteadily to a cabinet built into the capsule's hull and pulled out a spacesuit and helmet, which attached to the suit by interlocking metallic rings. He doubted that he needed the helmet, as the vehicle's readings showed the planet's atmosphere to be both breathable and safe.

Once suited up, he waited until the monitor confirmed the black cloud of ash had settled. Particulates seeping into the vehicle could damage the on-board electronics. He opened the capsule's main hatch and climbed out, jumping the last meter while holding onto a handle built into the exterior hull. He scanned the landscape before him. The ground beneath his feet consisted of fine black volcanic sand. Less than 100 meters away, the surface was covered with large, irregular stones that would have proven disastrous for a landing attempt. The capsule's automated guidance system had done well.

Benjamin removed his helmet and took his first breath of the planet's alien atmosphere. It was like Earth's, except the blast of hot air took his breath away. A temperature sensor built into the sleeve of his spacesuit read 105 degrees Fahrenheit. There was no wind and no discernible humidity.

Benjamin moved away from the capsule. The rock-strewn landscape extended in all directions, sloping gradually upward to rugged volcanic peaks in the distance. The three largest peaks, spaced almost equally apart, showed evidence of past lava flows radiating outward. Just above the horizon near one of the peaks was the brilliant blue star that was the planet's sun. It appeared no larger than Earth's sun, but the heat it produced even at low elevation was far more intense.

From the position of the sun in the sky, Benjamin estimated it was near noon, but at this high latitude determining how much daylight remained was difficult. It didn't matter though, as also looming in the sky was a nearly full moon. Its luminosity was muted now, but once the sun set, Benjamin had little doubt there would be sufficient light from this formidable orb. He set off to explore. Water would be the limiting factor, as the hot, dry conditions necessitated frequent hydration.

Camera in hand, Benjamin started toward the volcanic peak in the north to avoid having to stare into the bright sun. Before long he found himself walking along a sandy channel with few obstructions. Rocky slopes on either side of the channel obscured the sunlight, giving him relief from the relentless heat. The sandy course was caused by erosion. Water or some other flowing liquid had sculpted the landscape, creating the deep gouges through the surrounding volcanic rock. Benjamin's observations gave no indication of water in the atmosphere at the present time. Certainly the heat and dryness of the air would rapidly evaporate any moisture present.

The deepening channel forced him to remain within the rocky talus slopes that flanked him on either side. He took pictures along the way, although little appealed to him either artistically or scientifically. The best he could do was capture an unlikely combination of sunlight and shadow. Had he been on Earth, he'd have been alert for the occasional animal, or an anomalous burst of color from the rocks, but here the interminable sameness of the path before him did nothing to inspire him. There was no breeze and no odor, but he imagined the scent of sulfur, and attributed this to the hellish-like landscape fooling his visual and olfactory senses. Not really sure what he was looking for, he wondered how long he should continue. The blue sun was setting and the path darkening. The shadows changed from the sharp delineations caused by the sun to the more blended silhouettes shaped by the planet's bright moon.

As he was about to turn around, dreading the return through the same featureless channel, he felt a vibration beneath his feet and heard a distant rumble, like rolling thunder. Benjamin stopped to listen more carefully. The sound and vibration intensified and he experienced a growing fear that he had ventured into a region of unknown and possibly perilous hazards. He felt helplessly confined within the rock-strewn walls of the channel and craved a better vantage point for observing the catastrophic event taking place. Selecting a spot that appeared scalable, he began to scramble up, but each step only dislodged loose stones into the sandy channel. He continued his efforts, driven by curiosity and fear. Gradually, he made progress up the slope. His shins and knees were scraped mercilessly by the jagged stones, but the microfiber material of the spacesuit didn't tear or shred.

At last the slope became less steep and he made better time moving upward. Before long he was standing on level ground at the top of a ridge extending radially outward from the volcanic peak toward which he had been walking. From this position, he was able to see the source of the thunderous sound that now filled the air. The volcano before him was emitting a powerful stream of white extending high into the heavens. Benjamin was shocked into immobility by its awesome intensity. He stood watching and soon felt drops of moisture falling on his upturned face. Licking his lips, he confirmed the drops were water. The distant peak was a geyser, spewing tons of water and steam into the dusk sky. He settled into a depression in the rocky surface and sat down to watch.

The sky darkened rapidly as the sun set, but its light still struck the upper reaches of the fountain producing a majestic rainbow crowning the distant peak. The rainbow, brilliant against the night sky, was just the kind of paradoxical event Benjamin sought. Hands trembling, he reached for his camera to capture the scene. While adjusting the shutter speed and aperture to compensate for the varying shades and color intensities, his peripheral vision detected a new celestial glow forming. Elusive as it was, whenever he turned to see it more closely it disappeared. Only after the sky had darkened further did the light manifest itself as distinct curtains of green, magenta and red, undulating and oscillating across the sky from east to west. Benjamin recognized it as the aurora, and again he was challenged to adjust his camera setting to now capture the geyser, the nighttime rainbow, and the aurora. In the foreground was the mountain peak with its radial talus slopes barely illuminated by the muted light from the planet's moon. If he successfully captured the image, he'd have a single picture showing light produced by four distinct physical mechanisms. Indeed, the entire electromagnetic spectrum shone before him in all its glory, sculpted into a spectacular display unique to this alien planet.

For a long time he observed the spectacle. When the fountain finally subsided, it was completely dark except for the glow from the rising moon. The rainbow faded with the last drops of moisture in the atmosphere, but the aurora continued, the curtain of light now creating its own celestial show.

Benjamin decided it was time to make his way back to the capsule. He had solved the riddle of the planet's oxygen atmosphere, though others more scientifically disposed would have to confirm his conclusion. The core of the planet had to contain a reservoir of heated water and oxygen. The numerous volcanoes about the planet continually replenished the atmosphere even as it was swept away into space by the strong solar wind from the blue star. The planet could sustain life as long as the supply of oxygen beneath its surface lasted. Geothermal energy within the planet was necessary to force the water and oxygen periodically to the surface. If that were to diminish, the inhabitants would have to drill down to the oxygen to release it to the surface. By cultivating crops though, they could augment the oxygen supply through photosynthetic processes. However, there was little arable land, most of the surface being dominated by impenetrable volcanic rock.

Making his way back along the channel, Benjamin again felt

vibrations beneath his feet. He continued on, believing it to be another geyser, but the sound grew more intense. He didn't realize anything was wrong until the roar became a clatter, disturbingly close. Angry and disappointed with himself, he suddenly realized that the water emitted from the geyser was advancing on him through the channel. The rumbling was a flash flood, just like those on Earth. The physics of water was the same everywhere in the universe. Tons of it streamed down the channel from the volcanic peak carrying rocks and boulders like twigs. If he did not escape the onslaught, he would find himself among the insignificant masses being swept along helplessly by the hydraulic force of water and gravity.

His initial attempt to scramble up the slope to escape the deluge failed. Loose stones fell backward behind him and though he struggled frantically, he gained little ground. Just as the wall of rock and mud and water reached him, Benjamin managed to elevate himself just high enough to avoid the first tumbling stones. Flattening his body against the slope, he inched upward. When the roiling mass filled the channel from side to side, his feet were just above its turbulent surface. He clung there helplessly, hoping the water would rise no higher. He cursed his error in not anticipating the flood. The deafening roar filled his ears and brought tears to his eyes. He thought of his father and breathlessly apologized to him for his stupidity, and for disappointing him by failing on his first mission.

The water rose above his knees. He struggled to keep from being swept away. His feet were battered by rocks in the muddy stream. He alternately raised one foot then the other, seeking relief from the onslaught. Finally the water level began to subside. He still worried the water in the channel would erode away the stones below him and the entire wall he clung to would collapse into the stream, but somehow the integrity of the slope held. The water level receded and he allowed himself to be optimistic about his chance of survival. He dared not move until he was absolutely certain the unstable rocks beneath him would not suddenly give way. At last, he released his grip on the rocks and scrambled back down into the channel. There was still a layer of muddy water several inches deep, bubbling and churning in myriad tiny streams and whirlpools.

Benjamin stood and removed his camera from the belt upon which it had been attached. With trembling hands he took pictures of the remaining water percolating slowly into the sandy bottom of the channel. Disappointed he was only able to photograph the weak aftermath of the torrent, he started back, unsteadily making his way through the muddy concourse, avoiding the newly deposited rocks and boulders. The water level subsided further until all that remained was wet compacted sand, easier to negotiate than the softer dry sand he had walked on before. He was tired and shaky, and the planet's moon was too low on the horizon to provide adequate light on his path, but he couldn't help feeling that the ground around him was moving. He stopped and peered intently into the darkness. The surface was rippling in tiny wave-like motions no larger than his big toe. It was covered with tiny black creatures emerging from beneath the sand and moving laterally in corkscrew motions.

Benjamin's ears still rang from the roar of the flood, but after several moments of gazing at the little black amphibians he heard their diminutive cries. Part helpless plaints, part triumphant exclamations, the sounds emanating from the thousands of creatures combined to produce simultaneous feelings of supreme loneliness and boundless elation in Benjamin. Who knew how long they'd remained beneath the gloomy sands of the channel, waiting for the next burst of life-giving water to enable them to escape their dark and seemingly endless imprisonment? As he listened more closely, the disconnected sounds from the animals coalesced into a unique rhythm, not unlike the harmonic chorus of crickets Benjamin remembered hearing on Earth. As the coherence between their cries increased, the song of celebration they emitted became louder, and Benjamin thought sorrowfully of how useless his camera was in capturing the life process being carried out at his feet. The stark contrast between the frailty of their existence and the sheer joy of being above ground, wriggling through the muddy water, appealed to his sense of artistic juxtaposition. Yet the medium for capturing the moment probably did not exist, certainly not in the camera hooked to his belt. Nevertheless, he began photographing in video mode with the audio pick-up tuned as sensitively as possible. He reflected on how alien and eerie the sound would be when played back. The life cycle of these little amphibians transcended space and time and their song was a call to the universe, an ode to life in all its unlikely forms.

As the water in the channel percolated away into the ground, so did the animals. Their brief ritual completed, they returned to their sub-surface prisons. Benjamin wasn't sure whether the music and dance he'd witnessed had been associated with them being born, mating, or simply absorbing nutrients that would allow them to exist until the next flood. He deliberated only momentarily about digging one up and bringing it back to his capsule as a sample, but he could not bring himself to disturb even one of the creatures that had appeared. The sand beneath him might also contain other organisms and perhaps subterranean plant-life with which the creatures shared a symbiotic relationship. As an explorer he felt bound to investigate these possibilities, but as another solitary life form in the vast universe, he chose to leave this rare and beautiful ecosystem undisturbed. Indeed, the entrapment of the animals beneath the sand was not unlike the freezing process that enabled Benjamin to stay alive between those times he would be awoken to experience life once again, even if only briefly.

CHAPTER 11
— 18877 —

A hundred years after receiving the distress call from the mysterious vehicle heading toward Supply Ship 3, Arthur and Krystal underwent a routine unfreezing process to check the status of the supply ship's systems and review the data received in the intervening years. Taking her usual place at the control console, Krystal queried the computer for the status of the unknown vehicle. When the message "No data" appeared, Krystal turned to Arthur and said, "Her capsule is not transmitting anymore."

"When did that happen?"

Krystal entered commands and examined the stream of numbers that appeared. She frowned. "About 17 hours after the voice transmission we picked up."

"Is there any clue as to what happened?"

"No," Krystal replied. "Everything looked normal up until that time."

"She must have known something was wrong to sound as hopeless as she did." Arthur examined the numbers on the screen. "Send a follow-up message to Supply Ship 3. Tell them we lost contact with the vehicle. Ask them to be alert for vehicles in distress at the expected time of arrival we transmitted before. Request they alert all spacecraft in the area to intercept and board any unidentified capsule not transmitting signals. It's a long-shot, but there's a chance she survived."

"She might still be alive," Krystal agreed, "but she may not end up anywhere near Supply Ship 3. If she lost her navigation system along with the communication system, then she'll just move in a straight line until she encounters something along the way. Her course to Supply Ship 3 would not necessarily have been direct. It might have been toward a nearby star to take advantage of gravity-assisted acceleration."

"That's true. Then can you calculate a course from Supply Ship 5 to Supply Ship 3 to determine what her optimum route would've been? That way we can estimate what her heading was when she stopped transmitting."

Arthur stood behind Krystal as she worked. It was ironic. He'd joined the Union and left Earth to embrace the solitude that overwhelmed him after his wife died. Yet here thousands of years in the future and more than 4000 light-years from Earth he had found someone who made his loneliness as faint and distant as Earth and its life-giving sun. Krystal had been one of the first visitors to Supply Ship 6 and she lost no time engaging Arthur in a conversation lasting hours and touching on numerous topics. Arthur was especially intrigued to hear she had met Benjamin on the Union transfer station. Arthur already knew through Union communications that Benjamin had become a galactic explorer and was now on a voyage that would eventually bring him to Arthur's ship. He was amused when Krystal told him of her brief encounter with Benjamin. Though Krystal had always admired Arthur, her curiosity to meet him had become even more intense after talking with his son.

Krystal had spent six hours on Supply Ship 6 with Arthur, then returned to her vehicle and set a course toward her first planetary destination. She was only a few hundred light-years away when she'd been unfrozen by a coded Union command used only for emergencies. She exited her magnetocryogenic chamber and went to the control room to see what had happened. There she found a message from Arthur asking if she would care to be his partner on the supply ship. She accepted the offer, reprogrammed her vehicle, and headed back to Arthur, who welcomed her with unrestrained warmth and affection.

Arthur had been attracted not only by Krystal's dark beauty, but also her unique combination of astute intuitiveness and unsurpassed technical skills. Unlike the computer she so deftly commanded, Krystal was not only capable of precise reasoning and logic, she was also skilled at abstract analysis often requiring the relaxation of convention and the broadening of possibilities. It contrasted with Arthur's strength, which was based on firm adherence to the time-tested customs and practices of social science.

Indeed, his conservative approach to studying the similarities and differences among Earth's many cultures had served him well. His determination to apply well-proven analytical techniques gained him great respect. His work was not only praised by his peers, but easily communicated to the general public, giving power to ideas previously viewed as erudite, academic ramblings. Arthur and Krystal complemented each other, and together there were few challenges they were unable to overcome.

After a few minutes, Krystal completed her calculations and produced a display on the computer screen showing a map of the galaxy with the locations of the seven supply ships superimposed. Added to the display was a straight green line originating at Supply Ship 5 and extending toward the galactic center.

"The green line is her trajectory based on the assumption that her course was interrupted at the time the vehicle stopped transmitting data. Right now, she's passing Supply Ship 3 heading toward Supply Ship 1, but she'll pass by both unless she's intercepted."

Arthur nodded grimly. "Send a message to SS3. Let them know what her expected trajectory is."

Krystal shook her head. "Too late. By the time they receive our transmission, she'll be well past the ship. A vehicle in the vicinity of SS1 might have a better chance of rerouting and intercepting her in time."

"When will that be?" Arthur asked.

"Fifteen to twenty thousand years from now," Krystal answered.

"Send the message to SS1. And send a message to SS3 just in case. If their radar detected the vehicle passing by, ask them to send an update to SS1 on its expected location."

Arthur watched Krystal compose and transmit the message. He thought of Benjamin, probably speeding through space, frozen in his vehicle. He knew that perishing during the frozen stage of galactic voyages was a relatively rare event. He had heard of 38 deaths among Union members, but most of those occurred during the process of landing on and exploring other planets.

Thus far, Union efforts to find habitable planets had not borne fruit. Many contained valuable minerals and ores with the potential to be mined, but their inhabitability made mining an expensive and dangerous proposition. Arthur believed the true success of the Union's endeavors was the knowledge accumulated. The galactic explorers were merely information gatherers; the pay-off from the information would be realized many years in the future as scientists on Earth sorted through the volumes of data being returned.

Arthur and Krystal had studied with great interest what transpired on Earth in the first five thousand years after they left. He wanted to believe that civilization had escaped oblivion because of the knowledge obtained from space exploration. The observations made thus far confirmed that Earth was an extremely rare and unique planet. Only a small fraction of the galaxy had been explored, but it was increasingly clear that Earth's atmosphere possessed an unlikely combination of elements making the planet habitable.

Krystal completed the transmission and rose to stand next to Arthur. The screen still showed the predicted trajectory of the lost space vehicle. Before being frozen again for another hundred years, Krystal spent some time improving her computer programs. She had developed specialized routines that searched the incoming messages and flagged those most relevant to the topics and events she and Arthur were most intrigued by. That way, when they were unfrozen and returned to the ship, they could more easily find the information they were interested in. Of course, Arthur asked her to extract any transmissions pertaining to Benjamin, and each time they returned to the ship he waited breathlessly, dreading the possibility of receiving bad news about his son.

He had mixed feelings when he learned that Benjamin had joined the Union, but there was little he could do about it. He'd received the information thousands of years after Benjamin departed on his voyage. He knew by now Benjamin had visited Supply Ship 2 and then traveled on to a potentially habitable planet 2000 light years away from that location. He asked

Krystal to search incoming data and tag any information about planets in the vicinity of Supply Ship 2. He wanted to learn as much as possible about the worlds Benjamin might visit. Eventually his son's course would bring him to Supply Ship 6 and the two of them would be reunited after many thousands of years.

Chapter 12

— 20150 —

The first thing the Captain did upon being unfrozen was to look at the date display in his magnetocryogenic chamber. He was encouraged to see it did not read 22000 years. He, Brian, and Emily had agreed they would abandon their search for a habitable planet in that year unless they were successful in finding one meeting their requirements.

The second display he looked at was the one showing how much oxygen was left in his space capsule — only 52 hours worth. He'd have to work quickly if he was to unfreeze Emily and Brian to help him confirm the success of their experiment to create a habitable environment on an alien planet.

The experiment was Emily's idea. It involved launching canisters of material from Earth onto the surface of alien planets. Each canister contained a stew of organisms in a growth culture consisting of seeds, soil, bacteria, dead organic matter, fertilizer, and other substances selected to catalyze the chemical processes necessary for life. If conditions were right, this material would grow and spread, ultimately creating an Earth-like biosphere. The canisters had been frozen in a specialized vehicle from which they were ejected onto the surface of prospective planets, breaking open upon impact. Because they were carried in magnetocryogenic chambers similar to the cylinders the space travelers occupied, the material in the canisters was still biologically active when launched into the alien atmospheres.

While on Supply Ship 5, Brian and Emily identified eight prospective planets within a volume of space several hundred light-years across. They attempted to find worlds in the early stages of planetary evolution, similar to the conditions on Earth billions of years ago. They did not select planets already harboring extensive life. There was no guarantee that pre-existing life on other planets would be in any way compatible with organisms from Earth, particularly humans. Earth's atmosphere would not have evolved to its current oxygen-rich state without Earth-like organisms. The atmosphere and biosphere evolved together, creating conditions undoubtedly unique from any they might find on alien worlds. Emily's idea was to locate a lifeless planet and recreate Earth.

Water, of course, was essential. However, it needn't be on the surface in liquid form. A cold planet with abundant exposed or subsurface ice might grow warmer once a thriving biosphere took hold. The gradual heating would melt the ice and the resulting water would evaporate to initiate a hydrologic cycle irrigating the infant planet. Emily also specified that the planet have a magnetic field. Planetary magnetic fields, created by motion of molten iron in the cores, indicated the possibility of volcanism, plate tectonics, and other geologic processes that would give relief to a featureless planet. Having high points and low points was conducive to the formation of oceans, rivers, and lakes. Furthermore, the subsurface heat produced by molten cores could be a source of energy for the new civilization.

Emily knew it would take a long time for life to take hold once the canister of organic material was released on the planet's surface. Her idea was for the colonists to remain frozen for a few thousand years after the canisters were launched, in the hope that life forms survived and proliferated. Brian had programmed a course for the colonists that looped them around the eight planets during the waiting interval. Upon passing near the planets, automated telescopes and optical instruments on their vehicles made observations of the surface and atmosphere. When the observations indicated signs of life on any one of the planets, the Captain was to be automatically unfrozen to review the data. If the automated search routines did not identify a promising planet by the year 22000, then the colonists would return to Supply Ship 5 and reconsider their options.

Now, scanning the digital displays inside his magnetocryogenic chamber, the Captain tried not to be overly optimistic about the success of Emily's experiment. There might be other reasons the automatic unfreezing process was initiated prematurely. It could be an emergency or anomalous reading from one of the capsules in the group. He wouldn't know until he had exited the chamber and checked the data.

He pressed a button to open the hatch and propelled himself out into the control area of his capsule. He grabbed a handle on the wall to arrest his motion. Guiding himself to the console, he maneuvered into the chair and strapped himself in.

He was relieved to see no warning lights illuminated. He entered verbal commands to the computer and produced a radar image showing the location of the other vehicles. Satisfied that all appeared normal, he commanded the computer to show the data obtained during their most recent planetary fly-by, measurements of the temperature and composition of the planet's atmosphere, as well as other propertics Emily's search routine looked for to confirm life on the planet's surface. Besides the numerical data, the Captain requested a visible image of the planet. The picture that emerged made his heart skip a beat. He gazed in growing excitement at a glistening blue and beige disk wrapped in wispy white clouds and crowned with polar ice caps. Its similarity to Earth was striking, but what stopped the Captain's breath was a roughly circular patch of deep green occupying a portion of the beige solid surface. With another command, a red dot appeared showing the location at which the canister had landed. It was squarely within the area of green. Emily's experiment had succeeded. The life forms carried by the canister had taken hold and had grown and spread during the thousand years the Captain and his fellow colonists drifted through space nearby.

The Captain sent a command to unfreeze Brian. The two of them reviewed the data, both trying hard to contain their elation as they methodically analyzed the measurements. They considered unfreezing Emily as well, but that would require one of them to dock with her capsule to assist her in getting out of the containment cylinder and moving about the control room. They decided not to awaken her until after they had returned to the planet. It would take a few hundred years for the fleet of capsules to complete the loop and return. If their analysis of the preliminary data was correct, the green area would be even larger by the time they returned to the fledgling world.

CHAPTER 13
— 20731 —

A distinct aroma of alcohol wafted from the supply ship when Benjamin emerged from his capsule. He made his way to the galley in the artificial gravity portion of the ship. There he was met by a drawn and weary middle-aged man, barely fitting into his one-piece jump-suit. Benjamin was surprised. He had expected to see the same couple who greeted him during his earlier visit.

The morose man offered Benjamin a seat at the table. "Welcome aboard," he said dryly. "You're Benjamin, right? Benjamin Mizello. I read through your file during the last few hours before you got here." He placed some packages of food and an assortment of beverages in plastic squeeze bottles on the table. "I'm Steven Nutley, Galactic Explorer class of 2146." He reached across the table and shook Benjamin's hand.

"That's three years ahead of me," said Benjamin, wondering about the man's age. All the students he'd met at the Union training course had been fairly young. For this man to appear so old, he would've had to spend many years unfrozen. There weren't sufficient life support necessities on the space capsules or the supply ships to sustain a living, breathing, eating human for more than a year or two.

"You don't look familiar to me," Nutley said. "I heard of your father. Never met him though."

Benjamin shrugged and downed a container of reconstituted orange juice. Nutley watched him curiously until he had lowered the canister, then asked, "You don't happen to have any rum on your capsule, do you?"

"No," said Benjamin, adding a shake of his head to be more convincing.

Nutley ran a hand through his graying hair. "No, I thought not. I finished my supply during the last visit of an explorer. Must have been half a millennium ago. That's a long time without a drink." He coughed a laugh that was raspy and dripping with self pity.

"I don't understand," Benjamin said. "You're an explorer. Why are you taking care of the supply ship? Where are the Brinkleys?"

Nutley grunted. "They took off 2000 years ago."

"Took off? Took off where?" Benjamin asked.

"It's a long story," Nutley said. "Maybe you want to get some rest first. I read your report on the planet you visited. Interesting place. Not sure I could stand the heat."

Benjamin was wary, suspicious of the strange man. He decided not to spend more time on the supply ship than was necessary. He reached into a pocket of his jumpsuit and produced a memory device. "Here's a list of the fuel and other provisions I'll need to get replaced. I hope that won't be a problem."

"Depends on what it is," Nutley replied. "I wasn't trained to be a supply ship custodian. Not sure I've been rationing the supplies the way I should be."

Benjamin just stared back at him, still holding up the memory device.

"Tell you what," said Nutley. "I think I may be able to find a couple of beers somewhere in the pantry. Let's move into the control room and take a look at your list. You might want to review some of the data that came in during the last thousand years."

Benjamin nodded hesitantly and rose to follow Nutley into the control room. There were two desk chairs in front of the computer console. He took one and Nutley the other. Benjamin sipped the beer and began to relax.

Nutley was shaky at the console and appeared unfamiliar with the command language. Several times the computer did not respond to his words and he had to consult a well-worn book with a black leather cover suspended by a chain from the desk area. "Damn computer," he muttered. "The Brinkleys programmed it with their own language. If I lose that book, this piece of shit machine will be useless."

"Where are the Brinkleys?" Benjamin asked again.

"Who the hell knows," said Nutley without pause. "But if I can get this damn computer to work, I can show you where they might be."

After a series of additional commands that made the large screen come to life, an image of a star field appeared. With more words from Nutley, yellow lettering identified the brighter stars in the field. He spoke again and a green box appeared around one of the fainter points of light. "Maximum magnification," he added, and the backdrop of stars flew past them as the image zoomed into the area within the green box. A blue disc emerged in the center of the screen.

"That blue disc is a star about 1400 light-years from here. Next to it, that fainter object, is a planet. The Brinkleys are on their way to that planet."

Benjamin stared at the monitor for several moments. "How do you know? Did they tell you they were going there?"

"No. When I got here they'd already left, but there was enough information in the logs for me to put together what happened."

Nutley was silent. It seemed as though he had no more to say.

"What happened?" Benjamin finally asked.

Nutley settled into his chair, exhaling a current of alcohol-tinged air. Benjamin guessed there might still be some rum remaining on the ship. "You haven't reviewed any of the data from Earth since you left, have you?"

"No," Benjamin answered.

"Earth was having a rough time of it, as you might imagine. Global warming, food shortages, then nuclear war. The old girl was on her last legs. Then about 5000 years after we left, there was a sort of rebirth — evidence that civilization made a comeback. It's hard to tell how it happened. There wasn't too much communication from Earth then."

Benjamin listened intently. Nutley was speaking with emotionless detachment about events on Earth that probably resulted in the deaths of millions of people. How could he remain so dispassionate about the gloomy fate of a planet that had once been their home? Benjamin must have gone pale. He started to speak, but Nutley cut him off.

"Don't look so upset. It wasn't as bad as it sounds. Sure many people died during those times, but you'd be amazed at how resilient the old girl is."

"The old girl?" Benjamin stammered.

Nutley laughed. "I guess I still think of her as Mother Nature. She's a tough lady. It takes more than natural catastrophes and a few wars to do her in. Life hangs on."

Benjamin nodded, thinking of the little amphibians on the planet he had explored.

"When I was there, things were pretty stable already."

Benjamin's mouth dropped. "Wait. When you were there? What do you mean?"

"I went back," Nutley said, seemingly surprised at the question. "I was there for about fifteen years. You don't think I got this old frozen in a metal pipe, do you?"

Benjamin shook his head. "I didn't think…"

"The Union gave me a list of planets to check out within a few thousand light-years from Earth. The first two I visited were not very nice — not very nice at all. Both had primitive life forms, and maybe a bit of breathable air, but hell, I'll take Earth after a nuclear war over both of them. Just because there's life on a planet doesn't mean it's habitable for us. I'm talking about all kinds of natural phenomena that will ruin your day: deadly storms, places with too little water, too much water, swamps with quicksand, deserts with shifting dunes that will swallow up you and your capsule in the blink of an eye. You know what I'm talking about — mean, unfriendly places."

Benjamin nodded. Nutley's raspy voice seemed to fill the small room. When he paused, the silence was absolute save for the faint hum from the computer console over which Benjamin heard the pounding of his own heart. Though surrounded by the metal hull of the supply ship, he felt as though he were drifting unprotected in empty space, and the burden of that supreme loneliness rendered him speechless. Nutley was staring at the display. It seemed as though he'd said all he wanted to. Benjamin shook himself out of his reverie and asked, "So what was Earth like?"

Nutley shrugged. "It was okay."

"Okay?!" Benjamin repeated. "You're telling me you spent

fifteen years on Earth sometime in the last ten thousand years and all you have to say is that it was okay?"

Nutley turned back to Benjamin and pursed his lips as if deep in thought. Benjamin was reminded of a child just home from school being asked by a parent what happened in class that day.

"It's hard to explain. You have no idea how much can change on a planet in thousands of years."

Benjamin thought of the dioramas he'd seen with Ilsa at the Natural History museum.

"It took me a couple of years just to understand the language — and I was in the U. S. — or where the U. S. used to be. People even looked different — sort of evolved, if you know what I mean. I was an oddity. When I landed, I was treated like a celebrity. People still remembered the whole galactic exploration enterprise. I wasn't the first explorer to return to Earth. But after a while, the novelty wore off and I had to mainstream myself into their advanced society."

For a moment Benjamin wondered whether Nutley was making this entire tale up, or perhaps his rum-addled brain was confusing fact with fiction. "I'm trying to get a picture of what Earth was like. How did they live? What did they eat? How did they get around? What did they do for fun?"

"Hah! Fun!" Nutley exclaimed. "There's the rub. It turns out that Earth had become a serious sort of planet. The spirit of the people, their joy of living, had been sucked away. I guess it's understandable considering what the planet had been through. Sure there were all kinds of clever gadgets — neat new flying machines and robots that do everything. People were super-healthy, and when they got sick they went to a hospital — in one door and out another door in a few hours, good as new."

Benjamin thought about his father. Did he know about the new Earth? Perhaps he had abandoned his supply ship already and returned. He was sure his father would have sent him a message, but when and where would he actually receive it? "It does not sound so bad," Benjamin said, almost with regret. "Why did you leave?"

117

Nutley grimaced. "It just didn't suit me. It was..." and he paused, looking back at the field of stars on the display. "It was old."

"Old." Benjamin repeated.

"Yes, old and run-down." Nutley shuddered as if shaking off bothersome insects. "The infrastructure — buildings, houses, roads, bridges — all were ancient. Nothing could be rebuilt because the people were too worried about using up their remaining natural resources. That got them into trouble once, and they were reluctant to go down that path again. Plus, there was no adventure, no excitement. Sure everything was safe and secure and comfortable, but no one was interested in the future. There was video everywhere."

"Video?" Benjamin asked.

"Yeah, you know, like movies. Not just on TV or on the computer. Everywhere. In the walls, on the sidewalks, even in the clothing. It was like people lived in one world, but were totally immersed in another."

"So the videos showed movies?"

"Sometimes, but mostly they showed other people, other places, other jobs, other everything — anything that would allow humans to escape from their own limited reality. There wasn't one part of Earth that was unexplored, and people could see what was happening anywhere on the planet. But nothing was happening. You'd think they might get interested in space exploration. But no, no interest in space at all. No fascination looking up at the stars and wondering what's out there. They certainly had the smarts, the knowledge and technology to get into space, but no one was interested enough. Year after year I lived there with them, but after a while I said to myself, 'There has to be more to life than this boring routine. Give me a war, give me a volcanic eruption, an ozone hole, an incurable disease, a pandemic — anything to get these people reengaged in the realities of life.'"

Benjamin shook his head. "You're talking crazy, you know that, right?"

"Sure I know it. I'm exaggerating, but not much. The whole

planet was old and tired. Humans on Earth didn't want any part of risk, danger or excitement anymore."

Benjamin began to understand. Nutley was a galactic explorer. To return to Earth to find its problems solved and life humdrum and monotonous would seem an incredibly frightening future to him. It was no wonder he returned to space.

"What about the Brinkleys though?" Benjamin asked, "Did they know what was happening on Earth? How did they end up going to this other planet?" Benjamin nodded toward the video screen.

Nutley assumed a self-satisfied expression. "This is one of those tragedies that happen when it takes so long for information to travel from one place to another. It seems that sometime in that first 5000 years after we left Earth, during the time so catastrophic to civilization, there was a concerted effort to launch thousands of people into space. Astronomers had identified a planet about 5500 light-years away that was the spitting image of Earth in many ways. So confident were they about this planet, they undertook a mass exodus that made the Union's enterprise puny by comparison."

Benjamin shook his head. "If an evacuation that massive had taken place within the first 5000 years, it would've been all over the Union's communication network. Something like that would have been tagged as high priority. We'd have been automatically unfrozen when that message got to our capsules."

Nutley opened up another canister of beer. Benjamin wasn't sure where he was getting them from. "Wrong assumption. The group that left Earth at that time had nothing to do with the Union. It was an independent group. It's possible they knew about the Union communication network and could have sent a message, but they didn't. Think about it. When people hear of an undiscovered place that promises new life, new wealth, new opportunities, chances are they're going to keep it hush-hush. Those people were unlikely to alert Union explorers to this ripe young planet, fresh for the picking. Other ships could have gotten to the planet thousands of years before the vehicles from Earth. Colonies can grow mighty fast in a few thousand years. Look at our civilization. Big as that planet might be, the group from Earth did not want to arrive and find someone else already entrenched."

Benjamin nodded, seeing the truth in this. He had no doubt the travelers from Earth would want to be first on the planet they discovered. "Then how did the Brinkleys learn about it?"

"It just so happened that a Union space vehicle spotted the group with its long-range radar. That many vehicles traveling together would have a huge radar cross section and it was just the type of threat our radars are designed to detect. The guy on the Union vehicle was curious enough to track this group of objects, not really knowing what it was. When they finally approached the planet and started landing, he sent a message to the Brinkley's. He put himself in orbit about the planet and every hundred years or so would send an update. After a few hundred years, they saw this colony was going to be successful. The Brinkleys, bless their little souls, decided to abandon ship and take off to be part of the new world."

"And they didn't forward the information to other supply ships?"

"They did, but by the time other ships got the news and started making their own observations of the planet, conditions had already begun to deteriorate."

"Deteriorate?" Benjamin asked. "How?"

"The planet's sun is dying — very slowly. The radiation from the star is ebbing by a percent per century or so. Doesn't seem like a lot, but it's enough to bring on a mini-ice age in the blink of a planetary eye."

This time it was Benjamin's turn to down the remainder of his beer. He asked for another. "So the whole planet froze? Everyone?"

"No. Not yet anyway. Remember the image you're looking at here is fourteen hundred years old, but even at that time the people on the planet were still surviving. Now that I know where the planet is, I point the supply ship's antenna toward it periodically and collect enough signals from it to know there's still a modern civilization present. They're not trying to communicate with anyone, mind you. I'm just picking up stray signals from television and communication systems. But it has to be getting pretty cold there." Nutley shook his head. "Tragic, isn't it? They launch this huge exodus to a new planet because they believe their world is dying, only to find the new planet is dying too. On Earth there were ways to prevent the death spiral the planet was in. The people on Earth were in control. On that planet, they're doomed. There's nothing they can do to revive a dying sun."

"Couldn't they leave? They did it once. Why aren't they trying to do it again?"

"Good question. Maybe they are. Remember, we're looking into the past here. Maybe they've already left and they're returning to Earth. It's impossible to tell."

"And you think the Brinkleys landed there. By the time they got to the planet, they may have realized what was happening to it."

"The Brinkley's have not landed there yet." said Nutley. "It takes 2800 light years to get there from here. If the Brinkley's are lucky, they'll make measurements along the way and realize their mistake. Maybe they're on their way back here already."

Benjamin nodded solemnly. "So when you got here, the supply ship was empty?"

"Yes," said Nutley. "I've reported the abandonment on the secure Union communication link.

"And you decided to remain on the ship."

"I didn't decide to," Nutley said. "Read your manual again. There's a Union procedure to follow when encountering an empty supply ship. The explorer is to remain with the ship until replaced."

"But you could be here for thousands of years."

"Orders are orders," Nutley said. "Anyway, I've done my share of galactic planetary exploration, and I've done my second stint on Earth. I'm okay with hanging out here for a while. Sure wish I had more rum though." With that, Nutley rose and left the room.

Benjamin brooded over the situation, sipping his beer. He stared at the screen, trying to fast-forward the scene to determine what it might look like now. In the few minutes he sat alone, he made up his mind. When Nutley returned, Benjamin held up the memory device with the list of supplies he needed and said, "I'm going there. Download the exact coordinates of the planet onto this." Then as an afterthought he added, "In addition to the items listed, I'll also need some cold weather gear. I want to be prepared."

Nutley took the device from Benjamin and put it in a pocket of his jump-suit. "You might want to get some rest while I see to this. You're going to need it."

Benjamin offered Nutley reluctant thanks and rose from his chair. He strode from the room with Nutley still at the table, four empty canisters of beer in front of him. On the large monitor above him, the dying star glowed with a faint blue tint.

CHAPTER 14

— 21083 —

The Captain was the first to explore the planet where life from Emily's canisters had taken hold. He landed in an area just outside the green zone, which had grown significantly larger since he had first viewed it from space. He breathed heavily. Emily had warned him that the air was thinner and atmospheric pressure less than on Earth. She assured him they'd soon adjust to the change.

Low in the sky was an oddly colored sun. Squinting into its glare, the Captain perceived it to be more orange than Earth's sun, but he sensed no real difference in the amount of heat it provided. The planet had a rotation period of about 30 hours and the sun had just risen. He estimated about twelve more hours of daylight remaining.

Off in the distance, the Captain saw a line of green, the edge of the region of vegetation. Mindful that the other colonists were using up limited oxygen supplies on their space vehicles, the Captain strode without hesitation toward the vegetated area. Along the way, he saw mosses and lichens on rocks and occasional tufts of scrubby yellow grasses. The Captain scooped up a handful of dirt and plucked several spears of grass. He sifted the soil through his fingers, marveling at the familiarity in the weight and texture of the grains.

As he neared the line of green, the vegetation resolved itself into individual trees, tall and lush with foliage. If nothing else, the colony would have plenty of lumber to build with. The Captain hurried back to his vehicle and excitedly radioed Brian to begin the entry sequence for the colonists.

They had worked out a buddy system where the more physically capable colonists docked their vehicles to those carrying the ones needing help. After aiding the others, they returned to their own vehicles to prepare for entry. Brian kept track of the process. When each vehicle was ready, he transmitted commands to navigate them one by one into the planet's atmosphere. The lower pressure on the planet made the heat of reentry less than that on Earth. Though many of the colonists had physical disabilities, all were thoroughly trained and had passed endurance tests on flight simulators.

The Captain sat on the ground with a stalk of yellow grass in his mouth, his back against the space capsule, peering out through deep-set eyes at the arid plain where the others would be landing. The ground rose slightly toward a distant range of hills upon which the sun, hanging still low in the sky, cast dark shadows. From space he'd seen a vast ocean on the other side of those hills. The colonists would have to set up distilling machines there to extract fresh water from the sea, which probably contained excessive concentrations of salt and other minerals. Eventually, they'd have to devise a system to transport the water from the ocean to the forested area where they would build their homes. He felt a steady breeze. It might be strong enough to power wind-driven pumps, although the reduced pressure probably limited the efficiency of wind-powered devices.

The spread of vegetation in less than two thousand years amazed the Captain. It was no wonder life on Earth was so incredibly diverse after billions of years of evolution. This planet was an infant still. Emily had suggested calling it Aril, the name of the edible coating on seeds, from which life here had sprung. "Aril," the Captain said out loud and let the sound disperse in the wind.

There was a slight chill in the air, and the Captain worried about the colonists. All had brought along cold-weather clothing, but he suspected temperatures could drop substantially during the long nights, especially given the paucity of cloud cover. They would have to build fires, but he wondered whether they'd be difficult to sustain in the thin air. The more he thought, the greater the burden he felt. On Earth it'd been easy to imagine a better world. Food and fuel shortages, threats from global wars and terrorism, and the deteriorating climatic conditions made hope for long-term survival unrealistic and bleak. Was death on this infant planet more honorable than the end they'd have faced on Earth?

The Captain thought so, but the desperate souls who'd followed him to an uncertain future might not.

These were the moments when he needed encouragement from his wife Margery. Even before they'd decided to venture into space to establish a new colony, Margery had worked tirelessly with handicapped and disadvantaged children. Not able to have children of her own, she'd devoted her time to various religious and charitable organizations whose missions were to care for people on Earth unable to care for themselves. As Earth's problems became more severe, society's capacity to care for the weak diminished, but Margery persevered. Even after suffering a severe stroke and losing the ability to speak, Margery remained committed, enabling her husband to be steadfast in the face of impossible adversity.

Unlike his wife, the Captain had never really focused on any one thing. Having joined the merchant marine in his youth, he traveled the world before meeting Margery. Their union was the classic example of opposites attracting. He'd willingly yielded to her strong personality and resolute commitments. Though he gave up the merchant marine, he took various jobs that kept him close to the sea, many related to the off-shore oil industry. Margery must have known how easy it'd be to convince the Captain to travel into space. For him it was like returning to sea, another long journey to an exotic destination. When she suggested forming a group of the most unlikely space travelers one could imagine, the Captain didn't resist. The hardest part had been turning down those with severely crippling disabilities. Fortunately, Margery took charge of the selection process, while the Captain took over fund-raising. Though it did not come naturally to him, his worldly appearance and authoritative stature helped in acquiring the resources for their journey. Many organizations were relieved to have the Captain and his wife assume responsibility for many of the increasing population of needy people. The burden weighed heavily on him now, as he waited for the first of the group to descend to the surface of Aril. Their survival depended on the unproven capacity of an alien planet to sustain human life.

The first of the space vehicles entered the atmosphere, distinctly visible against the clear blue sky, a trail of white smoke in its wake. He sighed with relief when the parachute opened and the craft's descent slowed. Nearing the surface, four rocket engines ignited, breaking its fall as it touched the surface.

The Captain sprinted to the landing site. His wife emerged and climbed gingerly down from the hatch. The two embraced with excitement and relief, sharing a moment neither thought was possible. Detaching herself, Margery paced in a large circle, taking in the scene about her, arms outstretched in humility and awe. The Captain joined her and pointed to the sky. More vehicles drifted down on parachutes to land nearby.

Over the next few hours, Brian successfully coordinated the landings. His spacecraft was the last. He emerged to a grateful throng of colonists, who greeted him with applause and pats on the back. The Captain, savoring the joy of the moment, was encouraged by their infectious enthusiasm. The situation didn't seem as grim in light of their collective energy.

By late afternoon, they assembled under the shade of a spruce tree near a clearing covered with low grasses and shrubs, punctuated here and there with the trunks of trees toppled by wind and rain and age. The stillness and silence of this forested area was disconcerting. Animal life was absent on Aril because none had been included in the canisters. The Captain worried about this, unsure how important insects and birds might be to the cultivation of crops here. The plants originally deposited on Aril had thrived without these airborne fertilizing agents, but fruits and vegetables grown from the seeds the travelers carried with them might not fare as well. The Captain reminded himself that the space vehicles still carried enough fuel to lift off from the planet's surface and travel back to Earth or to a nearby supply ship.

Each colonist carried freeze-dried food to last one Earth-year. With sufficient water they'd have time to introduce agriculture to this virgin planet. Thus, the first topic of discussion at the assembly was which colonists would journey to the nearby ocean to set up the still for making fresh water. The others would remain behind to construct crude dwellings of sticks and grass as temporary shelters. The space vehicles basking in the sun just outside the perimeter of the forested area offered shelter in the evenings if temperatures became too severe. Although the craft would be insufferably hot during the day, their metal shells would slowly release the accumulated heat at night.

Of the four hundred colonists accompanying the Captain, half were healthy and strong enough to perform heavy manual labor. About a hundred had handicaps that kept them from performing anything but the simplest tasks. Some were unable to do any heavy lifting, but were healthy enough to assist in the care of those with severe ailments and handicaps. Many of them were teachers and their single-minded devotion to education made them an essential part of the population. The Captain's wife was among those. She became the leader of the group, assigning tasks as necessary. Brian was also in that group. He spent his time aiding the handicapped and educating the colonists on technical systems essential to the colony. He developed a wireless system to link the colonists and worked on a radio transmitter to communicate with nearby space vehicles. Always looking toward the future, Brian hoped to spread the word to other space voyagers about the emerging colony on Aril.

Brian also developed the colony's first calendar. Coincidentally, the rotation period of Aril was longer than Earth's by the same proportion the orbital period was shorter than Earth's. Thus, the total number of hours Aril's sun was above the horizon during the course of an Arilian year was the same as the number of daylight hours on Earth in one Earth-year.

Aril had no moon, so there was no need to have months, but Brian divided the Arilian year into twelve months anyway, each containing thirty Arilian days. As for seasons, Brian knew even before landing that Aril's rotational axis was nearly parallel to the axis of its orbit about the sun. That meant little change in the angle of the sun's radiation through the year and therefore no seasonal change. How this might impact growing seasons for crops remained to be seen. Brian decided he could always add seasons to his calendar later, after the cycle of crop growth and cultivation was known.

The Captain was one of fifty colonists who set out to explore the nearby ocean and construct the still for making fresh water. At the seashore, they were amazed at the crystal clarity of the water, and stunned upon discovering algae and primitive forms of marine organisms. This raised hopes there might be edible life in Aril's oceans, providing an unlimited source of food.

The distilling machine, made from sheets of plastic, was efficient because of the clear skies and long daylight hours. The lower atmospheric pressure also made it easier for water to vaporize over the ocean surface and condense on the plastic and trickle into buckets. Transporting the water proved more difficult. One colonist designed a wooden railway system to carry water to the summit of the hills separating the forest from the sea. Once at the summit, the water flowed freely down through a wooden sluice to the edge of the forest.

The same colonist, though crippled by cerebral palsy, walked with crutches and braces through the forest, identifying trees and bushes for use as building materials. His overriding principles became the mainstay of life on Aril: nothing was ever built that wouldn't last, and no material was ever used that couldn't be replenished. These two guidelines set the standard for all future infrastructure on the young planet.

The colonists constructed a lodge for communal gatherings, an A-frame with two wooden floors, including a conference room, a dining area, a small dispensary for those injured or sick, and an entertainment area. The lodge was windowless because they had no glass. A group of colonists was assigned to develop the technology for making glass from sand at the ocean's edge. After two years of testing, they finally succeeded, and windows were ceremoniously added to the lodge.

In spite of their efforts, colonists began to die of starvation and malnutrition soon after they exhausted the freeze-dried food brought with them. Though some crops grew, the quality of the vegetables was poor and the yield pitiful. By the end of the second Arilian year, two dozen colonists had perished. Their bodies were cremated after a ceremony led by the Captain. With each death, he looked more drained and weary. The colonists considered the possibility they would perish on Aril, one by one, with agonizing inevitability.

The supply of seeds they'd brought from Earth gradually diminished. Rice, corn, soy beans, and green leafy vegetables that grew so easily on Earth, barely survived on Aril. The plants introduced by the canister had more than a thousand years to adjust to the cycles of day and night on Aril and had adapted successfully. The seeds the colonists brought with them, on the other hand, did not have the benefit of time to counter the rhythm coded into their genetic make-up. The seedlings rapidly wilted and died, only surviving when carefully tended by the colonists both night and day. Many of the colonists grew up on farms, but that experience did not prepare them for agriculture on Aril.

In the midst of this despair, the first pregnancy on Aril was announced, and Brian proudly admitted he was the father. The colonists celebrated, though concerns were voiced about whether the baby would be normal and adequately fed. All the colonists gave up some of their rations for the pregnant mother. Before nine months had passed, a second pregnancy was announced. This time the celebration was more muted.

The colonists built a boat to explore the ocean, particularly the miles of shoreline lined with pristine beaches. They constructed nets and fishing poles, but never brought up more than simple forms of marine plant life, which was collected and used as fertilizer for the crops. Though this helped the plants grow, the colonists could not gather enough to make a big difference in crop yield.

A layer of fog sat over the sea for many days. The lower air pressure was conducive to its formation over the ocean and the surrounding land. In fact, most of the planet's precipitation was associated with condensation from the misty air.

Mushrooms became a food staple. They grew in the dark moist areas beneath the trunks and roots of large trees. A team of fifteen colonists was assigned to search for them, scouring ever deeper into the forest, but the supply soon decreased anyway. After one search, team members returned excitedly carrying an unidentified object covered with dirt and moss. In the communal lodge the Captain and other colonists removed the dirt to find the broken canister that had carried life forms from Earth to Aril. Curious about the site of the impact, the Captain asked to be led back to where the canister was found.

Hours later, a group of colonists stood at the hole from which the canister had been dug. The Captain excavated around the hole and noticed that the earthworms were more plentiful than in the soil where they'd been planting. Tossing dirt in the air, he noted the prevailing winds off the ocean carried dust deeper into the forest. On returning to the lodge, the Captain asked Brian to re-examine the data acquired on their space capsules. Together they sat baking in the stifling heat of Brian's vehicle as he started the computer and downloaded images of Aril from space.

With new maps, the Captain set out with a group of colonists to explore the forest farther east than they had previously ventured. The trees were taller with broad trunks and intertwining branches. Many were dead and fallen, indicating older woodland than the one they had settled in. The floor of the forest was littered with dead branches, tangled shrubs, and rotted leaves, making the group's progress slow. However, they were excited to discover rich moist loam beneath the undergrowth.

They continued farther east and the foliage thickened until further progress became impossible. As they were about to turn back, one of them stopped and bent to examine the plants at his feet. When the others approached, he rose holding a single yellow stalk. "This is maize," he pronounced.

Emily was the least surprised at the discovery of maize in the forest. She continually compared her inventory of plants found on Aril with the chemical and biological analysis of the contents of the canisters upon leaving Earth. Fully ninety percent of the plants in the canisters had managed to take hold on Aril.

With some regret, the colonists relocated their settlement east of where the canister had landed. Moving deeper into the forest renewed the problem of water transport. The simple rail system was no longer practical in the thicker forest. Yet, the abundance of plant life there was evidence for underground water, and they systematically excavated till they found it in ample quantities ready to be pumped from the ground. They had to use manual pumps because the wind wasn't sufficient to turn the large wooden blades of a windmill.

The ocean wasn't totally abandoned after the resettlement. The colonists continued to harvest the sea for algae and other marine plants used to fertilize the inland crops. Several canoe-like vessels were constructed, each large enough to carry a dozen colonists. The ocean-faring colonists continued to search the material brought up in their nets for signs of other animal life. Emily assured everyone that the canisters had carried the eggs of marine animals. If the algae and marine plants in Aril's ocean came from the canister, there was hope other life forms had survived as well. For those living near the ocean, the abandoned lodge remained a gathering place for colonists to share their ocean experiences. Brian added to his communication system, creating a single radio link from the lodge to the new settlement. In the evenings, the sea-going Arilians sat around the radio and communicated with their friends in the forest's interior. In turn the inland colonists relayed their new successes in growing and harvesting crops. Interestingly, the lodge became a favorite spot for couples from the forest who wanted a place to sanctify and consummate unions sprouting in the settlement. The seafarers provided ocean tours, where the newly joined colonists enjoyed the beauty of Aril's seashores and an unobstructed view of the setting sun.

CHAPTER 15
— 21090 —

The population of the colony on Aril was decreasing. They'd started with 420 colonists, but their numbers dropped to 300 after five years. As 50 of those were newborns, over one third of the original colonists had perished.

Deep within the forest, the colonists managed to cultivate a reliable crop of fruits and vegetables sufficient to keep them alive, if not well-fed. When harvest time came, they celebrated with food and music. The presence of children made it difficult for the colonists to grieve long for lost companions. Many of those who survived were the most handicapped. The children grew up respecting the elder colonists who could not run and jump and play as they did. Emily, most of all, was endeared by the children because of her profound knowledge of life in all its mysterious forms. In spite of her difficulty speaking, the children learned to understand her.

The Captain and his wife increasingly kept to themselves as the younger members of the colony took over the leadership roles. Brian and Emily remained fully engaged in the life of the colony. Brian improved the technical infrastructure with materials scavenged from the space vehicles. Emily, with her research and teaching skills, established a school that integrated exploration and education.

In the seventh year after they landed on Aril, the Captain's wife died. Weakened by her tireless efforts to help as well as by the stroke she had suffered, her health gradually deteriorated and she passed away in her husband's arms. Margery was cremated after a simple memorial ceremony. Her ashes were released in the grove with the ashes of others who died before her.

Crushed by his wife's passing, the Captain wandered aimlessly through the forests, unable to escape his sadness. Brian found him one cloudless day, sitting with his back against a space capsule, just as he had on that first day waiting for other colonists to land.

"You have to go," Brian said, standing over him.

The Captain just nodded.

Brian sat down. "I've been transmitting messages for six years now and waiting for an answer. I've heard nothing."

The Captain nodded again. The odds that a galactic exploration vehicle was near enough to receive Brian's message and respond were incredibly small.

"I just can't be sure whether anyone has picked up my transmissions," Brian continued. He paused for a long time, but the Captain said nothing.

"The only way we can be certain that someone knows about Aril is to deliver a message first hand."

The Captain fixed his deep-set gaze on Brian. "You want me to deliver a message personally?" he asked.

Brian shrugged. Finally, he said, "You could be back at Supply Ship 5 in about 8000 years. Tell Harding that we've established a successful colony on Aril, but we're struggling and need help."

The Captain chuckled. He slapped Brian on the back. "Ya know, I may be old, but I'm not dumb. Any help for Aril is thousands of years away. What good would that do?"

Brian remained serious. "Captain, I've never known you to lack vision. What is a thousand years in the lifetime of a civilization? We're babies here on galactic time scales. If and when others arrive, this colony won't even be middle aged. You and I and all the rest are just seeds, no more mature than the ones we brought from Earth. We've planted what could be a very large tree. We need to prepare for what the future will bring. This colony will need the diversity, fresh ideas, and new hope that might exist elsewhere in the galaxy."

The Captain lowered his head, humbled by Brian's wise words. He looked at Brian with the smile that had endeared him to so many of the colonists. "I'm not putting much stake in Aril's future if you send all the geezers into space the minute they start acting up."

This time it was Brian's turn to laugh.　·

The colonists had let Brian cannibalize their ships for electronic parts and fuel. Even with all the struggles and hardships, none seriously considered leaving Aril. The coldness of space had little to offer them now that they had grown accustomed to the limited pleasures of life on Aril. Prophetically though, Brian had left the Captain's ship intact, with enough fuel to return to space.

The Captain's send-off was bittersweet and touching. The colonists assembled on the plain where their space capsules had landed seven years earlier. The metallic structures baking in the heat contrasted sharply with the rolling sand hills that reached toward the unseen ocean shore. They all stood looking at the Captain for the last time, reflecting on the limited view of the universe their mortality restricted them to. They had traversed thousands of light-years of space and thousands of years of time, and yet they still represented only the tiniest specks of humanity in a universe ultimately filled with nothing more than empty space.

With a final wave, the Captain climbed into his capsule. The crowd waited solemnly as he performed a series of systems checks. Finally, the four jets that had guided the capsule to the surface ignited with a loud roar and the vehicle slowly ascended into the azure Arilian sky. The acceleration of the vehicle upward was only discernible by the rate at which it became smaller and smaller until it finally disappeared from view, seemingly absorbed into the atmosphere of their new home planet.

CHAPTER 16

— 23321 —

The first galactic explorers from Earth set out for a planet the Union had named Alpha. Alpha showed much promise for human habitability. It possessed a rich oxygen atmosphere and several oceans separated by land masses uniformly covered from pole to pole with deep green vegetation. Because Supply Ship 5 was along the route to Alpha, the explorers stopped there and were redirected to new destinations by the supply ship's custodian, Dr. Andrew Harding. They were easily convinced to go elsewhere because Harding was a well-known and highly ranked member of the Galactic Space Explorer's Union. Having taught many of the courses at the Union Academy, he had gained their respect and nurtured a strong following among the explorer fleet. From his critical post on Supply Ship 5, Harding was able to ensure no galactic explorer reached Alpha before Charles Stormer and his group. Had Captain Warner's companion Brian been allowed to view all Union communications on Supply Ship 5, he might have become suspicious of Dr. Harding's selective handling of information.

When Stormer and his 750 fellow travelers reached Alpha, he identified several higher elevation regions that were fairly flat and free of large trees or shrubs, favorable sites for landing vehicles. He selected four of his best men to accompany him to reconnoiter the terrain and assess the feasibility of establishing a colony on the planet. One by one their vehicles descended through the atmosphere and touched down on one of the more extensive highlands.

There was a slight breeze, warm and dry, smelling heavily of chlorophyll. A cloudless sky above them offered little hope of precipitation. From the highland, they saw the horizon in all directions. The miles and miles of continuous rolling hills covered by green vegetation left them awestruck. No one had appreciated the magnitude of the task they had undertaken — to carve a home from a planet where vegetation had enjoyed uncontrolled and undisturbed growth for millions of years.

Before venturing to explore further, Stormer and his men discussed how they might ensure they could find their way back once immersed in the dense green undergrowth. The planet had no magnetic field, so they could not use compasses. The sun was high overhead and didn't provide a point of reference to guide them back. They decided to use the time-proven method of breaking branches along the way.

Up close, the greenery proved to be a single type of plant, a vine-like shrub with large, oval-shaped leaves extending from branches connected to thick, woody trunks running horizontally along the ground. The earth beneath was completely in shadow and nothing grew in the gloomy darkness beneath the ubiquitous vine. Progress was slow. Sometimes the men had to scramble over the thick vines, and other times squeeze under them.

Stormer was in a foul mood. He'd read the message from Harding about Ilsa Montgomery and was still trying to figure out how she'd been able to escape the freezing process and take over control of the vehicle. He had underestimated the woman. There were other possibilities though. Perhaps she hadn't escaped and Harding had destroyed her capsule just to deny Stormer the pleasure of having her. He was at Harding's mercy, he realized. He even wondered if this was really the planet the Union identified as most promising for colonization. Control of a supply ship gave Harding information and resources Stormer didn't have.

Stormer had always wondered about Harding's motives for aiding the New Life efforts to establish a colony in space. He knew the man well enough, but he had no assurance he wasn't being betrayed. On Earth, Harding had offered his assistance in exchange for a hefty salary from New Life that rescued him from the financial obligations he had to his estranged wife and daughter. But here in space, monetary rewards were of no value. Harding instead thrived on the power he wielded within the Union enterprise. He'd always opposed the Union's vision, believing the pursuit of information ill-conceived and useless. Harding was more interested in his own Machiavellian ambitions for power. This aligned him well with Stormer, but how many other groups did Harding support? Was he waiting to see which new society evolved into one he approved of? Would he set himself up as its supreme leader? Or would he remain on the supply ship manipulating worlds and civilizations with god-like power and sentience?

After a half hour of sustained effort clearing a path through the dense foliage, Stormer halted the men. All were panting heavily and sweating. Their brief trek through the forest of Alpha exhausted them.

"How much more?" one of the men asked.

Stormer's face clouded with anger, but he controlled it. "Just far enough to make sure there are no surprises. We're not calling the others until we know this planet is safe."

"So far, all we've seen is this one plant and no animals at all," the man remarked.

He bent down and moved several branches away to better see the soil. He scooped up a handful and showed it to the others. "It's sand." He lay down on his stomach to crawl through the undergrowth. The horizontal vines dropped roots every six feet or so into the sandy ground. He tried to pull up a root, but it wouldn't budge. With a knife he made an incision along its length. Drops of moisture oozed forth. He tasted the liquid.

"There's water somewhere," he said.

Encouraged, the men moved on. The vines thickened and became an impenetrable tangle. The sky disappeared, occulted by the matted vegetation above them. Stormer drank water from his canteen. "Let's turn back. We need to plan what to do next," he said.

The men turned and followed the trail of broken branches in the direction from which they had come. The sun was lower in the sky and it would soon be dark.

Realizing the consequences if they were to get lost in this forest, they moved cautiously, making sure they were on the right course.

Stormer considered their options. With enough men, they could cut away the vegetation to make a large flat clearing for a colony. The wood would provide an unlimited supply of material to build homes with. The leaves could be chopped up for mulch to fertilize the crops. The absence of surface water meant wells would need to be dug and pumps constructed to tap into underground reservoirs. It fatigued him to think of all the work to be done before he could regain any semblance of the life he'd known on Earth. He might have done better remaining there and finding a way to deal with the authorities swiftly closing in on him. He reminded himself that he'd have been captured eventually and quite probably confined in prison for his remaining days.

They returned to their vehicles just as the sun was setting. Stormer entered his space capsule to transmit commands summoning another hundred men to begin the process of removing vegetation to clear an area large enough for the entire colony. While waiting for the additional men to arrive, he and the four others set up a camp at the edge of the thicket.

At night, the temperature on the planet dropped precipitously. The absence of cloud cover allowed the heat from the planet's surface to escape uninhibited. The men were forced to return to their capsules to enjoy the residual warmth radiating from the metallic hulls, but later in the night even that dissipated into the icy air. They cut twigs and branches to build a fire and, before long, a brilliant yellow blaze reached upward, the glow blotting out the starlight filling the alien sky.

Dawn brought another cloudless sky of endless blue, interrupted only by the dazzling brilliance of the merciless sun emerging over the horizon. The men prepared freeze-dried meals and weak coffee made from the leftover water in their canteens. Stormer ordered them to dig holes in the sandy ground in search of subsurface water. Leaving the physical labor to the younger, stronger men he explored the perimeter of the broad plain. There was no change in vegetation. The leafy vine dominated the landscape everywhere he went. He guessed it was just a matter of time before the parasitic plant covered the clearing as well, and he wondered only briefly why it hadn't yet done so. There was no way to tell the rate of growth of the plant. If the plain lacked underground water, then the men were wasting their time. They'd have to dig new holes where the vine had dropped roots into the ground. For every day they didn't find fresh water, the supply on their space capsules would dwindle alarmingly. He knew the nearest ocean was many days away.

Fortunately, before day's end, the excavators found water oozing through the dirt twelve feet below the surface. They dug the hole wider and deeper and prepared a dirt walkway from the surface down to the edge of the ever-growing pool forming in the bottom of the hole. That night the cold didn't depress them quite so much, and they eagerly built a fire around which they slept soundly, knowing that availability of fresh water on Alpha was no longer a problem.

Several days later, the other men arrived. The automatic piloting systems on the capsules worked well and kept the vehicles separated even as the density of the spacecraft on the flat plain increased. It took three days before all one hundred landed. Once they had, the men assembled to be briefed by Stormer, who presented his plan for clearing the vegetation. With some uneasiness, they accepted his plan and formed into teams to cut and remove the vegetation, sorting the debris into piles for later use. The smallest pieces were for mulch, the medium size fragments for building fires, and the largest pieces for construction.

Stormer was disappointed they'd been unable to find any other type of plant on Alpha. The resilient vine may have prevented other vegetation from growing. The lack of biodiversity was in striking contrast to Earth. The men had brought seeds, of course, to grow food products, but not plants to be used for building, making tools, rope, or clothing.

Another disconcerting aspect of Alpha was the repetitive monotony of the planet. They'd yet to see a cloud in the sky, and a mild wind blew incessantly from west to east. The surface lacked variation, both in color and elevation. Except for the oceans and barren highlands, it was dominated by continental areas covered in green vegetation, which Stormer now suspected was the same persistent plant they'd been battling. He wondered, in fact, if a single vine extended over the entire surface. Perhaps somewhere there was a main trunk to which all the branching foliage was connected.

After several weeks of arduous work, his men had made good progress in clearing the vegetation. The detritus was piled in multiple heaps, and Stormer felt there was sufficient clear space to experiment with growing the seeds they'd brought.

Suddenly one of the men approached him and reported smelling smoke. A group stood at the edge of the thicket trying to identify the source of the smell through the tangled shrubbery. Stormer instructed one to climb to the top of a space capsule to get a better view. From atop the vehicle, the man pivoted in all directions.

"I think I see smoke," he announced finally.

"Find binoculars," Stormer ordered.

He stood by nervously until the glasses were produced and handed up to the man on the capsule. Peering through them, he declared, "It's smoke all right. And it's black."

"How far away?" Stormer asked.

"Hard to tell," the man answered. "More than a mile — could be two or five. There's not much I can use for a point of reference."

"How could a fire start that far away?" Stormer asked no one in particular.

"It's downwind," answered one of the men at his side. "Embers could have floated up from last night's fires, landed somewhere, and just smoldered there until the right combination of heat and light set it off."

"I suppose we could just let it burn," Stormer said.

"Maybe," the man answered. "The wind will tend to move the fire away from us. On the other hand, the land slopes downward from here to there. Fires tend to climb upward, even if the prevailing winds are in the opposite direction."

Stormer worried. There was no way of knowing what a small fire in this vast forest might do. He prepared for the worst. "Let's make a wide firebreak between us and that fire. Have everyone work on removing vegetation for a hundred yards or more. Don't leave anything combustible. Hopefully, the fire will burn itself out. Who knows? It might end up helping us clear the vegetation."

"That should work — unless the wind shifts," the man said.

Stormer looked at him with annoyance. "In all the weeks we've been here, the wind hasn't changed direction. Why should it now?"

After the colonists cleared a firebreak, night fell and the wind shifted. To their dismay, gusts of warm air wafted toward them. The night sky was filled with glowing embers. The vast area of burning vegetation had produced a bubble of hot air and the resulting pressure difference between the regions caused an air flow that transported the heat and burning ash to the surrounding vegetation. The fire spread faster than anyone anticipated. The men watched helplessly as the orange glow diffused into the air around them. Sparks from the blaze lit the sky more brightly than the distant starlight, rapidly disappearing behind the blossoming smoke. Soon the first of the piles of cut vegetation caught fire. The speed of the fire filled the men with panic. Once the first pile caught, others started to burn with inevitable regularity.

Stormer needed no more impetus for abandoning the colony. Running quickly through the burning ash and panic-stricken men, he found his space capsule and climbed in. He initiated an abbreviated launch sequence, and moments later the glow from his rocket engines combined with the fiery air that hung over the plain as his capsule roared upward. When the men saw his vehicle ascending amidst the chaos of the fire, they all scrambled through the infrared darkness to find their own capsules. Unfortunately, many of the capsules were no longer approachable because of the heat. In desperation, they ran to the nearest vacant vehicle, but before they could enter others ran up with the same idea. Fights broke out among the men, eventually leading to vicious acts of brutality. The plain on which they had endeavored to build a settlement became a fiery battlefield. Bodies riddled the ground and soon the corpses caught fire, adding the sickening smell of burning flesh to the apocalyptic scene.

When his vehicle had escaped Alpha's gravitational field and entered an orbit about the planet, Stormer sat before the computer display too exhausted to think. Other vehicles escaped after him — 38 in all. He sent a message to the survivors advising them to rendezvous with the remaining members of their party, still frozen in an orbit safely distant from the warming rays of Alpha's sun.

As they departed, Stormer took one last look at Alpha through his space capsule's telescope. The entire planet was now smoldering, with a good fraction of its surface still covered with orange flames. Against the blackness of space, the planet resembled a glowing coal, which would continue to burn until all combustible material was gone and what remained was cold, lifeless ash.

When they had rejoined the others, he set a course to return to Supply Ship 5, leaving more than sixty men dead on the burning surface of Alpha.

CHAPTER 17

— 23513 —

Arilian civilization expanded relentlessly from its original location near the shores of Aril's vast and only ocean. The planet's single connected land mass covered two thirds of its surface and varied in elevation from sea level to 22000 feet. Between those extremes was a diverse array of topographic and geologic features, in many ways as rich as those on Earth. Lakes and running water courses of all types and sizes sculpted the landscape and created mini-climes that served as focal points for new Arilian colonies. Within the first 2000 years since the landing on Aril, villages, towns and cities spread across the planet almost from pole to pole. Between these population centers, Arilians were careful to preserve as much as possible the native state of the terrain. Because the plant life of Aril had a thousand years head start on its human counterpart, vegetation already blanketed the entire land surface. The oceans harbored simple forms of plant life on the surface and in the shallow coastal regions. The ocean depths, however, remained lifeless and barren.

Though more than 2400 years old, Arilian civilization was still young, with much to learn. It was a rash, upstart of a planet that was sorely conscious of its questionable Earth-based roots. The fifty offspring of the original settlers had been so busy struggling to survive, they had little time to sit and listen to the folklore of their elders. Instead, they and their descendants solved problems as they went along, creating laws, customs, religion, and traditions from the ground up. Only the vast library of books, documents, and electronic records that Brian had brought with him provided any grounding in the past. This archive was preserved with almost sacred care in a vast digital library built near the original landing spot. Before completing their education, all Arilian students were required to use the digital archive to study and report on some aspect of life on ancient Earth.

Little was known about what transpired on Earth beyond the

information in the archives. That historical record had a well-defined beginning and end that constituted a sort of tapestry, giving Arilians a more contextual view of individual events in the larger scheme of Earth civilization. Consequently, they were loath to adopt Earth's solutions to the challenges on their planet. A typical argument heard in Arilian political debates was, "That sounds like something they would do on Earth."

Regional governments across Aril were as different as the people and physiographic conditions over which they ruled. Yet they communicated well. The harmony was based on the shared notion that no region should undertake any activity that would impinge on its neighbors, and that resources should be shared. Each of the sub-cultures understood that it might not achieve the same quality of life as other regions had. Inhabitants of different regions had moved there by choice. They accepted from the outset that by moving away they were giving up certain comforts and ways of life they might not find in their new homes. They were not apt to look back and envy or resent the life styles of the people they left, many of whom were close friends and relatives.

Nevertheless, there had been two territorial wars in the first two thousand years of Arilian history. But these were unlike wars fought on Earth. Arilians had never pursued the art of designing deadly weapons because life was so precious on the planet and the governments understood what the ultimate outcome of such technology would be. For this reason, conflicts on Aril featured verbal abuse, malicious mischief, harassment, and fights with non-lethal weapons. None of the Arilian governments could afford standing armies, and wars were typically fought by militia and poorly organized government-backed groups. The level of emotion and intensity of conflict was similar to that on Earth, but the results were less deadly. Also, because conflicts on Aril seldom resulted in death, there was little reason to carry grudges through many generations. When two or three generations had died off, all memory of offenses was lost.

Thus, in spite of the occasional war, Aril was a pacifist planet. Violence and aggression were replaced by less destructive forms of fulfillment. The absence of animals on the planet other than humans meant that hunting and other endeavors that might encourage the perfection of lethal instincts were not practiced. Not only was there nothing to kill on Aril, there was also no opportunity for young impressionable Arilians to witness the act of killing in the animal kingdom.

The first murder committed on Aril occurred more than a hundred years after the planet was settled. No one knew exactly how to deal with it. Arilian law enforcement officials and representatives of the judicial system attacked the central archives in droves to study how murder had been dealt with on Earth, but that planet's lack of consistency and rationality in dealing with the crime offered little in the way of guidance. In the end, Arilians unanimously decided to exile murderers to regions of the planet they could not escape from, there to live in loneliness and isolation, with the only chance of returning to civilization dependent on demonstrated rehabilitation and improved potential to contribute to society.

Arilian religions were also unlike those on Earth, as Arilians insisted on inventing their own. Earth's religions didn't provide the guidance needed in confronting the challenges, threats, and opportunities unique to the new planet. Not that all Arilians agreed on what religion to follow: there were as many different religious sects as there were occupations on Aril. The differences among the religions were based on the distinctiveness of the communities they served, with much overlap between the religious sects and labor unions that were organized to maintain a healthy balance between employers and employees on Aril.

Through all the challenges of creating new governments, cultures, and societies across the Arilian globe, high priority was given to science. In addition to Brian, the aeronautical engineer, and Emily, the eminent exo-biologist, there were many others in the original colony who dabbled in diverse scientific study to varying depths of sophistication. As Aril had been founded by settlers afflicted from birth or by subsequent happenstance with debilitating diseases and handicaps, one important legacy passed down from the original settlers was a steadfast determination to understand and cure those afflictions. Medical science advanced quickly, profiting from the thousands of medical books and journals Brian had brought in digital form. The various gene defects that were present in the original colonists were addressed. Genetic manipulation was practiced early on and perfected. Recognizing the risks associated with a limited gene pool, Arilians quickly mastered the art of artificially introducing diversity into the genetic make-up of their progeny and they soon achieved longevity far greater than their ancestors on Earth.

Agricultural science ensured that Arilian crops were robust, resilient, nutritious, and sustainable. Genetic engineering gave Arilians the ability to create new foods that were nutritious, easy to grow, and tasty. Engineering skills were also imperative as Arilians struggled to build infrastructure from virtually nothing. Mining technology was developed with an eye toward safety, conservation, and preservation. Astronomical sciences held an important place in Arilian education, as stars were a source of wonder to all. Every Arilian could look at the heavens on any evening of the year and point to the constellation within which Earth was located.

Robust and reliable communication systems, a tradition begun by Brian and passed on from generation to generation, helped people in all parts of the planet stay connected through video and audio links that made use of wireless transmissions. Virtually no event took place in one location that was not able to be viewed elsewhere on the globe. So effective was the communication, that air travel between widely spaced locations was minimal. Arilians had weighed the cost, benefits, and risks of commercial air travel, drawing upon the historical records from Earth, and had decided to limit air transportation to trips that were essential. A publicly accessible ground transportation system involving automobiles, trains, and a diverse array of water craft gave Arilians many opportunities for exploring their planet without taking to the air.

The idea to send a radio message to Earth came from one of Aril's leading astronomers, Sigma DeAnthony. DeAnthony's talent for radio communication had been passed along to him from his maternal grandfather, a highly accomplished radio engineer. In reading the account of Aril's settlement, DeAnthony mused over Brian's preoccupation with communication systems. Examining digital photographs of Brian, DeAnthony saw a resemblance between Brian's moon-faced countenance and his own appearance. Though many generations had passed, it was still likely he was a direct descendant. The original colonists bore about 50 children and five of them were Brian's. Thus, there was a ten percent chance that he was descended from one of those five.

DeAnthony was obsessed with Earth and frequently visited the central archives in the memorial park, which Arilians had built at the site of the first colony. It consisted of several hundred acres of sculptured gardens, paved walkways, statuary, and fountains, at the center of which was a large amphitheater surrounding a bronze statue depicting a tall man with his arm around an elderly woman. The pair was flanked by a moon-faced youth and a slender young woman with arms drawn up and fists clenched under her chin. A plaque identified the figures of the four leaders of the early Arilian settlement. On monuments throughout the park were the names of all the original colonists. By international agreement, the park was designated the property of all nations, with equal access to every Arilian.

Near the park was a flat area of well tended lawn on which sat the remains of the space vehicles that had brought the original settlers. They had been protected through the millennia by heavy coats of water-repellant and weather-resistant enamel paint. Children played among the vehicles running on the lush grass, and climbing upon the mysterious structures.

In the archive, DeAnthony read a historical account written by Brian. The story of the Captain and his band of colonists began with the challenges they faced before leaving Earth, and told of the Captain's difficulties working with the Union, which threw obstacle after obstacle in his path, mostly consisting of administrative requirements, inspections, certifications, and massive paperwork intended to discourage all but insiders. Nevertheless, the Captain overcame these challenges and, in the end, the Union was happy to be rid of the persistent philanthropist and his wife.

Brian's account of the colonists' first stop at Supply Ship 5 was laced with sarcasm and resentment over the treatment they had received from Andrew Harding. DeAnthony wondered whether Harding still occupied the supply ship, sitting in the control room orchestrating events as if he were king of the galaxy. His curiosity drove him to argue successfully the case for building the largest radio telescope to date, proposing to build it on his own property, which was one of Aril's most productive vineyards. The cleverly-designed antenna received weak radio signals from space, while also serving as a network of arbors for his grape orchard. In addition to searching for signals from galactic explorer vehicles, DeAnthony also became interested in transmitting messages that could be detected by Andrew Harding's supply ship 4000 light-years away. To justify the cost of building the powerful transmitter, DeAnthony came up with a compelling argument: communication with a Union supply ship would open a permanent pathway for information that the supply ship gathered from the network of galactic explorers. Though it would take 8000 years before the information arrived, it would prove fascinating and useful to future generations of Arilians. Government officials argued that spending money for something so far in the future was useless, but DeAnthony accused these officials of being short-sighted and lacking vision, a criticism that Arilians were highly sensitive to. No one wanted to be reminded of where Aril would be had it not been for the brave foresight of the Captain and the original colonists.

DeAnthony went further in his arguments. He suggested the transmission include a request to forward a message to Earth — a message that would establish a link between the Arilian people and their distant ancestors. The day when the response from Earth was received would surely be one of awe and celebration.

After much debate, agreement was finally reached to send messages with information about Aril to the galactic supply ship and Earth. However, DeAnthony was not content with transmitting bland facts about Aril's people, governments, and culture. He considered sending a message that was more timeless, one that succinctly captured the essence of the Arilian persona. Should the message be respectful, acknowledging how much was known about Earth civilization and how it had served as the foundation for the Arilian way of life? Should it also be a unifying statement of religious universality, recognizing the greatness of Arilian faith while not minimizing Earth-based ideologies? Should it convey the sophistication of Arilian science, its breakthroughs in eliminating diseases and genetically-caused illnesses?

While the transmitter was being constructed, the question of message content was posed to the Arilian population and thousands of responses were submitted from all over the planet. It was left up to DeAnthony how to combine all these suggestions into a compact and meaningful message.

He spent many days walking through Aril's memorial park. He sat on a bench, before the statue of the Captain and his three companions, mulling over the message string. He also spent many hours in the library perusing the archives, hoping for some inspiration to guide his decision. With a digital notepad in hand, he walked out among the ancient space capsules that peppered the vast flat plane lying between the Memorial Park and the shores of Aril's ocean. He climbed to the top of one of the capsules and looked out over the jumble of vehicles. He jotted down the sentiments the Arilian people were attempting to convey in their suggestions. First on the list was pride, of which there was no shortage, but it was equally divided between personal pride and pride in their culture. Confidence was also present in the suggestions. Arilians appreciated how tenuous had been their beginnings, and all nurtured an appreciation for what they as humans could withstand and overcome. Charity, too, was pervasive in the text, as was an over-arching respect for others, even in the face of overwhelming obstacles. Arilians also articulated a tremendous respect for science, not only for how it could help solve seemingly impossible problems, but also in its ability to inspire curiosity and wonder. Finally, Arilians' respect for art in all its forms was apparent in the suggestions, as art was present in every facet of life on the planet.

Underpinning all these characteristics was the youthfulness of the Arilian civilization. They were naïve, optimistic, and altruistic. The pride they exhibited bordered on haughtiness. Their self-righteousness mimicked that of a teenager, as did their expectations for fairness and freedom. Arilians as a society had almost a hormone-driven aggressiveness in achieving that which they felt was their birthright.

DeAnthony puzzled over how to convey all of this, remembering also that Earth's language may have evolved very differently from the Arilian language. As soon as he realized the message had to be delivered in words from Earth's own history, the options narrowed considerably. Of all the Earth-originated sayings, the one that had impressed him most was one that had been at the heart of Aril's heritage. It was the one that had motivated the Captain, and was now permanently imbued in the Arilian persona.

DeAnthony made his decision, and the core of the message that was eventually sent to Andrew Harding on Supply Ship 5 and to Earth was:

> I am Aril.
> Give me your tired, your poor,
> Your huddled masses yearning to breathe free,
> The wretched refuse of your teeming shore.
> Send these, the homeless, tempest-tossed to me...

What better way to communicate the grandeur of a civilization than to send an offering to welcome and harbor the disadvantaged of other lands? It held the tacit assumption that Arilian civilization was secure enough in its own strength and superiority, while at the same time capturing the essence of charity. It conveyed the rare combination of youth and maturity, of pride and humility, and an acknowledgement of both good and evil in the universe. It embraced reality, without giving into its burden. It transcended time.

Following this simple message, DeAnthony transmitted the

obligatory data on Aril. He planned to transmit the message continuously for as long as he could keep the transmitter operating. The leading message would stay the same, while the latter part of the message would be updated periodically with new information. DeAnthony continued to transmit the message for the remainder of his life, taking steps in the meantime to mentor a string of Arilian students who would be dedicated to carrying on this important task for many years thereafter.

CHAPTER 18
— 25970 —

With a swift, practiced kick, Risto Jalonen launched himself from the containment cylinder as he had done dozens of times before. One of the earliest galactic explorers, he took his assignments seriously and didn't shy away from landing even on the most forbidding planets. He'd aged considerably because of the amount of time he spent unfrozen, exploring planets, repairing his space capsule, and spending time on supply ships.

Risto was a morose and introverted Finn, who embraced the lonely life of a galactic explorer. A mechanical genius, the skill he exercised in keeping his capsule functioning permitted him to take risks others wouldn't dare. He spoke little, and his silence was often misinterpreted as contempt by the supply ship custodians. On the contrary, however, he was intrinsically jovial and found enjoyment and fulfillment in even the most mundane and tedious tasks. His only weakness was an affinity for beer. It was the rationalization for everything he did. When recounting his experiences visiting other planets, his first statement had to do with the likelihood that one could make beer from whatever material he found there, organic or otherwise.

When deciding on his next destination, he typically sought out the bleakest and most inhospitable planets. He had incredible stamina and physical presence, and wasn't intimidated by the extremes in environmental conditions inevitable to a galactic explorer's experience. One of the planets he'd explored was a large limestone rock with a planetary scale network of subterranean caves filled with streams, lakes, and waterfalls. The lack of breathable air didn't deter him. He'd landed on the surface with as much oxygen as he could carry, which was considerable given the planet's weak gravity. He descended into the network using only his instincts to keep track of where he was heading and how to return. At the limit of his oxygen supply, he barely managed to return. The water and soil samples he brought back were analyzed on the supply ship and found to be completely devoid of organic life. Risto had shrugged it off with a chuckle, downed a canister of beer, and taken off for the next planet.

He was seated at his console reviewing the data on planets within a couple of thousand light-years of his current location when he saw a flagged message from Supply Ship 3 dated 23975 years. It read: "Unidentified vehicle with single female occupant on uncontrolled course toward galactic center. Vehicle has non-Union registry. Occupant unknown. Advise intercept and rescue. Estimated ephemeris to follow."

Risto asked the computer for subsequent messages. The software filtered through several thousand years of received signals to isolate another message, which read: "Errant vehicle detected by SS3 long-range radar 24036 years. Updated ephemeris attached. Request intercept and rescue."

With a few more commands, Risto brought up an intercept course for his own vehicle. He smiled grimly at the results displayed before him in graphic reality. To safely rendezvous with the out-of-control vehicle, his capsule would have to divert toward a nearby star where it could take advantage of a gravity assist to accelerate it on a nearly identical course to the other capsule. The estimated time at which he could dock with the target vehicle was 40334, fourteen thousand years in the future.

Risto groaned inwardly at the thought, but didn't hesitate. He commanded the computer to program the new course for his vehicle. He would have to defer his planetary explorations for a while, but a lone vehicle with a female occupant thousands of light-years from Earth was far more enticing than the lure of unexplored worlds.

Before returning to his magnetocryogenic chamber, Risto took one last look at the monitor of the computer. The galactic center was clearly visible as a luminous concentration of stars and scattered light from interstellar dust clouds, as varicolored and spectral as the stars themselves. It was possible, but highly unlikely, that other ships would try to rescue the woman. He took one last look at the monitor and then began preparations for freezing.

Chapter 19

— 28541 —

More than seven thousand years after leaving Aril, the Captain's vehicle approached Supply Ship 5 for the second time. The Captain was automatically unfrozen about an hour before docking at the supply ship. As he expected, Dr. Harding had also been automatically unfrozen at the approach of a galactic space vehicle. Harding greeted the Captain, looking much the same as he had during the Captain's last visit. In contrast, the seven years on Aril had marked the Captain's face with a weariness and sadness Harding hadn't expected. Without saying a word, he escorted the Captain to the simulated gravity portion of the supply ship and produced a thermos of rum from a cabinet in the galley.

The Captain took a long drink of the warming brew and dropped his head to the table and wept. Harding shook his head in a gesture that was part scolding and part sympathy. "It was madness, you know," he said. "Trying to establish a colony with a group of people so unfit for the rigors of spaceflight and colonization."

He paused and waited for a response, then asked, "Did they all die?"

The Captain looked up, his face streaked with tears.

"I need to enter it in the log," Harding explained coldly.

The Captain took another drink from the thermos and said, "They did not all die. When I left there were more than three hundred and they were doing okay. Not great, mind you, but okay."

Harding's face registered a combination of surprise and interest. "Then…" He left the question unfinished.

"I couldn't stay there after my wife died," the Captain explained. "I had to get away."

"I'm sorry," Harding said.

There was a long silence. Finally, the Captain asked, "You haven't heard from them, have you?"

"I don't think so. The computer would have alerted me. Of course, the antenna would have to be pointed in the right direction. It's constantly scanning, but it still may have missed something."

"It's been thousands of years since I left," the Captain said. "They've had plenty of time to develop the technology to send a strong enough signal. I was just hoping you might have heard from them."

Harding rose from his seat at the table. "Sit here and rest awhile. I'll enter the coordinates of your planet into the computer. It will search the data archives for a signal from that location at the normal transmitting frequencies."

After a while the Captain went to the control room and took a seat next to Harding. A brilliant field of stars filled the computer display before him. Exactly in the center, set off with red crosshairs, was a tiny point of light.

"That's where your planet is," Harding said. "If there's been a coherent signal from that point at any time, the ship's computer will have archived it. We'll know in a moment."

Several seconds later, a stream of letters appeared on the screen. There was little doubt about the coherence of the signal. The message read:

> I am Aril.
> Give me your tired, your poor,
> Your huddled masses yearning to breathe free,
> The wretched refuse of your teeming shore.
> Send these, the homeless, tempest-tossed to me…

Following that quote was a stream of text giving information about the population of Aril, its governments, arts, culture, and science. It ended with a request that any recipients of the message should forward it to Earth.

"Damn," the Captain muttered into his cylinder of rum. "Damn. They did it."

"Apparently so," said Harding, with a smirk.

The Captain turned to him. "Is there something you find amusing about that, Dr. Harding?"

"Not at all," replied Harding. "I'm just amused at their naiveté."

"I'm afraid I don't quite see anything naïve in that message," said the Captain, nodding toward the screen.

Harding leaned back in his chair and sighed. "Look at the date of the message, Captain. It was sent more than four thousand years ago. If I forward it to Earth, it will take another five thousand years. Did they actually believe that someone on Earth almost ten thousand years from the time the message was sent would jump in their spaceships to join them on their wonderful planet? Frankly, I find this message ridiculous beyond belief."

The Captain put the cylinder of rum on the computer console and rearranged his tall frame in the chair so he was facing directly at Harding. "First of all, Dr Harding, I object to your statement, 'If I forward it to Earth…'. You will forward that message to Earth. Second, I do not consider that message ridiculous or naïve. I see it as being an extremely altruistic offering of aid, a reaching out across space and time to others who may be less fortunate."

Harding glared back at the Captain. "You may see it that way if you wish, Captain, but I am a much more practical person. Many years have passed since that message was sent. Anything could have happened. For all we know, it could be a joke, a science experiment conducted by mischievous teenagers, a fraternity prank. Is that what you expect me to relay to Earth?"

"Was that message sent only once?" the Captain asked in return.

Harding sighed and turned back to the console and spoke one word to the computer, "More."

The screen before them refreshed. It was the same message, but now the subsequent information was different. Both the population of Aril and the time of transmission had changed. Harding repeated the command and the message with updated information reappeared. Harding turned to the Captain and sighed with resignation. "It appears this message was sent often — perhaps continuously. The supply ship received it every time its antennas were pointed in the right direction.

"Exactly," said the Captain, relaxing again back into his chair.

"Your attempt to establish a colony on this planet appears to have succeeded," Harding commented thoughtfully. "Still," he added, "what possible benefit might be derived from forwarding this message to Earth? We ourselves rarely hear from Earth. It's turned inward, no longer interested in galactic exploration. Recent data suggest that galactic explorers are viewed as myths of the ancient past, relics of an Earth so unfamiliar to the current inhabitants that we might as well be alien life forms."

"It surprises me to hear you say that," the Captain responded. "From what little I know about the Union, the whole idea was to inspire a new way of viewing space and time. It's Union creed that the current moment — a moment being thousands of years — is only a tiny part of a much larger truth. It's the trees, whereas the Union was striving to see the forest." The Captain paused, not comfortable with defending the Union, but elated over the survival of Arilian civilization.

"Don't lecture me about Union creed," Harding said harshly. "I was one of the founders. I remember very well the discussions that took place. There were always two sides to Union dogma. The lofty ideas presented to the public were politically motivated to ensure people with short-term vision did not interfere with Union efforts. Remember, the Union largely supplanted the government-driven space programs. It was a magnificent enterprise and ultimately supremely successful. But beneath it all was a much more practical vision for the future, one rooted in history and reality. Control is the foundation for stable societies. Creating something that stands the test of time requires a unity of purpose, a resolve to do things right, and a confidence and trust in the creative process. That was understood by many of us in the Union — not all, of course, but the bulk of the original founders believed this. And since we were the instructors of the explorer courses, we passed these ideas to the galactic force. Their efforts to explore other planets and transmit the observations they make in distant regions of the galaxy are just ways to kill time until a unique opportunity arises — the discovery of a habitable planet where the Union will rule uncontested. That frozen force out there," and here Harding pointed to the screen that once again showed a vast array of stars, "they're just waiting for a call from me to carry out that vision."

The Captain stared at the smug countenance of Harding and then with a gracefulness incongruous to his size and age rose from his chair. "Do you have any seeds?"

"Yes, of course," said Harding.

"I want all the seeds you can give me."

Harding shook his head. "I need them for the ship's gardens."

"You don't need all of them," the Captain responded. "Give me all you can. Give me seeds for flowering plants. I suspect you don't need flowers on the ship." Turning his back on Harding, the Captain strode toward the door.

"Where are you going?" Harding asked.

The Captain hesitated in the doorway, then turned back to Harding. "I'm going back to Aril. I came here to escape the memory of my lost wife and to see if I could get Union aid for my struggling colony. I now realize they don't need any help, especially from the Union. That jewel in space is my real home. I can at least bring them seeds. Get them for me, please."

Harding shrugged. "Suit yourself, Captain."

The Captain nodded toward Harding. It was a hard uncompromising look. "And forward the message from Aril to Earth, Dr. Harding."

After the Captain's vehicle departed, Harding remained at the console in his supply ship, staring blankly at the screen. He asked the computer to pan back to a view from above the galactic plane. The spiral arms of Earth's sector of the galaxy stood out from this vantage. He also had the computer superpose symbols indicating the locations of the seven Union supply ships, Earth, Aril, and the 1200 galactic explorers at their last reported positions. He updated the locations of the galactic vehicles based on an extrapolation from their positions and velocities in the past. He calculated how long it would take for all 1200 to reach Aril. "No, Captain, Warner, I will not be forwarding that message to Earth. Quite the contrary, in fact."

Using the keyboard on the console to avoid any misinterpretation of his words, he programmed the computer. Then he requested a display of the distribution of the vehicles 23,000, 30,000, 37,000, and 44,000 years in the future. After 23,000 years, only a small percentage of the vehicles would reach Aril. The number of vehicles at Aril doubled 30,000 years in the future, and doubled again 7,000 years after that. As he expected though, the number of vehicles arriving 44,000 years out did not double again, because by then most of the vehicles in the fleet would have arrived. Considering the tradeoffs, Harding decided that 37000 years in the future represented an optimum time when the bulk of the explorer fleet would arrive. Waiting longer for the few remaining explorers offered diminishing returns.

Harding prepared the command to all the explorers to rendezvous at Aril in the year 65,000. Before he sent the message, he deleted 200 recipients, who he suspected would question his directive. One of these was Benjamin Mizello. Also not on the list were all the supply ship custodians; they'd have to remain at their posts in case any of the travelers needed provisions on their way to Aril. Thus, Benjamin's father would not receive the message.

Harding's transmisson went out as a single packet. On reaching any galactic space vehicle, the message designated for that vehicle would be stripped off and the remainder of the packet relayed to all other vehicles in transmitting distance. Vehicles not on the recipient list could not interpret the message, but they would still relay the message to others. In this way, the message spread through the entire fleet like an elaborate system of tentacles. Harding flagged the message as "High Priority", meaning that, upon being received by the space vehicles, the occupants would be automatically unfrozen to read the transmission. Each would reprogram their vehicle's course according to Harding's orders.

Because Stormer was not part of the galactic explorer fleet, he would not receive the message. Harding was not concerned, because he knew Stormer was already on his way back to Supply Ship 5 with the survivors of their expedition to Alpha. When Stormer arrived back at the supply ship, Harding would tell him about Aril, and the gathering of the explorer fleet in 65000. This time Harding would accompany Stormer to make sure Aril did not suffer the same fate that befell Alpha.

CHAPTER 20
— 29915 —

The surface temperature where Benjamin landed was well below freezing. The wind blew with such force his space capsule was barely able to maintain an upright position, in spite of the four computer controlled rockets continuously compensating for the varying forces during descent. Blowing ice crystals stung his face as he exited the spacecraft and within moments the capsule was covered with a layer of rime that gave the hull a glassy blue sheen. The synthetic fiber suit he wore protected him from any physical harm the cold might cause, but it didn't prevent him from feeling the frigid temperatures.

Benjamin didn't have to walk far before he came to the first sign of civilization, a road, barely visible under an impenetrable layer of ice and snow. He followed the road cautiously, lest some speeding vehicle soundlessly and prematurely end his exploration of the planet. He remembered his visit to the Natural History Museum with Ilsa, where he had tried to calibrate how much change could take place in human physical appearance, culture, and language over thousands of years. It was impossible to imagine the type of people inhabiting this planet, even though he shared with them a common origin on Earth. He had not thought to bring any type of weapon; he could only hope that whoever he met wouldn't be hostile.

Before long he discerned the outline of numerous dome-shaped structures, too large and featureless to be homes. When he reached the nearest frost-covered dome, he scraped the ice away with his gloved hand to examine its surface. It was made of glass or transparent plastic, and through it he saw row upon row of plants growing on long, waist-high tables. They appeared well cared for. The leaves were a rich green color and all the stalks stood straight and firm. Benjamin was impressed. It must require a very efficient heating system to keep the interior temperature of the structure warm enough for plants to thrive.

He walked among the domes, every now and then stopping to peer inside. At one he heard a noise from within. Scraping away ice, he was startled to see another face looking back at him. It was small, a child's face, and it registered an equal measure of astonishment at seeing Benjamin. Looking beyond the face, Benjamin saw that the building was filled with children, running about and playing with a large ball, as if this were a playground or gymnasium.

Moments later, a group of children poured out from a door that magically appeared in the side of the dome. Surrounding Benjamin and chattering in a language he couldn't understand, they examined his clothing and the instruments that hung from his sleeves and belt. His camera equipment attracted particular attention. Behind the children was a man who approached Benjamin cautiously. He was short, stocky, and wearing a one-piece smock from neck to ankle. He had long, jet black hair, which fell with no particular design about his face, neck, and shoulders. His expression was grim, but not fearful or angry. He pointed to himself and pronounced a name that sounded like "Li Song." Benjamin answered by pointing to himself and pronouncing slowly, "Benjamin." The man nodded, apparently satisfied with this response. He turned to the children and, speaking in his language, motioned them back. They reluctantly went inside disappearing through the same door they had emerged from. The whole greeting took place in blowing ice and snow at temperatures that may have been deadly, but none of the inhabitants, children or adults, seemed the least bit discomforted.

Li Song walked toward the road, motioning for Benjamin to follow. Wondering if the man might understand him, Benjamin said, "Where are we going?" The man only responded by wagging a finger from side to side in front of Benjamin's face, by which Benjamin understood he was to follow and ask no questions.

Li Song led him to a smaller domed structure some distance away and knocked on a door like the one the children had exited from. It slid open revealing an elderly man wearing a long cloak similar to Li Song's. The man stood aside and welcomed them in.

The two men exchanged words, after which Li Song held up his hand in a farewell gesture to Benjamin. Benjamin returned the wave and found himself alone with the older man, who offered his hand and in hesitating English said, "I am Chen. I speak your language. You are one of those from up there?" He pointed toward the ceiling.

"Yes, I am Benjamin."

"Sit down, please." Chen motioned toward a wooden chair, one of several arranged in a circle surrounding a carpeted area. Just as he was seated, a woman entered. Like Chen, she was small, rotund, and elderly. Chen introduced her as his wife, Liang, and in English asked her to bring them tea.

Chen settled into a chair near Benjamin. Speaking slowly in broken, heavily accented English, he said, "Our village has never received a visitor from the sky before. Very few of us speak and understand the old language of those from space. I am the only one in this village."

"How do you know the old language?" Benjamin asked.

Chen shrugged. "My father taught me. He said it was important to know the ancient language and he forced me to learn it when I was very young, just as his father had made him learn it."

"It is the language of the galactic explorers," Benjamin said.

"Yes, and only today do I realize why it was important to learn it."

Benjamin nodded. "Your people have struggled on this planet."

Chen sighed and settled back in his chair. "It has never been easy for us. In the beginning, the planet was warm and plants grew everywhere. Our ancestors lived comfortably and our culture flourished. But then very slowly the planet became colder, a result of the fading of our sun's light. As the planet cooled, our machinery for generating power failed. Power from the sun, power from the wind, power from moving water — all became impractical as temperatures dropped below freezing. Construction, science, technology, all stagnated, as though frozen in time by the cold temperatures. Competition caused the population to break up into small towns and villages, each looking after its own needs.

Transportation and communication among the separate communities became unnecessary, as did governments and other global organizations. Over thousands of years, each town learned its own way to survive. Many did not. We know this because those remaining often travel here seeking warmth and shelter. We take them in and accept them as our own."

"How do you grow your plants in this cold weather?" Benjamin asked.

"We excavate the ground beneath each of the planting domes. Sufficient thermal energy is tapped from the planet's interior, and the plants have evolved to be extremely frost resistant as well."

Liang brought tea in ceramic cups. She poured some for Benjamin and Chen, then sat in one of the remaining chairs sipping from her own cup. The tea was hot and flavorful. Benjamin relaxed and soon found it difficult to suppress his yawns. Liang showed him to a small room in their house where a bed with fresh linen was waiting for him.

Benjamin spent the next several days with Chen and Liang, learning about their way of life. Li Song took him on tours of the town, showing him how they tended the crops under the domes. Benjamin found the children friendly and happy, and he was soon playing ball with them in the gymnasium. He spent time with Liang in the kitchen helping her prepare meals, observing her as she cooked vegetables in a large metallic skillet over an open fire fueled by frozen wood from the long-dead trees that surrounded the village. Liang also cooked a variety of fish that she took from a large freezer compartment built into the wall of the home.

One evening while eating dinner, Benjamin asked Chen where the fish came from. Chen explained that the fish were brought to the village by people he called Malanites, derived from their word for "furry ones". The Malanites fished for all the villages, delivering their catch frozen on a predetermined schedule. Chen consulted what appeared to be a calendar made from pebbles arranged on a small block of wood with rows of neatly inscribed holes. "There will be another delivery in two days. You will see the Malanites then."

Two days later, Benjamin was outside with Li Song, walking to the gymnasium when the frozen silence of the village was interrupted by the incongruous high-pitched whine of an engine. Li Song steered Benjamin to the side of the road as the sound intensified. Off in the distance, Benjamin saw a plume of snow rising into the air, blown laterally into a long sheath extending windward in the wake of the disturbance. The plume came closer and a few moments later Benjamin discerned a vehicle speeding toward them along the road, a quartet of headlights piercing the blowing snow before it. The vehicle was low and sleek, made from a sand-colored metallic substance. Whatever was propelling the vehicle over the snow was invisible, as the metal sides extended down to the ground. The vehicle reached the point where the road sloped upward and Benjamin expected to see it slip and slide over the icy surface, but it continued its approach with no discernible deviation in direction or speed. It passed Benjamin and Li Song and continued up the road toward the center of the village where it finally came to a stop. Three figures exited the vehicle and one of them circled around to open a hatch in the rear compartment. During this time, the townspeople had emerged from their homes and approached the vehicle where they queued up to receive packages of fish from the three Malanites.

Li Song motioned for Benjamin to follow and they trudged up the road and stood to one side watching the distribution of the frozen fish. The three Malanites wore single-piece cloth robes with hoods that covered their faces. They seemed to be unperturbed by the sub-zero temperatures and blowing snow.

When all the fish had been distributed, the Malanites climbed back into the vehicle and started the loud, whining engine. The vehicle spun in place 180 degrees and then accelerated swiftly, disappearing down the road in seconds amid a thick cloud of blowing snow. The noise of the engine faded gradually and the cold stillness of the town was restored.

Later that evening, Benjamin asked Chen where the Malanites lived.

"By the ocean, of course," the old man answered.

Benjamin was puzzled. "There are no oceans on this planet," he remarked. "At least none that aren't frozen."

"Yes, the oceans are covered with ice," Chen said. "But the Malanites make large holes in the ice and catch the fish that swim beneath."

Benjamin was curious. The Malanites seemed to be incredibly hardy and adaptive. "The Malanites give you fish," he said. "What do you give them in return?"

"We leave fruits and vegetables in a storage room outside of town," Chen answered. "The Malanites fill their vehicle on the way home."

"How far is the ocean?" Benjamin asked.

"About 30 km from here. It is a very difficult trip unless you have a Malanite snow machine."

"I'd like to see their village," Benjamin said.

"The Malanites are very reclusive. They may not want you to visit. Besides, they do not speak your language."

"Do they speak your language?"

"Yes," replied Chen.

"When will they return?"

"In about ten days."

"I will try to learn your language in the next ten days," Benjamin said with determination. "When they return, can you ask them if I can visit their village?"

"I will," Chen said. "But perhaps you will change your mind by then. It has been a long time since anyone visited the Malanites. It may not be safe."

Benjamin did not change his mind and ten days later he found himself in a Malanite snow machine careening across an uneven landscape of snow and ice strewn with dead trees and shrubs. In the driver's seat was Albon and next to him was his wife Iriana. Benjamin sat in the back seat with Albon's sister Bria. The noise of the vehicle made conversation impossible. Benjamin sat silently as the motion of the snow machine threw him alternately from one side to the other. Bria did not seem to mind the contact as his shoulder pressed against her. He felt strangely comforted by the feel of her body against his. Out of the corner of his eyes, he tried to see her face, but it remained hidden beneath the hood of her cloak.

An hour later, the vehicle came to a stop. Benjamin and his hosts exited onto a broad flat expanse of ice with snow blowing even more intensely than it had in Chen's village. Benjamin helped Albon unload the produce from the back of the snow machine, carrying it into a large storage room dug into the ground with walls supported by crudely cut timber. There were other Malanites nearby in similar vehicles, waiting to unload their cargo. Iriana and Bria walked off to a structure made entirely of compacted snow, similar to the igloos built by Inuits on Earth.

When they had unloaded all the produce, Albon led Benjamin on a tour of the surrounding region, speaking too rapidly for Benjamin to fully understand. He gathered that the Malanites lived adjacent to an ocean now permanently covered with ice. Venturing onto its surface, they came upon large holes that had been excavated revealing narrow channels of ocean water between jagged chunks of ice.

"These were fishing holes once," Albon explained. "Now the ocean is freezing again. We dig new holes when the fishing becomes poor."

"How do you fish?" Benjamin asked.

"We use nets. We drop the nets and wait until they fill with fish. Then we pull up the nets." Albon described this with expressive hand and arm gestures. Benjamin listened intently, nodding constantly to encourage Albon to continue. "Our newest fishing hole is farther away. We will go there tomorrow with the snow machine."

"That would be good. Thank you," said Benjamin politely.

"We will go to my home now and eat," said Albon.

The temperature in Albon's home was just slightly above freezing, as there was no source of heat anywhere in the dwelling. Iriana and Bria were in an area of the single-room home set aside for meals. They had both removed their hoods and Benjamin saw their faces were covered with coats of fine black hair about a half centimeter thick. When Albon removed his hood, Benjamin saw that the hair on his face was the same color and texture as the women's, but longer. Benjamin had already anticipated this and showed no surprise at their appearance. Chen had referred to them as the "furry ones", and it seemed reasonable that the humans on this harsh planet would have adapted to the cold temperatures with increased body hair. Bria seemed self-conscious, despite Benjamin's attempt to display no surprise at the unusual amounts of hair on her exposed skin. She kept her face turned away from him as she moved about in the kitchen.

The meal was a combination of fresh fruits and vegetables with strips of dried smoked fish. Benjamin sat across from Bria. She continued to be nervous, keeping her head down. The Malanites ate with their fingers and Benjamin followed their example.

"Do the others eat your dried fish?" he asked, not knowing how to refer to the people in Chen's village.

Albon shook his head. "They prefer to prepare fish their own way. They eat only fish that has been freshly cooked over their fires."

"You do not use fires to cook your fish?"

"No. Too hard to gather wood." Albon paused and then added, "The people who live in the village do not allow us to collect wood."

Benjamin stopped chewing a chunk of dried fish and asked, "Why?"

Albon sat back in his chair. He spoke to Benjamin as if to a child. "The land and that which grows upon it is theirs. The sea and that which lives within it is ours. We have been fishing the frozen oceans for many generations. Our children will do the same, as will their children."

"I understand," replied Benjamin. Out of the corner of his eye he noticed Bria's face lift and caught a glimpse of large opaline eyes looking at him curiously.

As if on cue, she and Iriana rose and began clearing the table. Bria's motions were brusque, and she clattered the dishes as she removed them from the table. When the two women were on the other side of the room, Benjamin commented to Albon, "Bria is not happy with me here."

Albon looked at the young woman, her back turned toward them. "She is young. She does not accept the way things are. She is unhappy with how we live. It bothers her that she has nothing better to look forward to — neither for her nor for her children. She is angry with Iriana and me because we do nothing to change who we are and what we do. She will learn with age. There is nothing we can do."

"Do you have children? Does Bria?"

"No. Iriana and I have no children yet. Nor does Bria. She has not found a mate. She may never find happiness taking a husband because it would mean she is setting a course toward a destination she knows too well. It is her choice."

Later that evening, Benjamin sat with the three Malanites and told them about Earth with the limited vocabulary he had learned. He tried to explain how explorers journeyed to the stars. Bria listened intently, eyes fixed on him in rapt attention. She seemed to be trying to communicate something that could not be said.

Later, Benjamin asked where he could go to relieve himself. Bria showed him the way, leading him out into the pitch-dark night. With the blowing snow, it would have been impossible for Benjamin to find his way. Bria took his hand and led him without hesitation into the stinging darkness.

In the outhouse, the total absence of light made it difficult for Benjamin to undress. It was freezing inside and the smell was unbearable. He finished quickly and donned his undergarments and thermal clothing, fumbling in the darkness with the zippers and snaps. When he emerged, Bria was waiting patiently for him outside.

"Thank you," he said.

She took his hand again and led him silently back to their house.

That night, Iriana gave Benjamin a thin cotton blanket. He slept on a crude mattress made of the same cotton cloth, but filled with a soft feathery material. Benjamin removed his outer garments, but kept his synthetic fiber underwear on for warmth. Still, he was cold through the long night and slept little. At some point, he heard the unmistakable sounds of Albon and Iriana making love on the other side of the room, near enough for him to hear their telltale moans and cries, as well as the soft whispering sighs afterward. He was aware that Bria, several meters away from him on her own mattress, undoubtedly heard everything as well.

The wind continued to howl throughout the evening. Benjamin dozed on and off and the night seemed endless. Finally, the icy walls of the house glowed faintly with an eerie blue color as the light from the rising sun strengthened. Benjamin heard his hosts moving about and rose from his bed to don his clothes. He said good morning to them and stepped out of the house to use the facilities again. The blizzard had finally stopped and he looked out over an endless sea of blindingly white ice and snow, interrupted only by scattered Malanite dwellings and an occasional windmill, not turning now that the gale had abated. Shielding his eyes from the brightness, Benjamin trudged off to the outhouse, noting the temperature had dropped with the clearing of the sky overhead. Although curious to observe the Malanites ice fishing, he knew the extreme cold would penetrate even the thick insulation of his thermal clothing.

After a breakfast consisting of more dried fish and fruit, he and Albon set off in the snow machine across the frozen surface of the ocean. Plumes of blowing snow in the distance to either side of them told him there were other Malanite vehicles on a similar course. Albon steered around large chunks of ice forced upward by the shifting tides of the ocean beneath. They passed many large holes in the ice, similar to the abandoned fishing hole Albon had shown him the previous evening. Albon explained that the fishing holes had to be dug increasingly farther from the shore, which suggested the ice covering the ocean was getting thicker, displacing the water and fish from the shallowest parts of the sea, forcing them progressively farther away from the Malanite dwellings. It depressed Benjamin to ponder the futility of the Malanites' plight. They and Chen's people were fighting to hold on to life on a planet whose sun could no longer sustain it. They went about their daily routines oblivious to the ultimate pointlessness of their endeavors. But what choice did they have really? Perhaps they all knew very well how hopeless the situation was, but also realized how little good it would do any of them to surrender to despair. He wished he could achieve the same level of acceptance they had. To them, his existence might seem just as bleak and hopeless. When they reached their destination, Benjamin saw that the active fishing hole was enormous — far larger than the abandoned ones they had passed, which probably had shrunk as they iced over again. Around the perimeter of the hole, other Malanites were casting their nets into the water. Some even ventured onto small ice floes floating on the surface of the water, and were drifting toward the center of the vast opening where the fishing might be better.

Albon joined a crew of other Malanite fishermen unfolding a large net that had been sitting on the ice. It had been covered with snow during the night and extracting it was a tedious job involving much tugging and kicking to free the fibers from their icy confinement. They now tossed it into the water in a practiced motion that maximized its extension away from the edge of the hole. When the net was fully deployed, the Malanites stood watching the sea surface with not much to do now but wait. Benjamin walked around the perimeter of the hole, attracting attention from the fishermen, who nodded his way but made no attempt to speak to him. Some of them were already pulling up nets filled with fish of different types.

The Malanites loaded the fish into large buckets arranged on the back of two special sleds. When one was full, it was pulled back toward the shore by a snow machine. By the time the buckets on the second sled were filled, the other sled had been brought back empty. This went on throughout the day and Benjamin marveled at how efficient the process was. He asked Albon what was done with the fish after they were taken away. Albon explained that they were brought back to the Malanite village where the women cleaned and packaged the fish for delivery to neighboring towns and villages.

By the afternoon, Benjamin was exhausted, even though he did little. He had to keep moving to stay warm. The men stopped only briefly to eat a lunch consisting of more dried fish and fruit. They carried canisters of fresh water. Albon shared his with Benjamin. During lunch, the men sat comfortably on mounds of snow. Benjamin mused at how well they had adapted to the frigid climate. The short, thick fur covering their bodies seemed sufficient to protect them from even the coldest temperatures. Benjamin knew it was impossible for evolution to have produced this adaptation in so little time. The Malanites' furriness resulted from the expression of a long suppressed gene in the human genome activated by environmental stresses. It was a spectacularly clever design built into the genetic code that had probably saved many organisms throughout the billions of years of life on Earth, and now also served to protect humans on this alien planet.

Late in the afternoon, the Malanites folded the nets again and started home. Benjamin and Albon arrived before Bria and Iriana, who returned later smelling strongly of fish. Albon asked Benjamin to wait outside until they had all changed their robes. Benjamin stood by the door looking out at the setting sun, slightly bluer than the surrounding sky, almost as invisible as the moon in daylight on Earth. Several minutes later, Bria emerged wearing a fresh robe and carrying a bundle of foul-smelling garments. Without saying a word to Benjamin, she walked away. Benjamin hesitated a moment and then caught up with her. He asked if he could walk with her and she nodded her okay, but she refused his offer to help her carry the garments. They walked to another ice building some distance away. Bria ducked inside, deposited the garments, and emerged several seconds later. Instead of heading back to the house, she led Benjamin away toward the icy ocean.

"You all work very hard," he said, trying to make conversation.

Bria looked at the ground, then turned her face toward him. "There is nothing else to do."

"I'm sorry," was all Benjamin could think to say, as if it were his fault. He felt the need to explain himself to her. "Life is very difficult here."

Bria stopped walking and turned to face him. "It is not the day to day life that is bad. It is knowing that things will never change that saddens me. It is the absence of something different to look forward to that makes it difficult to see the days pass by."

"But you never know what a new day will bring. Life always has surprises. Two days ago, you never imagined you would be standing here talking to an explorer from space." Benjamin smiled, hoping she would take the comment in the right way.

Bria stared into his eyes as if searching for something. Then she turned away and said, "Come."

They walked silently for several minutes and only stopped when they approached the edge of one of the abandoned ice holes, a large opening of still water not yet frozen over. With a single movement, Bria removed her robe and walked the remaining steps to the edge of the opening. Benjamin stood back and watched, her silhouette dark against the turquoise sky from which the sun had just departed. Her entire body was covered with soft fur, but her shape was very much that of a human female. He was only able to admire her beauty for a moment before she dove cleanly into the water and disappeared from view beneath the surface.

Benjamin hurried to the edge and in the fading light saw a dark shadow swimming smoothly under the water making graceful circles along the icy perimeter. Eventually, she lifted her head and, floating backward in the water, motioned for Benjamin to join her. Benjamin hesitated. Pieces of ice floated in the water. He wondered how quickly he would die if he entered the frigid liquid. He shook his head, but Bria continued to motion to him. Finally, Benjamin removed his thermal suit and the undergarments beneath. Once naked, there was little else to do but jump in. The shock he felt on entering would have rendered him unconscious, but he immediately felt the warmth of Bria's fur-covered body and her arms encompassed him. Benjamin wrapped his arms around her in return. Her fur provided enough buoyancy for them to float on the surface of the salty water without any arm or leg movements. They drifted together in that position while the water in the opening calmed. The arctic blue of the sky darkened above them and Benjamin closed his eyes, his head buried in the furry cleft of Bria's shoulder. The warmth of her breasts against him gave him a measure of comfort he had never known, and there in the freezing cold water under the fading light, Benjamin found contentment beyond anything he could have imagined.

That night, Benjamin and Bria slept together beneath the thin cotton blanket, and the inevitable happened. Hugging her from behind for warmth in the narrow bed, Benjamin became aroused. Bria unhesitatingly pressed herself against him and guided him into her. Soon their heavy breathing and moans matched those of Albon and Iriana. Later, Benjamin slept and dreamt of nothing.

When it was time for Benjamin to be delivered back to Chen's village, he sat with Albon, Iriana and Bria eating breakfast with unspoken thoughts hanging in the air. It was Albon who broke the impasse. "Do not consider the possibility of remaining with us," he said knowingly to Benjamin. "The weather has been mild lately. It will soon grow bitterly cold, and you would not survive." He nodded toward Bria, who was looking down at the table, her expression invisible to Benjamin. "Bria understands this. You have given her much enjoyment, and much to look forward to."

Benjamin looked up, puzzled.

"There is a good chance Bria will become pregnant with your child. The child will be either furry or hairless. If furry, Bria will raise the child. If not, she will keep the child until it is old enough to fend for itself. Then she will send it to one of the villages. They always believe it is one of their own from another village, and they will take the child in. It has happened before when one of them has mated with a Malanite. Bria will be happy to know that her child will be able to live in comfort, enjoying the benefits of their schools and reaping the rich harvest of their gardens."

Benjamin only nodded, speechless. He looked at Bria, who finally raised her head to return his gaze. There were tears in her eyes, but he detected no resentment, only a sad resolve.

Back in Chen's village, Benjamin embraced Albon, Iriana, and Bria, the last taking far too long before the curious eyes of the villagers. When he was reunited with Chen and Liang, Benjamin knew something had been altered in his relationship with them. They looked at him suspiciously, or so he imagined. He may have been projecting his own feelings, the awareness that he had been immutably altered by his time with the Malanites. Benjamin stayed only one more evening with Chen and Liang before announcing his intention to depart the planet. Saying his farewells to them and Li Song, Benjamin cleared the snow and ice from his capsule and entered with a final wave to the village on-lookers. He blasted off into the frigid blue sky, and as he ascended he knew Bria was near enough to see the rocket trail as it knifed through the heavens, aimed at the dying blue sun and the stars beyond.

CHAPTER 21
— 32220 —

Lindsay McAllister landed her space capsule in the Pacific Ocean, well offshore from what used to be the city of Los Angeles. She unfolded a small raft and paddled toward shore. Behind her, the vehicle sank slowly, until the last glint of sunlight reflecting from the metallic hull disappeared beneath the sea surface. She no longer needed the spacecraft that had been her home and prison for the last 30,000 years. She'd enjoyed the thrill of planetary exploration but had finally reached the point of dreading each descent, as she knew she'd have to lift off again. She feared the vehicle's rockets would fail and she'd be stranded on some lifeless world where she would die alone of asphyxiation or starvation. Though she had no idea what she'd encounter on Earth after so many years away, space exploration hadn't taken too many years off her life. She was still young and felt she could adapt to life on her home planet regardless of how much it had changed.

She navigated the small raft onto a deserted beach just as the sun was setting. She disembarked, carrying only a single backpack, and walked toward a low structure that extended as far as she could see along the length of the shore. The face of the building looked impenetrable, its bleak surface interrupted occasionally by windows covered to allow only faint slivers of light to emerge from within. She wondered how far she would have to walk before she found an entry to get past the imposing edifice. She kept as much as possible to the shadows, suspecting she would shock people she met.

Lindsay knew where she had to go. Before landing, she orbited Earth until her radio detected a signal from a ground transmitter at one of the official Union frequencies — a beacon with a unique code to guide explorers back to an ally on Earth. In the 22nd century, Union members had sworn to pass the code on to future generations. Lindsay realized how unlikely it was for this commitment to have survived through so many millennia, and she'd been pleasantly surprised when her receiver detected the signal. Unfortunately, it originated from the Griffith Park Observatory in the hills overlooking Los Angeles. With no open landing sites nearby, she was forced to land her vehicle offshore. Now she'd have to walk all night in the dark to reach the observatory before dawn. She was determined to avoid encounters with the local inhabitants, not knowing what they'd be like. She'd brought an electromagnetic pulse weapon with her, but she wasn't sure how effective such an ancient weapon might be in this city of the future.

Ironically, from where she stood on the beach, she found nothing futuristic about it. Los Angeles was a city turned upside down. The remains of an abandoned highway structure hung above the low-slung structures beneath. Access ramps leading up to the highway terminated abruptly in precipitous drops, with massive chunks of broken concrete strewn chaotically about.

She walked along the worn and crumbling building until she came to a narrow opening that provided access to the interior of the city. This path led to still more paths, each lined by walls that seemed as though they'd been carved through trash heaps. Using the computer-controlled navigation system built into her jumpsuit, Lindsay remained on a course that brought her steadily closer to her destination.

Though relieved to encounter no one, she felt uneasy at whatever kept people from venturing out of their crumbling abodes after dark. Her fears were well founded. The alleyway along which she walked led into a large courtyard bathed in an eerie blue light emanating from lamps in the undersurface of the elevated highway. Strange music rumbled in pitiless bass from an establishment where a group of very tall people stood rocking and swaying to the ear-splitting rhythm.

Lindsay froze in the shadow of the alley. Her first instinct was to turn around, but she'd have to backtrack to explore an alternate route, and she suspected any path she chose might return to this courtyard. It appeared to be a hub, where many paths met. Lindsay's navigation system pointed to a corridor, not far from where the group stood laughing, dancing, and talking in an unintelligible language. Occasionally, they drank from vessels that reflected the odd sapphire light from above.

She gripped her EMP weapon and strode surreptitiously across the courtyard in the direction of the dark corridor toward which her navigation system pointed. She'd almost reached the archway when she heard an exclamation from one of the group followed by an unusual lull in the conversation lasting several beats of the deafening music. Curiosity got the best of her and before entering the corridor she turned and locked eyes with a half dozen of the group, staring back at her in dazed wonderment. Her glance was quick, but she saw the distinctive oval-shapes of their faces and pale yellow tint to the eyes, which were large and cat-like.

Lindsay hastened her pace through the alley. She heard shouts behind her and broke into a slow trot. Her heavy backpack shook and something inside began to rattle loudly. She could not outrun her pursuers, and the noise of her pack made it impossible for her to elude them. In fearful desperation, she stopped, turned around, and fired her weapon at the underside of the road above. The blue electrified glow charged through the air, illuminating the alley with its own terrifying aura. In the flash, she saw her pursuers freeze in their tracks, yellow eyes cast upward at the streaking light overhead.

Lindsay didn't hesitate. She wheeled about and ran, hoping to outpace the crowd before they regained their resolve. Minutes later, she stopped and bent forward with hands on her knees to catch her breath. Once she had recovered, she listened for the sounds of running feet, but the stillness of the alleyway remained unbroken.

She continued through the narrow pathways, heading in the direction indicated by her guidance system. After several miles more, she realized she hadn't moved much closer to her destination because of the convoluted path she'd been on. She looked at the elevated road system above her, knowing she could make better time on that broad thoroughfare. The massive cylindrical piers on which the road sat were impossible to scale, and even if she were able to climb one, she'd just be confronted by the stark concrete underside of the structure.

Fortunately, beneath the concrete artery was a broad walkway leading eastward. Lindsay remained on it for as long as possible, relying on her navigation system to tell her when to turn northward toward the observatory. The homes here were in better condition than those she had passed earlier. All were built into an uninterrupted wall that was clean and newly painted. The doors were sturdy and well cared for. Lindsay saw narrow cracks of light escaping through opaque window coverings that made it impossible to see inside.

She made better time now and after a few hours of sustained effort found herself due south of her destination, but still four miles away. She looked at her watch, pleased to see there were still several hours before sunrise. She took a few minutes to eat and drink and then selected a path that led northward. After the openness of the walkway she'd been on, she was unnerved by the claustrophobic confinement of the narrow alley. The walls rose higher, blocking out the blue light cast from the undercarriage of the abandoned road system above her. Soon, there was only the hazy orange light cast by the murky L. A. sky. She removed a flashlight from her belt to illuminate the way.

An hour later, to her dismay, the alleyway dead-ended at a high, shear wall. So sudden and absolute was the obstruction that she wasted no time considering how she might get past it. Resolutely, she turned back, with diminishing hope she could reach the observatory before dawn.

She'd only taken a few steps when she was shocked to see a small boy standing before her. She fumbled to grab her EMP weapon, but stopped, detecting fear in the boy's yellow eyes. She brought her hand up and waved cautiously at him and was relieved when he returned the gesture. He spoke to her, but she understood nothing.

Lindsay decided her best way to communicate would be to show a picture of the observatory using the holographic display capability built into the computer of her jumpsuit. She held out her hands with palms up and a moment later a ghostly image of the observatory appeared. The boy looked at it, registering no surprise. He just nodded his head and motioned for Lindsay to follow him.

He led her back down the alley a short distance and then pushed against a wall covered with handprint-shaped depressions. A second later, a portion of the wall dissolved and the boy stepped through. Lindsay waited before entering until he motioned for her to follow.

She found herself in a long hallway with doors on both sides. This was obviously a vast apartment complex. The closeness of one door to another suggested the apartments were not very large and none could have exterior windows. She shuddered to think of the dismal living conditions of the city's inhabitants. For the first time, she regretted sinking her space capsule. She had not imagined how life on Earth could have degraded to such an extent.

Lindsay followed the boy through corridor after corridor. He walked with assurance, occasionally looking back to make sure she was still behind him. Several of the hallways ended at stairways that led upward to another level of dismal dwellings. She guessed she was gradually ascending the hillside that had once been undeveloped parkland surrounding the observatory. She wondered how the city's inhabitants could survive with so little room to move. After so much time in the galactic void, the density of humanity about her was unsettling.

She was panting audibly when the boy finally stopped at the bottom of another staircase. Instead of continuing up, he pointed to a doorway above and nodded at Lindsay. She walked slowly past him and climbed to the small landing in front of the door. She smiled back at the boy, waved, and turned to approach the door, searching for some means to open it. To her relief, the door slid smoothly aside to reveal an outdoor walkway. Standing on a waist-high wall, she gazed outward at the broad expanse of the city, brilliantly speckled with a sea of multi-colored lights interrupted only by the web of roads suspended above it. In the distance, the discrete points of light became more diffuse and at the horizon blended smoothly into the amber haze of the night sky.

"I am told a long time ago one could see the ocean from here."

The voice came from farther down the walkway. Lindsay saw the silhouette of a tall figure wearing a hooded robe.

"I wouldn't know," she said shakily. "This is my first time in Los Angeles."

"So that was its name then," the figure answered. "There has been much debate about that."

"What is it called now?" Lindsay asked.

There was a long pause. "Your question has no meaning for us. The world is all one place now."

"And a place that has lost track of its history. How could you not know what this city used to be called?"

"The events and facts from 30,000 years ago are of little import to us now. When you were on Earth, did you know the names of places 30 millennia in the past?"

"No, I suppose not," Lindsay answered, almost inaudibly.

The man walked toward her. When he was near, she saw his long, cleanly shaven face beneath the cloth hood that cast an oblique shadow like a mask extending from one eye to the opposite cheek.

"I am Gorin," he said, and bowed his head, his hands hidden within the robe.

"I am Lindsay. So it was your beacon that brought me here?"

"Yes. I've been expecting you. I asked the boy to keep an eye out for you." His English was heavily accented, but clear and precise. "I have carried out the charge as it was passed to me from my ancestors. I feel blessed that in all my family, I am the only one to be visited by an explorer."

Lindsay hesitated not knowing how to respond. She looked about her. "Is this the observatory? Do you live here?"

"It is a museum. As far as we know, it has always been more a museum than an observatory. We have little use for observatories. And yes, I live here. I am the museum's director."

Lindsay looked out at the expanse of lights again. "The city is so run down," she said.

"You are disappointed," Gorin replied, directing his gaze outward.

"I was expecting a very modern city."

"We have modern areas of the world. This is just not one of them. I'm sure in your day the entire Earth was not modern."

"No. Actually very little of it was, but Los Angeles was a great city with arts, culture, great wealth, magnificent homes, and huge skyscrapers."

"Many skyscrapers have come and gone since your time. Arts and culture — they are still here. Perhaps even more so than ever before. Do not let the quality of the living conditions fool you."

Lindsay tried to imagine the city she had walked through being fertile ground for creativity and imagination. "But what happened?" she asked.

Gorin took Lindsay's arm gently and led her on a slow stroll along the walkway. "Many millennia have passed since you were here on Earth. Since you departed, there were the great wars, then came the fall of the industrial empire, followed by the dis-invention of the internal combustion engine."

"That explains the abandoned roadways," Lindsay commented.

"Our technology made motorized vehicles superfluous. The tax paid to provide each individual with unlimited mobility became too much of a burden."

They stopped at a bench facing the city. There was a mild breeze and the lights before them twinkled. Removing her backpack, Lindsay sat beside Gorin, feeling safe and comfortable in the tranquility and isolation of the observatory.

"I suppose with all the wars, natural disasters, disease, and famine it's surprising there is even this much left of our civilization."

Gorin sighed. "You omitted the greatest challenge to humanity. Not to minimize the tragedy of millions of lost lives from the events you mention, but the biggest threat to civilization has always been human nature itself."

Gorin paused, and Lindsay sat patiently, wondering if he was waiting for some response from her. After several moments, he continued. "Wars, famine, and disease kill people, of course, but with many billions of people in the world there are always survivors. The mass of human population is as stubborn as the most resilient mold that grows upon the rocks in the coldest and most forbidding places on Earth. Many will cling to life, even in the face of incredible misfortune."

Gorin's voice seemed to be trembling. Lindsay was tempted to peer beneath the hood covering his face to see if he was crying, but he bowed his head, making such scrutiny impossible.

"The biggest threat to humanity will always be the way we behave toward one another in hard times. Pain and suffering are never eliminated. They are passed on from one to another inexorably. When the climate of Earth changed, the habitable regions shrunk. Instead of working together to help those whose homes were threatened, there were wars over the remaining tracts of land still suitable for habitation. Immigration laws became ruthlessly strict. Nations became more insular. Border violence strained the bonds between family and friends, between neighbors and nations, between races and religions. Mutual understanding and the spirit of unity became extinct.

"When the global economy collapsed, subjecting billions of people to abject poverty, there was no effort to equalize the wealth in the world. Those who had it became richer. Those who did not have it became poorer. Those in between stole, cheated, embezzled, and defrauded others to move up to the ranks of the prosperous and avoid sinking to the ranks of the deprived.

"When there was famine, there was no movement to share the world's supply of food. The fear of starvation made all people either predators or prey. More people died from the resulting conflicts than from lack of food. It was quite simply the desperation and panic that proved more fatal to humans than the failure of crops to produce the harvest.

"When disease struck, it certainly killed many millions of people, but far more devastating was the capture of disease agents to inflict mass murder on religious and political enemies. Nuclear weapons could destroy entire nations, but they never did. On the other hand, religious dogma was deadly, and the resulting conflicts changed the fabric of society over and over again, displacing entire populations, inducing patricide, genocide, and infanticide, killing people by the masses."

Gorin emitted a guttural sound that was almost a groan. The stillness about them was absolute. In the 22nd century there would have been the distant sounds of aircraft, cars, railroads, sirens. Here there was nothing.

"It is not weapons, germs, heat, cold, starvation that threaten our species. These things come and go. It is the persistent intolerance, persecution, hatred, bigotry, selfishness, stupidity, arrogance, and greed that will ultimately spell the end of the human race. That is the lesson 32000 years of civilization have taught us. In times of stress, one segment of the population victimizes the rest. When the number of victims becomes overwhelming, an upheaval of some type must occur, whether it is political, military, social, religious, or even technological — something must take place to restore the natural balance of society. Disease, famine, floods — these are only external agents that stress society, but it is the nature of the human psyche that brings it to the breaking point."

Lindsay had been on Earth only ten hours and was already depressed. She shivered. She almost yearned for the comforting oblivion of her magnetocryogenic chamber. Gorin rose and took her by the arm, leading her through a door farther down the walkway and into a broad hallway, the walls of which had a matte gray sheen resembling that of a video monitor. Lindsay was curious about what pictures the walls displayed to visitors of the museum. With a wave of Gorin's hand, a door to their left opened and they both entered a large room filled with oddly shaped tables and chairs and cupboards with glass panels revealing a variety of foods, including fresh meats, vegetables, and fruit. Gorin voiced commands Lindsay could not understand and produced two cups filled with a warm, sweetly pungent liquid. Lindsay and Gorin seated themselves at a table.

"So, Lindsay, tell me what galactic space travel has taught you."

Lindsay shook her head. "There's nothing out there. No lessons. No great cosmic truths. Hardly any life either — mostly just the cold, predictable products of chemistry and physics acting on the inanimate matter of the universe."

"As I expected," Gorin said. "Our civilization has only existed a short time relative to the age of the universe and I suspect it will not be around much longer. Any civilization out there will be just as impermanent. Such transience defies the search for extra-terrestrial life."

"Have you received news from other galactic explorers?" Lindsay asked, breathing in the soothing aroma of the hot liquid.

"How would I?" asked Gorin. He removed his hood. His face was heavily lined and the wisps of hair remaining on his head were uniformly white. Though he had the same yellow eyes as other Earthlings, age had softened their intensity.

"Haven't you received any messages from space?"

Gorin looked puzzled. "I don't understand. My equipment is only a beacon, transmitting and receiving at a single frequency. How would I receive messages?"

"I was hoping one of the receiving stations on Earth might still be operational. Or if not, perhaps the radio-telescope on the moon might still be sending data back to Earth."

Gorin shook his head in agitation. "I know of no such stations."

Lindsay became excited. "You mean you don't monitor the frequencies that enable you to pick up transmissions from the moon?"

"What frequencies? What transmissions?" Gorin was clearly upset now also.

Lindsay explained how the Union had put in place a communication network designed to endure through the millennia. Gorin was intrigued. "I guess that knowledge was lost sometime in the past. Do you know the frequencies of the lunar transmissions? The receiver here might be sensitive enough to detect them."

Lindsay rose from her chair. "Of course, I know them. When does the moon rise?"

Gorin pronounced a sequence of unidentifiable words and a

voice emanating from somewhere in the room responded immediately. "The moon is up now. Low on the horizon in the east," Gorin translated.

"Where is your receiver?" Lindsay asked.

"It doesn't matter," replied Gorin. I can command it from anywhere in the building. Just tell me what to do."

An hour later, Lindsay and Gorin listened to the audible rendition of the signal detected by Gorin's radio receiver. Lindsay shook her head recognizing the static as an indication that no signal was being detected. However, she wasn't discouraged because she knew the transmission from the moon would not be continuous. Lindsay and Gorin sat and talked, sipping their tea and listening to the raspy tone coming from the speakers in the museum's kitchen.

Soon, instead of static, the speakers emitted a modulated tone with a regular rhythmic background. "That's it!" Lindsay cried. "It's still working!"

Gorin rose and walked to the wall. With a single command, the surface became a screen down which a string of characters scrolled. Lindsay understood none of it and she urged Gorin to translate for her. A moment later, the message appeared in English on the wall. Lindsay recognized it as a report on the status of the instrument. Embedded in the text was the time at which the next full transmission would be sent. It would be in five hours, when the moon was almost directly overhead.

Lindsay spent the next few hours resting in a small room with only a bed. Lights, closets, washstand, and night table were all accessible as needed with a simple wave of the hand. Even the décor of the room could be changed by a single command, which Gorin selected for Lindsay as she didn't know the language.

She lay in the bed exhausted, but unable to sleep. Hanging her hopes and dreams on Earth, she had permanently cut herself off from Union comrades in space. She had underestimated how much she'd have to learn to adapt to civilization of the 330th century. How empty her life would be from now on? Where would she live? What would she do? She regretted ever having signed up to be a galactic explorer.

Eventually, she nodded off and awoke sometime later knowing she had slept too long. She rushed back to the kitchen where she found Gorin sitting with his head upon the table, hidden under the hood of his cloak. When she entered, he raised his head and nodded a greeting.

"Was there a transmission?" she asked.

He pointed to the wall where Lindsay saw an enlarged version of the display they had looked at earlier. "You were right. There was a long message containing all the latest transmissions received from space. It will take many hours to read and study all the data, but the message you see there was flagged as high priority."

Lindsay looked at the wall and read the brief message.

> I am Aril.
> Give me your tired, your poor,
> Your huddled masses yearning to breathe free,
> The wretched refuse of your teeming shore.
> Send these, the homeless, tempest-tossed to me...

"That message is followed by a long description of a planet named Aril that was colonized by a group from Earth thousands of years ago. I've been scanning the information. Aril..." Gorin stopped, apparently unable to find the right words.

"Aril what?" Lindsay asked impatiently.

Gorin rubbed a hand across his bald pate. "Aril sounds like a very nice planet."

Lindsay spent the next several days reading through the data on Aril, 8000 light-years away. It was a peace-loving planet with a youthful and positively spirited population. Preceding every message was the quote from the Statue of Liberty, which she learned from Gorin was still standing at the entrance to the harbor of the city that used to be called New York.

Gorin reported the discovery of the lunar telescope to officials around the world. The information streaming to Earth was collected and studied. The events occurring on Aril were followed by Earth's population as closely as they followed their own news. Eventually, Earthlings constructed large transmitters and began sending messages back to Aril, without even knowing whether there was a radio telescope on that planet sufficiently sensitive to receive the responses. Lindsay provided information about the locations of the Union Supply Ships, and messages were sent to those stations as well. Lindsay assured them the supply ships would forward the messages to Aril. However, the supply ship closest to Aril and most readily able to relay the message was the one occupied by Dr. Andrew Harding. By the time Earth's messages had reached the location of that supply ship, the large vessel was no longer there.

Lindsay stayed and lived at the museum with Gorin, who taught her the language of Earth and everything else she needed to know about the museum. Initially very reclusive, she gradually became more confident in meeting museum visitors. In fact, Lindsay herself became one of the most popular attractions because she was living proof of the reality of Earth's distant past.

When Gorin died, he left Lindsay in charge of the museum. It was a labor of love for her. She would never have her own children, but the boy, who had shown her the way to the museum her first day back on Earth, became her best friend and apprentice. He helped her perform her functions and learned from her the history of the Union's efforts to explore the galaxy. Although Lindsay's life did not unfold as she had expected, the events that took place during her second time on Earth validated the decisions she had made so long ago. As she grew older, Lindsay immersed herself more and more in the events on Aril, the planet that had become the embodiment of all she had missed out on during her long life.

CHAPTER 22
— 33963 —

Stormer returned to Supply Ship 5 looking worn out and disoriented, with black ash still marking his face and hands. He grabbed a canister of water from the galley, slouched into one of the chairs and drank thirstily, waiting for Harding, who bustled about the control room monitoring the ship's radar as it completed an automatic inventory of the remaining vehicles in Stormer's fleet. Harding knew that many of Stormer's group had not escaped the inferno on Alpha. When he joined Stormer in the galley, he sat at the table and rubbed his hands over his face as if he could reconfigure it. "You left almost seventy dead on Alpha — about fifteen percent of your men," he said to Stormer with disappointment and scorn.

Stormer stared back at Harding defiantly, "Why did you kill her?"

Harding hesitated until he realized what Stormer was talking about. "She was escaping."

"Impossible!" Stormer snapped back.

Harding pointed a thumb toward the control room. "I'll play back the data for you. About 24 hours after you left, I looked at the radar scan. One vehicle strayed from your fleet and headed in a different direction. It was hers."

Stormer wondered whether to demand the proof.

"Anyway, what's the point?" Harding continued. "She's only one person. We can afford to lose Ms. Montgomery, but what would happen if you'd lost all your men?"

"Do you think it's easy to colonize a planet?" Stormer shot back. "We were clearing vegetation. It was impenetrable. We worked all day in stifling heat, and then at night the temperature dropped below freezing. Did you want me to tell them they couldn't start fires to keep warm?"

Harding placed his palms on the table and scowled. "I thought you picked resourceful men who were experienced in living in the wilderness — tough men who know not to piss into the wind. Didn't anyone think the fires might spread?"

Stormer was silent for some time. Finally, through clenched teeth, he said, "What took place on that planet happened ten thousand years ago. There's nothing to be gained from any kind of recrimination, especially from someone on a comfortable supply ship with everything he needs just steps away. The least you could have done in all this time is find another habitable planet, because I'll be damned if I'm going to drift around the galaxy for the rest of my life."

"I've already found one," Harding said curtly. "This one should be easy to colonize. Someone else has done it for us." Harding rose from his chair. "Let's go to the control room."

On the large monitor, Harding displayed a star field and highlighted the location of one star with a yellow rectangle. "Back around 28,500, I had a visit from a Captain Warner. Ever heard of him?"

"No," answered Stormer, settling himself into a command console seat.

"It was his second visit here. The first time he came with a group of about 300 colonists, a bunch of misfits who had no business being in space, let alone colonizing a planet. But the second time he showed up, he told me the colony was surviving. I reviewed the message log over the previous ten thousand years and sure enough, this planet — Aril he called it — was sending messages out boasting about how wonderful their little world was and inviting others to visit."

Stormer raised his eyebrows. "Sounds very hospitable of them."

"Yes, and stupid too, if you ask me. They're just asking for trouble. Barely 4000 years old as a civilization and somehow they think they can save the universe, be a safe harbor for the flotsam of the galaxy."

Stormer turned to Harding, suddenly realizing where the man was heading with Aril. "Are you suggesting we take over this planet?"

Harding glared back. "It will be a lot easier than starting one from scratch."

"That's true, but thousands of years will have passed by the time I get there. The population will have grown, they will have governments, laws, religions, military — all of which may not tolerate the sort of colony I envision. I might just as well have stayed on Earth and dealt with the authorities there."

Harding stood and paced the room. Stormer could see the Union lecturer in his mannerisms, the confident, almost condescending, way he carried himself and spoke. "I've monitored their messages continuously since receiving the first transmission. They're very free with information, as if they want the universe to know how enlightened they are. Unfortunately for them, they're also a peace-loving culture. They have no military to speak of." Harding paused to let this information sink in, making a few more circuits around the small control room.

Stormer felt Harding's words had been carefully rehearsed, but now he appeared to be thinking. "We will have to precede our landing with a show of force — a demonstration of the power we have at our disposal should they interfere with our activities."

Stormer interrupted. "What do you mean 'our landing'?"

"I'm going with you. I've spent enough time on this supply ship, and this time I'm going to make sure the attempt to establish a colony is done right."

Stormer was troubled, but he put it aside. "What sort of demonstration of power are you talking about?" He asked.

"They have no space program to speak of — just a few communications satellites. We need to establish our dominance in space, to intimidate them by inserting our vehicles into orbits about the planet. There we can display the weapons we have. We need to take control of their communication systems also. We don't want them calling anyone for help. Then we land and deliver our terms to them, make sure they understand the consequences if they attempt to resist in any way."

Stormer shook his head. "But they'll outnumber us. I have less than four hundred men left. They could easily overpower us."

Harding was prepared for this. "More like 1200."

"How do you figure that?" asked Stormer.

"Companions of mine in the galactic explorer force — Union members I know I can count on for their loyalty."

"But they must be scattered all over the galaxy. It will take way too long to assemble them at Aril," Stormer objected.

"True," said Harding, changing the display on the monitor with a verbal command. The screen refreshed to show a broader view of the Union's quadrant of the galaxy. "As soon as I learned about Aril, I sent a message ordering most of the galactic explorer fleet to converge there." With the next verbal instruction from Harding, a multitude of red dots appeared on the screen. "Here are the projected locations of those galactic explorers at present. They're moving to rendezvous at Aril."

Stormer rose and backed away from the monitor to get a better view of the distribution of red dots. There was a noticeably heavier concentration in the vicinity of Aril, still outlined by the yellow rectangle. "When did you issue the command?" he asked.

"About 28500, when Captain Warner last visited."

Stormer poked his finger at the monitor. "Five thousand years ago and this is their current positions? At the rate your friends are converging, they won't arrive at Aril for a very long time."

"We will wait to invade Aril until 65000. By then, about 800 explorers will be in position."

"65000!" shouted Stormer. "We have to wait 30000 years for a planet to settle on?"

Harding only shrugged. "Aril is a sure bet. You could make maybe two or three more attempts at colonizing another planet in that time, but it's a long shot, given your dismal record." He paused to let the insult hang. Finally he added, in a more conciliatory tone, "Look, the galactic explorer force has been visiting planets all over this quadrant of the galaxy for 30000 years now and I have yet to hear about a habitable planet other than Aril. This may be our last chance for a long time."

Stormer shook his head. "Do you realize there is no way to tell what type of civilization there will be on Aril by 65000. They could evolve into a warfaring planet with advanced weapons and no tolerance for aliens, even those from Earth."

"We won't be landing on Aril as soon as we get there. We'll have time while we're waiting for the galactic explorers to arrive to make observations and update our knowledge of the planet and its people."

"And if they turn out to be hostile, then what? We tell 1200 people drifting along with us 'Sorry, only kidding'. Hope you did not mind wasting the last 30000 years."

Harding sighed. "I know Aril," he said. "I've studied their messages since they started transmitting. They're completely non-aggressive, anti-war and anti-technology. They refuse even to make use of valuable mineral deposits they know exist on the planet. They're afraid to embark on the same path that almost destroyed Earth. That philosophy has pervaded Arilian thought for thousands of years. It has been so ingrained in their collective psyche that it's second nature to them. It's not likely to change, no matter how much time passes." Harding paused, then said, "Besides, I have independent verification of that."

"From where?" Stormer asked.

Speaking slowly, Harding answered. "As soon as I learned about Aril, I asked one of the explorers in the vicinity to land on Aril and check it out. He was there for several months and sent a full report. He confirmed my expectations. Aril is a world of pacifist dreamers, who strive to live in harmony with their planet. They go about their petty business with an innocent euphoria that everything will work out in their favor if they live according to the rules they've followed since day one. It's ludicrous. It's pitiful. It's almost as if they need us to save them from themselves. I'm surprised an alien force hasn't already annihilated the whole Arilian population."

Stormer was still uneasy. "If we're going to invade an advanced civilization, why don't we just go back to Earth?"

Harding nodded toward the monitor. "Go back to Earth? Is that what you want to do?" He made a circuit of the room and returned to face Stormer. "Has it been that long since you were on Earth? When you want to pick a fruit from a tree, do you look for the old rotten ones ready to fall on the ground, or do you pick the nice, ripe ones, sweet and juicy? When you wanted a woman on Earth, did you look for some dried out old hag, or did you look for a beautiful, young woman, luscious and fertile? Earth has been raped many times over. There's nothing left there but a desiccated husk of a planet, barely able to keep the remaining population alive. Is that what you want to go back to?"

Stormer was speechless. He fell back into his chair and continued his examination of the display screen.

"Besides," continued Harding. "We have an ace in the hole."

Stormer swiveled his chair toward Harding and said, "What is that?"

"We're taking this supply ship with us," Harding answered.

Stormer found himself in the rare situation of being intimidated. Not only had Harding thought this out very carefully, he also had a superior intellect. Only after Harding's words fully sunk in did Stormer realize the implications. "You don't mean…"

Harding was nodding. "Yes. We'll use our nuclear weapons."

Stormer relaxed into his seat, the back-rest reclining with the weight. In orbit around Aril, the nuclear weapons on the supply ship represented an unimaginable threat. Harding could exercise unlimited nuclear blackmail to keep Arilians completely cooperative. For the first time, Stormer was beginning to believe the plan could work. He could think of no response. Finally, he said, "When do we leave?"

Arthur watched Krystal with admiration as she reviewed the data received during the last hundred years they'd been frozen. He paid close attention to her body language, hoping it would indicate news of Benjamin. When Krystal suddenly tensed, Arthur held his breath, fearing catastrophic news about his son. Finally, she muttered under her breath, "Interesting message from Earth."

Relieved, Arthur said, "It's interesting when we get any message from Earth at all."

"What do you expect?" said Krystal. "It's been 34,000 years since the galactic explorers left. I'm surprised there are still people on Earth who know we're out here."

"Say what you will about the Union, they managed to maintain a presence on Earth through all this time. Someday I'd like to sift through the data and try to piece together how the knowledge of the Union's exploration was passed on amid all the turmoil on Earth. Just the task of maintaining the official Union language through the millennia is unimaginable."

Krystal commanded the computer to display the message on the large monitor:

"From Earth to Aril: We have received your message and congratulate you on the successful colonization of your planet. Latest information and data on Earth follow. We welcome continued communication."

"What is Aril?" Arthur asked.

"I have no idea, but I can find out where it is. Once I've gotten its coordinates, I'll initiate a search to see if we missed any transmissions from its location."

Krystal looked at Arthur apologetically. Arthur trusted her to construct the automated search software. Her routines should have captured and flagged any message about a successful colonization.

"Is there any way Earth could have received a message that we missed?" Arthur asked.

"Lots," answered Krystal. "Aril could be closer to Earth than to us. Or even if it's farther away, Earth has the antenna on the far side of the moon that's more sensitive than our receivers. Also, the message from Aril could have been directed to Earth and not to us."

Arthur frowned. He estimated when the message from Earth was sent and added a few thousand years to account for the distance from Aril to Earth. Easily more than ten thousand years would have passed. It was discouraging. The fundamental principle that information can't travel faster than the speed of light put severe limitations on its usefulness. Whole civilizations could die out or be reborn during the time it took to pass messages between two different parts of the galaxy.

He once confronted Krystal with this dilemma, as she stubbornly adhered to the importance of information, regardless of how old or how irrelevant it might seem at the moment.

"Think of the galaxy as a big organism," she had answered. "The defining property of an organism is that the different parts are in continuous contact. Even the galaxy can act like a single being if there is a process to transfer information among all its different parts. It may take thousands of years to transmit information from one place in the galaxy to another, but that's only a long time relative to the human life span. Relative to the age of the galaxy, it's like the blink of an eye. Before, the galaxy was a disconnected array of celestial bodies. Now, by virtue of the communication network established by the Union, we've given life to the galaxy, a life force — a soul, you might call it.

"Communication brings together people, cultures, and planets in such a way that collectively they act as a single organism. The explorer network, the individual vehicles, the supply ships, and the rare colonies out there comprise a gigantic organism filling galactic space. The communication network that helps this huge organism survive is analogous in many ways to the human nervous system. The signals travel by electrical transmissions at nearly the speed of light. The control center for an organism is the brain, which receives and transmits signals, helping the various body parts perform their prescribed functions, as well as responding to stimuli, both benign and malicious. The fundamental difference between the galactic organism and our bodies is that it is so large the signals take much longer to move to and from the brain."

"That's a big difference," Arthur had commented.

"Are you sure?" replied Krystal. "Think about it. When we touch a hot object, the response is almost instantaneous because the signals travel back and forth so quickly, but not so quickly that it keeps us from getting burned. In our galactic organism, it means the control center, the brain, has to be more clever. Or maybe it's not so much a matter of cleverness, but adaptation. The human brain is wonderful at adapting to changes in the signals it receives from sensory organs. If we lose an eye, we lose depth perception, but the brain quickly adjusts to this change by developing other means to judge depth. If we lose sight totally, our hearing and sense of smell become more acute, compensating for the loss of visual information. If some neurological disease prolonged the time it took signals from sensory organs to travel to the brain, it would undoubtedly adapt by finding means of anticipating events. When you're blindfolded and made to walk through a room, your brain is instantly working out various scenarios to cope with the lack of information. The way our galactic organism adapts is by constructing complex procedures to deal with unexpected events — fall-back options, plans A, B, and C. And remember, data from the network is continually arriving, just as when we look into space the light from distant galaxies is always in sight. A constant stream of information pours in continuously. The challenge is to process that information usefully."

Arthur defended himself. "I'm used to dealing with people and cultures. You're talking about something that outlives civilizations. Different rules apply."

"Take it one step at a time," Krystal argued. "Look at civilization as an organism. Its control center is the collective human psyche that contains all the history of civilization at its core, just as every human brain has deep within it a remnant of the early humanoid mind around which it developed."

"You don't put much importance on the individual," Arthur had pointed out.

"Perhaps, but think about the fact that individual cells within the body die, reproduce, and regenerate, all to the benefit of the collective being. We don't mourn for their death. We're hardly aware that cellular life cycle is underway as we go about our business. Similarly, the galactic being goes about its business with little regard for the life and death of individual people, civilizations, or planets that in the distant past gave it life to begin with"

"You keep talking about a control center. Where is it?" Arthur asked.

"That's not clear yet," said Krystal. "It changes through the years. When we first left Earth, I would've said that it was on Earth — in the members of the Union who were responsible for receiving messages from the galactic exploration force and formulating responses. But I think that's changed. Earth seems to have abdicated control."

"To whom?"

"One of the supply ships, I suppose. Whichever one takes charge and assumes that responsibility. You have to accept the fact, Arthur, that because we are on the closest supply ship to Earth and because this one is a central node for all information transmitted within the Union's communication network, we — you and I — might actually be the brains of this big galactic animal."

Arthur had chuckled. It was definitely the kind of idea Krystal would be drawn to. "I'm flattered."

Krystal did not smile back. She just looked at him in a way he had learned meant she had no more to say.

Krystal tracked down the origin of the message from Aril. She turned to Arthur and, seeing him deep in thought, waited until he acknowledged her.

"Find out anything?" he asked.

"We never received the message from Aril, but I know what it said because it was appended to the message from Earth. Here it is." She gestured to the computer screen. Arthur read the quote from the Statue of Liberty in silence.

"Don't tell me anymore about messages becoming obsolete with time," Krystal chided.

"So where is Aril and why didn't we get the message?"

"We should have gotten the message," Krystal answered. "It was originally directed at two locations: Earth and Supply Ship 5. Supply Ship 5 should have forwarded it to us and we should've received it long ago. I checked. We received nothing from Harding except the normal chatter."

"But why wouldn't he forward to us something this important?"

Krystal peered at him, as if challenging him to answer his own question.

"You think Harding had some reason for not telling us about Aril," Arthur stated. Krystal continued to stare. "What do you think he has in mind?"

It was a rhetorical question, which Krystal did not answer.

"How do we handle this?" Arthur asked.

Krystal spun her chair around to face the monitor again. She brought up a map of the galaxy showing the location of the supply ships and the individual explorer vehicles as projected from the most recent data.

"First we send a query — nothing accusatory — just something so we know Harding is still doing his job. We don't want him on the defensive. Then we send a message to all galactic space vehicles and supply ships except for Harding's, asking for updated information on Supply Ship 5 — a routine status check. Once again, we don't want to raise alarm or suspicion. We also send a message to Aril advising that there's been a disruption in the galactic network and request they transmit future messages by routes that don't involve Supply Ship 5 — directly to us if possible. Finally, we should send a message back to Earth about our suspicions."

Krystal hesitated, then turned to Arthur. "How about it?"

"Sounds like a plan," returned Arthur, awed by the scope of her strategy.

He sat quietly as she worked. After a while, he felt her gazing at him again. He looked up, feeling himself absorbed in the blackness of her eyes. "What?" he asked.

"Don't worry. Benjamin is far away from Supply Ship 5. None of this could have any effect on him. Not yet anyway. As soon as I expect him to be in radar range, I'll send out a signal and confirm his approach."

"Thank you," Arthur said softly.

CHAPTER 24
— 36052 —

When the Captain regained consciousness in his magnetocryogenic chamber, he felt a surge of apprehension at the prospect of returning to Aril after so many millennia. He had no idea what he'd find on the planet he helped colonize. Fifteen thousand years was far too long to expect any historical retention of how the Arilian civilization began. It was possible he'd arrive a complete stranger, an alien being from a mysterious planet, hardly more than a myth in the minds of Arilians.

Feeling very old, he went about the routine of emerging from the cylinder and settling into the control room. Even in the weightlessness of the capsule, the mental and physical effort of moving about the small room made him weary and disheartened. He surveyed the images of Aril's surface taken by the capsule's instruments. He viewed a time lapse sequence on the video monitor, watching as the planet rotated under the light of its sun. What he saw left him puzzled and concerned. Other than the deep blue of Aril's single ocean, the remainder of the surface appeared to be overgrown with vegetation. He could see no sign of human presence. No cities, buildings, or roads were apparent amid the carpet of greenery. He shuddered with dread at what might have happened.

Finally, when he was about to land, a bright yellow light lit up on the control panel, an indicator that the capsule's radio was receiving a signal from the planet. With a verbal command, the Captain ordered the computer to lock onto the signal and initiate audio interpretation. An electronic voice came over the capsule's speakers, "This is Aril acknowledging approach of non-Union space capsule. Please identify yourself."

The Captain was relieved. Not only did the response indicate the inhabitants of Aril could still communicate at radio frequencies, it also signified they still spoke Union English. He stared at the images of Aril continuously changing in the time lapse display, then cleared his throat and tried to bring some moisture to his lips. Weakly, he responded, "This is Captain Lance Warner, requesting permission to land on Aril."

There was a long pause as he waited for an acknowledgement. The speaker crackled, "Roger, Captain Warner, advise landing at location indicated by our radio beacon at 4.4 GHz."

Having a beacon to guide his entry into Aril made landing easy. The Captain initiated the automated guidance system and secured himself in his seat in preparation for entry into the Arilian atmosphere. The digital messages he received gave no indication about whether the inhabitants were welcoming his arrival or just tolerating it. For all he knew, even the beacon signal he was trusting to guide him onto the planet's surface was a ruse designed to inhibit his landing, or even destroy him. He resolved to accept his fate regardless. At his age, he had little choice. If he was to die in the process of returning to the planet he helped discover, it would just be a fitting conclusion to a life that had been filled with irony. He closed his eyes and prepared for the inevitable buffeting upon entry into the atmosphere. He strained against the G-forces as the capsule decelerated, then waited in anticipation for the jolt of the parachute arresting the rapid descent of the vehicle. He breathed a sigh of relief when it opened, but his eyes remained closed for the remainder of the landing. After the capsule was sitting firmly on the surface and the engines had stopped, the Captain sat still for several seconds till he heard the voice on his radio: "Landing sequence complete."

The next words from the Arilian controller sent a warm chill up the Captain's spine. "Welcome home, Captain Warner."

Several hundred Arilian spectators surrounded the landing site. Oddly, entire families — men, women and children — had turned out to greet him. This was not an official greeting. It appeared more like a crowded family outing or a county fair. He exited the vehicle and stood awkwardly before them until he heard polite applause. He raised his hand nervously in a gesture that was half a wave and half salute. Many in the crowd waved and saluted back. The Captain smiled, gazing out at the throng.

A middle-aged woman accompanied by a bearded man approached. "It's a pleasure to meet you, Captain Warner," the woman said. "I am Philia and this is my husband Orvan. We have been given the honor of helping you become oriented to Aril."

The Captain had no trouble understanding the woman even though she spoke English with a strong, totally unfamiliar accent. "I appreciate the help," the Captain said softly. "I have to admit I am somewhat at a loss."

"That's quite understandable," Philia replied. "We'll take care of you, Captain. Please don't worry."

An older gentleman approached from the crowd. He was holding a cup. Nervously, he held it toward the Captain and with his eyes downward muttered shyly, "For you, Captain Warner. If you like…"

The Captain grasped the cup and raised it slowly to his lips. His hand trembled and he tried to steady the vessel. He smelled the unmistakable aroma of rum. "This is rum," he said. The old man just nodded with his eyes still cast downward. The Captain took a long swig of the sweet liquor and it nearly brought tears to his eyes. He swallowed slowly, letting the alcoholic warmth move through him with rejuvenating liquidity. He handed the cup back to the old man and gave him a grateful smile. The man finally looked up and locked eyes with the Captain, who felt a vague sense of familiarity. Gazing at the old man's moon-faced countenance and deep thoughtful eyes, the Capain felt as if he were seeing, after a very long time, an old friend.

Philia and Orvan took the Captain's arm and guided him through the crowd which parted respectfully before him. Several people shook his hands and patted his back. There was scattered applause. The Captain was tall compared to the people in the crowd. Arilians were large-boned and stout, with light clear complexions and sandy-colored hair. They moved slowly with a grace that spoke of inner peace and spiritual balance.

Orvan, Philia and the Captain boarded a small vehicle, which Orvan drove with verbal commands. It moved soundlessly and without vibration. They drove along a street made of a deep green substance with a soft porous sheen. The Captain realized why the surface of Aril had appeared to be completely covered by vegetation. Arilians had removed few trees in constructing their homes and roads. All buildings were erected within and around existing vegetation and none were tall enough to penetrate the crowns of the towering trees that covered the Arilian landscape. The silent vehicle threaded its way beneath a rich canopy of branches only broken by occasional clearings for parks filled with children. They encountered few other cars along the way, but Arilians on bicycles were everywhere, turning to look curiously at the Captain as he passed. The car pulled up in front of a two-story stone building with a simple sign that read "Hospital", a word that apparently had not changed from the ancient English language.

During the next several hours, the Captain was given an extensive physical examination in a medical facility more modern than any the Captain had experienced on Earth. Arilian physicians were thorough and thoughtful, using an assembly of instruments completely unrecognizable to the Captain. They guided him through a set of scanners and imagers that whirred and blinked, with displays scrolling numbers he could not comprehend. After the exam was complete, he waited in an office seated on a comfortable chair and sipped a drink reminiscent of orange juice, but thicker and sweeter. He was also given some nuts resembling almonds, savoring their salty crunchiness.

Two women and a man entered, dressed in what the Captain gathered was standard clothing for Arilians regardless of sex: ankle-length skirts made from a light cotton-like material, solid-colored, but each having a different hue. The only difference between male and female garb was that the shirts of the females were brightly colored with complex geometric prints, whereas the males wore solid-colored blouses. Arilians seemed to combine colors in ways that strayed from convention as much as possible without quite breaking the rules.

The three sat around the Captain smiling and attempting to be as friendly and non-threatening as possible. One of the women leaned forward and asked, "Captain, are you feeling okay?"

"Yes, thank you, I am," the Captain replied truthfully. He was inexplicably calm and carefree, and did not hesitate putting his fate in the hands of these kind, gentle people.

"We hope you won't mind spending the evening with Philia and Orvan and their family. They'll feed you and provide a comfortable place for you to sleep. Our physicians have determined there is nothing wrong with you that requires immediate attention. They can perform some procedures to extend your life by fifty Earth-years or so, but you may take your time considering whether you'd like to exercise that option. The only thing we ask is that you answer some questions tomorrow. We are very curious about what knowledge you've gained during your long absence."

"Knowledge?" the Captain responded quickly. "How much knowledge can I have? I left this planet 15,000 years ago and have been conscious for only about six hours during that time. What could I possibly know that would be of interest to you?"

The woman's smile did not waver. "Let us wait till tomorrow to discuss that." She stood and her two companions rose with her. She bowed demurely and said, "Good night, Captain. It's good to have you back."

Captain Warner just nodded, not knowing what to say. The three Arilians left in turn and Philia and Orvan entered the room smiling. Smiles seemed to be the default Arilian expression.

Philia and Orvan had two teenage children, or whatever the equivalent was in the Arilian lifespan. The Captain gave up trying to guess their ages after he learned that Philia and Orvan were in their fifties and expected to live another hundred or so Earth-years. Since the Arilian year was one and a half times longer than Earth years, the two parents were in their thirties in Arilian years. They'd live to be at least ninety. The longevity of Arilians eliminated enormous pressures to hurry, and they refrained from developing technology solely to save time. The Captain learned that Arilians were perfectly capable of building passenger jets that could transport them from one location to another in hours, but they preferred to take the highly efficient and quieter electric cars, though they took many days to go long distances. Bicycles were the transportation mode of choice, as the tree-shaded roads provided easy and pleasant routes to most destinations.

Although insect life had blossomed and even evolved since the Captain and his colonists first arrived from Earth, no more complex animals existed on the planet, other than humans. Arilians had developed the capability to engineer genes to produce any type of organism they desired, but they weighed such activity against the long-term benefits. The absence of animals on Aril, by and large, was more of a benefit than a hindrance. To replace the natural urge for nurturing that was just as prevalent in Arilian children as in Earth children, Arilians developed extremely sophisticated dolls and robotic toys.

Philia and Orvan's children were obsessively polite and respectful to the Captain, but it wasn't long before he overheard conversations suggesting they were just as rebellious as Earth children had been. Getting settled in the small room he'd been given, the Captain listened to the arguments and shouting, and he smiled with the comforting thought that some things never change. He prepared for dinner with a warm shower and then dressed in clothing the two teens selected for him amid much discussion and arguing. He and Margery had never had children, yet the familiarity and comfort he experienced with Philia and Orvan's family was inexplicably reassuring.

When he sat down for dinner, the Captain realized it was the first real meal he'd eaten in a very long while. His last meal had been with Brian, no more than a few days ago in his conscious time. It had been barely satisfying. At the time he left Aril, a well-balanced meal with all necessary spices was still not possible. The Captain remembered the seeds he'd brought with him from Harding's supply ship and he reminded himself to ask Philia and Orvan if they could recover them from the capsule.

Philia prepared a vegetarian meal served with cool fresh water. The Captain noticed bottles of wine in a cabinet near the kitchen, but it wasn't until the children had gone to bed that Orvan offered him a glass. It was as full and smooth as any he had ever tasted on Earth. When Orvan offered the Captain rum later in the evening, he actually turned it down in deference to the wine.

Captain Warner had no idea how tired he was until he collapsed on the bed that evening. The silence embracing him was even more complete than he'd experienced in deep space where the hum of the computers was ever present. He slept twelve hours straight before the glow of the early morning Arilian sun pierced the openings in Philia and Orvan's wooden shutters.

After breakfast, a car pulled up and the Captain was driven to an office building where again he was confronted by the two women and one man he'd met at the hospital. They introduced themselves as Lacee, Jeril, and Deana, who was clearly the spokesperson for the trio. She only deferred to the other two when uncertain how to respond.

"Captain," Deana said gently, "we have a detailed account of your time on Aril, compliments of your friend Brian, who had the foresight to leave thorough records of everything that transpired during his lifetime. That information has been carefully guarded and passed down from generation to generation."

The Captain nodded with a faint smile.

"Where did you go when you left Aril the last time, Captain Warner?"

"I went to a Union supply ship — number 5. I spoke to Andrew Harding."

"Could you tell us what you spoke about?"

"Certainly," the Captain replied. "We spoke about the message from Aril."

At this statement, the Arilians reacted by exchanging looks with raised eyebrows. "So our message was received by the supply ship?" Deana asked.

"Yes, it was. Dr. Harding had no idea about the transmission until I asked him to search his data to see if he had received anything from this location."

"And he had?"

"Yes, it was a quote from the inscription on the Statue of Liberty. Have you had a response from Earth?"

The three Arilians looked at each other. Deana answered. "No, we haven't."

The Captain did a quick calculation in his head. It was possible there hadn't been enough time for a response. "How about from Supply Ship 5? Did you hear from Dr. Harding?"

"We've had no response to our message at all." This time it was Jeril who answered.

The Captain stared at the three, thinking quickly, trying to understand the numerous possibilities. If Harding had sent any response back to Aril, it certainly would have been received by now. "Have you been listening for any return messages? Do you have receivers with enough sensitivity?"

Deana answered, "We have been monitoring continuously for many thousands of years using an extremely powerful radio-telescope designed by our famous astronomer Sigma de Anthony."

"Then Harding never replied to the message or forwarded it to Earth," the Captain said grimly. "I wonder why."

"We did get some response — sort of," said Deana. She consulted briefly with Lacee, who had been silent till now. Though she was probably the actual leader of the group, she was the least able to communicate. After terminating her chat with Lacee, Deana turned to the Captain and said, "We had a visitor many thousands of years ago — a galactic explorer."

The Captain was intrigued. "Who was…? What did…? Did this explorer make contact with anyone?"

"Oh, yes," Deana answered quickly. "He made no attempt to hide from the Arilians who greeted him. He actually lived here on Aril for many months. His name was Alexander Simpson. Do you know him?"

"No," the Captain answered, "but I didn't know many explorers. We traveled in different circles."

"He seemed very interested in learning about Arilian culture, government, politics. He was especially curious about our wars and how we fought them. He asked many questions about Arilian weapons, and the absence of any space program intrigued him."

The Captain experienced a growing uneasiness. It was true that explorers were trained to gather information, so it wasn't unusual that Alexander Simpson asked many questions. But when he considered the tone of the questions in light of Harding's failure to respond to the message from Aril, he felt something was amiss. The Arilians must have sensed his concern because Jeril asked, "Do you find it odd?"

The Captain shook his head. "Not particularly. The visit by itself is part of the mission that Union explorers are trained to execute. The kinds of questions he asked are not unusual, but I'm wondering why they were focused so much on wars and weapons. Of course, this happened a long time ago and the recollection of what actually took place may have been distorted through time. Maybe Mr. Simpson asked many more questions, but these are the ones that are most easily remembered."

Deana said politely, "Arilians are very careful record keepers. You may have noticed that there are no recording devices in this room, but the three of us will carefully write out our recollections of this conversation and we will meet and discuss them, combining them into a single report with all discrepancies and possible misunderstandings noted. We hope you don't mind, Captain."

The Captain smiled. "No, of course not. Brian was like that too."

Jeril said, "It is a common shortfall of all historical records. They suffer from being a reflection of the observer's point of view."

"I am very impressed by Aril and its people," said the Captain. "But I have no means to live and support myself here. I think I should return to space." The Captain could not conceal the dread in his voice. He choked up and looked about nervously.

"Captain," Deana said gently, "None of us would be here if it weren't for you. You will always have a home here. Thousands of Arilians would gladly offer you a place to stay. You should not feel obligated in any way to pay or reciprocate. For the next few weeks, or as long as you want, you will live with Philia and Orvan. They will show you our city and teach you about Aril and its people. At any time, you may choose another living situation and we will help you make that transition. It is an honor to serve you."

"Thank you," the Captain said, barely audible. Then a thought occurred to him. "I brought something with me from the supply ship. When I left Aril, the colonists were struggling to grow their crops. I thought I would bring back seeds. They're wrapped in plastic in my capsule. I don't suppose you need them anymore."

Lacee stood, approached the Captain, and placed a hand on his shoulder. "Captain, you will soon learn that Arilians cherish seeds of all kinds, and the gift of seeds is one of the most sincere gestures of friendship one Arilian can bestow upon another. You may think I am saying that to be polite, but in a few weeks you will understand. With your permission, we will enter your capsule and recover the seeds. Rest now, Captain, and be at ease. You are home now with your people."

With that the three Arilians rose to leave, but before they went through the door, he called, "Wait!" The three stopped and looked back at him. "I must tell you..." he paused, trying to choose his words carefully. "I'm puzzled about the galactic explorer who visited — not so much because of the questions he asked, but because his visit was followed by no other visits. I'd have expected news about a successful colony on Aril to be transmitted to all explorers and others would've arrived. There's a reason that didn't happen, just as there's a reason you have heard no response to your message from Earth or Supply Ship 5."

"What do you think it means?" asked Deana.

"I really don't know, but it's not right. I'm worried there may be a danger to Aril from space. I suggest you carefully monitor space around Aril to distances as far out as possible. Look for anything unusual and prepare yourselves. I'm not saying there's an immediate threat to Aril, but in the future there may be."

The Captain stopped and tried to gage the reaction to his warning. The Arilians stood silently exchanging glances. Finally, Lacee spoke. "We will heed your suggestion, Captain. We will also prepare ourselves should there be any threats from space, but please understand that Arilians are not accustomed to living in fear. We choose to enjoy every day for the peace and serenity it brings with the rising of our sun each day. That is just the way Arilian minds work, and it has served us well for many years."

"I understand," replied the Captain. "I'm sorry if I've alarmed you unnecessarily."

"No apology is necessary," said Lacey. "Thank you, Captain."

Despite the warm hospitality from Philia and Orvan, the Captain couldn't help feeling lonely and isolated. He was disoriented by the lack of familiarity with the people he met and places he visited. Given the gulf in time and space between Aril and Earth, it was incredible that he could live at all on Aril, but the attention required to adjust to the differences fatigued him. The only time he really relaxed was when he took walks. Arilian streets were quiet and cool, and there were many parks. He strolled along the pathways pretending he was back on Earth. Occasionally, Philia, Orvan, or even one or both of their two children would join him, pointing out sights along the way, naming the plants and flowers. The eeriest aspect of Aril was the lack of animal life. Birds and squirrels, common in the urban areas of Earth, were nowhere to be seen or heard. Occasionally, he'd see a flying insect — a fly, a gnat, or something vaguely resembling a bee — but that was all.

After about three weeks passed, Philia announced they were going on a road trip to visit other parts of Aril. The Captain made a weak attempt to remain at their house so as not to interfere with the family vacation, but they insisted he go along. Philia and Orvan didn't own their own vehicle; no Arilians did. Cars were checked out in the same way books were checked out from libraries on Earth.

The Captain appreciated the road trip. The Arilian landscape was much richer and variable than he had imagined. The small towns and farms they passed along the way resembled those on Earth, but the Captain was impressed at how new everything looked. Though fifteen millennia had passed since Aril was colonized, the buildings and other structures showed little sign of aging. When the Captain asked about this, Orvan told him that the Arilian approach to building had always been to either construct for the long term or not construct at all. Only the most durable stone was used and the wood was obtained from genetically engineered trees, with natural resistance to all sources of decay or wear.

The Captain was sufficiently distinctive in appearance that he stood out conspicuously wherever they traveled. Arilians were thrilled to be in his presence, but courteous enough not to impose on him or invade his privacy. The Captain had always been an introvert, relying on his wife to take responsibility for the social interactions that connected them to friends and family. His inability to strike up conversations with Arilians on his own underscored his feelings of loneliness and made him miss his wife more than ever.

On the third day of the journey, they were gliding smoothly through rolling farmland when they crowned the top of a hill and saw before them a huge building made of white stone. Surrounded by lush green landscaping, the starkness of the white façade made the structure stand out clearly. In front, four large metallic letters spelled "ARIL", each at least three meters tall, glittering in the sunlight. They stopped at the entrance to the building and a woman came out to greet them. She introduced herself as Ellena and said she would be the guide for their tour of Central Control.

The building was a large circular ring with a courtyard in the middle. The interior walls of the ring were lined with large video screens in front of desks populated by Arilians absorbed in watching the rapidly changing displays. The murmur of voices combined with the persistent low-frequency hum of machinery created a continuous background noise making it difficult for him to discern individual conversations, not that he would have understood as they all spoke the Arilian language.

Ellena led the Captain and his four Arilian companions into the courtyard where the noise was less and she could be heard well. Dense foliage in the courtyard concealed several large dish antennas mounted on pedestals.

Ellena motioned to a bench beneath a small tree and invited the Captain to sit, but he declined, preferring to move about. As they strolled along the pathways, Ellena said, "I know Philia and Orvan are familiar with Aril Central Control, but for the

Captain's sake I will take some time to describe the function of this facility. The concept is really very simple. Since the very beginning, Arilians have been concerned about the health of our planet. As a result, we have systematically deployed a vast array of monitoring instruments everywhere. I can describe the types of sensors we use but for now just imagine the planet is like a human body. The body has an intricate network of nerves that provide sensory information about the surrounding environment, as well as the internal physiological state of a person. In much the same way, our entire planet is populated with sensors that tell us continuously how Aril is 'feeling'. We monitor the ocean, the land, the atmosphere, the biosphere, and space. All the data we acquire is transmitted to small satellites orbiting Aril, where it is relayed through multiple communication pathways to the antennas you see in this courtyard.

"Even though Aril is divided into many sovereign countries, by international agreement all the data comes here regardless of where the observations are made. This facility is a country unto itself, a neutral entity belonging to no single nation, and equally accessible to all."

The Captain nodded, remembering Brian's ravenous appetite for information and the pains he took to acquire it. "You must have very sophisticated computers to be able to process all that data," he said.

"Absolutely. It is a uniquely clever computer, specifically designed for this task," Ellena said with pride. It's located beneath our feet and occupies the area of the building. Being underground allows us to keep the circuitry from overheating using only fans. The most intriguing aspect of the computer though is that it is modeled after the human brain."

The Captain smiled. "So the planet is Aril's body and the computer is Aril's brain?"

"Yes," replied Ellena. "And just like the human brain, the computer takes in data, while continuously querying archived and real-time data to detect anomalies or unusual situations. Based on the data it receives, it may reconfigure the remote sensors to improve the quality of the measurements. It also performs image processing to detect patterns or weak signals that may be obscured by noise. It correlates the data received from different places, looking for unexpected patterns, trends, and relationships. It compares the data to expected behavior, using theoretical models. It will also do this by comparing the information with data in our archives, i. e. past experience. Models are also used to determine the future state of the planet. The new data are matched against predictions. In other words, the computer anticipates what will happen based on previous experience and basic understanding of the phenomenon being observed. If the event is similar to a previous event, the computer will formulate a response based on that prior experience. This whole process will be archived in its entirety, so that the next time the event occurs, the computer does not have to go through the same analysis again to react. It develops an instinct, which allows it to respond without thinking the next time the event takes place. All of these activities are what our brains do continuously, consciously or subconsciously. Just like a human brain, the Arilian computer explores, learns, and discovers many times per day, every day of the year.

"Incredible," the Captain said.

"It is," said Ellena, "but what's even more amazing is how the computer works. It's designed very differently from computers you may be familiar with on Earth. This computer not only performs many of the same functions as the brain, it also mimics the brain in the way those functions are performed. As you know, your brain is divided into distinct parts that are responsible for different thought processes. There are areas of the brain dedicated to reasoning, emotions, short and long-term memory, learning, controlling autonomous body functions, etc. Our computer is designed in layers. You might think of them as virtual layers rather than physical layers. They mimic the organization of brain functions. The deeper layers are responsible for the more autonomous functions, while the outer layers take care of increasingly more analytical tasks. The beauty of this approach is that the design of each layer is customized to the specific task. For example, the layer responsible for straightforward analysis of data is optimized for digital number-crunching. The layer directly connected to the data streams is optimized for data manipulation and distribution. The more analytical functions are handled as complex logical tasks, such as image processing and pattern recognition. Of course, the different parts of the computer are not completely independent from each other. Data and other forms of information are constantly being transferred back and forth among the layers."

Orvan raised his hand as if in school, "If the computer is so capable, how come there are so many people working here?"

Ellena smiled. "We never depend on the computer to do everything, no matter how capable it may be. There are still functions the human brain can perform that computers cannot yet duplicate. Also, the technicians actually enter information into the computer verbally for later analysis. Furthermore, many of the people you see inside are students learning first-hand the physics, chemistry, and biology of our planet." She paused to see if there were more questions, then added, "If you're all ready to go inside, we can look at some of the stations."

Ellena led them back into the building. They walked along the corridor flanked by display monitors. All were set on black backgrounds upon which charts and numerical data stood out in fine lines of red, green, yellow and white. Some monitors were dedicated to specific instruments, each with their own distinctive display of axes, lines, bars, and symbols. Other monitors displayed the output of models and data processing routines. Every now and then, Ellena asked one of the technicians to alter the display and demonstrate the options available for viewing the results. Some of the younger Arilians were noticeably nervous because of the Captain's presence. He suspected his visit had been announced ahead of time.

At the far side of the building, diametrically opposite the entry door, the corridor terminated in a wall with another door, above which a red light glowed. Ellena stopped the group and said, "Behind this door is everyone's favorite display. We can't enter until the light changes to green because stray light entering the room disrupts the holographic imaging process."

When the light turned green, they entered a large room with a raised platform in the center. A number of technicians sat along the walls before computer monitors. Ellena whispered to one of them, who spoke a command to his console. Immediately, the room lights faded and all the monitors went black. A hazy glow appeared in the center of the room above the pedestal. After several seconds, the light resolved itself into an image of Aril floating in three-dimensional clarity in mid-air before them. The sphere was three meters across, and looked much like the image of Aril the Captain had seen from space, except this three-dimensional rendering made the model more palpable and real. Ellena explained that the technicians could call up any data they were interested in: air and ocean temperatures, wind velocities, atmospheric pressure, surface strain on the planet's crust, gravitational and magnetic fields, all in real time — information Arilian scientists might wish to use to gage the state of the planet.

Ellena asked for a display of archived data showing in a time lapse sequence the effects of a volcanic eruption from 45 years earlier. The volcanic eruption was not a local phenomenon. The sequence showed that anomalies in many different properties occurred before, during, and after the actual event, some completely unexpected and inexplicable. The data showed how strongly every aspect of the planet was linked and how the entire planet responded almost organically to a single localized event.

They exited the holographic room through an outer door that led to the back side of the building. Because the structure had been built on the crest of a hill, the land sloped downward in a checkerboard of farms. A rare cloud in the Arilian sky cast a single shadow that drifted wraith-like over the multi-hued crops. There was a mild breeze smelling moist and sweet.

The tour complete, Ellena led the group around the outer perimeter of the building. The Captain strolled beside her, his hands clasped behind his back. "I'm very impressed, but tell me what happens if you see a problem developing. It's one thing to observe an anomaly; it's another to know what to do about it."

"You're absolutely right, Captain," Ellena answered, "and you are probably astute enough to realize that Arilians are extremely reluctant to interfere with natural processes. When our technicians observe a potentially harmful trend in any critical property of the environment, it is reported to a special committee. Based on the severity of the threat, we conduct a study that may take from one to five years. The study may involve a single group of investigators or a global team of researchers. We not only study the natural phenomenon at the root of the problem, but all aspects of the planet that may be affected."

It was late afternoon when they returned to their vehicle and drove for several hours before stopping at a lodge. After a satisfying dinner, Orvan asked the Captain if he was comfortable resuming their journey very early the next morning. The Captain agreed. In his room, the wonders of the day did not prevent the oblivion of sleep from descending upon him.

The next day, they drove on a winding road that ascended into dense old forest land, where many trees had fallen and dead trunks and stumps littered the ground. They stopped and walked into the forest. The ground was a thick carpet of dead leaves and pine needles. Though similar to the forests of Earth, there was an eerie silence here owing to the absence of animals. The Captain had never realized how much animal life in a forest transformed it into something with a living essence, providing a level of animation not possible with plants alone.

Back in the car again, the upward sloping terrain leveled out into a broad forested plain. In his comfortable seat watching the trees slide hypnotically by, the Captain dozed off. Sometime later he woke to the unmistakable smell of salt-laden ocean air. The vehicle turned off onto a smaller side road, where the trees were farther apart and the ground was covered with a thin sprinkling of sand. The smell of the sea grew stronger as the vehicle came to a gate made of black iron suspended between pillars of stone. An archway of larger stones bore the English words "ARIL MEMORIAL GROVE. The vehicle stopped and the Captain exited on trembling legs. He knew where he was. He walked shakily to the portal and with a gentle push, the iron gate swung open. A raised wooden walkway led deeper into the grove.

Philia walked behind him. He turned to look at her, a questioning look in his eyes. "Yes, Captain, this grove is where your wife's ashes were spread, along with those of all the original colonists. Take your time. We will be here waiting for you."

The Captain nodded and strolled along the path, remembering when he'd watched his wife's ashes dispersed in the young forest. For him, it had happened less than a year ago and the memory was still fresh in his mind, which struggled to come to grips with the disparity between the two time scales. He began to doubt his memory. His mind tried to assimilate the facts by giving them a dream-like quality. The more he wrestled with the truth, the more unbelievable it became. Only when he reached a large stone off the side of the path well inside the grove did his sense of reality return. Inscribed on the stone were the names of each original colonist. He traced his fingers over the inscriptions for his wife, Brian, Emily, and the rest of his companions. At that moment, he knew where he wanted to live on Aril — near the Memorial Grove — to be close to his wife and comrades. The Arilians understood this and had anticipated his visit to the Grove would be the homecoming he was seeking.

When he returned to the vehicle, Philia, Orvan and their two children greeted him with wordless embraces. They continued their drive and a half hour later gazed out at Aril's only ocean. They weren't alone, as the beach was a popular spot for vacationing Arilians. Philia explained that the sea was still unable to sustain animal life forms. Nevertheless, Arilians had developed a sophisticated marine fleet for transportation, research, exploration, and tourism. The last time the Captain saw the ocean, he'd felt disappointed that it offered so little to sustain the struggling colonists. Now, Arilians were enjoying the sea, free from the desperate hope of finding a source of food from its depths.

The last stop for the Captain that day was the Arilian Memorial Park and Library. He, Philia, Orvan and the children strolled through the lush garden to its center, where the Captain was humbled by the statue of him, his wife, Brian, and Emily that had stood for many thousands of years. He glanced at the statue only briefly and moved away, overwhelmed with the unanticipated honor he had achieved in Arilian folklore.

The library held all the data Brian had brought from Earth and collected during their voyage. It also contained his personal memoir, which the Captain took some time to scan, resolving to read it fully another time.

At dinner that evening, Philia confessed to the Captain that they'd timed their vacation so as to be at the Aril Memorial Park for the most important of all Arilian holidays, the Festival of Seeds, when Arilians celebrated the miracle of the seed. Seeds were at the heart of Arilian survival from the beginning. Philia broke it to the Captain that he'd be guest of honor at the ceremony the next day. After all the hospitality he'd been shown, the Captain had little excuse to refuse the tribute.

But the next day he had second thoughts. The extent of the crowd attending the ceremony amazed him. Arilians were everywhere. The grown-ups huddled in conversing bunches, while the children scurried among them like so many electrons in a lattice of atoms. At the amphitheater where the Captain's statue stood, a band played lively music. Orvan went off with the two teens to enjoy the festival attractions, while Philia guided the Captain toward the stage.

The official ceremony began with a song composed for the festival many millennia ago. After the band played the first few bars, the crowd became quiet and all eyes turned upward. The Captain followed their gazes and saw two dozen hot air balloons drifting toward them against the brilliant blue sky. They descended gracefully and landed among the crowds amid cheers and shouts. Arilians lined up at each and waited patiently as four at a time boarded the gondolas to take short rides. Once airborne, the passengers released bags of seeds and those below watched as the tiny flecks caught the wind and drifted away.

Finally, it was the Captain's turn. He boarded with Philia and two youngsters, who instructed him how to release the seeds. As they fell on those below, the Arilians lifted their arms and began a loud chant the Captain could not understand. The tempo of the band music changed to match the chant and soon the entire crowd was bouncing up and down to the infectious rhythm. It seemed incongruous for the austere and well-mannered Arilians to lose themselves in the music, caught up in an ecstasy that was almost primitive. The chant continued as the Captain's balloon landed.

Philia led him back to the stage, where he was invited to sit with several dignitaries. One of them rose and after quieting the crowd, began his speech. The Captain understood nothing, but surmised the oration was about him. Whenever the speaker gestured toward him, the crowd roared its approval. After two more speeches in a similar vain, the band played again, but this time in a subdued rhythm suitable to a parade or procession. Children climbed the stairs leading to the stage and one by one walked up to the Captain and presented him with gourds split open down the middle. In the hollow of the gourds were multi-colored seeds. The children placed them at the Captain's feet, bowed smartly to him, and walked off. The Captain smiled broadly at each of the children, remembering the canisters of organic material Emily had designed for launching onto the surface of planets. He had no doubt that the ritual dated back to tales the early Arilians told their children about how the planet was made habitable. When the procession ended, a guitar-like instrument played a lively melodic tune, timeless in its harmony, beat, and composition, and suddenly the Captain was transported back to the day he sat on the empty Arilian plain and watched the colonists land, silvery parachutes glistening above them, not unlike the balloons, now aloft and fading into the distance.

The Captain moved to a home for elderly Arilians close to the Memorial Grove and Park. Often when he strolled through the gardens, children ran to him and grabbed his hands. He told them tales of those early days on Aril, speaking slowly and mixing Arilian and English words. They listened attentively, their eyes squinting up at him against the glare of the sky above.

The Captain learned that Arilians had mastered medical science well enough to program their own deaths. By controlling the genetic coding that brought on aging, Arilians could easily live more than 150 years, if they chose. Decisions were entirely up to the individual, but the elderly were given counseling on how to optimize their quality of life and recognize diminishing returns if they went on living. Once an elderly person made the decision to die, their bodies were programmed with a terminal illness that brought death quickly and painlessly. The program could also be disrupted at any time if the person had a change of heart, but that seldom happened. The exact day of death was not known, but every day the person lived thereafter was lived to the fullest. The Captain knew when his time had come and his request to die peacefully was expertly granted by his physicians. He died quietly in his sleep one night dreaming of his wife and the many happy years they'd spent together on two planets.

The three Arilians who interviewed the Captain in the hospital wrote independent accounts of their conversation with him. They then got together to resolve the differences in their accounts so that only one version was entered into Arilian archives. The words the Captain spoke during his second visit to Aril were studied extensively by future generations of Arilian historians. His last remarks were interpreted as a prophecy and for thousands of years after the Captain's second visit, Arilian eyes turned upward fearing the prophecy would come true. And although tens of thousands of years passed with no visitors arriving from space, the prophecy inspired a resurgence of astronomical sciences, and Arilian astronomers constructed ever more powerful telescopes. Astronomy was a required subject for all Arilian school children, and many devoted their lives to the study of the heavens. In this way, Arilians continued their vigil through the years and little that happened in space escaped their view.

CHAPTER 25

— 40041 —

Krystal was reviewing the output of one of the many programs she'd written that detected anomalies in the data from explorer vehicles. Normally, the program identified space capsules from which transmission ceased because the vehicle had moved too far from the supply ship. However, this time it identified an interruption in the signal from a Union supply ship — number 5.

Krystal completed her examination of the data received in the last century, but detected no other anomalies. When Arthur joined her sometime later, she greeted him with a curt statement, "Transmissions from Supply Ship 5 stopped about 6000 years ago."

Arthur took his seat at the control console next to Krystal and looked up at the monitor displaying the galaxy as seen from above with the locations of the supply ships indicated by yellow circles. The disruption of a signal from one of the supply ships could only be caused by damage to or loss of the supply ship itself — in either case an extremely serious event. Supply ships were major hubs in the Union's communication system and critical life support sites for the galactic explorer fleet. Although explorers could always freeze themselves and move on to the next nearest supply ship, if their food and oxygen were already at critical levels, they would not always be able to survive the extra stop along the way.

"So I guess we never received a response from SS5 to the message we sent after hearing about Aril from Earth."

"No," answered Krystal. She was entering commands on the console keyboard and changing the display. Numerous small green circles appeared, each indicating the location of a galactic explorer vehicle.

"And what about the inquiries we sent to all the Union space vehicles? Any response from them?"

"Most haven't responded at all. Those that have reported nothing abnormal."

"Have you lost transmission from any of them in the last hundred years?"

"No," replied Krystal, but Arthur suspected she may not have heard his question. She seemed to be absorbed in something else. On the monitor, the green circles turned on and off as Krystal entered commands, Arthur wondered what she was looking for, but he knew better than to interrupt her while she was so completely engaged in her analysis.

Finally, she sat back in her chair, the display of vehicle locations frozen in the last configuration she had called up. "Interesting," she said.

"What's going on?" Arthur asked.

"I'm not sure." Krystal picked up a laser pointer and directed the beam onto the monitor. "Every time we receive a message from one of the Union's vehicles, it comes with complete information about the location, heading, and velocity of that vehicle. That's enough information to compute where the vehicle will be at the time of its next transmission. The calculation is very accurate and usually there is no discrepancy between the calculated location and the actual location at sometime in the future, but it happened in one case during the last hundred years."

"That doesn't seem so anomalous," Arthur said. "Certainly there are going to be times when an explorer changes course for one reason or another during any one hundred year interval."

"True, but it made me curious about how often it happens. I don't usually collect those statistics, but I decided to look back through the last ten thousand years of data to determine the frequency of the discrepancy. I found that almost every vehicle has changed its course during that time."

"And you think that's more than expected?"

"Hard to say, but I made another calculation. For every discrepancy I found in the last ten thousand years, I determined the amplitude and direction of the error. Here's what it looks like." Krystal hit a key on the console and next to each green circle representing a vehicle there appeared arrows of varying lengths. "Notice anything odd about those errors?" she asked Arthur.

Arthur peered at the display, then shook his head.

"All the arrows are pointing in the same direction. If the discrepancies were caused by explorers changing course, you would expect the direction of the discrepancy to be random. What this shows is that at different times in the last ten thousand years, almost all of the vehicles changed course in the same direction."

Krystal's skill at deduction amazed Arthur. He had no idea what inspired her to travel down the avenues of investigation she chose. Of the myriad ways she might explore the volumes of data coming into the supply ship, she always managed to select the approach that yielded the richest results. He supposed it was because she had developed all the software that analyzed the data received by the ship. That narrowed down the number of possibilities for manual analysis of the information in search of anomalies or patterns. Still, Krystal seemed to have an uncanny ability to uncover trends that most humans and no machines could match. He looked at her with a puzzled expression and said, "Krystal, what made you think to perform this calculation?"

Krystal smiled. "If you have to know, I'll tell you. Whenever there is a discrepancy in the calculated location, I always look at the direction of the error. When I looked at the one that occurred in the last hundred years, I remembered it was in the same direction as the last one, which was a few hundred years ago. Those two events occurred many years apart in real time, but to me they were just a few days apart. It was still fresh in my memory. The similarity in the errors in the last two calculations made me curious about the errors associated with previous events. It was a hunch that paid off."

Arthur nodded, then asked, "So what does it mean? What would make all of them change course in the same direction?"

"That's even more interesting," Krystal replied. "Did you notice where all the arrows are pointed? Let me help you." With additional entries on the keyboard, she extended the length of each of the arrows. Arthur could see that all the lines converged to a single point. "Do you know where all the arrows are pointing to?"

Arthur said, "No," but he had an uneasy feeling he was unable to verbalize.

"Aril," Krystal said. "It appears that at some time in the last ten thousand years all these vehicles changed course toward Aril." Anticipating more questions, Krystal continued. "If you're wondering how that might have happened, consider this as well."

She entered more commands and next to each vehicle appeared a five-digit numeral. "Those are the years the changes in course occurred. You can see a pattern in the numbers. The times the vehicles changed course are consistent with a scenario where a message was sent out from a single location. As each vehicle received the message, it changed course."

"What location did the message originate from?" asked Arthur.

"Supply Ship 5," answered Krystal. "The farther away from Supply Ship 5 the vehicles were, the longer it took the message to reach them and the course changes to be made. It's like a wave in a pond expanding outward in a circular shape. As the wave reached each vehicle, that vehicle executed the change in course."

Arthur could only gaze at the monitor, trying to assimilate the information Krystal was giving him. He knew it was futile trying to keep up with her train of thought. It was as if she were playing a game of speed chess and was already several moves ahead.

"I can use these times to estimate when the message to change course was sent out. It was around the year 28540."

"So you're saying that a message was sent from Supply Ship 5 in 28540 that made all these vehicles change course and head for Aril. Then 6000 years later the supply ship stopped transmitting."

Krystal nodded. "Except that not all the vehicles the message wave passed over changed their courses. Some have not — either because they decided not to or because Harding did not send the message to them. He can customize the recipients of the message in whatever way he chooses."

"Can you give me a list of the ones that did not change course?"

"Sure. I know what you're thinking. If Harding can selectively send a message to all his allies in the explorer fleet, then so can we."

"Exactly."

"At the time Harding sent his message, did he know about the message from Aril?"

"Almost certainly. The message from Aril to Earth left the planet around 23500. SS5 is less than 4000 light years from Aril. If they sent the message to SS5 at the same time, it would have reached Harding well before he sent the message out to his explorer friends."

"What could he have told them to get them all to follow his instructions?"

Krystal shrugged. "He could have told them he needed help, that he was under attack from an alien planet. Or he could have told them a new wonderful world had been found and they should all abandon their missions and head for paradise. Or..." Krystal hesitated searching for the right words.

"Or what?" Arthur prodded.

"Or it might have been prearranged that when a planet was found that was ripe for the taking, they would all meet there and..." she stopped.

"...and invade. Is that what you're trying to say? Harding and his followers in the Union planned in advance to invade and take over the first habitable planet they came across?"

"It's just one of the possibilities," Krystal said. "You're the social scientist. Is this within the realm of what a human being would do?"

Arthur didn't answer. "So then Benjamin didn't get this message?"

"Benjamin is still pretty far away from Aril. The message has not reached him yet, but my guess is he wasn't on the invitation list."

"What about the message we sent to all the vehicles near us? We must have some friends among them who would let us know what's going on."

"But they don't know what's going on either. Remember, they didn't get the message. As far as they're concerned everything in the galaxy is as it should be."

"So when will all those vehicles get to Aril?"

"Different times. They'll start arriving within a few thousand years or so and keep showing up for the next twenty thousand years. Some that are farther out and haven't even gotten the message yet will take even longer to show up."

"That's not what I would call an invasion," Arthur remarked.

Krystal shrugged. "No, it doesn't make sense, but I still don't trust Harding. If he wasn't up to something devious, he wouldn't have been so selective about whom he sent the message to."

Arthur sighed. "What can we do?"

Krystal considered this as she continued to stare at the monitor. "One possibility is to send a warning message to Aril, but they won't receive it unless they have a sensitive enough antenna that happens to be pointed toward us at the right time. The other option is to ask one of the Union explorers to travel to Aril to deliver a warning in person."

"Are there any close enough to us to get the message?"

"A few." Krystal was back at the keyboard and the display was changing rapidly.

"Send them a message. Give them a complete description of what's happening and request they proceed to Aril immediately to warn the inhabitants about a potential hostile attack. Make them priority messages so the explorers will be automatically unfrozen upon receipt."

"Do you want to see the message before I send it?"

"No," Arthur answered immediately. He knew Krystal could craft a message far better than he could. As an afterthought, he added, "While you're at it, send a message to Earth. Let them know what's going on. I'm sure there's nothing they can do to help, but it can't hurt."

"Not unless there's still someone on Earth working with Harding."

Arthur thought about this and then said, "Let's take that chance. Send the message to Earth. At least we'll know that someone else is aware of what Harding is up to."

Krystal nodded and turned back to her keyboard. Arthur rose and moved behind her to massage her neck. "Do you ever get the feeling we're alone in the universe?"

Krystal leaned her head and planted a kiss on the back of Arthur's hand. "Yes, but that's the same way I felt on Earth," and she went back to her typing.

CHAPTER 26
— 40323 —

Steven Nutley was unfrozen by the priority message from Andrew Harding. Priority messages did not come often. Typically, the hundred-year intervals between his visits to the supply ship were only interrupted by the arrival of galactic explorers, and that occurred only rarely. Previously, when he'd been unfrozen automatically upon the receipt of a priority message, they'd been false alarms, or news from other galactic explorers he had no interest in. He always grumbled about the valuable oxygen used up during the time it took him to start up the capsule's computers to access the message. Of course, now that he was custodian of Supply Ship 2, he had less reason to worry about oxygen and food supplies. The supply ship had more than enough to sustain him and it was constantly producing more.

This time, as he read the message, he was immediately intrigued by the sender. He knew Harding was custodian of Supply Ship 5, 12000 light-years away. A message from Harding was somewhat mystifying. It must have been routed through many other spacecraft before finding its way to this part of the galaxy. He brought the message up on his display screen:

"Union mission aborted. Proceed immediately to coordinates below for rendezvous with galactic explorer fleet in year 65000. Suspect traitorous elements within galactic fleet. For your eyes only. Do not forward or reply. – Andrew Harding"

Nutley read the message again to be sure he had understood it correctly. He wasn't sure which part of the message confused him more, that the Union had aborted its mission after so many years, or the suggestion of treachery among the explorer fleet. Although he'd hoped for many years he might be offered an escape from the endless burden of exploring planets and watching after the supply ship, he wasn't sure now how he felt about being offered the opportunity to break away. It wasn't clear from Harding's message what was at the location he was being directed to. He didn't like the idea of abandoning the supply ship, where at least he could be sure critical life support supplies were at hand.

He replayed all the messages received by the capsule during the time he'd been frozen to see if there was some indication of the events that had led up to this order from Harding, but there was nothing. Before following Harding's directive, Nutley decided he would visit the supply ship again. It was possible the ship had received messages that had not been forwarded to his capsule. Nutley reminded himself that the Union was not a military organization. There were no formal ranks, only an unspoken acknowledgement that some of the members had more authority than others. Senior members of the Union and supply ship custodians were normally respected and their advice followed. Harding was both, and Nutley had to presume there was a very sound justification for this directive.

After Benjamin Mizello visited the supply ship, Nutley thought a great deal about Arthur Mizello. Although he respected the diplomat, his experience and success did not mean he was prepared to be assigned such an important position in the Union's fleet. Harding had demonstrated his knowledge of the Union, the vehicles, and the explorer force over many years as an instructor at the Union academy. He had befriended many of the trainees and helped them through the demanding courses the Union required. Nutley knew he did not necessarily have to follow Harding's directive, but he was inclined to do so.

When he returned to the supply ship, he immediately went to the control room to examine all the new messages received since his last visit to the ship. As he expected, there were none. Just to be sure he hadn't missed some important content within earlier messages, he reviewed transmissions received during the last ten thousand years. It was a tedious task because he had never figured out how to use any of the Brinkleys' automated search routines for interesting messages. He scanned the messages as they scrolled down the control room display monitor. There was nothing but the routine transmissions from galactic explorers providing information about planets they'd visited. Included in that was the report from Benjamin Mizello received in year 34507 describing his visit to the planet the Brinkleys had departed for. The report had depressed Nutley and made him question even more the sanity of the Union mission.

He continued perusing the messages in chronological order until he stopped at a message from Earth he must have previously overlooked. He read it carefully as the import of the words struck him. A planet had been successfully colonized by a non-Union group of space travelers from Earth. He cursed himself that he had totally missed the message when it first arrived. Whoever sent it from Earth did not use the Union protocol for priority transmissions that would have alerted recipients of its importance. Given the number of messages being continuously received by the supply ships, flagging the critical ones was essential. The message from Earth included the location of the new planet, which had been named Aril. Nutley's immediate thought was to compare the location of Aril with the location Harding had requested they all meet, but when he attempted to bring up Harding's message on the supply ship's computer, he found it was not there. For some reason, Harding had not transmitted the message to the supply ship. That was strange because if the Union was aborting its mission, it certainly would want the supply ships to also assemble with the rest of the fleet. Was there some reason Harding did not want to include Supply Ship 2? At the time Harding sent the message, he certainly would have known about the Brinkleys abandoning the ship. Perhaps he thought no one had replaced them. Nutley had sent out a message to all the other supply ships notifying them that he was assuming command of the ship, but maybe Harding had not received it.

Nutley had to return to his capsule to bring up Harding's message again. He transferred it to a memory device, which he carried back to the supply ship control room. When he displayed Harding's message along with the coordinates of the rendezvous point, he confirmed what he had suspected. The coordinates matched the location of Aril. Harding was ordering all the galactic explorers to meet at Aril in the year 65000. A quick calculation told Nutley he could just barely make it to Aril by that date. All of his uncertainty disappeared as he considered the possibility that this new planet might offer him the escape he had always been seeking. Although the option to return to Earth was always there, he had tried that once and the outcome had been disappointing. Aril, on the other hand, represented a new frontier, and Nutley was excited about the possibilities it might offer for starting a new life.

He was preparing to board his capsule and depart the supply ship when a thought suddenly occurred to him. Why abandon the supply ship? If the Union mission had been cancelled and all the explorers were being ordered to Aril, what purpose would the supply ship serve thousands of light years away? He did not have to consider the option very long. He programmed the automatic navigation system to guide the ship to Aril. He would travel in his own capsule, shadowing the larger ship's course. He'd arrive at Aril in time for the rendezvous with Harding and the rest of the explorer fleet bearing an unexpected gift, a fully stocked and armed Union supply ship. Whatever Harding's plan was for Aril, the supply ship would be very useful. Nutley went to the galley to retrieve a canister of his dwindling supply of rum and then set to work preparing the ship.

CHAPTER 27

— 40761 —

The interception of a vehicle moving at extremely high speeds was risky business. Risto Jalonen had programmed his capsule to awaken him several hours before. The capsule he'd been pursuing was traveling significantly slower than his. He had to decelerate gradually over the previous hundred years to match the velocities of the two spacecraft at the time of the rendezvous. The docking procedure was automated, but Risto preferred to do that manually to avoid any unexpected mishaps.

Risto had been unfrozen about 4000 years earlier by a priority message from Andrew Harding. He'd felt a twinge of disappointment upon learning that the Union was abandoning its mission. Risto was not sure he was ready to give up the adrenalin rush he felt on finding and exploring new worlds. Yet he respected Andrew Harding and felt compelled to heed the order to change course and head for the location indicated in the message. On the other hand, if he'd done as directed, he would have had to give up his rescue mission. Not one to leave anything unfinished, Risto had performed some quick calculations and determined that he could complete his interception of the wayward vehicle and still have time to meet up with Harding and the others by the year 65000. He had returned to his magnetocryogenic chamber and resumed his chase of the mystery space capsule.

Now, strapped into his seat at the control console, he watched as his capsule approached the other, listening to the hiss of rocket jets that helped orient his vehicle for docking. The other capsule must have been spinning slowly because he could sense the rotational acceleration of his own vehicle as it spun itself up till the two capsules were pirouetting about one another. On the monitor, he saw the broad base of the conical section of the other vehicle. The corresponding portion of his capsule would come closer until, upon contact, lock together via strong electromagnets built into the hulls of both vehicles. That would hold the vehicles together until mechanical connecting devices joined them tightly enough to prevent any air leakage from either craft. The moment he felt the gentle bump as the two vehicles connected, a row of green indicator lights appeared on the control console confirming the docking had been successful.

He unstrapped himself and floated away from the seat, guiding himself toward the docking hatch at the back end of the capsule. He pressed a button next to it and a wide opening appeared iris-style revealing the outer hull of the vehicle he had been pursuing for thousands of years. It was pockmarked with tiny holes and abrasions, the result of continuous bombardment by microscope particles through the millennia.

If there was someone conscious in the other vehicle, the docking hatch of that craft would have been opened from the other side allowing the two interiors to connect. Without that, he had to open the hatch manually. It was likely the other vehicle was not pressurized; when the hatch opened, air from Risto's craft would rush explosively into the adjacent vacuum. To avoid that, he'd have to open a valve in the hull allowing pressure to slowly equalize between the two vehicles. It was located behind thick metal panels secured with numerous small screws. Risto used an electronic drill to methodically remove them one by one until the panel floated away revealing the valve behind. He turned the valve and listened to the loud hiss as air rushed from his vehicle into the other. He did not like losing all that oxygen, but he had checked before to make sure he had an ample supply. He wondered how much oxygen the other capsule still had.

Risto removed another panel concealing a handle to manually open the circular hatch. When the pressure had equalized, he turned the handle and the iris opened slowly. Several minutes later he was staring at the interior of the mystery vehicle.

The first thing he noted was the spacecraft was not of Union design. Though similar in layout, he saw differences in the arrangement of the display panels and control electronics. These differences were merely cosmetic; the inner circuitry and computer systems were probably very similar to that of the Union vehicles.

The second thing he noted was that the other spacecraft had no power at all. Even when the occupants of galactic exploration vehicles were frozen, some computer systems remained active using the tiny amounts of electricity generated as the vehicle traveled through the plasmas and fields of interstellar space. But on this vehicle, the entire electrical system was not functioning. He knew of only one cause for such a total breakdown in electronics and that was an electromagnetic pulse, EMP, either from a natural source or from a weapon carried on a space vehicle.

Risto set about inspecting the damage. Working at the computer console with a flashlight in one hand and the drill in the other, he removed the panels that allowed access to the internal circuitry of the spacecraft. He was conscious that several meters away was a frozen human. He resisted the temptation to open the chamber because that would jeopardize the safety of the individual inside. He had to get the magnetocryogenic system working again first. Once the intense magnetic field was applied, the body could begin safely defrosting.

Risto worked quickly and assuredly. Any other explorer would have had far less experience in actually performing the necessary tasks. But Risto had done them so often on his own vehicle for one reason or another that it had become second nature. Like the Union vehicles, this capsule had repair parts for the critical power and life support systems.

First, he restored power to the control room lighting system so he could work without the flashlight. He then repaired the onboard computers by replacing all the burned out circuit boards. He was more certain now that EMP had caused the failure because of the type and extent of the damage he found in the electronics. Within a half hour, the computer was running again, and while it went through its routine start-up procedures, he worked on the control circuitry for the freezing chamber. No more than an hour later, the capsule was fully functioning again and Risto was ready to initiate the unfreezing process. What he had failed to consider during the repair was how to confront the passenger if the unfreezing process succeeded.

When Ilsa awoke, the fear and dread she felt when she'd been frozen 28000 years earlier returned as if only moments had passed. Curiously, she remembered exactly where she was and why she was there. Waking up from being frozen was unlike waking up from a deep sleep. There was no disorientation because nothing psychologically or physiologically had taken place during the time the body was frozen. Thus, Ilsa's first thought was whether she had gone anywhere at all since being frozen. A moment later, she heard the hatch open and bright light from the control room flooded the chamber. Then she heard a voice ask, "Are you okay?"

The shock of hearing another person in the capsule made her start and she twisted her head to see who it was, but in the weightlessness of the chamber the movement caused her to bump into the interior of the confined space. She felt a hand on her shoulder and she screamed, as whoever was out there attempted to pull her from the tube. Her fear made her draw back into the chamber, but there was little room for retreat.

"It is okay. I will not hurt you," the voice said. It was a man's voice, faintly accented, but distinct enough from Stormer's Eastern European lilt to give her some comfort. She brought one hand up and grasped the man's hand which was trying to find some part of her anatomy to hold onto. She felt the man tug gently.

"Straighten your body, please, and make it as rigid as possible." She did as she was told and felt herself slide through the opening into the brightly lit interior of the control room. She twisted her body around to see the man, but by the time she'd executed the maneuver he had his back to her and was rummaging through the compartment that held her clothing. He extracted the jumpsuit she had worn only briefly during her time in the control room and handed it to her without turning around. He then moved off to another compartment to locate food and water while she struggled to put on the jumpsuit, which twisted uncontrollably in the absence of gravity.

Once fully clothed, she grasped a handle on the bulkhead of the capsule and steadied herself to get a better look at the man who had pulled her out of the chamber. She noticed the opening in the side of the capsule that revealed the interior of another vehicle attached to hers. She was so completely confused at the situation she could not even think of a question to ask. A short distance away from her she noticed the medallion on its colorful necklace floating and twisting gracefully in midair. She asked, "Are you the old woman's son?"

"I think not," the man replied. "My mother died when she was still young."

"Where am I?" Ilsa asked.

The man hesitated, glancing around the interior of the capsule. "There are many ways one might answer that question. You are a long way from Earth in a space capsule. Your vehicle was drifting without power for many years."

"Without power..." Ilsa repeated softly, trying to understand the meaning of the words.

"How did you get here?"

"I was kidnapped," Ilsa stammered. She looked hard at the man to detect his reaction. He was stout and heavily built. He had thinning blond hair and a beard. His eyes were blue and only partially visible behind lids closed as if looking into bright light. They were not threatening or unfriendly eyes, but she saw potential for uncontrolled intensity.

"Kidnapped by whom?" he asked.

"Stormer," Ilsa answered, not sure if any more explanation was needed. At that moment, the medallion floated into her view again a meter from her eyes. She reached out to grab it, but it was too far and she did not want to release her hold on the handle fixed to the bulkhead. The man noticed the attempt and in one smooth motion propelled himself across the room and caught the necklace in one hand. Arresting his momentum with the other hand before impacting one of the storage compartments, he hovered before her and placed the necklace in Ilsa's outstretched grasp. Then he pushed himself back across the room to a less threatening distance. Ilsa swung the necklace around and placed it over her head.

"Who is Stormer?"

"Charles Stormer, the head of New Life Enterprises. I went to interview him in the desert. He drugged me and put me on this space capsule against my will." She said it as if it had happened only hours ago, and for her it had.

The man watched her silently for several moments, then motioned to the seat in front of the control console. "You will feel better strapped into the seat. You should have some food and water."

The offer was sufficient to put Ilsa at ease. The man was more considerate than his scruffy appearance might suggest. She released her hold on the handle and floated in place wondering how to get over to the console. The man had anticipated her problem and drifted over to her. He bounced gracefully off the bulkhead behind her, grabbed her hand on the rebound, and together they drifted back across the room. Ilsa pulled herself into the seat, and he grabbed the restraining straps to buckle her in. After completing the task, his face loomed before her. "I am Risto," he said, and then moved away.

"I am Ilsa Montgomery." Ilsa paused and then added, "Thank you."

She drank and ate, wondering what she should tell Risto. She was not sure how much she could trust him. Was he one of Stormer's men, one of his paramilitary force? He had said he did not know Stormer. "Are you in the Union?" she asked.

"Yes, of course," Risto answered. "I received a message about an unidentified vehicle in distress. I've been pursuing you for about 15000 years."

"I'm sorry," was all Ilsa could think to say.

"Tell me how you came to be drifting through space without power. Start from the beginning."

"I can tell you what I know, but there is a lot I don't understand myself." She told him about New Life and Stormer's plan to colonize a planet with a group of specially recruited men and women.

Risto listened carefully without interrupting her until she came to the part about being unfrozen by Stormer on a larger space vehicle. "Excuse me, would you describe this ship you were taken to?"

"It had a long corridor that I had to float through after Stormer took me out of the capsule. At the end of the corridor was a ladder that I climbed down and then I was in a room with gravity. There was a man in charge of the ship. His name was Harding."

"Andrew Harding? Dr. Andrew Harding?" asked Risto.

"I believe so," said Ilsa. "He said he was one of the founders of the Union."

"And he and Stormer were working together?"

"Yes, very much so. I asked Dr. Harding what his role was and he told me it was information control. He collected information and used it to make sure no one interfered with Stormer and his attempt to colonize a planet. I had the feeling there was a planet that only Stormer and Harding knew about. I believe that's where we were going when we left the larger ship." Ilsa went on to tell him about how she had escaped the freezing chamber in time to change course using the medallion. This intrigued Risto.

"May I see it?" he asked.

Ilsa removed the necklace and handed it to Risto. He floated over to the console next to her and inserted the ceramic rectangle into the slot Ilsa had used. Then he pressed a key on the console and a stream of text appeared on the monitor before them. Risto scanned the lines and said, "This is a rendezvous plan. Where did you get it?"

Ilsa explained about her visit to the IGET Conference and how Benjamin had purchased the necklace from the old woman.

"This Benjamin — you said he was a Union member."

"In training at the time. Do you know him? His name was Benjamin Mizello."

"No, I don't know him, but I know his father." Risto removed the medallion from the slot and handed it back to Ilsa. "You are sure you selected SS3 as your destination and the computer confirmed the selection?"

"Yes. It even displayed the time of arrival. I remember it very clearly because it seems like only moments ago. I remember it was 8000 years away. Now here I am 28000 years later." Ilsa's voice began to break. The hopelessness of her situation made her weak and she tried to put it out of her mind.

"You would never have gotten to Supply Ship 3," Risto said. "Sometime after you were frozen your vehicle was disabled, most probably by a blast from an EMP weapon."

"EMP weapon?" Ilsa repeated slowly.

"A weapon that fires a burst of electromagnetic energy, strong enough to destroy the electronic circuitry within the vehicle. It did not harm you, but all the spacecraft systems ceased to operate. You were drifting through space with no navigation and no control — also no defense against particles in space that might strike your vehicle and destroy it and you. It was just a matter of time before that happened. Either that or your vehicle would have been captured by the gravitational field of a nearby star and pulled gradually into it."

"I owe you my life," Ilsa said. She knew it was true, but it was difficult to get the words out. "Except I don't have much of a life now anymore." She could no longer hold back her tears. She sobbed silently into her hands.

"We will discuss your options later," Risto said, placing a gentle hand on her shoulder. "It may not be as hopeless as you think. However, I want to be sure about Dr. Andrew Harding's part in this."

Ilsa recovered and told Risto how she had attacked Stormer in the supply ship and that Harding had grabbed her and thrown her against the wall. When she finished recounting the events, he said, "It may very well have been Harding that fired the EMP weapon at your capsule. If he observed your vehicle veering off course, he may have decided to disable it, killing you in the process."

"That would not surprise me," Ilsa said. "He struck me as the kind of person capable of destroying anyone who interfered with his plans."

"Yes, that might be, but I and many others in the Union have a great deal of respect for Harding. He was an excellent mentor and leader."

"Perhaps," Ilsa responded, "but with a dark side, as so many men of power have."

Risto remained quiet for some time. "Several thousand years ago, I received a message that was sent to the entire fleet of Union explorers. It was from Harding, and it directed us to rendezvous in the year 65000. Do you know anything about that?"

"No. All he mentioned was that he made sure no one else in the Union knew about the planet Stormer was heading toward."

With a gentle push against the control console, Risto floated over to the opening between the two spacecraft. After peering into the interior of his own vehicle, he turned back toward Ilsa and said, "We are using valuable oxygen supplies that we may need later. I have a suggestion. Your options are few, but your situation is not hopeless. Your best option is to return to Earth, but not until you have determined it is safe to do so. I can program your vehicle to take you to Supply Ship 6, which is where Arthur Mizello is. He will have the latest information about Earth and can advise you on whether you should return there. Arthur Mizello is a good man. He will help you. I will send a message to Mizello's supply ship alerting him that you are on the way. I will also tell him about the message I received from Harding giving the time and place for the Union fleet to assemble. Arthur Mizello may not be aware of this order."

Ilsa dreaded the thought of getting back in the freezing chamber for many thousands of years more. The loneliness of that prospect, even though she knew she would not be conscious of it, was overwhelming to her. In the minutes she had gotten to know Risto, she felt an attachment that she was reluctant to lose. "What will you do?" she asked.

"I will go to the rendezvous that Dr. Harding has ordered. I would like to have a better idea of his intent." He paused, looking intently at her. "You will be fine. I will do some additional checks to make sure your vehicle is working properly. Before you know it, you will be on Supply Ship 6 with Arthur Mizello. I will have to ask you to let me sit at the console while I perform some safety tests and reprogram your flight plan."

Ilsa nodded and dutifully removed the shoulder straps to yield the seat at the console to Risto. She floated away toward the hatch separating the two vehicles and hovered there steadying herself with her hands clinging to the opening. She watched Risto work, admiring the assuredness with which he manipulated the controls. She still could not believe how much had happened to her in a length of time that seemed like only hours. Was this what it was like to be insane? Was there a mental disorder in which people closed their eyes and opened them again a moment later to see that the world had totally changed in that brief instant? Was this not the ultimate nightmare, to lose consciousness and awaken an instant later to see a different face looming before one's eyes, or hands grasping and pulling at one's body? She thought about Benjamin and wondered if his father would know where he was. Had Benjamin found what he was looking for in the extreme contrasts that he'd always deemed so stimulating? Had he settled down on some planet ages ago and lived a bizarre but rewarding life that was full of contrasts — hot and cold, old and young, good and bad? How futile were her thoughts when there was so little she could do. She was at the mercy of the universe and the immutable laws of space and time. She would meet Benjamin's father in a span of time equal to the entire length of recorded history on Earth. Her only grounding with reality was in watching Risto confidently working at the capsule's computer with a concentration that insulated him from the futility of wondering what would happen next. She envied his absorption in the task. At one time, she had been able to be equally absorbed in the articles she was writing for publication, but now that activity seemed absurdly ridiculous, and she puzzled that it had once been so consuming. To break the spiral down which her thoughts were tumbling, she pushed herself back to where Risto was seated and asked if he would explain to her what he was doing. She knew she would understand very little, but at least it would be a diversion from her mental meanderings.

When he finished, Risto told her she would have to return to the chamber. He would remain in his own capsule while she undressed and reentered the tube on her own. She thanked him with a hand shake at which time he took the opportunity to teach her the official Union hand shake that prevented uncontrolled motion in weightless conditions. She smiled at him and thanked him again. Before he left her, he said, "Ms. Montgomery, I was wondering if you would be willing to give the medallion to me."

Ilsa's hand went to the ceramic rectangle and she held it tightly. "What for?" she asked.

"I may encounter the son of the old woman when I rendezvous with Harding. I can give it to him."

The request seemed reasonable to Ilsa and she reluctantly removed the necklace and handed it to Risto. He took it from her and examined it closely. He found a clasp on the necklace and unhooked it to remove the medallion. Then he closed the clasp and returned the necklace to Ilsa. "You may want to keep this."

"Yes," Ilsa said. "I would like to very much."

With that he turned and propelled himself with one graceful motion through the hatch and disappeared into his capsule. Ilsa undressed and stored the jumpsuit and necklace back in the clothing compartment. Then she opened the hatch to the freezing chamber and slipped inside. Extending herself rigidly in the tube she waited, taking note of the readings on the interior displays. Several minutes later, the ceramic pins extended to position her body in the center and she heard the familiar hum of the capacitors charging up in preparation for the magnetic freezing procedure. She watched the digits count down the time, then heard the loud bang and felt the intense electromagnetic shock, which she had totally forgotten about the last time and would forget about once more upon awakening.

Risto watched Ilsa's capsule separate from his on the computer monitor. He checked the status of all her vehicle's systems one last time. Then he composed a message for Arthur Mizello reporting that he had successfully rescued the female on the non-Union space vehicle and had repaired her capsule and programmed it to take her to Supply Ship 6. He added that he was following the directive he'd received from Andrew Harding to rendezvous with him and the Union fleet in the year 65000. He appended Harding's message to his own. Once he was satisfied he had completed his mission, Risto prepared himself for the long voyage to meet with Harding that would take nearly 25000 years.

CHAPTER 28
— 43141 —

Since the age of four, Elliott Von Digby had been fascinated by the signals received by Aril's only operating radio-telescope. Not being a professional astronomer by trade, he had more freedom to explore the weak and complex signals being detected from space. By Arilian law, all data from the telescope and other scientific instruments were made available for public use without restriction. Aril had adopted an unusual approach to handling data and other forms of information. The idea of retaining data in stationary electronic storage devices was abhorrent to Arilians, who regarded knowledge as something that had to keep moving lest it stagnate. Data was treated like water in a stream. As long as it was in motion it was safe to drink. Standing water grew old and became a nesting ground for harmful agents. For this reason, Arilians constructed a global network of transmitting and receiving stations that constantly streamed huge amounts of data from one to the other. At any given time, more information filled the atmosphere around the planet than was stored in stationary sites on the ground. To access the data, Arilians simply tapped into the information passing by, just as they might tap into a current of electricity to power the lights in their homes.

Data from all sources were continually added to the Arilian bit streams crisscrossing the planet. Bottlenecks were rare, and when they occurred they were dealt with by adding new relay stations. Because of the multiply redundant pathways over which the data were transmitted, information was seldom lost. Those who used the data were encouraged to add it back into the stream when their projects were completed, just as water might be recycled after it was used. The difference was that the more data was used, the more it would be replicated. Some Arilians worried about the unnecessary duplication of heavily used data that would result, but others argued that it was the best way to ensure preservation of the most useful and important information. It was survival of the fittest applied to knowledge, which was as important to Arilians as the air they breathed.

Elliott Von Digby was particularly interested in finding messages from the ancient fleet of galactic explorers reported to be still present throughout the galaxy. According to the historical records he'd studied, the galactic exploration vehicles were constantly moving through space, and it was unlikely that the radio-telescope would be fortuitously pointing in the right direction at the right time to receive a direct communication from the tiny spacecraft. Also, powerful as the telescope was, it could only detect signals from the small vehicles if they were within about 100 light-years of Aril. The large supply ships, however, had strong enough transmitters that their signals could be readily detected, especially because they were at fixed locations, and the ancient records contained information about their coordinates in space. Elliott knew that the supply ships would relay all communications received from the exploration vehicles. Therefore, Elliott paid close attention to see if there was a message hidden in the data from the radio-telescope when its antenna was pointed toward one of the supply ships

After years of steadfast effort, Elliott was finally rewarded when his data acquisition program flagged a coherent signal from the location of one of the legendary supply ships. As expected, the message was written in the ancient language of the Galactic Explorers Union. Elliott had learned the language once, but did not subsequently have any opportunities to use it. It took him several hours to translate and he went over the text a second time to make sure he had done it correctly. The message was from Supply Ship 6 and it warned of possible disruptions to the Union communication network. It also advised that Aril should report any suspicious visits by galactic explorers.

Elliott realized he had to bring the message to the attention of the authorities, but he was not sure anyone would pay attention to him, or even believe he had actually been able to extract the data, convert it to text, and translate it all on his own. He had no friends or relatives in positions of authority, nor did he have any connections to anyone who might have access to those high enough in the Arilian government. Fortunately, Elliott understood enough about how the Arilian data network functioned to take advantage of its peculiar features. Thus, he methodically extracted the same data from the radio-telescope and immediately reinserted it back into the Arilian atmospheric bit stream. Each time he did, he increased the volume of space the message occupied in the network. By repeating this continuously over several weeks, the message from Arthur Mizello's supply ship achieved a dominant presence in the dynamic Arilian data reservoir. It wasn't long before any Arilian browsing the network would eventually come upon the warning message from space dutifully translated by Elliott Von Digby.

The reaction from Arilians once the message had reached the proper authorities was typical. In their methodical and deliberate way, they analyzed and discussed the message, particularly in light of Captain Warner's prophecy of long ago. Arilians weighed all possible options available to the planet as a response. A worldwide research program was initiated to prepare Aril for an attack from space. It would be a multi-faceted approach involving surveillance, defense, logistical support, psycho-sociological preparation, steps to mitigate risk, and fall-back strategies.

While undertaking these activities, Arilians paid closer attention to the radio transmissions coming from the supply ships and Earth. Although subsequent messages provided little additional information about the possible conquest of the planet, reading the latest events from Earth and space made them feel less alone in the universe. Despite enormous efforts to observe signs of the invading force, Arilian astronomers detected nothing that could be perceived of as a threat. One activity that was discussed but never implemented was the establishment of a space program and the development of a space-based defense system. After much consideration, Arilians decided that the impact of such a program on their economy and environment would jeopardize the well-being of the planet far more than an invasion from space that may or may not take place.

Elliott Von Digby, of course, achieved worldwide recognition for the role he played in discovering the message. He was interviewed frequently, and his name and picture appeared in the popular media. He was even invited to give lectures at universities, where he was questioned about his methodology, particularly the automated search routines he had developed to search the data streams.

One of the measures the Arilians decided to take in response to the warning was to construct a gigantic transmitter powerful enough to send a message directly to Earth. Through thousands of years, Arilians had kept in sporadic touch with Earth whenever there was sufficient interest to invest in the cost of building a new transmitter. They believed that the relationship between the two planets was still friendly and that sending a message inquiring about the possibility of an invasion was a harmless and prudent thing to do. To honor Elliott, they allowed him to craft a separate message of his own. Elliott considered this for some time and finally came up with a short note saying, "I am Elliott Von Digby from the planet Aril. I am interested in learning more about Earth. Please write."

Of course, it would take approximately 16000 years for Elliott to receive a response from Earth, but he could not quite comprehend the impossibility of that event. After all, Elliott Von Digby was only the equivalent of 10 Earth-years old.

CHAPTER 29
— 43680 —

The greenhouse gardens of Union supply ships were set in large rotating cylinders at one end of the spacecraft. The rotation created an artificial gravity equal to one-third Earth's, enough to keep the soil from floating away, but not so strong as to impede the growth of plants. The rotation axis of the cylinder pointed directly at the star around which the ship orbited. The end of the cylinder contained transparent crystalline windows that allowed the starlight to fall upon an array of mirrors angled to reflect the light radially away from the axis of the ship onto the plants. The total area of the inner surface of the cylinder was about a half acre. The greenhouse was a self-contained biosphere, with plants and insects balanced to maintain oxygen, carbon dioxide, and water levels within the cylinder for thousands of years, allowing them to be bled off to the living quarters of the ship as needed. When food supplies diminished, the custodians cultivated food crops, to be harvested, processed, and placed in cold storage for future use.

The greenhouse offered an excellent vantage point to gaze at the star about which the supply ship orbited. It was a luminous disk, a fraction of the size of Earth's sun. Though the intensity of the light was lower than that of the sun, the cumulative effect was sufficient to keep the greenhouse at a comfortable temperature. Arthur and Krystal had installed seats to look out at the celestial vista before them. As the cylinder rotated, the surrounding stars circled about the primary one, just as circumpolar stars spin about the North Star at Earth's pole.

Benjamin and his father sat in the greenhouse watching the dizzying pirouette of stars. Neither knew how to begin the impending conversation. When he'd awoken in his magnetocryogenic chamber, his first thought had been of his father, who after over forty thousand years was only several meters away. Benjamin had the same difficulty dealing with his mother's death as his father. Conflicting feelings of guilt and abandonment made it impossible for either of them to fully accept the tragic and pre-mature death of someone they relied upon so deeply. By joining the Union, Benjamin had followed his father's lead. He anticipated a long conversation with his father that might offer a measure of comfort.

That hope was quickly dashed when he had climbed down into the ship's living quarters where he was shocked to see a middle-aged woman with jet-black hair leaning nervously against the bulkhead. He recognized her as the woman he'd spoken to on the Union transfer station before he departed from Earth. When he learned that she was now his father's partner, the conversation he'd looked forward to became suddenly meaningless and inappropriate. He felt betrayed. The dark-haired woman looked uneasy under Benjamin's resentful gaze.

Later, after the three of them had spent several hours in the control room going over recent events, Benjamin could still not come to grips with the obvious affection between his father and this woman. When they all decided to get some rest, Arthur offered to show Benjamin the greenhouse, knowing there was something weighing heavily on his son's mind. They sat before the crystalline windows gazing at the circling stars outside the glass.

"Krystal seems very nice," Benjamin said, wiping a bead of sweat from his forehead. The humidity inside the greenhouse was always high. "Totally different from Mom," he added softly, "but I guess that's the way it happens."

Arthur leaned forward with his elbows on his knees. "Do you really think she's different from your mom? What makes you say that?"

"She's an engineer. She works with numbers, data, machines. Mom loved plants, flowers, music and art."

"Do you think I've betrayed your mother in some way?"

"No," Benjamin replied unconvincingly.

"Why did you join the Union?" Arthur asked.

Benjamin looked sharply at him. "I'm not sure. At one time, I thought I knew, but I don't know now."

"What was the reason at the time?"

Benjamin looked at his father, wondering how frank he should be. He shook his head, stood, and walked to the window. His breath condensed on the cool surface. "Mom would have liked it here."

Arthur rose and stood beside his son. "Are you sure?"

"Yes. The greenhouse, the spectacular view, and the wonderful isolation would all inspire her sense of beauty."

Now it was Arthur who shook his head. "You're wrong. Your mother hated the isolation. All those years she accompanied me on my trips to the most primitive and godforsaken parts of the world, living with poor, desperate, suffering people — it was torture for her. Eventually it killed her."

"I don't remember it that way," replied Benjamin. "I remember her art. Wherever we were, she'd find a way of creating something pleasing from whatever she had to work with."

Arthur smiled. "That was just her way of coping, but did you ever stop to think that her creations were striking because they were crafted in the bleakest, ugliest places on Earth. Taken elsewhere the same pieces of art would be bland and uninspiring?"

"No. Maybe. Does it matter?"

"I'm not trying to detract from what your mom did. I'm trying to draw a parallel. Your mom motivated me. By finding beauty in the midst of ugliness, she challenged me to find hope in people and places where everyone else saw only despair. You're a photographer. What do you look for? Contrast — to let the subject stand out from the background? People want order from chaos. One has no meaning without the other. Musicians create sound that stands out from noise. Engineers, like Krystal also extract signal from noise. Your mom and Krystal are not so different. Krystal looks at information, most of which is garbage, bland uninteresting drivel. Like your mom, she isn't satisfied with that, so she uses her intelligence, intuition, and the tools at her disposal to extract larger truths.

"I didn't travel to space to find Krystal. I wanted to get away from Earth because there wasn't anywhere I could go there that didn't remind me of your mom. I needed to escape the bittersweet memories. Space was perfect. But then Krystal showed up. In her own way, she reminded me of your mother's dedication to beauty. Ultimately, everyone has the same goal in life: to be surrounded by love and loveliness, no matter what form it takes — art, music, enlightenment. When you find someone who can be a partner in that endeavor, then let that person into your life completely. You can't go wrong."

"I thought you needed me," Benjamin said quietly. "That's why I joined. I knew how much Mom's death crushed you and that you blamed yourself for it. I didn't want you to face that blame alone."

"I did need you. I still do, but not in the way you believe. To know that I've nurtured in you the values your mom wanted you to have — that's what I need, and you've satisfied me more than I could ever have imagined. Every time I see your photographs I'm convinced. We've taught you well: that there is beauty in the world as long as one has the sensitivity to detect it. Now, in the middle of the galaxy, Krystal has taught me that there is beauty even in empty space. It's everywhere around us."

Arthur looked at the swirling stars outside and added, "It isn't just beauty that you can see." He held up two hands spaced about six inches apart as if he was holding an imaginary box. "Do you see this volume of space? Krystal could build a tiny receiver and put it right here between my hands, and do you know what she could extract from that seemingly empty bit of space? An amount of information far beyond anything you can imagine. And it's not static; it's dynamic, changing, and often miraculous and inexplicable. We build transmitters that send electromagnetic waves into space and suddenly space is no longer a vacuum. Can you see the awesome wonder in that? I know you can, Benjamin, because we raised you to. At least, your mom did anyway."

Benjamin's eyes locked on his father's. "I'm lost, Dad. I don't know what I want out of life anymore."

"You were a serious child," Arthur said. "It's not surprising. You grew up at a time when the Earth was dealing with impossibly difficult challenges. And I did nothing to make it easier for you.

252

By taking you to the most desperate and squalid places on Earth, I robbed you of the joys childhood normally brings. You never learned how to ignore the suffering around you. It's no wonder you're lost. You've never had the opportunity to think about yourself first. It's time you started doing that."

Benjamin gestured out the window to the empty space beyond. "Where do you suppose I start?" he asked, unable to disguise the irony in his voice.

Arthur drew in a deep breath and sighed. He waited several moments, then said, "On Aril."

"Aril?" Benjamin repeated.

"Believe me, I'm very reluctant to send you there. All evidence points to the likelihood that Harding and a large fraction of the Union fleet are planning aggressive action. It could be dangerous for you. If Harding wanted you involved, you'd have received the same transmission as all the others. You will not be welcome there, but you may be able to help. At the least, you can observe and send messages back here to let us know what's happening. You might even be able to warn the Arilians and prevent Harding from doing harm."

Benjamin nodded, not enthusiastically, but with understanding. Going to Aril might not resolve his personal confusion, but it would engage him sufficiently for now. "I'll go," he said finally.

"Of course you will," responded Arthur, and the two of them embraced as the stars outside completed one more circuit about the glowing orb that provided the supply ship its life force.

CHAPTER 30
— 48049 —

More than four thousand years later, Krystal performed a routine scan of data received during the past hundred years. First, she used the program that looked for discrepancies between the current and projected locations of vehicles to determine if any of the galactic explorers had changed course. As she expected, she found none. More than eight hundred galactic explorers were still heading toward Aril. Next, she checked for any high priority messages, or those that contained specific keywords or phrases. The result was an urgent message from a galactic explorer named Risto Jalonen. Within minutes of seeing it she called Arthur to the control room to show it to him. It read:

"Female occupant of errant vehicle, Ilsa Montgomery, rescued as requested. Subject on course for Supply Ship 6. Estimated arrival 55277. Please confirm abortion of Union mission and rendezvous at designated location in year 65000."

"Just as we suspected," Arthur said. Now we know the time this assembly is taking place. Apparently, Risto Jalonen was one of the explorers instructed to proceed to the 'designated location'."

Krystal turned to him with an expression of concern he was not used to seeing. "This is serious, Arthur. It's one thing to make speculations based on data, but now we know for a fact that a supply ship custodian is planning to invade a sovereign planet. Did you suspect Harding was capable of this?"

"Now that I know, it really comes as no surprise. Anyone who wields power on a small scale doesn't shrink from expanding his control when the opportunity presents itself. Harding has almost the entire Union fleet at his disposal."

"He has a supply ship too. My guess is that SS5 is on its way to Aril."

"How do we stop this?" Arthur asked.

"We could send a message to the fleet, but I doubt they'd listen. They've got their orders from Harding."

"I sent my son to Aril," Arthur said quietly.

"You knew there might be danger, and Benjamin knew it too. I'm sure he'll be careful."

"Is it too late to warn him?"

Krystal nodded. "He's too far away. We could try to relay the message through other vehicles, but then they'd know that Benjamin is coming."

"Maybe we should go there," Arthur suggested.

Krystal shook her head vigorously. "We can't abandon the supply ship, and we can't take it with us. Other explorers are out there who haven't received the message and might show up here for supplies. And don't forget the woman who was rescued. She's on her way here too. Because of her, we know when Harding is planning his invasion of Aril."

Arthur held up a hand. "You're right. You're right. Then there's only one way we can help, but it's a long shot. We need to send a message to Earth. They know about Aril. They might have an interest in ensuring its safety."

"It will take a long time for our message to get to Earth, and still longer for help to arrive. I doubt Aril and Earth are still communicating. Remember, they forwarded Aril's message to us in the first place. Why would they have stopped forwarding subsequent messages?"

Arthur shrugged. The intermittent communication between their ship and Earth was an endless source of speculation by Krystal and Arthur. Thousands of years would go by with no messages, then there'd be a flurry of them. It was not unlike two people trying to maintain a long distance relationship over many years. Each would wonder about lapses in response and try to outwait the other so as not to convey more information than might be appropriate. It was like a galactic scale courtship ritual.

In the case of Earth, there were more reasons that communication would be discontinued than there were factors that might sustain it. The powerful antennas and sensitive radio receivers could cease to operate because of deterioration or age. Or perhaps the cost of operating the instruments could not be born by the struggling civilizations on Earth. It was also likely that people on Earth had totally forgotten about the existence of the Union and its fleet through the millennia. Then there was the very real possibility that no one on Earth could understand the language used by the Union fleet. The messages sent by Krystal and Arthur may be no more than gibberish to those on Earth receiving them. It was conceivable the chain of knowledge passed on by Union members was interrupted by war, disease, or the failure to bear children who might carry on the tradition.

"When did we receive the last message from Earth?" Arthur asked.

Krystal typed in commands. "16000 years ago," she said.

"16000 years," Arthur repeated. "How much could change on Earth in that much time?"

"Everything," Krystal answered.

"We don't have other options," Arthur said. "Send a message to Earth and tell them what's going on. Emphasize our suspicions. Tell them that Aril is defenseless against an attack from space."

"How do you know they're defenseless?" Krystal asked.

"I don't, but do you think Earth will help if they're not?"

Krystal was shaking her head. "It's tragic, you know. The Union communication system is being threatened. The Union in all its wisdom made one huge mistake. Putting a supply ship in the hands of one person made that critical network hub a single point failure. Harding has jeopardized the whole Union mission just by manipulating information and impeding communication. The system that functioned like a single organism for millennia is now no more than a disconnected collection of space hardware and lost souls."

"Don't give up yet," Arthur said, surprised that the tables had turned and he now had to play the optimist. "Let's continue applying the strategy that you implemented — fight fire with fire. Can you generate a list of the Union explorers that have not changed course? They're probably the ones that Harding feels won't listen to him."

"Sure," said Krystal.

"Then, in addition to sending the message to Earth, let's also send messages to those explorers. Tell them all to proceed immediately to Aril and to provide whatever assistance the planet may need."

"Good idea," said Krystal.

"And you might as well send the message to all the supply ships we can reach from here. It's not clear where the other supply ship custodians stand on this, but it can't make things much worse if they hear our plea for help. Send a message to Aril that there is a possibility of hostile action around the year 65000. Tell them to only allow explorers to land on the planet if they use my name. Finally, see if you can get a message to Risto Jalonen. Send him a copy of the list of explorers not in Harding's camp. Request that he keep in touch with us by transmitting messages through explorer vehicles on that list. Keep repeating the message to all possible recipients as frequently as our power system permits."

"Roger, Captain," Krystal said, with a ghost of a smile on her lips. "You're beginning to get the hang of this."

"It doesn't come naturally," said Arthur.

"Oh, but it's very natural," replied Krystal. "Don't you see what's happening? Take a step back and look. Harding and Stormer represent a threat to this huge, galactic-scale organism the Union gave life to. They have launched a viral attack on the whole system, not just Aril. Viruses attack organisms by making believe they are something else. They mess with an organism's internal communication system causing organs to malfunction. The body's response to that attack is to send specialized cells to destroy the infection."

"That would be our friends in the Union," Arthur said, half jokingly.

"That's one part of it, but don't forget about Benjamin, who's heading to Aril to help, as will our friend Risto. And if Earth sends help, then the overall response to this threat is truly global and organic in nature. These are antibodies on a grand scale."

"Very interesting, Krystal, and since we're orchestrating this, does that mean we're the hypothalmus in your big animal."

Krystal gave Arthur a light slap with the back of her hand. "Very funny. I'll tell you what we are another time. Right now I've got work to do."

CHAPTER 31
— 48000-52000 —

On Earth, it was a new age. It was an age of alchemy, as if human history had come full circle and civilization had finally achieved the dreams of ancient mystics. It was an age of reconstruction, enabled by the development of microscopic robots with the capability to transform disordered masses of material into complex engineering structures.

Early experiments had shown that customized molecules could be chemically programmed to break down the crystalline structure of matter, reorganize the lattice holding substances together, and catalyze the growth of new structures. There were only two drawbacks to the process. First, breaking chemical bonds in stable materials consumed large amounts of energy. The little robots were too small to carry their own power source, so engineers designed special energy-carrying robots. They were programmed to transfer their chemical energy to fabricating robots, after which they were carried away by a non-reactive liquid to be later recycled and used again to transport more energy. Continuous power had to be supplied to maintain the cycle. The process did not really become practical until small nuclear power plants were designed to provide the requisite energy.

The second drawback to the process was that it worked very slowly. Engineers justifiably feared that rapid processes, once initiated, would be difficult to control. All attempts to speed up transmutation led to near catastrophic results. Initially, people had little interest in projects that would take longer than their lifespans to complete. Eventually though, societies came to appreciate the merits of technology that would benefit future generations without great expense to the current population.

The first successful demonstration of the new engineering technique was accomplished on a beach. A test tube carrying millions of invisible builder molecules was poured onto the sand and then left alone. Twelve years later, a beautifully intricate castle stood at the site where the test tube had been emptied — not a castle made of sand, but one of brilliantly colored glass.

After that, engineers embarked on more ambitious demonstrations of the technology. Truckloads of material were dumped on an open field with a handful of robotic builders added to the mix. Several years later, a complete house stood at the site, with windows of glass and a roof made of a new water and heat resistant composite material.

Eventually, the robots were designed to decompose existing structures and then rebuild them from the transmuted material. These robots were put to use restoring much of the aging and failing infrastructure on Earth. Entire cities — buildings, roads, bridges — were deconstructed over the course of many decades to be born again, strong enough to withstand weather, oxidation, earthquakes, and the slow degradation of age. A collection of designer robots released at a landfill could, within ten years, convert it to a playground, a shopping mall or a sports stadium.

The next big advance in robotic building technology was reverse engineering. For extremely complex manufacturing tasks, the first unit would be constructed manually by a team of engineers. Once it had been completed and tested, miniature robots were released that broke it apart molecule by molecule, atom by atom. In so doing, the little robots retained the knowledge of how to assemble the product again. These memory robots would link up with the manufacturing robots and years later, the item would be rolling off an assembly line at a slow but steady rate.

Given the success of these engineering feats, Earth's population relaxed after thousands of years in the clutches of despair. So slow was the process of rebuilding, that people went about their business forgetting that reconstruction projects were taking place all over the world. Somewhere back in the shadows of the collective psyche, however, people understood that the world was getting better — that homelessness and intolerable living conditions were being eradicated. This did wonders to eliminate jealousy, strife, and wars. The change did not occur overnight, but enough improvement happened during a person's lifetime to inspire unprecedented worldwide optimism.

While Earth was undergoing a global facelift, there was little interest in space. No longer were attempts made to communicate with Aril. The memory of the Union and its effort to explore the galaxy faded. Occasionally, teachers or scientists tried to resurrect interest in astronomy and space, but the general population was too absorbed with the astonishing transformations taking place on Earth. Even the long-standing fascination with extraterrestrial life languished as Earthlings witnessed their own planet being transformed into a custom-built paradise.

Then in the 50th millennium, a young woman, Marian Clement, wrote a thesis for her doctorate degree in Multidisciplinary Studies, a catch-all academic discipline for students who were bright but could not always focus. Marion was the great granddaughter of a man who claimed to belong to an ancient secret society of space explorers. Piqued by his strange tales, Marion studied the history of space exploration using ancient databases, extremely difficult to find and extract information from.

After years of research, she produced a thesis documenting the rise and fall of galactic exploration. She began with travel to the moon, Mars, and planets within the solar system. She then explained how magnetocryogenics made it possible for humans to embark on longer space voyages, and she finished by describing the Galactic Explorers Union, with its single-person capsules and self-contained supply ships. She even rediscovered the now defunct radio-telescope on the far side of the moon. She speculated that Union secrets, including its vast knowledge base and language, had been successfully passed on through many generations. She was sure her great grandfather was an heir to this legacy.

Her thesis described the rumored expedition from Earth that colonized a planet around a star whose luminosity was fading rapidly. She also reported on Aril, an apparently successful colonization of another planet by a ragtag group of exiles from Earth. She included the uplifting message from Aril, received by Earth in the year 31720, which began with a quote from the Statue of Liberty, an ancient structure that still stood in New York Harbor.

She noted that Earth had sent messages to Aril for many years, but correspondence ceased when the last of the ground-based radio-telescopes was no longer operational. Marian speculated the Union explorers might still be out there. Through painstaking investigation, she uncovered historical accounts of strange people who claimed to have come from space and spoke in an unknown language. Some of these strangers disappeared, while others were assimilated into the local culture and lived out their lives without making any further claims about their puzzling origin.

The main point of Marian's thesis was that the failure to find alternate homes for the desperate people of Earth inspired the age of reconstruction. Once people accepted the idea that space offered no alternate home for humanity, they were more motivated to find solutions using the resources at hand. The thesis was excellent and Marian received her doctoral degree with honors.

No more would have come of it had it not been for another ambitious test of the microscopic robot technology — building a permanent base on the moon.

An international team of engineers assembled and built a self-contained moon-base on the sands of the Kalahari Desert. Then they released billions of memory robots at the site and in two years the moon-base was deconstructed. The tiny robots were collected, placed in a rocket, transported to the surface of the moon, and released along with a small nuclear reactor that provided energy for the construction project. Eighty years later, an exact duplicate of the Kalahari base was ready for human habitation on the moon.

In the subsequent hundred years, the base was permanently occupied by rotating teams selected from a global pool of candidates based on proposals they submitted explaining how they would use their time on the moon. Most proposed scientific research projects, but some offered to spend the time in artistic pursuits — painting, writing, photography, sculpture. A young radio engineer, who had read Marian's thesis describing the telescope on the far side of the moon, proposed to restore the instrument to search for signals from space. His proposal was accepted and he spent the next several years on the moon renovating the telescope, which only needed replacement of optical fibers damaged by meteor impact. Once it was operational, he programmed it to look for messages from one of the ancient galactic explorers.

The first message from space was detected 90 years after Marion wrote her thesis, but thanks to the increasing human life span, she was still alive. She had taught her great grand-children everything she knew about the Union, and they became instant celebrities as the news of the survival of the galactic explorer fleet spread. It produced a revival of interest in the Union, and courses in its official language were taught in universities everywhere.

Earth responded to the first message, which happened to be from Supply Ship 4, though everyone realized it would be 10000 years before they would receive an answer in return. They continued to monitor messages from the Union network. The Union had mandated that all messages to Earth contain enough information about scheduled transmissions from its supply ships so that once any message was received, the observer knew exactly where and when to look for subsequent transmissions.

As for messages from Aril, none were received for many more years. Finally, in the year 51348, an urgent message from the young planet appeared inquiring whether Earth knew of plans for an invasion of Aril by an unidentified space force. Enigmatically, it concluded with a brief note from an Arilian named Elliott Von Digby, requesting that someone on Earth write back, as if he were seeking an intergalactic pen pal.

There was much speculation on Earth about what had happened to Aril in the time since the message was transmitted. Eventually, the communication was forgotten, but the radio-telescope continued to operate, searching for other signals from the Union supply ships that related the wondrous exploits of the galactic explorers.

Three hundred years passed after that. Then a message from Supply Ship 6 was received containing a plea for help, claiming that a large part of the galactic fleet was en route to Aril to attack the planet. Before, it had been easy for people on Earth to ignore what was happening on Aril. The earlier message had been just an inquiry about whether Earth knew of plans for such a siege. The new message specified the year the attack would take place. Still, most on Earth were not inclined to act. Other than routine flights to the moon, Earth had lost all capabilities to venture into deep space. Without magnetocryogenic technology, it was impossible. Despite the appeal from Aril, Earthlings were too comfortable in their indestructible homes to intervene in events so far away.

Many more decades passed until a generation of rebellious young people took up Aril as the poster-child for the complacency and neglect of Earth's population. Ignoring the pleas of other humans, even as far away as Aril, was an example of how people had dug their collective heads in the sand and lost the values that were the foundation of humanity. From demonstrations on college campuses, the rallying cry of "Save Aril Now!" was broadcast around the world.

The debate would have gone on indefinitely with neither side budging were it not for a discovery made in the Gobi desert. Townspeople there were transforming the desert sand to new homes using commercial micro-robots when they spotted, buried in the ground, a galactic space vehicle, left by one of the explorers who had returned to Earth and decided to stay. The vehicle was dug up and transported to a nearby city where it was placed in a popular museum. Thousands of people visited the ancient spacecraft before someone wondered whether it was possible to use the robotic technology to reverse engineer it. Because the process would destroy the spacecraft, it was resisted by those who saw the vehicle as an irreplaceable monument to be preserved at all costs.

Again there was a stalemate until a group of students at a nearby university pointed out that once the craft was reverse engineered, it could be mass produced for a rescue mission to Aril. They argued that preserving an old relic was not as important as rescuing Aril from space invaders. The students prevailed and the spacecraft was moved from the museum to a large manufacturing plant. Before the memory robots were put into action, a number of modifications to the spacecraft were made. Most important of these was replacing much of the metal in the vehicle's hull with more lightweight and durable composite materials. This was essential as the vehicles had to reach Aril in 12000 years if they were to get there by 65000. A twenty five percent reduction in the mass would enable the spacecraft to travel much faster than the ancient models.

Technicians made the modifications and released the memory robots on the prototype vehicle. Two years later, nothing remained of the structure but a mass of dark powder on the floor. The memory robots were collected and set to work duplicating the galactic space vehicles. The process was extremely slow, but in a little over a thousand years, three hundred vehicles were ready for the voyage to Aril.

The fleet was to be led by a command ship engineers had modeled after the Union supply ships, but much more sophisticated. One important difference was that it carried on-board freezing chambers for a crew of thirty, not possible on Union ships because heat from the life support systems would slowly seep into the cylinders and kill the occupants. The composite materials of the new command ship provided much better thermal isolation.

The command ship was built on Earth and subjected to the onslaught of billions of memory robots. The robots were then launched in a rocket to the moon where they slowly reproduced the large craft. The ship was launched directly into space from the lunar surface, taking advantage of the reduced gravity on the moon. After more than a thousand years in the making, the command ship, along with the three hundred individual spacecraft, began the 12000 year journey to Aril.

CHAPTER 32

— 55277 —

When Ilsa awoke, she remembered Risto's instructions about which indicator lights and numbers to check first. As she did this, the hatch above her head hissed open, just as it had at the end of her two previous journeys. This time, the voice she heard was a woman's, "Ms. Montgomery, my name is Krystal. May I help you out?"

Ilsa nodded and felt hands grab her by the shoulders and pull her gently through the opening. In the dim lights of the control room, she saw floating next to her a middle aged woman with black hair and dark penetrating eyes. She held a garment that drifted uncontrollably. Somehow Krystal managed to maneuver the listless cloth around Ilsa and secure it with snaps. "You can change into a more comfortable garment once we get someplace with gravity," the woman said.

Ilsa murmured a thank you and followed Krystal, using the handles to pull herself along the cylindrical corridor. When they descended the ladder into the artificial gravity portion of the supply ship, Krystal handed Ilsa a jump-suit and helped her into it. She then led Ilsa to the galley, where Ilsa was reminded of the harsh treatment she'd received from Harding and Stormer, seemingly only a few hours ago. She shuddered.

Krystal offered Ilsa food and water, saying little, as if she were avoiding conversation. Ilsa ate silently, deep in thought, experiencing an overwhelming weariness. When she finished, Krystal said, "I'll show you where you can rest. When you're up to it, Mr. Mizello and I would like to talk to you." She peered at Ilsa and then added, "Only if you care to."

Ilsa bowed her head and looked at her hands resting on the table, shaking visibly.

"I can give you medication," Krystal said. "You may be in shock."

"No, I'm okay," returned Ilsa. "I just need to rest."

And she did. Once she reclined on the bed in the quiet comfort of her sleeping quarters, overcome by exhaustion, she slept for many hours, dreaming of Earth as if she had been there yesterday.

Ilsa awoke and returned to the galley. Krystal was at the table sitting next to an elderly man with thinning gray hair. As he rose to greet her, she immediately saw the resemblance to Benjamin. He was an older, more rugged, version of his son. He smiled warmly and offered his hand. "Welcome to Union Supply Ship 6. I'm Arthur Mizello. You can call me Arthur. You've already met Krystal. May I call you Ilsa?"

Ilsa nodded and took a seat at the table. Krystal brought more food, but Ilsa had little appetite and could only nibble at what may have been scrambled eggs. Arthur spoke: "We've had a fairly complete report from Risto Jalonen on what happened. I'm very sorry. Those of us who volunteered to explore the galaxy were fully aware of what we were doing. Even with that, we all experienced a horrible dread the first time we woke from freezing and realized the world we knew was impossibly far away and gone forever. I can only imagine what it must have been like for you. Krystal and I will help you adjust, but I'm afraid we're powerless to reverse what's been done. And if I understand correctly, hundreds of other women have faced or will face the same terror you have. Anything you can tell us about Harding and Stormer may help them."

Ilsa mentally played back the events at the New Life compound in the Mojave Desert. There was very little of relevance, only the unmistakable reality that Stormer had executed a crime of human trafficking on a galactic scale. It was insidious in its ultimate goal of establishing a colony with kidnapped women and a band of ruthless mercenaries, but even more despicable because it was mercilessly irreversible. The women he'd tricked into coming along on the voyage now had little else to live for except being slaves to Stormer and his men.

Ilsa told her story and Krystal typed at a keyboard before a monitor with a split screen. The left side of the display contained a transcription of Ilsa's exact words as recorded by voice recognition software. On the right side of the screen, Krystal entered her own comments at various times, sometimes correcting errors in the transcription, sometimes noting Ilsa's expression or mood. This kept Krystal apart from the easy rapport Arthur had established with Ilsa, who remembered more and more details as she relaxed. When she'd finished, Arthur sighed heavily and glanced at Krystal. "We have to get this information to the Arilians. They have to know what kind of people they're threatened by. It's not just the galactic explorers converging on their planet. Stormer has his own paramilitary group leading the invasion."

"Who are the Arilians?" Ilsa asked, looking confused.

"They're descendants from a group of travelers from Earth who colonized a planet they named Aril. The colony thrived and now Harding and Stormer are planning to invade and take over the planet."

"How far away is Aril? Can they be stopped?"

Krystal answered, "A message from here to Aril will take 8000 Earth years to arrive. It will get there before Harding's army assembles, but we can't be sure the Arilians will be listening for our message." She seemed about to say more, but she stopped and looked at Arthur.

Arthur said quietly, "My son is on his way there."

Ilsa felt a flutter within her. In a voice she could barely control, she asked, "How is Benjamin? Have you seen him?"

Arthur looked up quickly. "Do you know Benjamin?"

Ilsa tried to control her emotions. "I met him at a conference in Washington, while he was studying to become a space explorer." She stopped. The brief explanation did not capture the depth of her friendship with Benjamin.

Arthur sensed there was more to the story. "Benjamin is fine. He was here and doing well." He looked at Krystal for assurance and continued. "He was distracted — as though he had something on his mind he couldn't articulate."

Ilsa smiled. "That's what he said about his last conversation with you. He was sure you were trying to tell him something, but he hadn't been receptive enough. He was anxious to see you again."

Arthur peered at Ilsa intently. "You and Benjamin must have been very close if he confided that to you."

"You have a wonderful son, Mr. Mizello."

"Thank you." Arthur rose from his seat and paced back and forth. "Ms. Montgomery, you will need to consider what you want to do now. Please don't feel rushed into making a decision. I'm afraid there are only three options for you — return to Earth, go on to Aril, or stay here on this supply ship for as long as you wish."

Ilsa answered without hesitating. "I want to go where Benjamin is. Can you help me get there?"

Arthur sat down again, facing her. "Yes, we can, but you must understand that Benjamin will have gotten there long before you. If he decides to remain on Aril, he will be long dead before you arrive. Aril appears to be an extremely friendly and hospitable planet, but many thousands of years will have passed by the time you arrive there. If Stormer and Harding prevail, Aril may not be the kind of place you want to go to."

Ilsa looked at her hands, which were trembling again. The possibility of stumbling back into Stormer's clutches terrifed her. So unusual was her situation, she was unable to make a decision based on reason. She had no recourse but to rely on her emotions. "I just want to be where Benjamin is," she said. The words came out as a whisper, and she wiped away a tear from her eye.

Arthur took her hands in his. They were warm and comforting. "We will get you to Aril, and we'll send a message to them with your course and arrival time. We'll request that if they have any contact with Benjamin, they should let him know that you're on the way there. He'll know what to do. You'll see him again."

Krystal added, "We can also program your vehicle to return to this supply ship. If anything goes wrong when you arrive at Aril, you'll be able to easily turn around and come back here."

Ilsa nodded.

Over the next several hours, she sat with Krystal as the older woman prepared messages for Aril and for Earth. They contained Ilsa's complete account of her time with Stormer and Harding. Krystal performed the same checks on her space capsule as Risto had, and like Risto, Krystal instructed Ilsa on the various functions of the on-board computer.

Feeling more comfortable with Krystal, Ilsa remarked, "Benjamin didn't say anything about his father having a partner on the supply ship."

Without missing a beat, Krystal replied, "He couldn't have known. I started out as one of the explorers. I visited the supply ship and Arthur and I both found something that was missing in our lives."

"Were you here when Benjamin came?"

"Yes." Krystal seemed to anticipate Ilsa's next question. "He didn't take it well. He and Arthur had a long talk, after which Benjamin decided to go to Aril."

"He keeps a lot inside him," Ilsa said.

"Much like his father." Krystal finished replacing a panel that concealed an array of circuit boards after diligently checking each one with a wireless circuit probe. "Arthur wouldn't say it, but he was very glad you decided to travel to Aril to meet Benjamin. There's an emptiness in Benjamin that you can fill."

Ilsa smiled. "I certainly understand emptiness," she said.

After a few fitful hours of sleep, Ilsa found herself again preparing to be inserted into the magnetocryogenic chamber that had been her home for all but a tiny fraction of the last 50000 years. She waited nervously for the loud bang of the electromagnets, wondering what she'd find the next time she regained consciousness.

CHAPTER 33
— 57215 —

Risto Jalonen underwent an automatic unfreezing process after his vehicle received a high priority message from Arthur Mizello. Had he known what Mizello's reaction would be to his message inquiring about the orders he received from Harding, Risto may have reconsidered sending it. Now Mizello was requesting Risto's aid in preventing Harding and his ally Charles Stormer from undertaking their attack on a mystery planet called Aril. From the message, Risto learned that Harding had omitted a couple of hundred explorers because they could not be trusted to aid him, and now Arthur Mizello was soliciting help from those left out of Harding's plans. More disturbingly, Arthur had told these men that Risto would coordinate their actions upon reaching Aril. The idea of commanding two hundred galactic explorers was scary enough for Risto, who had successfully avoided all positions of responsibility thus far in his life, but to lead them against a thousand others in the explorer fleet was entirely outside his comfort zone. He knew nothing about Harding's plans or how and why he could or should prevent their execution. For all he knew, Mizello had gone crazy from the isolation of being a supply ship custodian and had made up the entire threat as a means to discredit Harding.

Risto had been disturbed after speaking to Ilsa Montgomery. He didn't think of himself as a good man. His vices on Earth stemmed from the excessive time he spent drinking in bars. Had it not been for the Union, he would have self-destructed at an early age, or found himself in a foreign jail. Still, he understood there was a difference between his transgressions and the evil that Ilsa Montgomery had described. He was comfortable with the idea that humans were imperfect, but he had little tolerance for the type of malevolence that impels one person to deceive and prey upon others. The light Ms. Montgomery shed on Dr. Harding's character caused Risto to feel doubly offended: he himself had nearly been drawn into Harding's deception. The more he pondered the situation, the more uneasy he felt. He supposed that if forced to lead a small group of explorers in an effort to prevent Harding from taking over a defenseless planet, he would know what to do.

Risto was still 7000 years from Aril. He returned to his magnetocryogenic chamber, planning to reassess the situation upon his arrival at the endangered planet.

Chapter 34

— 58004 —

Arthur and Krystal were unfrozen by a priority communication. Krystal reached the supply ship first and was already in the control room looking triumphantly at the message displayed on the monitor.

"What's going on?" Arthur asked, taking his usual seat next to her.

"It's a message from Earth. They've launched a fleet of three hundred vehicles to help Aril."

Arthur read the message. "I honestly believed it would never happen. I'm amazed."

"It was a gamble and it paid off," Krystal replied.

"Hang on," said Arthur, still peering at the screen. "Look at the date of the message — 52653. They won't get there in time."

"Read the rest," Krystal responded. "They expect to be at Aril around 64500."

"That's impossible," said Arthur. "They can't travel that fast."

"Arthur, it's been more than 50000 years since we left Earth. Don't you think improvements in space technology have taken place over that much time?"

"Then that's even better news. They may not have any trouble dealing with Stormer and Harding."

"Let me show you a display I created," said Krystal. She replaced the message on the monitor with a picture of the galaxy from above. Colored symbols appeared among the stars. She zoomed in to the sector of the galaxy occupied by the Union's fleet of explorers.

"The red symbols represent Harding's galactic explorers heading toward Aril. The yellow symbols are where I believe Stormer's army is located. The blue symbols show where the Earth fleet is. I also included two star-shaped symbols showing where Benjamin and Ilsa are. That's the situation at the present time. I'll start an animation that shows the motion of all the vehicles in the future."

Arthur watched as the symbols moved toward Aril, converging at the planet at different times — first Stormer and Harding with the supply ship and their fleet of 750 space vehicles, then the symbols representing the galactic explorers, followed by Benjamin and the fleet from Earth, and finally the two hundred galactic explorer vehicles dispatched by Arthur and Krystal.

"All will reach Aril early in the 65th millennium. What does this remind you of?" Krystal asked and repeated the animation.

"Beats me," said Arthur, perplexed.

"Use your imagination."

Arthur watched the movie repeat. "It looks like an invasion. But that's because I know it's an invasion."

"It's an invasion, and the response to the invasion."

"True," said Arthur with exasperation. "What's your point?"

Krystal made the image pan out again to include the entire galaxy. The colored symbols remained, but now clustered in one part of the image. "Imagine the galaxy is an organism — a huge spiral shaped life form. Then imagine that Harding and Stormer represent some malicious parasite or infection attacking part of the organism. The organism's response is to launch a defense represented by Benjamin, the two hundred explorers, and the Earth fleet. Doesn't it remind you of biology class and the animations of how the human body releases white blood cells at the site of an infection to destroy the intruding cells?"

"I should have known," said Arthur.

"Yes, you should have," said Krystal, derisively. "Because of the system the Union established, we're able to initiate a collective response, just as living things do."

"Cute," said Arthur. Krystal animated the display again. "Uh oh, there's more, right?" Arthur asked.

Krystal nodded with an amused expression on her face. "In human anatomy, the brain receives messages from different parts of the body and then tells the body how to respond. Like it or not, Arthur, this supply ship has become the brain of the organism you're looking at on the screen."

"I don't like it," responded Arthur."

"Well, too bad, because you've got the job."

Arthur continued to stare blankly at the screen. "So where's the heart and soul of your organism?"

"There's no heart in the literal sense, but I believe it has a soul. Life and being are inseparable, regardless of form. The brain and body are inextricably linked, part of an integral whole that defines the way in which the world is perceived. It requires every part functioning together to be the unique individual that defines the being and its soul."

"So you believe our little supply ship is part of the galaxy's soul?"

"Not the whole galaxy yet. Just the part spanned by the Union network. The soul resides in all the individual living beings that comprise it. You and I and this supply ship, represent the conscience of the organism because we've made decisions based on our concept of right and wrong. We're the ones who orchestrated the response to the threat based on our notions of good and evil.

"Tens of thousands of years in the future, the entire galaxy, and eventually the known universe, will also have a unique soul, made up of all the beings linked together by virtue of having the same origin and through the tenuous communication network that binds them. The network gives the universe life and a unique soul."

"Be careful," Arthur said. "You're entering the domain of God."

Krystal thought for a while before she answered. "At the point when there's a centralized command post that senses everything and is able to control what happens in the universe, to the extent possible by physical laws, then it does assume God-like properties. By the same analogy, the brain is God for each person. If we were individual cells in the human body, would we not worship the brain because of its ability to know and control what happens next? Thanks to the Union, there is a God in this sector of the galaxy, and, like it or not, Arthur, it's us."

Chapter 35

— 64000 - 65000 —

The orange star around which Aril orbited was young, slightly smaller than the Sun and with a lower surface temperature. The resulting difference in the rate at which it burned hydrogen fuel in its core meant that its lifespan would be twice that of the Sun. Aril's star was still surrounded by remnants of the cloud of debris from which it had formed. The Captain and his fellow colonists had made extensive use of their anti-impact weaponry to prevent destruction by collisions with ambient particles.

Harding, Stormer, and Stormer's army traveled together, escorting the supply ship. Upon nearing Aril, they inserted their vehicles in an orbit about the planet sufficiently far as to be undetectable by any ground-based observing systems. The debris-filled space environment about Aril would have made it difficult for Arilian observers to distinguish the spacecraft from surrounding objects in any case. From their orbits, they could reach Aril in just a few days. On firing their retrorockets they'd fall rapidly inward under the influence of Aril's gravitational field.

By 64000, more than eight hundred explorer vehicles had arrived. Harding ordered them to remain in a more distant orbit where the abundance of small planetoids and asteroids was even greater. Harding also advised the explorers to turn off the beacons that routinely transmitted the position of their vehicles to other Union spacecraft in the vicinity.

Harding and Stormer unfroze themselves every hundred years to check the status of the force using the supply ship's long range radar. The Union vehicles had a unique radar signature that enabled them to be distinguished from the surrounding objects. During one status check, Harding was surprised by a message from a Union explorer named Steven Nutley, who claimed to have with him Supply Ship 3. Harding had kept the supply ship custodians ignorant of the invasion plan as they would have questioned his message asserting that the Union mission had been aborted.

Although puzzled by the arrival of another supply ship, Harding realized that two ships would enhance the threat to Aril. He responded to the message ordering Nutley to depart from the orbit he shared with the gathering fleet of explorers and continue to Aril. Ten days later, when Nutley arrived, Harding instructed him to bring the ship into the same orbit as his supply ship occupied, but at the opposite side of the planet. Then Harding told Stormer to take several of his men and board the other supply ship to ensure Nutley could be trusted. Stormer unfroze two of his men to accompany him.

Nutley was waiting for his visitors in the entry room at the foot of the access ladder. He looked surprised to see two of the men carrying weapons and none wearing official Union uniforms. Nonetheless, he invited the men to the galley where he related the story of how he gained possession of the supply ship.

All the while Nutley spoke, Stormer eyed him carefully. Stormer found him to be a gullible man with unquestioning trust in Harding. It was easy for Stormer to convince him that Harding was rescuing a planet settled by colonists from Earth who had split into warring factions that threatened the survival of everyone. So willing was Nutley to help that Stormer decided to leave him in charge of the supply ship rather than replace him with one of his own men. Supply ships were extremely complex systems and it was important that someone be on board who could make use of those capabilities if they were needed. Stormer left one of his men with Nutley to assist and take control of the ship if Nutley proved undependable.

When Benjamin awoke in his magnetocryogenic chamber, an array of red lights told him there was an imminent threat to his vehicle. He propelled himself out of his cylinder and bounced painfully against the hull as he fought to gain control of his body twisting in the weightlessness of the capsule. He reached the command console and managed to strap himself into the chair. He brought up the radar display to search for nearby objects. There was a single blip on the screen less than 3 km away. The distance did not change with each radar scan, and Benjamin surmised the object was traveling with him at the same speed. That the object had gotten so near without being detected earlier puzzled him. He guessed it was fairly small. It lacked the characteristic radar signature of a Union vehicle. Benjamin scanned the radio frequencies and locked on a signal at a Union band. The message was transmitted in the official Union language:

> "This is Earth Fleet Command. Request you follow
> instructions below to dock with Earth command ship.
> Your father sends his greetings."

Benjamin breathed out rapidly and smiled. He replied in acknowledgment, but was confused because the instructions were identical to the process for docking with a supply ship. He found it hard to believe that the small object in his radar display could be that large. He was surprised when the image from his capsule's telescope confirmed its true dimensions. Mystified by his radar's inability to detect the object sooner, he made the necessary preparations for docking with the ship from Earth.

Two hours later, he entered a large spacecraft, constructed very much like a Union supply ship, but with noticeable differences. He was greeted by a tall man in a blue jumpsuit who guided him to the artificial gravity portion of the ship. Benjamin found himself with a group of men and women dressed in the same sapphire garments as the man who had met him. On each of the uniforms, above the right breast pocket, was a vivid decal displaying planet Earth, very much as Benjamin remembered it from long ago. However, the appearance of the men and women about him was unlike anything he recalled from Earth. They were uniformly tall, male and female alike, with thick dark hair and skin the color of mocha. Their postures were somewhat stooped, as if they'd grown used to looking down on others, and the bone structure of their faces was unusual, almost disorienting to Benjamin. Though he understood intellectually that these beings were from Earth, he saw them as aliens. Perhaps the most disorienting aspect of their features were the iridescent amber eyes that seemed to glow from under the shadows of well-formed brows. Benjamin remembered the people he'd met on the planet with the dying sun. They'd evolved far faster than could be expected by random mutation and natural selection. They'd most likely been transformed by environmental stresses that activated genes to help the species adapt more quickly than could be explained by slow, random evolutionary processes. Benjamin wondered what had produced these beings, whose eyes were like those of a tiger, skin was almost leather, and posture and gait reminiscent of a giraffe on two legs. The overall effect was extremely intimidating, and Benjamin found himself humble and submissive in their presence.

They led him to the briefing room and introduced him to the commander of the Earth fleet, Admiral Julian Chase. Their Union English was heavily accented and they struggled with many words. After 60000 years, English was obsolete. These travelers from Earth had probably learned just enough of the language to be able to communicate.

Admiral Chase explained that they were sent to defend Aril from invasion by a force of galactic explorer vehicles led by Andrew Harding. He told Benjamin how the vehicles from Earth had been designed after the galactic explorer vehicles using tiny specialized chemical robots. Benjamin listened, fascinated by the way the vehicles had been manufactured, and marveling at the technology that made such a feat possible.

Admiral Chase was a methodical and meticulous man. Having never experienced any sort of combat, particularly in space, he'd spent many years studying historical accounts of wars throughout Earth's history. Unaware of the nature of the threat they faced, he had no idea which wars would be similar to the impending conflict, and he knew nothing about the battlefield on which the war would be fought. He hoped to learn something from Benjamin to help him prepare.

Unfortunately, Benjamin only knew what he'd learned in his Union training courses, which Admiral Chase had also studied. Nevertheless, Benjamin talked with him and his crew for many hours, exchanging information about what each knew, and in the end, the commander seemed satisfied. He invited Benjamin to accompany the fleet, providing advice and aid as needed. Benjamin agreed, but insisted on traveling in his own vehicle. Admiral Chase looked disturbed and explained that the vehicles from Earth traveled twenty-five percent faster than the Union vehicles because they were made from a lighter, non-metallic composite material. This also explained why the spacecraft from Earth created a minimal radar echo, allowing them to approach much closer to Union spacecraft before detection. Not caring to arrive at Aril hundreds of years after Admiral Chase's fleet, Benjamin agreed to remain on the command ship, frozen in one of the on-board magnetocryogenic chambers.

Nearing Aril, Risto Jalonen was unfrozen by the same high-priority message from Harding that the other explorers received, advising him to remain in a distant orbit, disable the on-board beacon routinely broadcasting the vehicle's location, and await further instructions. Risto was little disposed to follow Harding's orders. He was curious about the status of the two hundred galactic explorers Arthur Mizello had sent to Aril to intervene, as the planet was now only a fraction of a light year away. Having been given no specific direction on where exactly to wait, they were scattered in different orbits. They'd all made independent decisions based on their own judgments of the amount of thermal radiation they could endure near Aril's sun, as well as on the density of particles in the surrounding planetary environment. Through the years, other planets circling Aril's sun had scooped up great quantities of debris through gravitational attraction. Many of the explorers were congregated in the relatively empty doughnut-shaped rings through which these planets moved. As instructed by Arthur Mizello, the explorers had sent messages to Risto advising him of the orbit they occupied. Risto's radio receiver also picked up messages to him from Aril, because they had been advised by Mizello that he was an ally who could be trusted. The Arilians were hopefully awaiting a rescue fleet from Earth.

Risto did not have the patience to untangle the babble of

messages to determine what his strategy should be, and he was in no state of mind to command the explorers sent by Mizello. Instead, he programmed his vehicle to follow Harding's supply ship. Risto's radar confirmed that Harding and Stormer's fleet of 750 vehicles had begun their gradual spiral inward to Aril. It was a fairly easy task for Risto to follow this fleet on its approach to the planet, as the radio transmissions between those vehicles gave him all the information he needed. He programmed his navigation system to track their course and prepared to freeze himself so as not to use valuable food and oxygen during the intervening time.

Harding, Stormer, and their fleet occupied an orbit similar to those of geosynchronous weather satellites on Earth. The vehicles moved about Aril at the same rate as the planet spun on its axis such that they remained above a fixed location on the globe. Harding's supply ship remained over the site he and Stormer had selected for landing. This would allow them to communicate with each other continuously once Stormer was on the surface. The other vehicles were distributed in orbits selected to be as inconspicuous as possible. They would not remain in orbit long, because they'd soon be descending to the planet. Only the three hundred women would remain frozen in orbit until the occupation of Aril was completed. Before the descent, Harding and Stormer met on the supply ship to finalize their strategy, but on entering the control room they were alerted to a high priority message from the Arilians. It said,

> "Welcome to Aril. Please identify yourselves and state the purpose of your visit to our planet. Landing instructions will follow."

Seeing no reason to delay the invasion any longer, Harding sent a message back requesting approval for four members of his party to land. He received an immediate reply granting permission. Then he told Stormer to select three men from his paramilitary force and prepare for landing on Aril.

After the four men had landed, they were greeted by a wary

and concerned group of Arilian officials, who nonetheless maintained a façade of civility and politeness. Stormer and his men remained on Aril for several days enjoying Arilian hospitality. On the fourth day of their visit, Stormer broke the news that a large fleet of colonists from Earth would be landing on the planet and would need food and shelter while establishing a new settlement. When the Arilians expressed reluctance to allow this intrusion, Stormer lost no time presenting them with an ultimatum backed by the threat of nuclear attack from two Union supply ships currently in orbit. Practical as Arilians were, and largely unfamiliar with the concept of invasion, they agreed to Stormer's demands without hesitation. Indeed, many Arilians were curious about the ancient Earthlings, who now wanted to live among them. Hospitality had been at the core of the Arilian value system since the beginning, even though the ancient prophecy of Captain Warner had always been surrounded by a veil of doom and foreboding.

A few days later, Arilians stood on hillsides to witness the arrival of Stormer's fleet. Underestimating the impact the landings would have, they had offered a large tract of prime farmland as the landing site. At first, the on-lookers were awed by the miracle of seeing the scores of spacecraft descending from the sky. However, as they burned large scorches in the lush farmland, the spectacle soon became unbearable, and Arilians gathered their families to return home. Many hours later, four hundred vehicles littered the land and nothing was left of the crops that had been growing so vigorously before. Stormer assembled his men and released them with instructions to infiltrate the surrounding towns to ensure there would be no Arilian resistance to their eventual take-over. He himself took four men and headed for a nearby farmhouse where he could set up a command headquarters.

It did not take the fleet from Earth long to locate the two supply ships and the three hundred smaller vehicles circling Aril in synchronized orbits. Benjamin and the commander were surprised to see two supply ships. They had been relying on information from Benjamin's father, relayed from a galactic explorer involved in a rescue mission of a wayward vehicle. The presence of two supply ships was disconcerting because now they had to imagine what other errors and omissions the information was suffering from. It was also troubling that they could find no evidence for the presence of the 800 galactic explorers Harding had diverted to Aril. Admiral Chase had used his ship's surveillance systems and had sent out members of his fleet to search, but the spacecraft could not be found. Either they had not yet arrived, or they were waiting someplace sufficiently far from Aril to be undetectable. Even more alarming was the possibility that they'd already landed on Aril. The uncertainty about the progress of the invasion made it difficult for Admiral Chase to develop a strategy to intervene.

When they were close enough to Aril for radio contact, they began receiving urgent messages from the planet, broadcast in Union English. Benjamin and Admiral Chase were alarmed to learn Charles Stormer had landed with 400 heavily armed men and taken over several Arilian farming villages. They responded to the messages from the planet, announcing their arrival and requesting regular status updates. As for trying to find Harding's force of galactic explorers, they began to develop a plan they hoped would trick Harding into revealing where they were.

As Risto Jalonen approached Aril, his radar detected two Union supply ships orbiting the planet. By monitoring radio transmissions, Risto learned that Stormer and his small army had already landed on Aril and were firmly entrenched in several Arilian towns. He knew also that Harding still occupied one of the supply ships to maintain the nuclear threat over the planet. Jalonen was curious about Steven Nutley, a fellow explorer and now the custodian of a Union supply ship, which was orbiting Aril diametrically opposite Harding's ship.

Risto navigated his vehicle to approach Nutley's ship and radioed a message identifying himself as a galactic explorer and requesting permission to board. Nutley must have been surprised and confused by the message, as several minutes of silence ensued. Finally, Nutley sent a response giving Risto clearance to dock.

After boarding, Risto followed Nutley to the galley where he was surprised to see a man in a non-Union uniform carrying an EMP weapon pointed squarely at him. Risto wondered how long he had before they realized he was not an ally. He suspected the man with the weapon would wait only briefly before becoming suspicious and then immobilize or kill him.

Risto announced that he had something important to show them, but needed access to the ship's computer. The three men moved to the control room, where Risto took a seat at the console. With several key strokes, all the lights in the small room went out and Risto charged across the room throwing his full body weight against the man holding the weapon. Globes of blue iridescent light ricocheted at blinding speed off the hull as the man fired wildly in panic. The stocky Finn was used to fighting in seaport bars and easily overpowered Nutley — smelling strongly of rum — and the armed man, who seemed to have little experience in hand to hand combat. Risto wrested the EMP weapon from him and shouted a command making the lights come back on. He fired the weapon twice without hesitation and the two men fell into a silent paralyzed repose. Within five minutes of entering the supply ship, Risto had gained control of the vehicle. He sat before the console and prepared to monitor the activities taking place on and around Aril.

Using the ship's more powerful radar and communication systems, he displayed the space around Aril. Like Harding's ship, the radar system could detect and uniquely identify the 800 Union vehicles in Harding's force in their distant orbit. He added their locations to the display, using a special symbol. Risto then confirmed the presence of the Earth fleet from radio transmissions in a language he could not understand. However, much as he tried, he was unable to locate any radar echoes, except from the ship that was in direct communication with Aril. It seemed to be a spacecraft somewhat smaller than a supply ship. The transmissions though suggested there were many more vehicles than his radar could detect. It was possible the Earth vehicles were dispersed among the thousands of other objects in the vicinity so as to be as inconspicuous as possible. He considered sending a message to the vehicle from Earth, but was reluctant to broadcast the fact that he had taken over the second Union supply ship, fearing that Harding would intercept the transmission. Taken together, the display gave Risto little information upon which to act. He decided to hold his position until it was clear how to proceed.

Andrew Harding, alone on his supply ship, also monitored events on and about Aril. He was in constant communication with Stormer, who reported that Arilians were being cooperative, if not overly welcoming. Stormer was still working to identify a suitable region of Aril they could occupy and defend. Overall, Harding was pleased that everything seemed to be going according to plan. Stormer and his men were firmly entrenched among the Arilians, who would not interfere because of the nuclear threat from the two supply ships about the planet. The Union fleet was in a distant orbit, ready to aid in the invasion of Aril if necessary. If they were not needed, Harding would unfreeze them later and give them the option to join them on Aril or resume their futile exploration of the galaxy. Finally, the three hundred women brought from Earth by Stormer were still safely frozen, sharing the orbit with the two supply ships. When the time was right, Harding would send a command unfreezing them and giving them instructions on how to prepare for entry into Aril's atmosphere. The arrival of the women on Aril would be the culmination of a grand plan for starting a new society that Harding and Stormer had conceived of more than 60000 years earlier.

CHAPTER 36

— 65000 —

Stormer also was satisfied with the progress his paramilitary force made in the three weeks since landing on Aril. He firmly held the three main towns in the vicinity of the landing site. Because Arilians had no weapons, it had been easy for his men to take over the primary transportation, communication, and power systems. Their only means of defense was to badger Stormer with questions about what they were doing and why. Arilians wanted rational explanations, but the events transpiring in the three towns defied their understanding of expected behavior. Why a group of individuals would want to assume control over a town was inexplicable to them. The townspeople initially appealed for help from nearby cities, but Stormer's men quickly quelled those communications.

Very soon after Stormer and his men landed, the Arilians removed all the women and children from the three towns, sending them to friends and relatives in outlying areas. The invading party was outraged and continually harassed the Arilians who remained behind. After several days, even they began to move away. Packing as many belongings as they could carry, they left the towns by foot, by bicycle, and in the few electric cars they could steal from Stormer's men. Before long, the invading force inhabited most of the homes in the towns, and the days and evenings were filled with the wild revelry of victory celebrations. Stormer knew the men were growing impatient for the arrival of the women and he decided to give the go-ahead to Harding. His only remaining concern was taking measures to prevent an attack from Arilians, if they ever generated the resolve to launch one. He posted guards at the roads leading into the populated areas, but with all the celebrating the sentinels could not be trusted. Still, he reasoned that once the women arrived, it would be easier to organize the men for a better defense.

Harding received the news from Stormer with ever increasing satisfaction. He was getting ready to unfreeze the women when red alarm lights lit up his console indicating the ship's radar had picked up an unexpected echo. It often detected small meteoroids and asteroids in Aril's crowded space environment. Typically, they crossed the path of his ship harmlessly, disappearing from view in a matter of minutes. But this time the radar showed an object approaching slowly from behind, at a speed eerily matched to his. The object closed the distance to his ship at a steady rate. Harding armed the ship's EMP weapon, but before he had a chance to fire, a light on the radio receiver glowed red, indicating an incoming message. Harding displayed it:

> "This is Earth Fleet Command requesting permission to board your ship."

Momentarily shocked into immobility, Harding read the message again. He could not believe the approaching vehicle was from Earth, nor could he imagine the single small object being any kind of fleet command. He thought about firing his plasma weapon at the ship, but held off. He entered commands to direct the ship's external telescope at the object. Seconds later, an image appeared revealing an object similar in size and shape to a Union supply ship. The size of the spacecraft was incompatible with the weakness of the radar echo. The ship should have been detected at a distance of several million kilometers. This spacecraft was only a few kilometers away.

Harding armed his plasma weapon, then entered a reply:

> "Permission denied. Withdraw immediately or defensive actions will be taken."

He received no reply. The vehicle continued to approach. Harding sent another message:

> "This is a Union supply ship under the command of Dr. Andrew Harding. Cease your approach immediately."

Still no answer. The spacecraft closed the remaining distance to his ship. In desperation, Harding typed another message

> "Nuclear weapons are armed and ready for firing, targeted for the largest cities on Aril, and will be launched in one minute unless you cease your approach and withdraw."

Harding stared at the display, trying to discern any change. After several moments, the vehicle stopped and then noticeably withdrew, its radar echo diminishing. Harding sighed with relief, though he knew he'd only delayed the threat. He transmitted a message to Nutley in Supply Ship 3 at a secure Union frequency.

> "Hostile ship in my vicinity. Locate, pursue, and attack with all available weaponry."

Nutley was close enough to receive Harding's message instantaneously, but it would take the ship several days to move to Harding's vicinity. The maneuver required accelerating into a higher orbit and then decelerating back into the orbit of Harding's ship at just the right moment. The reply from Nutley came in one word: "Acknowledged."

Harding had bought time with the threat of nuclear attack on Aril and soon Nutley would arrive and tilt the scales in their favor. He wondered why the ship from Earth had shown up. Was it possible these Earth vehicles were protecting Aril? Had there been some treaty between the two planets? If that was the case, why hadn't he heard about it? It was also possible that Earth had somehow learned of his plans and sent a fleet to Aril to intercede on Aril's behalf. But how could they have obtained that information? It must have been many thousands of years earlier, unless the Earth fleet was already in space somewhere and had intercepted his communications. And where was the Earth fleet and how large a force was it? Had the commander from Earth been bluffing, or perhaps he had just made a mistake in using the Union language that was unfamiliar to him?

Harding could not take a chance that the Earth commander's statement had been an error. He had to act on the assumption there were other ships from Earth in the vicinity as part of an opposition force. He composed a message to summon the Union explorers in their distant orbit about Aril's star. Within a few weeks, the 800-strong Union fleet would be at Aril to help out, but he needed to ensure there was no interference from the Earth vessel until then.

As he puzzled over the problem, he remembered the Arilians had a constellation of communication satellites in orbit around the planet to relay transmissions from one location on the planet to another. Although Stormer and his men had taken control of the communication systems within the towns they were occupying, the satellites made it possible for individual Arilians to transmit information to others on the planet who would then keep the fleet from Earth advised. Harding cursed himself for not remembering that the first rule of conquest is to cripple the enemy's command and control systems. He first considered destroying the communication satellites one by one using his EMP weapon, but then he conceived a more elegant solution that would serve two purposes. A well placed nuclear detonation in Aril's atmosphere would create a region of damaging high energy radiation through which all the satellites would eventually pass, resulting in the destruction of all their electronic circuitry. At the same time, the detonation of a nuclear weapon would be a striking display of the devastating power of the device. Harding armed one and calculated the appropriate trajectory and blast point for the device. Then he sent a message to Stormer telling him what he was about to do. He advised his ally to maintain control of the Arilian towns and hold any remaining Arilians hostage. Eventually, the intruders from Earth would lose contact with the planet and be forced to take actions based on ignorance instead of intelligence. By that time, the remaining explorer fleet would be approaching. He doubted the Earth fleet would maintain its resolve in the presence of that force.

The detonation of a nuclear weapon in Aril's atmosphere produced panic among the entire population. It occurred on the daylight side of the planet, but its effects were observed globally. Arilians looked up at the expanding circle of light, whose size and intensity increased until it was brighter than their sun. Many were temporarily blinded by the flash, having been transfixed into staring at it too long. The shock wave produced blasts of superheated air over the surface below. Arilians were familiar with nuclear power through their study of Earth history, but none could imagine the awesome intensity of the explosion. Although the detonation was high enough in the atmosphere that it injured no one and did little damage to infrastructure, it drove home the imminent threat from the invaders above them. Awoken from their complacency by the event, Arilians attempted to communicate among themselves, but it was no longer possible because of the loss of their space-based systems.

Wearing dark glasses, Stormer watched the detonation uneasily. He was disturbed that Harding had to resort to using a nuclear weapon so soon. Harding's trigger-happy approach would raise the stakes and make Stormer and his men more vulnerable to reprisal attacks. Like Harding, he was puzzled by the unexpected arrival of the ship from Earth. It was a rude awakening. He was becoming increasingly lulled by the comfort and ease of life on Aril. He was impressed by the prosperity and health of the Arilian people, as well as the natural beauty of the planet. It was ideal for their purposes. Elegantly manicured trees and flowers were everywhere and the air was clean and crisp. There was no shortage of food or water, and the Arilians for the most part were very accommodating. The only adversity was the disappearance of all the women and children from the towns surrounding the landing site. When questioned, the Arilians freely admitted they had been moved to the nearest city because of their fear of the invaders. It was an understandable reaction his men could only grumble about. They saw it as a temporary delay in enjoying the spoils of war. But that was not the worst of their experience. One day, they all suffered from severe intestinal cramps, probably from eating too much of the unfamiliar Arilian food. They spent most of the evening becoming adept at the functionality of the planet-friendly Arilian toilets.

Now the smooth and uncomplicated takeover of Aril was muddled by the arrival of a fleet from Earth and the explosion of a nuclear weapon in Aril's atmosphere. Given the situation, Stormer took Harding's suggestion and commanded his men to capture as many Arilian hostages as possible.

When Risto heard that Harding had exploded a nuclear weapon in Aril's atmosphere and summoned the Union force for aid, he realized he could no longer delay action. He'd received and acknowledged the order from Harding commanding him to confront and destroy an unidentified threat, but he hadn't moved the supply ship. He was reluctant to take tactical measures, especially since he had little resources other than the two hundred Union explorers scattered in random orbits about Aril. Risto wondered what the Earth fleet had done to provoke Harding's use of a nuclear weapon. He did not want to make the same mistake by acting too hastily.

Risto knew at some point he'd have to engage the explorers Arthur Mizello entrusted him with. That enormous responsibility was a burden to him. The Union had not prepared him to command one group of explorers to attack another, and the spacecraft were not designed for battle in space. They were only ponderously maneuverable because their rockets were designed for low thrust over long periods of time. The weapons were specifically engineered for firing at objects directly in front to avoid potential collisions. They had no capability to fire at threats approaching from the side or behind. If those handicaps were not limiting enough, they only had sufficient oxygen to last at most ten days. If combat lasted longer, which was likely given the time and distances in space, then all the participants in the conflict would die of asphyxiation before any victory. It would be like a battle at sea involving armadas of sinking ships. All were doomed regardless of how skillfully and valiantly they fought.

While he pondered the problem, he brought up a display of

the anticipated trajectory of the explorer vehicles Harding had summoned. Each spacecraft would follow a loose spiral bringing it gradually closer to Aril's orbit to ensure its capture by the planet's gravitational field. While approaching, the explorers occupying the spacecraft would remain frozen to conserve oxygen. That would be the time they'd be most vulnerable to attack. If they were approached from a direction perpendicular to their course, their vehicles' collision avoidance systems would not activate. The occupants of the vehicles would not be automatically unfrozen if there was a threat that could be handled automatically. On the other hand, the attacking spacecraft approaching from the side would see the vehicle crossing its path as a hazard to be neutralized. For an object the size of a galactic space vehicle, all destructive weapons would be used: laser, plasma, EMP, and ballistic. The combination would destroy the craft and kill the explorer inside. Risto could not accept the slaughter of a fellow explorer helplessly frozen, regardless of what was at stake. Of course, if the explorer in the attacking vehicle was awake, then the automated defense system could be disabled. By using only the EMP weapon, the target vehicle would be disabled while leaving the occupant unharmed, just as had happened to Ilsa Montgomery.

To implement this plan, the 200 attacking explorers would have to be unfrozen so they could pilot their vehicles manually. If planned properly, explorers could be unfrozen in a carefully calculated sequence. Each could execute attacks on Harding's force, disable as many of those vehicles as possible, and then end up at Risto's supply ship for replenishment of oxygen. It was an incredibly complex logistics problem that could be worked out with the information Risto had about the orbital motion of the attacking and target vehicles.

Without delay, Risto devised an attack sequence that took into account the trajectory of the vehicles in Harding's fleet, the orbits of the 200 explorers sent by Arthur Mizello, and the remaining oxygen supply of each. He had to ensure all could complete their missions and get to Supply Ship 2 with oxygen to spare. At one time, such a programming task would have taken months to complete, but the advanced computer on the supply ship was able to interpret and carry out semantic commands and construct customized software. Risto only had to tell the computer what he wanted. When the program was complete, he executed a simulated run to validate the expected outcome.

After that, he wrote instructions to all 200 vehicles, making sure the explorers were aware of the attack and withdrawal sequence. More importantly, they had to be convinced the mission they were given was both sound and justified. For that, Risto documented the entire history of the invasion of Aril, beginning with Ilsa Montgomery's investigation of New Life on Earth and culminating with the occupation of Aril by Charles Stormer and his paramilitary force. The supply ship's computer held the supporting documentation the explorers would want to review before adhering to Risto's directives. By the time he appended these documents, his message was so long it would take several minutes to transmit, and with 200 to send, Risto lost no time initiating the communications. He would have to remain alert for the inevitable questions the galactic explorers would ask. He had not slept for the last twenty hours. He went to the galley and made some coffee, wishing he could have a beer instead. Much as he wanted to participate in the attack, Risto knew he had to remain on the supply ship. He regretted he would only be a spectator once the explorers engaged Harding's fleet.

Benjamin and Admiral Chase were shocked when they learned of the nuclear detonation. At first they experienced a moment of dread, believing the weapon struck the planet's surface, but subsequent observations made it obvious what Harding's intent had been. Aril's global communication system had been disrupted after the explosion. With no further information from the villages occupied by Stormer, all the Arilians could do was transmit messages repeating the account of everything that had occurred after the invasion began. Included in the transmissions was a copy of the original message received from Arthur Mizello on Supply

Ship 6 containing more detailed information on the planned invasion. Admiral Chase summoned Benjamin, along with other crew members, to meet in the briefing room. They'd hoped that by making their presence known, they'd force Harding into calling in the galactic explorers, but none of those vehicles had appeared. They questioned the veracity of Arthur Mizello's report on the diversion of the fleet.

Benjamin and Admiral Chase again mulled over their options. They knew that a direct assault on Harding might force him to launch more nuclear weapons. Although the Earth command ship might disable one or two of those weapons after they were launched, several would make it to the surface and result in millions of deaths.

Benjamin was concerned about the growing violence displayed by Stormer's men toward the Arilians. He urged the Earth fleet to land on the planet and overcome Stormer's force in a surprise attack. Admiral Chase believed Harding would detect the entry of the vehicles into Aril's atmosphere and resort to his nuclear arsenal. Benjamin assured him that the low radar cross section of the Earth vehicles would make it less likely they would be seen landing. The Admiral reminded him that the entry of so many vehicles into Aril's atmosphere would produce a visual signature that made radar detection unnecessary. They could not agree on a sound plan, and the Earth commander suggested they wait for one more Arilian day.

Before he retired to his sleeping quarters, Benjamin asked for an electronic version of the message recently received from Aril. He wanted to re-read the message from his father, which the Arilians had forwarded to the Earth fleet. Since the message had probably been crafted by Krystal, he knew it would be exhaustively detailed and thorough.

Benjamin lay in bed reading the message on the monitor, struggling to remain awake at the hypnotic scrolling of the text. He'd almost dozed off, when a stream of characters made him sit up. He blinked to clear his vision, but the text had scrolled off the screen. A verbal command backed up the text and he read through it carefully. His heart leaped when he saw the name Ilsa Montgomery in the message. Not believing what he'd seen, he backed up the text again and read through it one more time. The information about the invasion of Aril had been provided by a Union explorer named Risto Jalonen, who had rescued an errant space vehicle carrying a passenger named Ilsa Montgomery. He repaired her spacecraft, put her back on the vehicle, and set her on a course to Supply Ship 6. Ilsa Montgomery had shown up on Arthur Mizello's supply ship sixteen thousand years later and given a full account of everything that had happened to her. Fueled by this astonishing information, Benjamin spent the next several hours reading Krystal's transcription of Ilsa's story. The complete message ended with the statement that Ilsa was on her way to Aril in the hope that Benjamin would be there.

Benjamin's heart was throbbing in a way he hadn't experienced since he was a teenager. In the time since he last saw Ilsa, she had been in his thoughts and dreams continuously. He knew enough about her to easily conceive of the fulfillment he might have found with her had he remained on Earth. That she had decided on her own to travel across thousands of light-years in the hope of meeting him was the ultimate statement of love. Suddenly his life, the meaning of which he'd increasingly questioned, had new purpose. He should have been thinking of ways to save Aril, but it was impossible to keep from thinking of Ilsa. Fleetingly, he considered leaving Aril to rendezvous with her to pick up their courtship where they'd left off, but he knew Ilsa would be extremely disappointed with him, especially given the horror she was subjected to at the hands of Stormer and Harding.

Rereading the message, he confirmed that Ilsa was still about seven thousand years from Aril. If he could find a way to end the conquest of the planet, he'd still have plenty of time to return to space to intercept her before her arrival. He could not, of course, wait for her on Aril, as he would age and be dead before she reached the planet. All possibilities cycled through his mind as he sat on the edge of his bed completely unable to sleep now. There was still a part of the message he wanted to review again. It was

Ilsa's description of her visit to the New Life compound in the desert. Her instincts about Stormer had been correct, but she had not realized that Stormer was planning to extend his human trafficking network into space. Having stumbled across that knowledge, Stormer kidnapped her and brought her along with the rest of the women he had coerced and misled into joining his group. Benjamin read the message repeatedly, almost as if by doing so he could bring Ilsa closer to him. Eventually, he nodded off in a fitful sleep punctuated by bizarre dreams that made little sense and left him feeling restless and unsettled.

CHAPTER 37
— 65000 —

While taking care of galactic explorers arriving to refuel and replenish oxygen, Risto followed the battle between the two groups of explorers — if battle is what it could be called, because those in Harding's fleet remained nothing more than frozen baggage aboard their spacecraft. The 200 explorers under Risto's command needed only to navigate their vehicles to intercept the others. Their forward looking radar systems locked onto the traversing objects in advance. At that point, the explorers fired their EMP weapons and the pulse struck the opposing vehicles with unfailing accuracy.

Risto's computer display showed each encounter as the motion of color-coded symbols moving against a background containing thousands of other objects. After being struck by an EMP pulse, the color of the symbol representing that vehicle changed, indicating its power and electrical systems had been disabled. One by one, Harding's fleet was rendered harmless and defenseless. Risto hoped the crippled vehicles continued on their courses to be safely drawn into stable orbits about Aril. Without collision avoidance systems, there was a risk the vehicles might be struck by other objects, but that was unlikely as long as the frozen occupants were rescued within several weeks. Space vehicles orbiting Earth in the 22nd century survived for many years without active systems to protect them from impacts. The interplanetary environment around Earth was sufficiently empty to tolerate such risks. Was that true for Aril as well?

Confident his plan had been successful, Risto began composing a message to the Earth fleet. He suspected its command ship was the lone echo his ship's radar detected. He directed his message to it in Union English hoping those on board would understand. Like the message he'd crafted to send to the 200 explorers, Risto was careful to include all information he could assemble to assure the Earthlings he could be trusted and had accomplished a critical undertaking in the defense of Aril. After that, he sent another message to his 200 comrades, now safely in orbit about the planet. They'd freeze themselves again and wait for further orders from him. Risto waited for a reply from the Earth ship, exhausted and overwhelmed by the reality of what he had accomplished.

Benjamin awoke with a start, angry with himself for falling asleep at such a critical time. The full import of what he'd learned from the transcript of Ilsa's visit to the New Life compound came back to him with a rush. He rose and hurried into the control room where Admiral Chase and his crew were excitedly reviewing a message from a galactic explorer named Risto Jalonen. Benjamin recognized the name immediately as the explorer who rescued Ilsa. Apparently, Jalonen had taken possession of one of the two supply ships Harding had brought to Aril and then successfully commanded a force of two hundred galactic explorers against Harding's force four times larger. At first they didn't believe the report, but their electronic surveillance confirmed the presence of hundreds of inert Union vehicles orbiting Aril.

Encouraged by the news, Admiral Chase proposed a direct attack on Harding's supply ship. If it was destroyed, at least the nuclear threat would be removed. Benjamin objected. "That's too risky. If Stormer knows the supply ship has been attacked, he may start killing the Arilians he's holding hostage."

"I'm not sure we have a choice," replied Admiral Chase, "He's already used one nuclear weapon without any provocation from us. There's nothing to stop him from repeating that. The losses may be far worse if we don't destroy his ship now."

"There may be another way," Benjamin said.

"What way is that?" asked Admiral Chase.

"Can you get me onto Harding's ship?"

The commander shook his head. "His ship's radar will detect our approach."

"Even if I used one of your vehicles? They have a smaller radar cross section. I might be able to dock without being observed."

"The cross section is smaller, but it will still be detectable once it's close enough to the supply ship."

"Can we destroy his radar antenna?" Benjamin asked.

"Too dangerous," the commander replied. "As soon as he knows we've done that, he will have to assume he's being attacked. Can't you just send him a message?"

Benjamin paced back and forth in the briefing room. "This is a hostage situation. We need to get inside the mind of the person who's holding the threat. I need to understand where he's coming from. I can't do that sending messages back and forth."

The commander nodded. He looked at the monitor in the briefing room, noting the locations of the vehicles in his fleet. "There may be a way to get you on the ship," he said thoughtfully. "We create a diversion by deploying a half dozen of our vehicles close enough to Harding's ship so his radar detects them. They will approach from his port and starboard, keeping his attention focused there, while you attempt docking aft."

Benjamin was skeptical. Even if he was successful in docking with the larger ship, Harding might notice at the last minute and lock the access door preventing Benjamin from proceeding farther. On the other hand, once Benjamin identified himself, Harding might be intrigued enough to engage him in conversation. Benjamin could not anticipate how Harding would react to the situation. It might work. He reviewed the plan with Admiral Chase one more time, then prepared to board one of the spare vehicles attached to the command ship.

Harding was woken by an alarm from the ship's radar. Glancing at the display before him, he saw six blips on the screen. These six echoes were as close as the Earth command ship had been, yet their radar signatures were much smaller. The ship's telescope, pointed to the objects, showed six vehicles, identical in size and appearance to the Union explorer spacecraft. Yet his ship's radar had not tagged them as explorer vehicles. Were some of the galactic explorers already arriving to help? Why had they not contacted him? To his relief, the six vehicles were not moving any closer. He transmitted a message on Union communication channels:

"This is Andrew Harding on Union Supply Ship 5.
Please identify yourselves."

There was no response for several minutes. Harding transmitted the message again. He waited, staring at the blips on the screen, willing them to go away. He was about to arm his plasma weapons when he noticed the indicator on the console showing that a vehicle was docked at the supply ship. When had that happened? In panic, he checked the docking station video camera. To his horror, a man emerged from the access port of a docked vehicle. Harding immediately entered a command that closed off the docking station from the artificial gravity portion of the ship. Harding grabbed a weapon to confront the man, but did not want to leave the control console while the six unidentified vehicles were so close. He watched the man float through the corridor from the docking station. As he came nearer to the video camera, Harding saw the intruder wore a Union uniform. He was hopeful the man was an explorer arriving to aid him. He pressed a button to activate the speaker in the corridor. "This is Andrew Harding. Identify yourself and state your business."

The man in the image looked momentarily confused, but then found the camera mounted flush in the cylindrical wall of the corridor. Steadying himself and looking squarely into the lens, the man said, "I am Benjamin Mizello. I came to talk."

Harding smiled grimly. He recognized the name immediately. Just before leaving Earth he'd heard that Arthur Mizello's son had joined the Union. Then, over the next twenty thousand years, he'd picked up communications about Benjamin's activities in space. The unexpected appearance of the Earth fleet now made sense. Arthur Mizello must have noticed the disappearance of Supply Ship 5 and alerted Earth about anomalous movement of the galactic explorer fleet. It was difficult for Harding to believe that this had prompted a rescue fleet from Earth to travel across the galaxy, but there were many thousands of years in the interim during which other factors may have entered into the decision. And somewhere and sometime, Arthur Mizello's son had allied himself with the Earth fleet. Harding spoke through the ship's speaker again. "I don't talk until the six vehicles near my ship withdraw."

As Harding expected, Benjamin was in radio contact with those vehicles. After several minutes the six ships receded beyond radar range. "I'm opening the entryway, Mr. Mizello. Please join me in the ship's control room. I will be armed. I trust you are not."

Benjamin lifted his arms to show there was nothing hidden anywhere on his jumpsuit. Harding said, "You may proceed, but just to make sure, I am setting the nuclear weapons to launch automatically in 30 minutes. The operation of this supply ship and the launch of the nuclear weapons are under my control through coded commands only I know. If anything happens to me, there is nothing you can do to prevent the launch of these weapons."

Benjamin nodded emphatically, placing his head to fill the video image. Then with a gentle push, he propelled himself down the corridor toward the access ladder that led to the gravity controlled portion of the ship.

Benjamin found Harding seated in the control room. The only other chair in the room was the one right next to him. Benjamin waited for a nod from Harding before taking the seat. Harding told him to fasten the lap and shoulder straps. "That will discourage you from any sudden movements, should you be tempted to do something foolish."

"Fair enough," said Benjamin.

"If you'll excuse me, I need a moment to lock the remaining docking sites to prevent any of your colleagues from boarding. How is it those vehicles could approach so closely before my radar detected them?"

Benjamin was tempted to tell Harding about the composite material of the Earth spacecraft, but thought better of it. "I don't know. Is your radar working properly?"

"Don't be coy with me, Mr. Mizello," Harding shot back angrily. "Otherwise, I will end this conversation immediately and dispose of you."

"Then don't ask me questions about the Earth fleet," Benjamin returned. "I didn't come here to provide you military intelligence."

Harding backed off. "Why did you come here?"

"To convince you to cease your attack on Aril."

"Too late," said Harding. "Even if you were to change my mind, Stormer's men are in complete control on the surface. They no longer need the threat of nuclear attack to hold their position. Right now, it's the intrusion from Earth's fleet that is creating the greatest peril to Aril. If they hadn't arrived, I'd be on the ground already, enjoying Arilian hospitality."

"Are you sure you could maintain your hold on Aril. Eventually they'd find a way to reclaim what you've taken possession of."

"You haven't done your homework, Mr. Mizello. The Arilians are completely passive and possess no weapons to speak of. It would be foolish of them to attack Stormer's well-armed men. Besides, they'll soon learn that if they leave us alone, they can go about their business as if we weren't there. Other than food, supplies and services we'll need occasionally, we ask only to be free to live in our own way on a small part of their planet."

"Yes," Benjamin said wryly. "With a group of women kidnapped from Earth."

Harding smiled. "The statute of limitations has certainly passed on that crime. Anyway, that was Stormer's addition to the plan. It was an idea that made a lot of sense, too. How can we start a colony without young women to produce the next generations of humans?"

"Any means to an end ," said Benjamin. "Regardless of how many you hurt."

"We didn't plan to take over a planet already settled. Originally, we intended to colonize our own planet, one the Union had identified early on and was a well kept secret. Unfortunately, that planet was not as ideal as observations suggested. That's when we decided to investigate Aril as an alternate site."

"So you decided to exploit people who were successful where you failed, not caring how intrinsically evil that is."

"Evil is a relative term. Don't you think?" said Harding,

assuming an air of maturity and superiority that was intended to intimidate Benjamin.

"Relative," Benjamin repeated thoughtfully. "Meaning that if you're the perpetrator of the evil, it might not be so bad, whereas if you're the victim, no crime could be worse."

"What is it you want to say, Mr Mizello?" Harding said through gritted teeth.

"I want to understand. You see, Dr. Harding, I'm not so different from my father. That's what always motivated him — attempting to understand what drove others to do what they do. You, for example, went through some difficult times that ultimately may have scarred you."

"Mr. Mizello, I refuse to talk about my life…"

Unperturbed, Benjamin went on. "Your wife left you — another man, wasn't it? She abandoned you with a teenage girl, who then grew up to despise you. She could not stand the fame and wealth you acquired by leading a powerful corporate entity that sucked the life blood out of the world's disadvantaged. She became quite the wild child, didn't she? The media attention, the scandals…"

"Mr. Mizello, I'm warning you…"

"Amanda — that was her name, wasn't it? Amanda Harding."

Harding rose and in the same motion back-handed Benjamin across the face with sufficient force to spin the chair around. "That's enough!" he roared.

Benjamin, tasting blood on his lip, said, "Why don't you start sending the women down to Aril now? I'm sure it's safe with Stormer and his men in control there. They must be looking forward to having those women after all this time. Of course, you may be interested to know that one of them is Amanda Harding."

Harding sat down suddenly. "What the hell are you talking about?"

"Ilsa Montgomery. I think you know her. She was an investigative journalist kidnapped by Stormer while she was visiting his compound in the desert."

"Ilsa Montgomery is dead!" Harding shouted.

"Not so. She was rescued and sent to my father's supply ship where she gave a full account of what happened to her. I read it last night. While she was at the New Life compound, she saw a list of the residents. One of them was Amanda Harding. The name sounded familiar to her and she intended to check into it when she returned home, which she never did. She made the connection when she met you here on this ship. Still, she thought it might be a coincidence that one of Stormer's women had the same name as your daughter. What do you think?"

"You're crazy," Harding hissed.

"Maybe so." replied Benjamin. "Why don't you check the names of the women in those vehicles? Maybe Ms. Montgomery made a mistake. Maybe it was a different Amanda Harding who joined New Life. It's not that unusual a name." He paused to stare into Harding's eyes, which had suddenly gone blank. "Ah, you don't have the list of names, do you? Do you think there's a reason Stormer never shared the names of the women with you?"

"I never asked to see the list. That was his business. Anyway, he knew he could never get away with bringing my daughter. As soon as I found out…"

"Yes, yes," Benjamin interrupted. "You'd have killed him the minute you knew."

Harding turned to look at the monitor as if he could see Stormer there. Benjamin imagined what Harding was feeling. Benjamin had experienced similar shock just hours ago when he learned Ilsa was still alive. But astonishment had been mixed with elation, whereas Harding's must certainly be mixed with indescribable dread.

"Of course, maybe Stormer doesn't care if you find out. Maybe he'll just have you killed the moment you step foot on Aril. You're of no use to him anymore really."

Harding rose and walked across the room, then back again. "That bastard," he whispered. "I'll kill him."

"Disarm the nuclear weapons and we will help you," Benjamin said quietly.

Harding glared at Benjamin. "I don't need your help."

"Really?" said Benjamin, feigning admiration. "How will you do it on your own? Stormer commands the mercenaries down there."

Harding was pacing again. "I'm not alone." He paused to look at the monitor before them. "I'll have help."

Benjamin followed his gaze to the display. "Are you talking about the Union explorers you brought here?"

Harding turned to him abruptly, visibly disturbed, but saying nothing.

"It's rather hard to hide a large force of space vehicles. I can assure you, they are in no position to come to your assistance."

"Impossible!" growled Harding, and he sat at the console and typed commands into the keyboard, searching for signs of the arriving fleet, but failing to find any.

Benjamin said softly, "I repeat my offer. Work with us and we'll make sure your daughter is safe and Stormer is rendered harmless."

Harding dropped his head to the console. Benjamin couldn't tell if he was weeping or just exhausted.

"What do you want me to do?" he said, raising his head, without looking at Benjamin.

Stormer's men stood on the hillsides surrounding the site where the women were landing. There was much ribald merriment as the men joked about what they would do after so many thousands of years without female companionship. Stormer watched the scene with mixed feelings of disgust and relief, unsure whether he could control the men with or without the women. Their arrival had a symbolic meaning: with them the population of the colony would grow. Their numbers would increase rapidly and their offspring would soon become dominant over the weak Arilians. The future of the human race as Earth knew it in the 22nd century was contained in the vehicles that now descended through the Arilian atmosphere.

The spacecraft arrived at a faster rate than Stormer expected. Harding must have seen some reason for haste because one vehicle followed within a minute of the previous one, their parachutes billowing brilliantly against the clear blue sky.

Triumphant shouts from the men broke the morning stillness. The spacecraft landed with blazing rockets that churned up clouds of dust where Arilian crops once thrived. The cheering heightened as the ports of the spacecraft opened. The men could hardly contain their excitement when the women emerged and walked toward them through the settling haze of rocket-disturbed debris. But something was wrong. The women approaching amid the black clouds were tall and gawky, walking with a strange gait. The shouts subsided and turned to hushed murmurs. Were these strange creatures the women Stormer had brought? Or had 60000 years of being frozen in space transformed them into hideous mutants?

Stormer was as puzzled as the men were. What had gone wrong? Had alien beings possessed the bodies of the women he'd brought from Earth? Had the nuclear explosion in Aril's atmosphere altered them? As the aliens came closer, the men were shocked into silence and immobility. There were hundreds of the aliens now and they fanned out and surrounded his men. Most of Stormer's men had not brought their weapons. The few that had fumbled to raise them to aim at the monstrous beings, but no sooner had they gotten their weapons positioned, than they were engulfed by balls of blue flame shot from weapons the aliens produced from behind their backs. Paralyzed and still glowing faintly with blue light, the men who'd been shot toppled over and lay motionless. Upon seeing this, the remainder of Stormer's men raised their hands in a gesture they hoped conveyed surrender to the creatures surrounding them.

His men defeated, Stormer backed away down the slope behind him toward the farm house in which he'd been living. When he was safely inside, he radioed Harding. "I need your immediate help. Aliens in the women's space vehicles overpowered my men."

Harding's voice broke through the static. "They're not aliens. They're from Earth, and I sent them." A strange coldness edged Harding's voice.

"From Earth?" Stormer shouted back. "Why would you send them here?"

"Why did you kidnap my daughter and bring her along with your other whores?"

So that was it. How had Harding found out? Stormer thought quickly. "She came on her own volition."

"And you didn't think it was important enough to tell me?"

"She asked me not to, and I honored her request." Stormer answered.

"Since when did you start caring about honor? When she said she wanted to come along, did she know she was going to be a slave to paramilitary hoodlums?" Harding did not wait for an answer. There could be no answer. "The force from Earth has been instructed to take you and your men prisoners. I suggest you put up no resistance."

Stormer terminated the transmission. He was stunned by how quickly the situation had reversed and irate that Harding was letting his emotions get the better of him. Stormer had not anticipated Harding would accompany him to colonize a new planet. He was supposed to stay on the supply ship. He was never to know about Amanda being among the women who had been deceived.

Stormer had few options. He knew the Union fleet was not far away in space, but they'd never side with him against Harding. He could go to the Arilians for help, but it was doubtful they were so forgiving as to aid him. The only remaining alternative was Nutley in the other supply ship. Switching frequencies, Stormer shouted into the radio, "Nutley, I need you to direct a nuclear weapon at my location. Arm it and prepare for firing. Then wait for my instructions."

After a moment of static, he heard a slightly accented voice reply, "Sorry, Mr. Stormer. Mr. Nutley is unable to speak right now, nor is the man you left here to assist him. This is galactic explorer Risto Jalonen. I have taken control of this supply ship. Have a nice day." The transmission ended with a loud squawk.

Stormer sat and rubbed both hands over his face. Defeated, he contemplated taking his own life with the EMP weapon at his side. Instead, he exercised his last resort. He was out the door in two steps and began a furious run across the Arilian countryside. The orange sun was high in the sky and he felt its intense heat as he ran toward where his space vehicle waited at the spot he'd landed weeks ago. He glanced behind him, but saw none of the Earthlings in pursuit. Just as he reached the spacecraft, a man stepped out from behind it and aimed a weapon at his chest. He was dressed in a Union jumpsuit and above his pocket was embossed the name "Mizello". Stormer instinctively did what he'd just observed his men do — he raised his hands in surrender and ended the invasion of Aril.

CHAPTER 38
— 65000 —

No lives were lost in the battle for control of Aril. The entire conflict was resolved on the basis of a single piece of information obtained 63000 years earlier and transmitted by electronic and human means over thousands of light-years. At the victory celebration, a multitude of humanoid races gathered before the statue of Captain Warner at the Arilian Memorial Park. Those of the Arilian race were uniformly short and stout, round-faced with shocks of unruly red or blond hair. The lack of diversity among the Arilians was the result of the limited gene pool from which they'd begun. The near in-breeding that occurred among the first few generations on the planet would have produced numerous birth defects had Arilians not advanced their medical science quickly enough to prevent this.

The modern day Earthlings represented another race, markedly distinct from their 22nd century ancestors. They were tall, dark-skinned and gaunt, with thick brown or black hair covering their heads like plush carpet. After many millennia of interracial marriages on Earth, all race-related variations in appearance had been washed out. There were undoubtedly subtle differences those from Earth could easily discern, but to the Arilians and the people from ancient Earth, all the modern day Earthlings looked alike.

The greatest diversity in the crowd was among the 22nd century Earthlings, particularly the kidnapped women attending the ceremony, who hailed from all over the ancient world. They'd been safely brought down to the surface to be cared for by female Arilians, helping them recover from the shock and disorientation that crippled them. They stood huddled together looking dazed, struggling to come to grips with the events that transpired in what seemed to them only minutes. One of the women was not standing with the others. Amanda Harding stood next to her father, who held her tightly. He was flanked by two members of the

Earth fleet, but the guards were hardly necessary since all aggressiveness had gone out of him like air from a balloon. Now he was just an old, weary relic from an ancient human race on the brink of extinction.

Looking similar, but perhaps less willing to accept his fate, was Stormer, standing on the opposite side of the stage from Harding and with his own pair of guards. He wore no restraints of any kind, nor did the men of his paramilitary force who had also been allowed to attend the celebration. Though loosely guarded, it was clear they lacked the motivation, amidst a sea of alien faces, to initiate any kind of resistance or uprising.

Also among the crowd were a couple of hundred members of the galactic explorer fleet. Once they'd been told what Harding had done, they all unhesitatingly recanted their support for the de facto leader of the Union force. They were given the choice to land on Aril and become assimilated into Arilian society, or to remain in their vehicles to resume their exploration of the galaxy. They were also offered the opportunity to visit Aril before making their decision.

Benjamin stood center-stage with Admiral Chase and a small group of Arilians who represented the planetary governments. A band played, as was the Arilian custom for any gathering or celebration. Looking out at the crowd, Benjamin admired the stoicism with which they accepted the damage and hardship done to them by Harding, Stormer, and their men. It would take years to repair the devastation inflicted on their fields and their homes.

Absent from the celebration was Risto Jalonen, who chose to remain in space caring for Supply Ship 2. Not one for pomp and circumstance, he volunteered to pilot the ship back to its station 12000 light-years away. The members of the Union fleet who chose to continue exploring the galaxy would need the supply ship to resume their endless mission. Before he left, the Arilians launched Harding's space capsule, unoccupied, to dock with Risto's supply ship. Harding no longer needed his spacecraft anyway. Inside the capsule, Risto found a half dozen large pressurized containers filled with Arilian ale, one of the best beers Risto ever tasted. He stored the containers carefully on the supply ship so he could enjoy the brew for many thousands of years to come.

At a signal from the Arilians, the music ceased and an Arilian official stepped forward and spoke rapidly in the native language neither Benjamin nor others from Earth understood. He introduced another member of the Arilian delegation, a woman with curly yellow hair, wearing a long red robe, and sporting an unwavering smile. She carried a portable electronic device which she activated and placed on the podium. Clearing her voice, she spoke in the official Union language, understandable only to the non-Arilians.

"My name is Tarina. I am humbled by the honor to speak to you on behalf of the unified governments of Aril." Switching to Arilian, she said, "My apologies to Arilians in the audience who do not understand the Union language. You may read the text of my speech on your translators." Most of the Arilians carried the same portable device Tarina had placed on the podium.

"The unified governments of Aril thank the fleet from Earth for helping rescue our planet. We understand the courage and commitment it must have taken to leave family and friends on Earth forever to embark on a space voyage of highly uncertain outcome. Our planet was founded by just such a group of adventurers.

"Many thousands of years ago, Captain Lance Warner, who you see behind us, came to Aril a second time and made a prophecy. He said Aril would be invaded by evil men from Earth. That prophecy came true, but what the Captain failed to predict was that Aril would be saved by others from Earth, more enlightened than earlier Earthlings and more committed to ensuring that malevolent forces in the galaxy do not prevail.

"We are pleased to offer the full extent of Arilian hospitality as an expression of our gratitude. Those from Earth who wish to remain on Aril are free to do so. Those who wish to leave may help themselves to whatever they might need on the long voyage into space. We extend this offer not only to the members of the Earth fleet, but also to the men and women brought here by Dr. Harding and Mr. Stormer."

At this point Tarina turned to address Stormer's men, who stood together off to one side. "The unified governments of Aril suggest that you men also thank the fleet from Earth, for it is probably true they saved your lives as well. You see, Arilians may have no weapons, but we are not as defenseless as you may believe. Having mastered the art of medical science, we have the ability to engineer viruses of any kind we wish. Your intestinal problems of several nights ago were not the result of your consumption of Arilian food. We introduced a virus to demonstrate our ability to manipulate biological agents. There was no danger in this virus spreading to Arilians because our genetic make-up has had many thousands of years to differentiate from the humans we descended from. If the lives of Arilians had at anytime been threatened by you, we would not have hesitated to release more deadly strains of viruses in your midst." There were murmurs and grumbling from among the men. Tarina turned away from them and faced the Arilian crowd again. The fixed smile on her face turned mischievous. "There was considerable debate among us before resorting to the introduction of the intestinal illness among the intruders. Most of the objection came from our chefs, whose excessive pride prevented them from agreeing to bear the blame for the resulting stomach ailments." Sporadic chuckling was heard from the crowd of Arilians.

"Although the Captain's prophecy was not quite complete, he inspired Arilians to look toward the heavens. Since that time, Arilian astronomy has thrived and the last few thousand years have seen marvelous breakthroughs in our knowledge of the galaxy. In honor of our guests from Earth, I am pleased to announce some of those to you today. First, every Arilian knows the history of how our planet was founded. The canisters released from space vehicles to seed life on suitable planets to this day inspired the origin of Aril's most popular holiday, "The Festival of Seeds". But the story of the canisters did not end with the founding of Aril. Our astronomers have made careful observations of the other seven planets on which the canisters were launched. Four more of those planets now show definite evidence of life forms similar to ours and possessing oxygen-rich atmospheres. We will gladly share with our friends from Earth the locations of these planets so they might explore them more thoroughly."

Tarina surveyed the crowd assessing the response, as though looking for encouragement to continue. It was Benjamin who decided to clap first. He had no idea if clapping was an acceptable custom to Arilians, but it seemed to catch on and before long the entire throng was applauding, including the men in Stormer's militia, who suddenly felt it was important to please their Arilian hosts.

Tarina smiled more broadly now and raised her arms to quiet the crowd. When there was silence again, she continued. "The miracle does not stop there however. Our astronomers have also found many other planetary systems that have properties suggestive of life. The atmospheres of those planets show evidence for abundant water and oxygen. The locations of these planets have been carefully determined and what we've found is that they are localized to a well-defined sector of our galaxy. Both Earth and Aril are on the outskirts of that sector, at the border of a region where there is an abundance of planets with the basic chemical constituents necessary for life. Through their research, Arilian astronomers have learned that long ago, a supernova explosion blasted these building blocks of life into a portion of the galaxy where planets were being formed from the celestial dust surrounding young stars. The supernova planted a garden of planets, all of which possessed the chemical make-up necessary to produce life forms. For those planets that were at the optimum distance from their central stars, the habitable zone, the advent of living organisms was just a matter of time." Tarina paused again. This time there was no hesitation and the entire crowd applauded loudly. When the noise subsided, Tarina said, "Here again, we invite our friends from Earth to share this exciting discovery and help us further explore the thousands of new worlds within this galactic garden."

The excitement conveyed by Tarina, her inspirational words, and the interminable smile on her face appealed to Arilians and

Earthlings alike. In some strange way, her words inexplicably re-united the multiple races of humans. By drawing their attention away from Aril and transporting them to an imaginary garden of life-bearing planets, she'd found a common cause for celebration. In just that short a time, the plight of Harding and Stormer be-came absurdly insignificant, and what had started out as a cele-bration of victory now became a celebration of life in all its forms. Tarina did not speak for a long time, savoring the silence, a silence the entire crowd respected.

Finally, she continued. "I have one more piece of news. This may seem less profound by comparison, but it is especially mean-ingful to Arilians. It is something our government officials have known about for thousands of years, but it is a secret that's been kept carefully hidden. Our oceanographers have been nurturing and protecting a small area on the floor of our ocean where new animal life forms have been discovered. After billions of years of being completely barren, life, in its unique and unpredictable way, has emerged from the hydrated sediments on the ocean floor." Tarina's smile glowed. "We are a long way from seeing the mighty leviathans of Earth's oceans leaping into the Arilian sky, but it will happen someday. For those of us who will not be around to see it, we can imagine it, for there is nothing Arilians do better than imagine."

A burst of applause followed this announcement, but there was also grumbling from some of the Arilians. Tarina seemed to notice this and she held up her arms to quell the disturbance. The smile on her face turned mischievous again as she said, "Arilians thrive on sharing. From the beginning, we've shared everything among our people. Keeping the secret of the Arilian ocean for so long has not been easy, but those privy to the secret all agreed the newly discovered ocean life was too tenuous. They feared making the announcement prematurely. Now, the survival of those living organisms is more certain."

This seemed to satisfy the Arilians and their mumbling faded away. Tarina continued, "And now let us celebrate all there is to celebrate on this fine day, and let us welcome our new friends from space. Tonight when you look at the heavens, consider that Aril is no longer alone. A new age has begun on this planet and we are all very fortunate to bear witness to it."

More applause followed and the band played again. Benjamin found himself caught up in the excitement and was shoved along by the crowd, which had begun to disperse. He was able to see Harding separated from his daughter and whisked away with Stormer by the guards from Earth. The two men looked meek, helpless, and defeated. Benjamin wondered whether it would be Arilian justice or Earth justice that finally had to deal with them.

Benjamin remained on Aril for several more weeks, joining Admiral Chase and others in the Earth fleet on a tour of the planet, beginning with the Memorial Park, Central Library and Archives, and the Memorial Grove. Benjamin stood by the stones honoring the Captain and his wife, the memory of the tall man he'd met at the IGET Conference still remarkably fresh in his mind. Around the stones, the Arilians maintained an extensive garden of brilliant flowering plants, descendants from the seeds Captain Warner brought back with him upon his return to Aril.

Their tour of Aril ended at the Arilian Central Control facility, which greatly impressed the visitors from Earth. Admiral Chase speculated that the difficult times Earth had undergone through the millennia had placed humans in a position where they had to rely heavily on technology to engineer the planet to keep it habitable. The Arilian approach was to monitor the planet closely and apply appropriate measures as necessary to relieve potential stresses and hazards while control was still possible.

It was a typically hot, dry Arilian day with crystal blue skies when Benjamin boarded his space capsule and took off to rendezvous with the supply ship that had once been Andrew Harding's charge. He had agreed to take responsibility for the ship until a replacement for Harding had been selected. He would have regretted leaving the serene security of Arilian civilization had he not been looking forward to seeing Ilsa again. He still had not completely come to grips with her survival after having already accepted the reality of leaving her behind forever on Earth. But somehow she endured being kidnapped, found her way to his father's supply ship, and now was on a capsule heading toward Aril. His father had sent information about the course her vehicle would take, so it was a simple task for Benjamin to intercept her along the way. Once he was close enough, the supply ship's radio would pick up the beacon signal that all vehicles transmitted continuously. By sending a coded command to her capsule, it would automatically change its course and adjust its speed to safely dock with the supply ship. When he had programmed that into the ship's computer, Benjamin returned to his capsule and separated from the supply ship, moving several kilometers away where he would remain for the next three thousand years until he and Ilsa were reunited.

This time, the hands that guided Ilsa out of the magnetocryogenic chamber were Benjamin's. He was carrying a robe for her that hung in the air like a frozen banner, but Ilsa ignored it. Instead, she drew Benjamin to her and wrapped herself around him, hugging him tightly with her head buried into his shoulder. It was the most comforting sensation she'd felt in a very long time, and he seemed to understand its importance as he made no attempt to alter the arrangement. Only when they'd drifted into the metal bulkhead of the command room did she push away from him, one hand wiping away the tears flowing freely down her cheeks. Holding hands, they drifted in a dream-like fluidity toward the ladder that had previously led her to the frightening encounter with Harding and Stormer.

Once within the confines of gravity, Ilsa donned a jumpsuit and the two of them went to the galley where they had much to talk about. In the stronger light of the dining area, she saw that Benjamin looked much older than he had appeared when they'd met at the IGET Conference. He assured her that the total amount of time he'd spent unfrozen amounted to no more than a few months, but the experiences he had during that period aged him in a way that defied the laws of chronology. When they had talked in Washington, DC, she lectured him as though he were an immature young man, prone to rash decisions and self-destructive impulses. Now, she couldn't imagine conversing with him that way, and she found herself drawn even more to his self-confidence and inner strength, especially since his intrinsic kindness and humility somehow remained intact.

Eventually, they reached a point in the conversation when it was necessary to discuss their future. Benjamin told Ilsa about Aril, and for her the friendly, young planet seemed a far more attractive option than returning to Earth. But when she heard about the garden of habitable planets the Arilian astronomers had found, she was intrigued. The Arilians, the Earth Fleet Commander, and Benjamin had discussed a strategy for redeploying the Union supply ships to be better placed for exploration of this region of the galaxy. A message was sent to Arthur Mizello suggesting the change and if he approved, he'd forward it to Earth and the other supply ships. In another thirty or forty thousand years, the supply ships would be distributed in a line along the galaxy's Orion Arm, beginning at Earth, passing near Aril, and traversing the planetary garden. The galactic explorers would be similarly reassigned and the new sector of the galaxy would provide endless opportunities for discovering and exploring new habitable worlds, and perhaps planets with intelligent life.

Benjamin's enthusiasm while describing the garden of planets the Arilians had discovered must have been infectious because Ilsa soon found herself lost in wild imaginings of what those other worlds might be like. Whatever thoughts she had of returning to Earth with Benjamin were dwarfed beneath the wonder and excitement galactic exploration offered. The freezing technology made the explorers the equivalent of giants on Earth, who with great strides could be in New York at one moment and Paris the next. As an investigative journalist she had been motivated by the desire to expose those who represented the most evil aspects of the human race. Now, those injustices were far away in space and time and her view of goodness and evil took on galactic dimensions.

Benjamin led Ilsa into the greenhouse of the supply ship. Walking among the crops, he explained how the self-contained biosphere could be sustained indefinitely, fed only by the energy it received from stellar radiation and the plasmas of interstellar space. Ilsa felt dizzy when she peered out through the transparent windows of the greenhouse at the field of stars making circular orbits as the cylindrical section of the supply ship spun about the ship's axis. She imagined she and Benjamin were spiraling downward into a bottomless pit lined with brilliant lights, descending constantly, yet never reaching the bottom. Love was like that, and she let herself fall into it.

CHAPTER 40
— 72218 —

"Do you still feel like God," Arthur asked Krystal.

She smacked his arm. "I never said I was God." They were sitting on the bench in the greenhouse looking at the stars relentlessly circling the large central star that had fueled the supply ship for more than 60000 years. Arthur put his arm around her. The air in the greenhouse was cool and damp, smelling of soil, compost, and chlorophyll.

"I'm going to miss this star," Arthur said. They had received the full account of the invasion of Aril and the proposed plan to redeploy the supply ships to the region of the galaxy 5000 light-years on the opposite side of Aril, deep within the area that was called the galactic garden. Benjamin, if he decided to remain on Supply Ship 5, would be stationed 5000 light-years even deeper into this sector of the galaxy. His ship would be the primary hub for the galactic travelers systematically exploring those planets.

"I'll try to find another star just like this one," Krystal said.

Arthur shook his head. "They're all different. Trillions of them out there and no two the same. Just like people. Just like planets."

Krystal yawned. She'd been working at her computer for the last sixteen hours. She and Arthur carefully worked out the redeployment of the Union fleet, and crafted a detailed plan for the movement of the ships. If all went well, the new configuration of supply ships would be in place before the year 100000. At the last minute, before the messages were transmitted, Krystal made one last adjustment to the instructions sent to Supply Ship 4. Then she joined Arthur in the greenhouse where he was tending the plants.

Chapter 41
— 89555 —

On Supply Ship 4, an old lady, who set out from Earth 87000 years earlier on a mission of love, is finally reunited with her only son. She has traveled farther than any of the galactic explorers — her journey only interrupted by stops at Union supply ships according to a rendezvous plan recorded on medallions she gave to space travelers departing Earth in the 22nd century. At each supply ship, she waited for several days, hoping her son would show up. And when he didn't, she boarded her capsule again and departed to the next destination.

She was terrified upon arriving at the location of Supply Ship 5 when she found the spacecraft was not there. Alone and lacking any information about the fleet, she resolutely returned to her magnetocryogenic chamber and continued on to Supply Ship 7. Once again, she was disappointed when her son failed to meet her.

Her next rendezvous point was Supply Ship 4, where she found her son at last.

Although Supply Ship 4 was to be redeployed to the region of the galaxy around the planet Aril, Krystal Charbeau had sent instructions that the ship not relocate until after the arrival of an old woman from ancient Earth. Risto Jalonen had found the woman's son among the Union explorers orbiting Aril and gave him Ilsa's medallion. The son set off immediately to meet his mother, and Risto sent a message to Arthur Mizello's ship. Krystal had calculated when the old lady and her son would reach the ship and sent instructions that the supply ship not move until after the reunion took place.

The old woman makes peace with her son, which is an easy matter given the time and place. They sit in the supply ship and reminisce about their life on Earth, the young man's father, and the difficulty they had after his death. When they both exhaust all ways to prolong the conversation, they retire to their quarters to rest. Soon, the woman will board her vehicle again, this time to return to Earth to live out her remaining years. The young man will head back to Aril to be part of the Union fleet that will explore the thousands of planets that lay within the galaxy's garden of life.

CPSIA information can be obtained at www.ICGtesting.com
Printed in the USA
BVOW011728291211

279252BV00002B/12/P